"Actually, there is another thing," he said quietly. His eyes seemed to darken as he allowed them to travel from her face down to her feet. Slowly. "I also want your promise to at least try and keep to that style of speech which corresponds with your clothing."

Considering that she had just been subjected to another one of his lordship's outrageously intimate *oglings,* Mattie had more than a few reservations about entering into any agreements whatsoever! Nonetheless, thinking it prudent, she kept the thought to herself. *"D'accord,"* she answered brusquely.

Still, it seems he had one more proviso to add. "Oh, and I say there, Mattie?" This time, a flicker of some lighter shade of blue sparkled down at her. "If you would be so good, I also wish you to understand that I would appreciate it greatly if you would, henceforth, avoid all those 'sir's' and 'my lord's.' Address me simply as 'Vincent.' I don't think—no, I could not possibly bear it if I was again to hear myself referred to as"—his massive shoulders commenced a slight shaking while his voice came out sounding strangled—" 'your *worship.' "*

It was that same light she had seen gleaming from his eyes when she had accepted his "introduction" at the Ellengoods'. This time, she knew what it was. He was funning her!

She had no fault to find with that. "Agreed!" she gurgled, succumbing to a burst of laughter while the earl looked on indulgently.

Catching her breath, Mattie fell silent. Again, she discovered his eye dark upon hers. The warm night air carried the scent of late summer flowers to her nostrils and also another similar fragrance, that of his lordship's tangy, masculine scent. These elements, combined with something in the earl's stance, caused Mattie to feel strangely uneasy . . .

An Alluring Deceit

Melissa Lynn Jones

ZEBRA BOOKS
KENSINGTON PUBLISHING CORP.

ZEBRA BOOKS are published by

Kensington Publishing Corp.
475 Park Avenue South
New York, NY 10016

Zebra and the Z logo Reg. U.S. Pat & TM Off.

First Printing: December, 1993

Printed in the United States of America

Chapter One

"Oomphf!"

Tiny Madeleine Serinier managed to keep to her feet for less than half a backward step before collapsing to an awkward seat on the pavement. She gawked rather stupidly at the obstacle which had sent her sprawling: six feet of masculine solidity.

"Sorry, lad. No damage, I trust? Here, let me help you up."

So saying, the large gentleman in the elegantly cut coat of dark green superfine extended Mattie his hand. Absurdly, she noticed that his shirt cuffs were marvelously white, his gloves perfectly fitted . . . and that the hand he proffered was just about the size of her entire face.

"Steady on, lad. Lad? I say there, you aren't hurt, are you?"

Although in truth a trifle dazed, Mattie recognized the man's deepened tones as indicative of his concern. She also heard herself referred to as "lad," but since her current attire included baggy tan knee breeches, an over-long vest beneath a loosely fitted brown jacket, and a soft, fawn-colored slouch hat, his reference was not unexpected. It was a very good thing to be so dressed, too, for in her rôle as Matt-the-delivery-boy, she needn't fret over the many yards of petticoat a nineteen-year-old young lady would otherwise have had tossed all awry by such mishap. Wouldn't *that* have made a fine sight to scandalize Mayfair's passersby!

Collecting her scattered wits, Mattie reached for a hold to pull herself up. In one part of her mind, she registered the pleasant feel of fine leather as the gentleman's gloved hand wrapped wholly around hers, even as her nostrils quivered at the faint trace of some tangy scent. Sandalwood, she thought it. Still, she was not so distracted as to forget the courtesies due. Regaining her feet, she snatched off her hat to reveal cropped, baby-fine curls of sparkling black—her hair, lashes, and delicately winged eyebrows in distinct contrast to the pale purity of her skin.

"Oh, I'm tip-top an' tearin' fine!" she proclaimed in deliberate Cockney inflections. She gave private thanks for the natural huskiness of voice which provided additional support to her imposture. Words all but tumbled over themselves as she rushed on. "An' it were all me own fault, o' course—never think otherwise! Sometimes I do gets in too much of a hurry. Yer knows how it be some days." Unaware of it, her speech then smoothed into more refined accents. "But you, sir, you weren't injured?"

A rich chuckle supplied answer.

Realizing the ridiculousness of her query, since the broad-shouldered gentleman easily would make up two of someone her size, Mattie grinned in return. "Well, I suppose not," she acknowledged. "Even so, sir, you have my apologies. My carelessness has delayed you, if nothing else."

She promptly made the gentleman a very pretty bow, unconcerned that this latest action might be viewed by the good citizens of London's most fashionable district as, if not precisely scandalous, at the least, highly presuming. Common delivery boys did not go about bowing in form to their betters, after all.

But the large man in the exquisite coat seemed to find nothing amiss. "No harm done, lad. There is nowhere in particular I need be at the moment. Nothing to signify, at any rate."

His words came lightly, at his ease, and yet Mattie couldn't help but question a certain stillness which seemed to settle over him. There was something not altogether right about his look, an odd quality which didn't quite match his tone. Intrigued, she made a quick examination of his strong, squared jaw; his beautifully curved mouth; the broad forehead beneath thick, satiny waves of dark blond hair—none of which explained the discrepancy.

Could it be something about the eyes then?

Ah, yes. But what was it? She searched the dark, jewel-blue color of the eyes facing her.

Before she could decide on an explanation for what it was that so disturbed her, though, the gentleman spoke yet again. "Here, this should take care of it," he said quietly. With that, his look began to solidify into something recognizable.

Perforce, Mattie dropped her gaze to the bright coin held forth. She hadn't even noticed when he had pulled it from his pocket, being too caught up in trying to analyze his expression. Appalled, she realized that he was offering her money; she'd stood silent for so long, he must have assumed it was what she expected.

Alors! How perfectly awful! she thought in horrified silence. A tide of embarrassment washed through her.

Apparently, the elegantly dressed gentleman perceived her disquiet. "Sorry," he murmured, frowning slightly as he whisked the coin out of sight. "I've made you uncomfortable, haven't I? I only meant to—"

"Aw, yer meant what?" she challenged, cutting short his explanation. She felt inexplicably angered and so reacted in immediate defense, not pausing to wonder exactly what she thought was under attack. Drawing the sweeping arch of her silky black brows into a fine scowl, she reverted to the accents common for a youth of the streets.

With her particular talent for mimicry, she also readily incorporated those liberties of expression enjoyed by the opposite sex. "Be yer thinkin' yerself obliged to give a reward to any ol' idiot who caroms into your path?" she jibed. "Well, dish me! Just what sort o' chucklehead notion is that! An' there's no need to get all stiffly on your stiffs, I'm sure," she added gruffly when she noticed that, at the fall of each reproachful word from her, the gentleman seemed to distance himself, becoming progressively more and more remote. Nervously, but without taking her eyes from his face, she fidgeted with the hem of her coat.

Her brave speech served to check him, however. For long moments he stared back at her, his widely spaced eyes of deepest Kashmir blue suddenly relit—alive!— yet mightily displeased. Perhaps such vulgarities of speech did not often come his way, or possibly he was incensed at being called to account by a mere scrap of an errand boy. Whatever caused the change in his expression, though, for the first time in their encounter, Mattie feared that she'd given offense.

Then, his cheek twitched just slightly. It was her only warning before a wonderfully powerful thump landed across her slim shoulders. His face relaxing with humor, he said, "Well, well! That makes two hits you've dealt me, lad, and not many can claim such a feat. Vincent Charles Houghton, Earl of Staffield, and very much at your service." The corners of his mouth lifted further, and he tipped the curved brim of his tall-crowned beaver hat to her.

In light of this distinct condescension after her surely outrageous temerity, Mattie's upset disappeared as quickly as it had come. Not to be outdone, she swept her own floppy-brimmed hat to the pavement with the grace of a polished courtier. "Matt Serinier," she announced. "*Your* servant, milord. So, it's a truce, is it?" she asked hopefully, drawing herself gracefully erect. She was pleased to note that the distant, off-putting look had vanished from his face.

"Indeed, yes. Truce, bantling." The gentleman's smile was sincere.

"Then that's all right and tight!" Relieved, Mattie clapped her hat back atop her black curls.

With clear, sherry-brown eyes, she then glanced up to judge the amount of light left showing above the rooftops. "So, an' with yer permission, milord, I'd best be gettin' along me way. It's gettin' late, it is, an' my last delivery ran a bit late, yer sees." Angling her head to give his lordship a last measuring look, she tossed him another cheeky grin before whirling around and starting away at a trot.

She wove her way skillfully in and out through the pedestrians along St. James's Street. Moving swiftly, her speed in no wise reduced by her accident, she dodged apprentices, porters, and sober-faced men of business who were likewise hastening to finish the day's tasks before the supper hour. She didn't see the earl's warm smile change into one of bemusement as he watched her quick, darting movements.

Thoughtfully, his eyes followed her progress until she reached the turning at the end of the street.

Without so much as a single backward glance, Mattie entered Pall Mall and continued rapidly up toward the Strand. There was one more stop she was anxious to make before she left the area, and the singular honor paid her by the exchange of names with a titled gentleman was out of her mind in a trice. As usual, she was in far too much of a hurry even to think of looking behind her.

Indeed, it had been nearly two weeks since she had last spoken with Mr. Biggersley, and she was anxious to reach his carpet warehouse before it came closing time. There was a particular item resting in the shopkeeper's window which she needed to check, an unusually fine specimen of the weavers' art. And she was dreadfully afraid that she would arrive too late, or that the carpet she'd been saving so long for would be gone.

If only it hadn't sold, she prayed with every step, if only she would find it still hanging in its place of honor in the front window of the Biggersley Carpet Warehouse. For without that carpet, she was sure, Tante Agathe would spend another London winter trying to disguise the pain caused by hard floors and rooms entirely too cool and damp for comfort.

Oh, their small lodgings were kept warm enough on wintertime nights by a generous scoop of coals left to smolder on the grate. Their single hearth gave out adequate heat to warm the apartment's main room, also Mattie's minuscule sleeping closet. But no matter how

10

hard she tried, Mattie couldn't seem to convince her great-aunt Agathe to keep the fire built up during the day. Certainly, before leaving each morning to go to her place of employment, Mattie would check to see that the scuttle was filled and a fire left burning vigorously on the grate; and yet, by the time she returned home in the evening, she would find a hearth grown cold and rooms that were decidedly chill.

She would also find a cheerfully unrepentant old lady.

Mattie could beg, plead, and argue however much she liked, but it seemed nothing would induce her *grand-tante* to maintain a fire when alone. The old dear was determined to do whatever she could to increase their savings, so long as the discomfort was only to herself.

"But there was no need for a fire today," Tante would reply to all Mattie's remonstrances, even as Mattie would set about relighting the coals. *"Vraiment,"* the old lady would blithely continue, "the weather was very fine out, and only in this past hour has it become a trifle chilly. You mustn't so concern yourself, dear!"

But Mattie couldn't disregard her great-aunt's increasing stiffness and shortened steps so easily. To be sure, Tante Agathe's constant little economies scared her half to death.

Mattie wanted . . . No. She *needed* that carpet.

Mr. Biggersley was just stepping outside to secure his shutters when Mattie skidded to a halt in front of his warehouse. A neat building on Burleigh Street, just behind Exeter 'Change, Mr. Biggersley's shop prided itself on holding the city's largest and most prestigious collection of fine old carpets, as well as an impressive selection of new ones.

"Why, Matt, 'tis good to see you, boy," the merchant greeted her fondly when she came up alongside him.

"I've been wondering when you'd take a minute to stop by for a visit. Come to see the Brussels, have you?" Merry eyes above plump cheeks mirrored Mattie's glowing smile. "Yes, it's still here," he reassured her.

"There've been no offers, then?" She made a polite show of concern.

"As if you really wished it gone," he teased. "No, I'd say there's not much danger of anyone purchasing it for the present. Fine carpets like this one don't sell in a day, you know!" He stepped farther out onto the pavement to join her in an admiring appraisal of his wares.

What held their attention in the shop's front window was a double-wide, tightly woven carpet known as a "Brussels," so-named for that city where the uniquely looped weave was first produced. Expensive in terms of both the time spent in manufacture and in the materials used, a Brussels carpet required one full thickness of stout woolen yarn for each color in the surface design. The Brussels displayed in the front window of the Biggersley Carpet Warehouse boasted a base color of soft apple green; a border using two darker greens; a central rosette pattern with interesting additions of blood red, maroon, and dark pink; with an occasional autumn-gold yarn to add depth and warmth to the whole. Altogether, the finished product was thicker than any two of Mattie's fingers and very costly, indeed.

"It's beautiful," she breathed out in awe.

"Then why is it that you won't let me set it back for you, boy? You know I don't mind, for so I've told you time and again." Mr. Biggersley's look bespoke genuine puzzlement.

His suggestion was tempting, too, and Mattie frowned while she considered it. Finally, she sighed and shook her head. "No, 'twouldn't be right. I'll have enough money to meet yer price before too much longer, I 'spect, but I still lack fer a mite. 'Course, I 'preciate yer willingness more'n anything," she added on a huskier note. "But my wantin' to buy is no reason for yer not makin' a sale, if'n yer should gets the chance."

The shop owner acknowledged her words with a brisk nod of approval. "You're a long-headed one, now ain't you, boy? Not many would understand a trades-man's position like you do. Even so, my offer holds good anytime you say. But tell me something, Matt—for in truth, I've wondered about it these past many months—why is it so important for you to have this par-ticular carpet, or a Brussels, come to that? I have other carpets which aren't nearly so expensive, meaning you likely could buy one today without all this waiting. What makes you insist on something that costs so dear?"

Mattie studied draped expanses of apple green as she gave answer. "I have to have it for *ma tante*—er, m' aunt, that is. Actually, she's my great-aunt, having been wife to my grandfather's brother. Anyways, she and I looks after one another now that the rest of our family is gone. But the important thing is, Mr. Biggersley, that she's gettin' on in years and last winter suffered the rheumatism somethin' awful. It's her knees, yer under-stand, brought on 'cause we live close by the river where it comes up foggy an' all pretty regular." Her small face, reflected in the glass, for an instant looked almost sad. Then she brightened. "But this here's the very thing needed to turn the trick. Stap me if it ain't! Thick enough to ease her steps and large enough to cover every inch of flooring—from her favorite sittin' chair to the hearth!"

"But surely, Matt, I have others inside which would serve your purpose just as well," the shopkeeper reminded kindly.

Peering through the glass, Mattie responded in wistful tones. "No. 'Twouldn't be the same. For yer sees, Mr. Biggersley, there's somethin' else special about it. It has precisely that shade of green which m' aunt once told me she had in her room as a girl. 'New leaves, touched with blue sky,' she described it. An' I just know this is the color she spoke of, so it'd mean everything to her if she could have it round her once again." Mattie jammed one hand into the pocket of her brown worsted jacket, then turned to face the merchant. "So, p'rhaps yer can understand if it just *has* to be this one."

The plump-faced shopkeeper considered this explanation while he looked down at the comely youth. A full head shorter than his own five-feet-and-six, the boy would be considered too pretty, and of a too-delicate construction, were it not for the uncompromising straightness of both his posture and his mien. Mr. Biggersley admired, too, the youngster's forthright and honest address. Thus, he felt himself justified for having told what was, by strict definition, a lie.

There had been, in fact, two serious inquiries about the Brussels in the window. In both cases, however, Mr. Biggersley had given out the excuse that the carpet was meant for display purposes only. Being a shrewd businessman, he had managed to turn the interested parties to account, nonetheless, leading one customer to buy a lovely Aubusson rug, and the other a fine red Axminster.

So what if the price he had quoted young Matt was no more than his dealer's cost. Just whose concern was that? Mr. Biggersley considered that satisfying the youngster's very real desires made profit enough. Still, he couldn't help fearing that for a mere errand boy, even one with such high a degree of dedication as Matt seemed to have, the expense required was too much. "Well, I'll have to grant that the shade is unusual, Matt. All the same, at the price I'm asking . . . ?"

Mattie replied with decision. "Oh, I'll have wherewithal and soon as soon may be! I've way more'n half the amount set by already, and since summer's just beginnin', I'm sure to raise the recruits before the weather turns nasty again. I'll be in to make the purchase afore ever yer knows it!"

"And it will be here waiting," Mr. Biggersley stoutly affirmed.

"Oh! But Mr. Biggersley, you mustn't—"

"Matt, my boy, it's like I said before." He reached over and gave her hat a friendly tug. "Those who can appreciate a fine carpet like this one don't come along every day."

And Tante Agathe is just such a one, Mattie thought.

An aristocrat, accustomed to the greatest luxury before the Revolution, Agathe de Serinier had known only deprivation since. She had lost her husband to the Jacobins, what remained of her property to Napoleon, and had very nearly lost her little great-niece-by-marriage before managing their escape to England. And when she and little Mattie had finally made it to safety in London, they had found themselves welcomed into a community of other aristocratic émigrés who huddled together in gentile poverty, pathetically close to the fashionable districts, where they pined for better days.

Making an assessment of the situation—and their meager funds—the then-fifty-eight-year-old Frenchwoman promptly dropped the *de* in her name, along with all other reference to her rightful title. She dropped her noble acquaintances as well. Refusing to join her more despairing countrymen, she immediately took young Mattie by the hand and moved south to the far side of the Thames. She went to where industry and hope abounded.

In Southwark, Agathe Serinier found them a new place alongside the energetic bourgeoisie. Allowing no snobbish notions to deter her, she busied herself by taking in work trimming pretty gowns meant for others, with hands that remained thankfully supple and skilled with their needle. And when Mattie turned thirteen, she too had taken an employment with Marie Leteuil, the modiste who purchased Agathe Serinier's exquisite embroidery. So, between Mattie's enterprising efforts, which resulted in a nice little salary, and her great-aunt's unstinting industry, they managed to earn enough to live in reasonable comfort, all the while carefully saving a growing fund for the future.

But the senior Serinier forever persisted in cutting corners to shorten the time until they could expand into a full partnership with the dressmaker. It was a plan all agreed would serve them well in due course, for Mme. Leteuil was in favor of any arrangement which would afford her the opportunity of moving to a better business location, while Tante wanted herself and her great-niece to have the advantage of sharing in the increased profits brought thereby. Unfortunately, Tante seemed prepared to go any length for the sake of this dream, so long as her little Madeleine wasn't made to suffer.

But Mattie did suffer. She felt every pain-filled effort as Tante Agathe moved with a false show of ease around their small, two-room apartment during the long cold months of winter.

Mattie pushed her small fists deeper into her coat pockets. She allowed herself to be reassured by Mr. Biggersley's confidence that she would soon have her heart's desire, made possible since Tante insisted that all tips which came her way were hers for her very own use. And tips there were for an enterprising lad! Prompt, polite service brought the coins rolling in.

With that thought, Mattie jumped to recall the time. She took leave of the carpet store owner and directed her steps toward a very different part of town.

Joining the afternoon traffic crossing Blackfriars Bridge into London's southern districts, Mattie made swift progress to a short row of rents situated behind the King's Head yard. Her straight little nose crinkled in protest at the rude smells surrounding the area, even as she obtained her destination: a small shop marked by a modest sign promising ladies gowns made à la mode.

The bell over the door scarcely ceased its jangling before her employer peeked out and came bustling forward to greet her return. Mme. Leteuil's welcome rapidly changed into something more like elation, when Mattie reported on the day's main transaction, involving a notoriously clutch-fisted client.

"De plus? Incroyable!" exclaimed the neatly dressed, middle-aged Frenchwoman. She slapped her palm to her forehead in amazement.

Mattie was swift to answer in the same language. "But of course, Madame." Matter-of-factly, she withdrew a small receipt book from an inner pocket of her vest. At the same time, she brought out a neat stack of currency. "Mrs. Hawes knew to expect me, for I explained the matter to her yesterday when I delivered up her new gown. I had simply to remind her that the advantage of our low prices depends upon each customer's prompt payment, and that nowhere else could she expect to find better work, *n'est-ce pas?* Six years I have had the responsibility for collecting bills due; have you ever known me to fail? Come, come. There is nothing to excite yourself over, Madame."

"Ah, Mattie, *il est un miracle, néanmoins.*"

Mattie shrugged her slim shoulders in typical Gallic style. "It is hardly a miracle that clients should pay their debts, surely. You work hard to have an order ready on time, as do your assistants, my Tante Agathe, and me as well. Why shouldn't Mrs. Hawes do us the same courtesy?"

"*C'est incroyable!*" exulted Mme. Leteuil yet again, her arms waving about in excitement.

"Ah, but then, there is one other thing I should perhaps mention to you." Mattie grinned wickedly in remembrance. "I am bound to say that Mrs. Hawes is not nearly such a tight-fist as we had heard her to be, for just yesterday I had a generous *pourboire* from her very own hand for my services. Of course, that was before I told her to expect me back so soon. Today, I must admit, she was not quite so forthcoming after paying out her bill." Mattie assumed a moue of mock disappointment.

Her employer had to laugh. "Ah, Mattie, Mattie," she scolded with affection, sufficiently calmed by her laughter to switch into speaking English. "It amazes me that you had anything at all from that one. My only hope is that you continue successful with your sweet young face and your boy's dress. I hate to think how I should manage without you."

At this, Mattie glanced about, anxiously putting a finger to her lips. She realized her own speech had been unguarded since entering the shop. "Brigitte?" she whispered softly.

The older woman made a quick, dismissive motion. "Not to concern yourself, *ma petite*. She and Claudine have already gone upstairs to their room, finished with their work for the day. Brigitte mentioned something about a new lotion which was sure to make them both into rare beauties overnight, so it is unlikely that they will interrupt us while you change your clothing. Six years," she mused. "Six whole years and not even your *grand-tante* has discovered our ruse."

"Sacrebleu!" Mattie closed her eyes and gave an involuntary shudder. In perfect English, with no trace of her earlier Cockney accents, she declared, "Now there is the real miracle, Madame. Tante Agathe is fair-minded, indeed, but it was difficult enough convincing her to let me come here as a seamstress, without her having to accept this as well!" Removing her soft felt hat, she pointedly swept it down her costume.

Deep creases split the distance between Mme. Leteuil's thick, half-moon-shaped eyebrows. She held her hands out, palms upward, in an attitude of pleading. "But what else could we do, Mattie? Try hard as I may, I can still see no other way for us to—"

Shushing her on a throaty chuckle, Mattie grasped the modiste's outstretched hands. She gave them a reassuring squeeze. "Oh, there's no need to say it, Madame. I am perfectly well aware that I am the worst needlewoman ever to push a pin through cloth. You could never have afforded to keep me on as a seamstress, no matter your loyalty to Tante Agathe. For do you not remember that first task you set me? It was to baste a length of point lace onto an unfinished hem, if I recall correctly. I also recall that two hours after I'd started, I had somehow snapped a needle, snarled an entire roll of expensive silk thread, and had tangled up the lace so impossibly that you finally had to cut it."

"*Oui, oui. Quel horreur!*" Mme. Leteuil answered feelingly.

"Oh, yes. You said those words exactly," Mattie gurgled.

The dressmaker heaved a sigh. "And your *grand-tante* is such a fine needlewoman, too. The work I send her always comes back perfection itself. No one does such fine embroidered trims as Agathe Serinier. I cannot, no, I really cannot comprehend how it is that you have none of her talent. None!"

"But you remember how it was," Mattie prompted. "After my parents died at the hands of the Jacobins"— she gave an involuntary shudder—"the servants who remained loyal to my family sent me away to a small village in Gironde. There, I was given shelter by a sweet old cleric who made pretense of being my uncle. The good Père Gilles taught me much, including the English language, but I learned precious little of the domestic arts during those years. And then, when Tante at last discovered my whereabouts, I was already twelve years old. It never occurred to her that a young girl's education could be so lacking as to exclude the art of stitchery. When I talked her into permitting me to apply to you for work, she assumed that someone had already given me the proper instruction."

Mme. Leteuil shook her head and made soft tisking noises with her tongue. "But your *grand-tante* is, truly, such a good and honest woman. I do not like our having served her such a trick."

"But there was no other choice, Madame," came

Mattie's husky-voiced reply. "For months on end, we both tried our best to make a decent seamstress out of me, until you finally insisted that I must suffer crossed eyes, or at the very least be equipped with three thumbs. The idea for me to make your deliveries was the only solution we could devise for rendering me useful. We also decided that dressed as a female, even a very young one, I wouldn't be able to go about the streets so freely."

Madame's heavy eyebrows rose high in alarm. "But of course, such a thing would never serve! Wearing skirts to walk the few blocks here to my shop from your lodgings every day is one thing, but for a *jeune fille,* a young girl, to go alone into the city is a different matter altogether!"

"Just so. But things have worked themselves out well enough, I think?"

"Mais oui, I cannot disagree. My profits are improved every year, since the customers do not need to come here so often." Marie Leteuil wrinkled her long narrow nose in a gesture similar to Mattie's earlier one of distaste for the local aroma. She next added in bracing notes, "But you, my little one, you have your own special talents. You have a way of seeing to it that we're paid right on time for every purchase. Why, I doubt any shop in the city has accounts so up-to-date! Although if we want our luck to endure," she then cautioned, glancing up to the old round-cased clock hanging on the showroom wall, "it is time we got you ready for your return home. Madame *la Marquise* will be missing you."

This reminder of her great-aunt's position under the *ancien régime* spurred Mattie to a recollection of her afternoon's introduction to a member of the English nobility. What was it again? The Earl of Stafford? . . . Stamfield? Mattie wasn't sure. But she clearly recalled the concern in his voice, the pleasant warmth of his smile, and the unnamed thing which had, for a time, dulled his eyes.

She had identified it, finally.

It was deadly, positively crushing, boredom.

Chapter Two

Vincent Charles Houghton, the Earl of Staffield, glanced over at the brown cut-velvet draperies which prevented so much as a hint of daylight from seeping its way through. He took a long, slow sip of Madeira before transferring his playing cards over to his other hand. Absently, he reached down to tug at the thick gold chain attached to the sueded leather loop just above his watch pocket, extracting a slim, chased-gold timepiece. Using the edge of his thumb, he sprang open the dial cover to lazily remark the hour to his companions.

"It's going close on seven, gentlemen. So what's it next to be? Boulton's Chop House for a rump and a dozen, or straight on as planned to Westminster Pit?"

Directly across the *tapis vert* sat a leanly built, hatchet-nosed fellow. He slouched in his seat, his long sharp-edged jaw tucked deep into his shoulder. Left to his own devices since being dealt out at the last raise in stakes, he seemed intent on making a count of the many silver whip points speared into the breast of his beautifully fashioned, sedge-colored coat. The glittering barbs marched up his chest in a perpendicular line, ascending almost to the edge of his exquisitely styled, sateen-lined collar. Mr. Schweitzer, the maker of this once-superb garment, would undoubtedly cringe at the profanation.

"Too early for supper," this Tulip of the Turf mumbled preoccupiedly. "Don't like to dine before nine, y' know." Returning his full attention to the matter at hand, he concentrated on making a minute adjustment to a whip point adjudged slightly out of line.

Another athletic-looking gentleman, this one much heavier in build and wearing burgundy Bath coating over a red Loretto silk waistcoat, was placed at Vincent's right. He looked up from his cards to suggest, "Why not get ourselves a quartern of stingo at the Crown and Cushion after this hand? We can hie over to the Pit afterward. No use in going too early, since the serious betting won't start till eight or so. Zounds! I hear they're setting a Brazilian monkey against Seagrave's terrier tonight. Should be quite a match! I doubt it'll be much past ten before it's all over, though, so we can sup afterward, think you?" He glanced round at his fellows to see if everyone was agreeable.

A fourth at their table, his sun-browned face and hands marking him as yet another member of the Corinthian set, held the seat on Vincent's left. He affected a green silk eye-shade, its brim stiffened with wire. The contraption was set well back on the gentleman's head, its serious use evidently forgotten.

With the punctilious methodology common to those approaching a certain state of inebriety, the green-visored gentleman carefully laid his playing cards, face down, on the table. Ignoring the discussion, he counted out his remaining chips, then bent his head to commence a search through his pockets. Peering owlishly at the assortment of crumpled pound notes and the odd smattering of coins eventually discovered, he brought the whole amount forward. He began making stacks of what was left of his painted wooden counters, adding in the various-sized coins and paper currency in a precise and finicking manner.

"Challenge," he announced, then hiccoughed loudly.

Sir Guy Chittenham, the powerfully built, burgundy-clad gentleman, scowled and reexamined his hand. He had called for two new cards at his last turn, and now seemed put into a dilemma over whether to exchange more cards or drop out, whether to meet or exceed the bet.

Vincent observed each of his table companions by turns. He barely managed to contain a sigh as he lazed back in his seat, his eyelids feeling thick and heavily weighted of a sudden. Obliged to idleness while he awaited Sir Guy's decision, he ruminated over how many evenings he had sat here in White's exclusive gentlemen's club, whiling away an ever-lengthening series of slow-moving hours as he watched Sir Guy frown over his cards in just that particular way. How many times had he seen Lord Maines toy with the spare whip points he always wore stuck into his coat, and watched his friend Mr. Evant imbibe glass after glass, until he could hardly hold to his seat?

Restlessly, the earl stretched his long, muscular legs beneath the table. He had scant interest in the play, despite the growing amount at risk, and feared that tonight's contest at Westminster Pit would prove even less entertaining.

Who cared, really, whether a monkey could best a bull terrier? Besides which, it was the type of event which invariably left Vincent feeling somewhat discomfited, even guilty. The idea of men setting animals against each other, animals which had to be unnaturally baited before they would fight, was a trifle disgusting, to his mind. It was all done for sport, of course; although lately, he had found himself wanting to eschew such excursions.

Oh, he didn't have to go, certainly. There were other, more entertaining *divertissements*. To be sure, one could switch to dicing if the cards continued too predictable.

Vincent spared a dilatory glance for his accumulated winnings—mute evidence of the day's prowess with the pasteboards. The sight brought him no pleasure. But if setting a wager didn't please, either here or at the Pit, well, he could always remain at the Crown and Cushion, bending an elbow with whatever company he found there.

The earl downed a deeper sip of his Madeira. His attention continued to wander while Sir Guy dithered over the cards.

With his eyes half closed, Vincent acknowledged an encroaching element of unimportance, of wasted days, causing unwonted shadows of late. The old excitement of a night on the town, the thrill of high stakes and dangerous risks, didn't seem to exhilarate the way it once had done, and worse, he realized that the odd moment of unhappy introspection was becoming more and more frequent. . . .

By God! Sitting straighter in his chair, Vincent gave himself a stern mental shake. Was he become some brooding moralist? He, who had always prided himself on being a man who lived life unto its very hilt? Never say so! Dark blue eyes sparkled in self-directed anger. Vincent made himself a silent vow to enjoy himself tonight, be it at the Pit, the gin shop, or wherever else his fancy might take him!

Then, another activity worth considering occurred.

Lady Hedgewick would be at the Bessborough rout party later tonight, so she had told him with an altogether *killing* look yesterday when he'd stopped for a moment beside her carriage in Hyde Park. Free to take her pleasures as she wished after having birthed a son for the Hedgewick barony, her ladyship seemed to expect that the Earl of Staffield would consider her notice most flattering. In truth, nearly any man would. And more especially since, in addition to her unmatched beauty, she was known for the highest selectivity in choosing her lovers—*exclusivity* being the ultimate goal amongst people of *ton*. So. Should he put it to the touch tonight?

Not that Vincent was overly impressed by the baroness's having singled him out. The lady had a reputation for regarding only those men whose titles ranked above her husband's. It was a quality which this particular earl failed to find especially praiseworthy. He did think it interesting, though, that Lady Hedgewick considered his earldom so important, when a mere errand boy hadn't seemed overly concerned.

This thought put Vincent in mind of the young lad whom he had encountered earlier, the boy with the glistening black curls and the gaily impudent grin. *He* hadn't been greatly awed by a title. The words "chucklehead notion" sang through Vincent's head, while the faintest of smiles touched his lips.

And just why should it be, he wondered, somewhat less happily, that more people couldn't see him as the lad had seemed to do? Why shouldn't he be accredited simply as a person, without assessing the value of the honors bestowed upon him at birth? God knew, he had done nothing to deserve élite status!

Sometimes, Vincent bethought himself, the world made no sense. No sense at all.

Movement at his right put an end to these musings. Sir Guy apparently had made up his mind. Tossing out sufficient chips to match Mr. Evant's bet, the brawny sportsman in the burgundy cloth coat then moved to increase the wager as, with a cunning look, he plunked down a whole rouleau of guineas. The gold coins were wrapped in a string-tied bag of dark red morel felt.

The rolled coins sounded heavily on the tabletop. A dull thud reverberated all the way to the ends of the room.

Bored club members, disturbed by the noise, looked about them for the source of the sound. Within seconds, all eyes focused on the telltale coin sack. Those gentlemen not currently engaged in play jumped up and hurried over to better see what went forward, while those whose games forbade them to rise snapped their cards shut tight against their chests, even as they anxiously twisted about in their seats. Whispered comments grew in volume as avid eyes slued from man to man.

Impassively, the earl matched Sir Guy's bet. He exchanged not a single card.

Several of the younger clubmen seemed much elated by his cool, decisive move. Their low-voiced buzzings rose to an excited pitch as they dodged about the cardroom, grasping acquaintances by the arm to give voice to their speculations. Equally attentive, if more staid of movement, the older gentlemen, too, collected in numbers around the earl's table. Soon, new bets were being eagerly offered along the sides. Age was no barrier as gambling fever struck full force.

Mr. Evant seemed unaware of the growing tumult. He remained for some minutes in strict perusal of his cards.

Their arrangement must have pleased, for he finally called for a pen and paper and set himself to painstakingly preparing a marker meant to add to the bet. Passing his chit to the Earl of Staffield—as was proper since his lordship was acting as their dealer—he said distinctly, "Challenge again."

The surrounding din grew louder.

More alert to their many observers, Sir Guy studied his cards with a sly expression. At length, he drew out the coins needed to match Mr. Evant's investment. Then, for good measure, he threw in still another weighty roll of golden boys.

As before, a deep thud sounded on the tabletop.

An elated roar swept up to the ceiling and bounced down along the walls. Men slapped their fellows across the back, shouting out their approval! A game of deep brag was unusual at White's, and the clubmen seemed scarcely able to contain their joy. Fast and furious, new bets were impetuously offered and accepted.

Vincent observed the outrageous to-do, at the same time wishing he could feel something of the same fervor. Instead, he felt strangely closed in, oppressed by all the excitement. He exhaled a long, slow breath and pulled his feet nearer to his chair. Disdaining so much as a peek at his cards, he selected the appropriate amount needed to stay in the game and pushed it to the table's center.

In turn, Mr. Evant looked again at his own cards. Giving an inane grin, he removed his silk eye-shade, laid down his cards, and positioned the green visor atop the lot. Still grinning, he called loudly for a side bet and added an order for wine-of-choice all around.

Only two now remained in the game: Sir Guy and the Earl of Staffield.

The additional wagering became frenzied as newcomers moved in to join those nearest the table. The crowd increased with amazing swiftness as word of the game reached the club's other rooms. The subsequent amounts bet on the game attained phenomenal heights.

Chortling in triumph, Sir Guy at last called the bet. "B'gad, Vincent, I have you this time!" He looked round gleefully at his supporters. "Just look you here—I hold a trio of eights! You'll not beat that, I'll be bound!" Beaming with delight, Sir Guy fanned out his cards, face up, and reached for the jumbled pile of notes, coins, and counters.

Before he could gather his winnings, however, Vincent spread open his own hand. Four queens winked up at the overhead lamp: two of them inked in black, and two in the brightest of reds.

"Well, bless me, har-har!" the would-be winner guffawed, disregarding the many moans of dismay from his backers. "Why, I'm all done up! No thief could've cleaned me out better. But what a bang-up hand it is that scorched me! Zounds!" Smiling hugely, Sir Guy called over to the Corinthian of the sedge-colored coat. "Well, Nick, what think you of my being beaten, and by such a *go* of a hand?" He seemed more thrilled by the winning cards than Vincent did himself.

Nicholas Porterby, Viscount Maines, left off fiddling with his whip points. A wry smile flickered across his narrow face. "Oh, really, Sir Guy," he drawled, "what else could one possibly expect? Our friend always comes the eagle, 'specially where the ladies are involved." With just a trace of envy in his voice, he added, "And you must know that Lady Luck is little different from any other demoiselle, charmed by a good-looking phiz. We'd best to just be grateful we weren't completely *cleared* like poor Evant here." The viscount gestured toward their potative friend, now snoring softly, his head at rest on the green baize table covering.

Mr. Evant continued oblivious even when the more fortunate gamesters made the earl a rousing cheer. Indeed, most of the clubmen had backed Lord Staffield as the winner, for such was his reputation. In their elation, several of the younger gentlemen even dared make so bold as to come forward with loud calls of "Jolly good show, Vince!" and "We can trust Ol' Invincible to know what's what, eh, fellows?"

Still, Mr. Evant didn't stir.

Irritated for no reason he could think of, Vincent stood to his height. One dark, dispassionate look sent their collective audience back to attend whatever prior matters had concerned them. Summoning the club's steward, the earl then undertook to pay for the wine Mr. Evant had so recklessly ordered, after which, he picked up the green silk eye-shade and placed it inside his own coat for safekeeping. Without anyone's notice, he also slipped a wad of pound notes into the sleeping man's pocket.

Gently, he shook Mr. Evant by the shoulder. "It's suppertime for you, my friend," he said softly. "Come, man, it's time we were off."

Mr. Evant mumbled something incomprehensible, without raising his head.

"Nick? Guy?" The earl nodded meaningfully to the two.

Understanding the implied request, Sir Guy came forward to help Vincent lift Mr. Evant to his feet. Lord Maines eased the impeding chair out of their path. Together, they assisted the intoxicated gentleman from the room, collecting their stylish, high-crowned beaver hats and their fine leather gloves from a liveried footman along the way.

By the time the party reached the out-of-doors, Mr. Evant was holding his own.

Even as the four gamesters made their way down St. James's Street, a half-grown girl wearing thick, black cotton stockings beneath a calf-length dress skipped merrily through the early evening streets of Southwark. An overlarge mob cap of some soft white material sat squash atop her head, and a voluminous blue-and-white-striped pinafore, fastened by one large button at the back, swung loosely from her shoulders. Neatly blacked ankle boots with crisscrossed lacings covered her small, swiftly moving feet.

She appeared to be no more than eleven or, possibly, twelve years in age, judging from her piquant little face and her slender, unformed body of rather less than adult size. Indeed, there was nothing to distinguish this particular child from a thousand others girls who toiled daily in the many manufactories south of the Thames. She was an ordinary girl from her head to her toes, prosaic in all respects; that is, unless one happened to notice that she whistled a merry little tune under her breath as she made her way homeward. Not too many females ventured to learn that particular skill.

But then, Mademoiselle Madeleine Serinier was up to almost anything.

At Williams Court, Mattie turned in and trotted up the worn stone steps fronting an old but sturdily built rooming house. Rapping a three-two rhythm as she passed by the landlady's door to let her know that she'd returned, she then sped up the three sets of stairs which angled toward the top floor.

"Tante, I'm home!" she chirruped as she rushed inside the uppermost apartment. She hastened over to give her great-aunt an energetic hug.

In a wooden-armed Windsor chair, placed beside a cluttered work table set before the room's single window, Agathe Serinier responded in melodic, faintly French accents. "And so you are at that, my little one. I see your day went well." She raised her strongly modeled chin to accept her great-niece's hug.

Of generous proportions, Mattie's great-aunt was not at all of that sort referred to as "fat." Instead, the senior Serinier's firm figure was more rightly termed *substantial*. Her erect posture in the chintz-cushioned chair bespoke the dignified noblewoman, as did her well-defined features and her impeccably coroneted salt-and-pepper hair, worn under a high lace cap in that style popularized during the reign of Louis Quinze. Coffee brown eyes beneath sharply arched brows, along with her beautifully shaped and purposefully engaged hands, proved the elder Serinier to be a woman of both breeding and of character.

"Oh, a fine day, indeed!" Mattie declared, giving a glad little smile. Her smile broadened as she recalled the Brussels safely fixed behind the polished panes of Mr. Biggersley's shop window.

Mattie bent to touch the gay yellow threads forming a delicate pattern beneath her *grand-tante*'s quick fingers. The waning light was just sufficient to distinguish one thread from the other, and she delighted anew in her great-aunt's skill. She felt a familiar stirring of pride.

Agathe Serinier had another matter on her mind, however. Glancing out of the window at the failing light, she said in her sweet, musical voice, "You do not forget that today is Thursday, Madeleine?" Tante was the only one who called her Madeleine.

Spreading wide the folds of her pinafore, Mattie stepped back and spun about, very like the young girl she pretended to be. Bright, expressive eyes lit with anticipation. "Thursday!" she crowed. "And that means no cook's chores for us tonight. I'm to fetch our dinners ready-made from Mrs. Canaday's Pot House! It's cock-a-leekie soup, honied carrots, mutton pâtés, and matelotte; also, Mrs. Canaday's best light bread, and all the salad I can fit into my pail. I'm as good as there already."

So saying, she went to rummage behind the faded calico skirting tacked to the edges of a bare-topped deal table in one corner of the room. She soon found what was wanted, bringing up two sizable tin containers, each one fitted with a sturdy wire handle. One for small beer, the other for holding their dinners, Mattie took a moment to check her pockets for the needed coins before scurrying back out of doors.

Just as the evening shadows melded together, she returned. She set the two pails, much heavier now with Mrs. Canaday's wares, on top of the sanded surface of the deal table. She knelt to search out plates, mugs, and their few eating utensils stored underneath, and after arranging these items precisely, she went to the opposite corner of the room to pull out a long flat box from under Tante Agathe's narrow cot.

Reverently, Mattie lifted the hinged lid and withdrew two snowy-white damask napkins. Each was marked in rich gold thread at the outermost corner with the *écusson* of the de Serinier house. She brought them over to the table and laid them out, before lighting a single slender rushlight in its twisted blacked-iron stand. This, she fixed exactly in middle of the table. She next cautiously filled their mugs with beer, taking care not to spill.

"All is ready," she said at last, giving her kinswoman the nod.

Tante Agathe put aside her sewing and took up a plain walnut cane. Moving with slow, dignified grace, she came to take a seat at the table.

In utter silence, Mattie apportioned their dinners from the neatly packed pail. Never once did she allow a carelessly wielded spoon to yield up noise. Finished with the serving, she sat down opposite her great-aunt and placed her napkin in her lap. Surreptitiously, Mattie then reached for a corner of the table skirting to employ as a cover for the fine white damask, wanting nothing to mar its pristine surface.

In the language of their homeland, Tante commenced a very proper dinner conversation. She included a description of Molière's last play, a lively comparison between the elderly woman's memory of French theatre and her ideas about the current English productions, as lately read about in the newspapers, followed by a request for Mattie's opinion on Scott's newest poem. While the subject matter might change from one week to the next, all was done according to the regular Thursday night ritual. It was the only time, in fact, that Tante Agathe permitted French to be spoken between them, since she held to the idea that they should otherwise embrace the language of their new homeland.

After the last morsel was eaten and Mattie had neatly stacked the dishes by the door for washing at the common pump in the back courtyard on the morrow, Tante

Agathe made her way back to her seat by the window. She gestured for Mattie to bring up another chair.

First bringing the rushlight over to the small worktable by Tante's elbow, Mattie went to fetch one of the slat-backed dining chairs. She positioned it comfortably near. And when her great-aunt launched into a rapid-fire series of questions, Mattie answered each just as rapidly with the proper way to phrase a social invitation and the polite forms of address for each level of the nobility— French and English, written and spoken. Tante encouraged her to a recitation of the correct seating for guests at a formal dinner party, an outline of the duties of both a guest and a hostess at various types of functions, the expected amount for the vails requisite with different sorts of service . . .

And so forth, and so on. Just as it went on this one night of every week.

When the rushlight burned down nearly to its end, Mattie hopped up to set a new stem. The next hour would be much more entertaining for a young lady who found it difficult to remain still for any length. The time for sitting rigidly upright and politely patient was ended. Now, it was time for the second set of lessons.

On Tante's command, Mattie began a sequence of curtsies, each one graduating in deference until she made her final practice bow to a royal. Without faltering in the slightest, she arose smoothly from this last when her great-aunt gave her the word. Her execution was flawless.

"Perfection. Sans défauts," Tante Agathe breathed in appreciation. *"Eh bien,* Madeleine," she cried softly, *"eh bien, la polonaise!"*

Obediently, while Tante hummed the three-quarter-timed measures to the ancient court dance, Mattie performed the steps. Actually more of a procession than a dance, the polonaise required subtly intricate motions made *en promenade*. Mattie fulfilled each stately movement, through the Coup de Talon, the Chassé Coupé, the Pas de Valse, and the Pas de Basque, performing each step of the dance with extreme precision and, more importantly, with elaborate style. Barely able, in the small room, to keep her arms fully extended to the sides as required, she nevertheless managed her turns and transfers with exquisite grace.

Mattie knew that, for the moment at least, her great-aunt was lost to any awareness of the blue-and-white poplin billowing out in the larger of their apartment's two tiny rooms. Tante didn't see thick-soled black shoes, nor even the overlarge mobcap covering her great-niece's dark glossy curls. Instead, she saw satins and lace, slippers of soft Morocco leather, tall plumed headdresses, and jewels of great price. The old lady envisioned a grand ballroom, rich with the sounds of gay laughter and fine music, a place where the enjoyment of leisure had become an art. All this, Mattie sensed without being told.

At the end, Tante Agathe gave a soft sniff and wiped a hint of moisture from the corners of her eyes. *"Merveilleux, ma petite,"* she murmured proudly.

Mattie smiled. Not that she felt any real desire to be dressed in silks or fine feathers like those her great-aunt imagined for her. Neither did she think that a knowledge of formal dance nor of orders of precedence was anything needful for her future. She was content with life as it was. Nonetheless, she understood why Tante was so insistent. The old lady believed that such instruction was entirely practical, considering elegant manners to be a brilliant achievement of civilization. Tante stoutly maintained that her little Madeleine should develop an appreciation for the niceties of gracious living.

Mademoiselle Serinier wasn't altogether certain about the correctness of this reasoning—although dinner parties and plays did sound rather nice—but she accepted absolutely that her *grand-tante* saw the lessons as a necessity. More to the point, she recognized that the old dear was never so happy as when giving out her instructions. It was reason enough to participate in their Thursday custom with enthusiasm.

Attending to the dishwashing the next morning, Mattie scrubbed away at the remainders of last night's dinner while her thoughts drifted over Tante's latest lecture on the subject of vails.

Tipping was a fact of life, as Mattie knew to her profit. To be sure, she rejoiced in every opportunity for an active lad to earn that little bit extra. The money was especially important since every coin, every half-pence, brought her closer to the amount needed for the carpet in Mr. Biggersley's shop window. Copper pennies added up to make silver shillings, and with slightly less than a hundred more of those, the beautiful Brussels would be hers.

A vague frown marred Mattie's forehead when she next recalled how a certain lord had been entirely too quick with the mint sauce just yesterday. The earl had offered her a coin, and a whole shilling at that, merely because *she* had charged smack into *him*. What had made him think she was entitled to his money, money she'd in no way earned? He hadn't looked like a green 'un, unused to town ways. Rather, he had appeared downright knowing.

Perhaps it was because she'd sat there on the pavement for so long that he'd taken her for a spooney. He might well have felt sorry for a presumed defect in her intelligence; she had certainly stared up at him long enough for him to have formed that opinion. What a fool she must have appeared!

Mattie pumped a fresh stream of water and rubbed harder at the inside of the tin pail currently undergoing the process of cleansing. She wrinkled her dainty nose in disgust.

A little smile followed. She remembered what had happened next, the way his lordship had accepted her pert refusal and had even given out his name. *What the Jack Adams was it anyway?* She wasn't certain. But his eyes against the tanned skin of his face had glowed the most beautiful shade of dark blue, of that she was very sure. Oh, yes. His eyes she remembered well—and she wondered about them most of all.

Not given to introspection in the ordinary way, Mattie spared a moment to consider whether she could have been mistaken in her interpretation of his lordship's look. She had judged it more than simple boredom, since for long moments he had seemed hideously detached, despite his pleasant speech. And just as if he were someone she had known for a lifetime, Mattie had read his face with surety.

Shaking her dark curls with a snap, she decided she wasn't wrong about what she had seen.

This, in turn, led to the next question. Why such appalling apathy, such a look of unendurable weariness? He was obviously well-favored, an acknowledged peer of the realm, and to her alert eye, his clothing marked him as quite well-to-do besides. How could such a person feel bored?

Someone like herself might better have reason. A displaced French noblewoman with a menial employment, she alternated her part as an insignificant errand boy with that of a stumpy, half-grown girl. There might be some excuse if she felt the banality of such a routine. Instead, she learned something new almost daily, made friends in great numbers, and had acquaintances galore. Busy as she was with trotting around town, she exulted in her easy camaraderie with this one and that, and she knew herself well thought of by all.

True, she couldn't discuss playwrights with young Billy Tomkins, who did the deliveries for the stationer on Wardours Street, but neither could Tante Agathe enlighten her on the latest in *canting*, the vulgar slang used in the streets. Both were topics worthy of interest. Mr. Biggersley had admitted her into many of the secrets of appraising a fine rug, Mrs. Frobisher at Covent Garden Market had taught her the best way to tell a good pine, and the old charley on watch at Chandler Street had a fund of the wittiest jokes ever. All of her friends were enjoyed for whatever they could contribute. In return, Mattie served as a willing and sympathetic listener and was known as a quick one to lend a hand.

The world was full of fascinating people with untold knowledge. Most definitely, it was! Now that she gave it her serious consideration, too, Mattie marveled that anyone could fail to be involved with the lives of those around them. It was unthinkable to feel disinterested or detached. Each soul had its own thoughts, its own troubles and triumphs, just begging to be shared.

Shaking her dark curls yet again, this time in dismissal, Mattie put the earl from her mind. She wiped the last fork dry and gathered up the dishes. A few minutes later, she dashed back out of the building, pinafore a-flying. She was off to Mme. Leteuil's with nary a second to spare.

Once outfitted in her boy's attire, Mattie scampered through the mazelike streets of London, bringing in new fabrics from the big import houses at the mouth of the river and picking up orders for matching thread at the dyers. On the following day, she delivered packages to Mme. Leteuil's customers scattered throughout the city, with only one errand taking her to the West End. And even though she was alert for the sight, Mattie failed to encounter the earl.

She had to shrug off a flicker of disappointment when, after several more days had passed, she still didn't see him.

Chapter Three

"Coo-oey! Would ya' fasten yer peepers on that?"

Billy Tomkins, Kevin Howe, and "Matt" stopped to gawk in wonderment at the great red and yellow lozenge-paneled balloon just passing beyond the massive dome of St. Paul's Cathedral. Young Billy, a dark-haired boy of rather awkward thinness as his arms and legs sprouted to their adult length, had been the first to spot it when they rounded the corner of Carter Lane. As one, the trio joined in giving loud hurrahs for the thrilling spectacle.

The shortest of the three, though half again older than the youths' ages of thirteen years apiece, Mattie stood on tiptoe and made several little hopping leaps to keep the magnificent globe within sight for as long as she could.

"Ye gods," she at last swore in admiration.

"Look at 'er go!" the sandy-haired Kevin shrilled nearly at the same time. "Oin't it the foinest thing? Why, I bet she could toike a fellow all the way ter the moon, whatcher think!" He seemed about to burst with excitement.

Mattie turned and tweaked her broad-faced, freckle-nosed friend's cap. "Naw," she derided, "an' yer a bloody fool for the very idea, Kevin Howe. 'Tain't possible, I says. 'Sides which, I've heard tell that the higher up yer goes in one of them contraptions, the colder and colder it gets. Yer'd freeze yer back pockets off afore yer'd made it half the distance."

"Matt's gotcha there," Billy Tomkins put in wisely. He bobbed his head with such vigor as to send his long, blunt-cut hair swinging. A trifle nearsighted, Billy rounded raisin-dark eyes to pass along the benefit of his experience. "You'll remember that big balloon exhibition in the park late last summer?" he directed. "Well, I was there, and one o' them famous air-ree-o-nauts told me personal as 'ow 'e nearly froze somethin' awful on one trip, seein' as 'ow 'e let the burner get too fierce, sendin' the balloon away up too 'igh. Said 'e finally had ta shut the fire off completely and come a-fallin' to the ground all in a 'eap. Broke 'is bleedin' arm, 'e did."

"Aow, yer oin't just sayin' that?" Kevin asked.

"S'truth," said Mattie straightly. "I heard 'bout it the next day m'self. Leastways, though, it makes a right toppin' sight to see, don't it?"

Mattie had the knack of mimicking her two friends' speech patterns and could swallow her ending *g*'s with the best. She usually refrained from dropping her aitches like dark-haired Billy, and from *oi*-ing her *i*'s like the fair-skinned Kevin, although, on the whole, she delighted in the idiom of London's street-raised kiddies. She copied their accents for the sheer joy of it and so as not to appear too odd in their company.

Without another word being spoken and everyone apparently in agreement, the three remained where they were until the last speck of red-and-yellow silk floated from view. Hot air balloons were a novelty which invariably took youthful imaginations soaring along with them.

Billy Tomkins suddenly recalled that it was a working day, with time a precious thing. He took his two friends in charge, reminding them that if they were to have a spot of coffee together at the Bluebell as planned, they would have to hurry. "An' the last one there's an ol' goose's rump!" he caroled merrily over his shoulder.

He started off in a sprint down the street, Kevin and "Matt" right behind.

Over their cups and buns a short while later, Mattie thought to make use of the opportunity to solicit a bit of information from her two friends. Both boys were above the usual cut, having obtained enough schooling to read, and they knew the city well. Young Billy carried specially engraved stationery to some of the best houses in Mayfair, while Kevin's employment, distributing handbills for Astley's famous circus, brought him into contact with a still larger part of the city. Either boy might be able to help her. In deliberately casual tones, she inquired, "Say now, I don't s'pose one of yer, by chance, happens to know of an earl who's chaunted as Stamfield or maybe Stafford, does yer?"

"An earl?" squeaked Kevin, his adolescent high-low voice sounding like a cartwheel in urgent need of the grease. Hot coffee sloshed over his freckle-skinned knuckles. With a bang, he dropped the dish onto the scarred surface of the table. Ignoring the mishap, his short, turned-up nose twitched in dismay. "Naow, Matt, how'd yer suppose our loikes 'ud be knowin' anythin' about *earls?* They has their ways, and we has ours! Whatcher wants ter know fer, anyways?"

Mattie scraped one neatly trimmed fingernail against a small chip in the handle of her own cup. She wasn't sure how to answer Kevin's question; more than that, she suspected that any attempt to explain would be met with well-merited ridicule. Still, she refused to let it go.

"Well," she muttered, "I sort of stumbled into this partic'lar one some days past. Less than thirty in years, I'd say, and a goodly sized, remarkable grand fellow he was. I knew I hadn't got the name straight, but you could be in the right of it, thinking 'tis none o' my business."

"Oi'll say it oin't!" Kevin pushed out his broad chin pugnaciously.

Mattie felt an unexpected surge of disappointment course through her. As though her meeting with the earl had happened but an hour since, the large, elegantly dressed gentleman with the deep blue eyes made a picture which persisted in cropping up in her mind at odd intervals. She recalled how his lordship's face had seemed to warm after she had twitted him and the answering warmth she had felt at his smile. Most of all, though, she wanted to see if that wearisome look she'd discovered lurking within his eyes was still there, or if it had been merely a temporary thing, now forgotten.

Peering across the table, Billy Tomkins cleared his throat. He fixed Mattie with a serious look. "Yer'd be meanin' Lord Staffield, then," he said sagely. "But Matt, anyone who knows anythin' could tell ya' as 'ow that one's an out-and-outer. Why, 'e's known all about town as the 'Invincible Vince,' seein' as 'ow 'e's a tearin' great Nonesuch. Ol' Invincible takes up any sportin' wager, they say, and wins it fair and square. Whether it be in the boxin' ring, toolin' a bang-up rig, a matter o' blades or even pistols, I tells ya true, the man's unbeatable! But ya must be 'avin' us on, Matt. Ya couldn't be meanin' ya actually met 'im, could ya?"

"Ah-ha!" she cheered in triumph, her mask of indifference vanishing on the instant. "Oh, I *knew* the name was somethin' like that. Staffield. Staf*field!* Yes, that's it! A tall man with hair about the color of Kevin's here ... er, well, maybe a shade or two off," she judged, comparing the latter's lank and sandy-colored wisps with the memory of the sun-gilt thickness of dark gold. "But yer says he's a famous Nonesuch? I doubt it could be the same fellow I mean, then." Her voice faded as she heaved a small sigh. "No," she continued more slowly, "the man I met seemed to be a withdrawn type of fellow, the kind to have few friends."

Then, remembering that the large gentleman had given out his first name as Vincent, she took heart and said, "Still an' all, it might be him, Billy. Tell me more 'bout this Staffield fellow, so's I can tell if it's the same 'un I came across."

Nothing loath, the dark-haired boy dredged up story after story of Lord Staffield's daring. Billy Tomkins ever prided himself on being in-the-know and so included spirited accounts of the earl's mastery of the reins, his reputation for coolness at the gaming tables, and a report on his superb style in the field of honor.

It was mention of this last which sent Mattie into shivers. She found the thought of *that* sort of notoriety chilling. Dueling might well be illegal, but because it was virtually unheard of for a jury to bring in a conviction for such an offense, the activity was frightfully common.

Misinterpreting her reaction, Kevin gave a light cuff to her upper arm. "Naow, Matt," he cautioned, "if'n yer really came across such a prime 'un, he'd never have a word ter spend on one such as us, naow, would he? 'Tis more'n any could be expected ter believe!"

46

"Well, yer can believe it or not as it suits yer, Kevin Howe." She sniffed with indignation. "But if it is the same fellow, then I do so know him. More'n that, *he* knows *me.*" Smiling widely to take the sting out of her words, she reached over and returned the pale-haired, freckle-faced boy an affectionate shove.

When this proved effective in making him grin back at her, the three friends downed their coffee and hungrily dabbed up the last crumbs from their buns. It was time they set back out to attend their respective businesses. At Carter Street they broke apart, each on his own separate errand.

Mattie headed back toward Mme. Leteuil's. As she trotted along the pavement, she spared a brief thought for what her friend Billy had told her. Was it possible that the gentleman she had encountered was the sort of neck-or-nothing sporting man described? Was the tall gentleman with the sapphire blue eyes a roistering Man-About-Town?

But no, she concluded. He couldn't be. For despite the fleeting look of boredom he'd worn—a hallmark of wastrels, she knew—his lordship hadn't looked in the least dissipated. Dismal or disillusioned, perhaps, but not dissipated. His sun-warmed complexion had glowed with good health, and he had been so very, very kind. He had willingly helped her to her feet and had inquired after her well-being. Why, he had even taken her chiding in good part.

A man known as the "Invincible Vince" would instead have harsh creases stamped into his face. Cynicism, not ennui, would rule his days. Such a man would never think to trouble himself with being polite to a clumsy errand boy; a man like that would ignore her totally!

Having thus convinced herself that she still hadn't got the name right, Mattie gave up further speculation and hurried along her way. Unless something new had occurred at the dressmaker's in the last two hours, she had no more duties on this side of the river today. A very good day it had been, too. Even after a deduction for the coffee she'd shared with her friends, she'd earned a full shilling since the morn.

She arrived at the shop just in time to see Madame disappearing around the other side of the building, apparently off on a concern of her own. That left only Brigitte and Claudine minding the shop.

"Heigh-ho!" Mattie called loudly as she burst in through the front door.

Assuming a menacing air, she brandished an imaginary pistol. She pushed through the curtain which separated the workroom from the front area, surprising Madame's two assistants in their tasks. With her arm extended threateningly, she mimed two pulls of the trigger fired up at the ceiling.

"*Boom! Boom!* Yer mine fer the ransoming, me pretties, so step ye lively there!"

Startled, Brigitte dropped her needle, leaving its long green thread to trail haphazardly behind. Claudine loosed her hold on a card of lace to clap both hands over her mouth.

Mattie bellowed out in her deepest voice, "Two such fine beauties should bring a heavy purse, for it's Incomparables ye both be! Ne'er have I seen the likes of yer jet black hair, yer skin as smooth as any newborn babe's, and yer eyes like fresh-shaved chocolate. Lips like cherries, ripe and red; why, a man is not a man who doesn't long to steal a kiss!" She swept off her hat and made a leg in homage.

Giggling madly, the two shop assistants fell in with the spirit of the game. *"Non, non!"* shrieked Brigitte. "Please not to harm us, *monsieur,* for we are only the two poorest girls and there can be none to save us!" She threw out her slender hands in supplication, the perfection of her features all the more adorable for her expression of pretended dismay.

Plump and pretty, if not such a beauty as her elder sister, Claudine only giggled all the harder. She was not so comfortable with English as Brigitte, but it was plain to see that she was equally pleased with "Matt's" caperings.

Mattie often teased the pair in similar manner since they seemed to enjoy it so. More importantly, it helped in giving her an appearance of young masculinity, since Brigitte and Claudine were not in on the secret of her disguise. They had no knowledge that the shop's errand boy was in any way related to the Agathe Serinier who did such wonderful needlework; being from the provinces themselves, they were left to suppose that Serinier was a common name in other parts of France. The grand old city of Paris, for example, was naught but a mystery to them. They had come directly from Alsace to London during the Peace of Amiens. Being simple girls, they had no idea that young Matt was, in fact, a "Mattie" who exchanged her clothing every day after they had gone up to their room.

Mme. Leteuil had advised against telling them the whole when the two girls arrived last April. Recognizing them as a giddy pair, Madame was afraid that they might let something slip to the aristocratic *marquise* if they should meet her one day or, equally dangerous, to someone else who knew Mattie's great-aunt.

Not that there was much chance of the girls ever seeing the creator of the beautiful embroideries which Mattie dispatched back and forth. Nor was it likely that Tante Agathe would venture far from home herself of late, since to manage the three flights of stairs down to the street required more assistance than little Mattie could offer. But Mme. Leteuil was ever a woman of discretion. She insisted that the young grisettes be told nothing, not even that Mattie spoke more than a smattering of French.

On several points Mattie admired the sisters. Brigitte was tall and lovely in both face and form; she had but to crook her little finger to bring forth a string of admirers. And although she excelled in games of the heart, her favorite flirt was a jolly young man just finishing his apprenticeship to the Messrs. Gunter as a baker in the renowned confectionery shop in Berkeley Square. Brigitte's young man had proposed to her less than a month ago, and the romantic-minded young seamstress had ecstatically agreed. Even now, Brigitte awaited her family's permission to marry her Mr. Wilson.

Claudine, on the other hand, was rather stout of body and merely average in height. However, her round open face made way for laughter on the slightest of pretexts, while her halting English was charming when she could be induced to speak. And like her sister, she also had a particular gentleman caller. On Sundays like clockwork, Claudine and her beau walked out together, arm-in-arm. She giggled and preened before his nervous compliments, for he was a young man of solemn aspect. Claudine and, indeed, everyone else expected him to make a declaration most any day.

Sometimes, Mattie wished that she, too, could enjoy the attentions of a young man above the age of thirteen. Brigitte recalled her from such maunderings. "You should be in the *théâtre,* Matt," she proclaimed, recovering her needle and thread. "For one so small to look so very fierce is a great talent, I think. Yes, yes! You should go upon the stage!" She seemed delighted with her idea.

Mattie dropped her imaginary pistol and acted as though she had just sustained a shot to the heart. Grabbing her chest as if in great pain, she fell to her knees, head drooping, and said in a gravel-voiced moan, "I am wounded unto death by these cruel words. I give it my all and what happens? I am accused of playacting. Playacting? Why, I have never so much as set foot inside a theatre, I do assure you."

"But how *injuste.* How unfair!" Brigitte at once exclaimed. "Everyone must go at least once to see a fine *comédie* or a great drama. The *belle danse,* the *costumes*—Matt, you would love it so!"

Claudine, giggling, reached over and pulled at her sister's sleeve. She winked at Brigitte, Mattie could swear to it, passing the other girl a look of sly intelligence. With a sudden, answering look, Brigitte snapped her mouth shut. The pair of them commenced smiling at Mattie in the most fatuous way imaginable.

Mattie couldn't think what the two were up to. Obviously, it was something they didn't want her to know about; the girls acted as if they had just held a private and very significant conversation—one which seemed to concern herself!

Unwilling to pry into their secrets, however, she only shrugged her slim shoulders and said, "So, enough of this foolery. Where has Madame got off to? Am I so late in returning that she has been forced to undertake my duties?"

Brigitte's expression at once turned grave. "But no, it

is nothing like that, Matt. Mme. Leteuil went only to the posting office one street over. It's nearly five o'clock, and she wanted to send off another *lettre* for us before the end of the day's collection." Neither Brigitte nor her sister could read or write, but Mme. Leteuil was faithful about penning letters to their mother for them.

"Oh, Brigitte," Mattie sympathized in immediate understanding. "I do hope the mail gets through this time, for you've not heard from your parents since when— March? And June is nearly spent. Oh, that horrid, horrid Napoleon! He agrees to make peace only last year, and already he's broken the treaty beyond mending. You and Claudine are left with no way to be sure of contacting your family. I am so sorry for it!"

"Not of ze greatest importance," Claudine entered slowly, striving mightily to speak in the unfamiliar tongue. "Eet ees only zat we meess our parents muchly. But zay have no danger, I zink. Mostly, eet ees ze young men who weell suffer eef *le petit général* goes on ze march again."

"And remember—our young men are here," Brigitte added with complaisance.

"Why, and so they are," Mattie agreed.

Then, for no reason at all, the image of a large gentleman with dark blue eyes made a picture in her mind.

Chapter Four

With a sweet smile, Tante Agathe held up a newly completed gown. "Happy birthday, Madeleine!"

Halted in her customary rush across the room, Mattie's lips formed a surprised *O*. She had just come from Mme. Leteuil's shop, finished with her work for the day, unsuspecting that Tante Agathe was bent on marking the occasion of her twentieth birthday with ceremony.

Mattie stared at the soft folds of rose-colored silk cascading from her great-aunt's hands. In the late-afternoon's light, the fabric gleamed with shell pink embroidery, enhanced by an occasional, bright silver thread. The needlework formed an intricate pattern of whorls and points which covered the bodice completely, then flared, spreading out to extend a third of the way down the narrow skirt. Short, cap-style sleeves poufed above a high bandeau waistline, where a long sash, in the deepest shade of rose, was knotted at the front. Two shallow tiers of rich flouncing, picked out in silver and also trimmed in deep rose, subtly finished out the garment.

A beautiful gown, incredibly beautiful, the delicate

tints of pink-on-rose, so daintily touched with silver, would add elegant inches to a natural denizen of Lilliput. It was a perfect dream of a dress.

Mattie remained speechless for long moments. Never, she decided, had anyone received such a gift! Her *grand-tante* had obviously intended it for a surprise, and Mattie knew that her dazed reaction would not give cause for disappointment. Even as she went to feel of the shimmering fabric, though, she felt a quick rise of protest at the expense it represented.

"Oh, Tante, I really didn't need anything this grand," she demurred. "It will likely take weeks and weeks for our savings to recover and— 'Pon my soul!" she suddenly burst out as knowledgeable fingers identified the costly material. "This is purest floss silk!"

"Why, and so it is," the old lady affirmed, the lacy cap above her smoothly coroneted hair gently bobbing up and down. "But you needn't feel concerned, Madeleine, for Mme. Leteuil found the cloth among the bolt ends at the mercer's warehouse, meaning that the price required was but nominal. Madame, of course, made up the fabric, while I did the finish work—so really, your gift is made of spare moments and very little more. As for what money I did use, our savings have no value if we sacrifice the present entirely. I do not forget that for you, little one, the future is now. But that is not all," she added on a note of triumph. Reaching under her chair, she produced a pair of sixteen-button gloves sewn from fine white kid, also a pair of exquisitely embroidered, rose-colored slippers.

Mattie's breath came out in a whoosh. "Oh, my. Oh, my! You have, truly, made this the best birthday ever. I don't know what to say!" With only a modicum of caution for the gown resting in her great-aunt's lap, Mattie bent to impress great kisses on the old lady's cheeks, first one side and then the other. Almost to herself, she opined, "Madame must have spent hours and hours . . . *You* were put to such trouble . . ."

Mattie had to stop and draw a calming breath. A gather of moisture was tickling her eyes and her voice threatened to tremble. She accepted the dress from her great-aunt's hands, the delicate fabric deliciously sensuous under her fingers. It made her feel like quite the young lady—a young lady with twenty years to her credit.

Hugging the fragile silk against her slim figure, she twirled gracefully around the room. "Ta-DUM-de-dum, ta-DUM-dee-dee!" she sang, her contralto voice velvety as she spun.

She then paused in midswing on a thought. The price of the fabric might well have been small, but what about the other gifts? She could contribute some share, at least.

Prepared to do just that, Mattie disguised her interest as she asked in apparent idleness, "And how, pray, did you two conspirators manage the gloves and shoes, *ma chère* Tante? Don't try to tell me that they were among the odds and ends at the mercer's, for I'll never believe such a taradiddle." She slid on a glove with a show of admiring its fit, then held up a slipper, seemingly to better examine the fine needlework swirling through the prettily dyed leather.

Her great-aunt rendered up an innocent look to match Mattie's own. "Well, if you would know, Madeleine, Mme. Leteuil discovered the gloves in a secondhand shop, priced at the veriest pittance. I had asked her some weeks ago to keep an eye open for something appropriate for your birthday, and so when she found the gloves, obviously unworn and in a size quite useless for most, she knew that they would answer. Actually, they were my first purchase and gave what me the idea for the rest."

Only partially relieved, Mattie felt she had to know the full extent of the debit. She could curtail her habit of indulging herself weekly at the Bluebell with Billy and Kevin, needs be, and would gladly do so rather than set back Tante's plans for a partnership with the dressmaker. Keeping her tones light, she inquired, "But how managed you the slippers, then? They look to be made to my measure."

Agathe Serinier gave no sign of noticing any particular point to these questions. Indeed, she and her great-niece were in the habit of discussing all matters financial, and she seemed pleased to answer. "Now those were an especially fine piece of luck. We had them from the new shoemaker on Upper Thames's Street, so you are right in thinking them specially made. It happens that he came to Madame's shop to solicit her good offices in recommending his work to her clients. She agreed to his request, *if* he would first supply her with a sample of his wares."

Mattie broke into a laugh. "Oh, clever Madame! I daresay, there is none so sharp as she in matters of business! Am I obliged, then, to allow this pretty pair of slippers to reside for a time on the display shelves before I can wear them? Is that the agreement?"

"Madeleine, it is no such thing!" Tante scolded. "Mme. Leteuil simply advised the shoemaker that she admired his skill and would be happy to do him the service. She then volunteered my needlework on another pair of shoes to go into his own shop window, provided we should have *two* pairs in return."

Shaking with laughter, at the same time Mattie

clicked her tongue in disapproval. "Shameless. Shameless! The both of you!" Being a true Frenchwoman herself, however, she was pleased by her mentors' shrewdness in effecting such a good bargain.

She took the gloves, gown, and slippers to lay out in state across her great-aunt's cot. Mattie stepped back to admire her gifts before remembering one other present. Reaching into the pocket of her pinafore, she pulled out a green square of imprinted pasteboard.

Agathe Serinier leaned forward in her chair. "But what do you have there, my little one? It looks to be some sort of an admission ticket."

"This," Mattie replied importantly, passing the item over for inspection, "is my permit for entry to the Theatre-Royal, Hay-market, on the night of July 6. It is a present from Brigitte and Claudine. They had the idea from something I'd said about my never having seen a play, and they managed their secret for nearly a week—right up until today. Oh, a huge effort for those two, I assure you. Still, I can hardly believe it! Me. At the Theatre-Royal!" Again she twirled about the room, her face alive with excitement.

Such finery. Such wonderfully feminine luxury! Moreover, money was not at issue, so the coins and pound notes tucked away beneath the mattress in Mattie's tiny sleeping closet would be unneeded for her to fully enjoy today's unlooked-for bounty. She could hardly contain herself for the joy of it.

"A fitting occasion then," said Tante Agathe, giving her great-niece an indulgent smile. "You really do understand the reason behind my choice of gifts, just as I had hoped you might. I intended them as a reminder that you are a young lady of breeding, one who can hold her head high in any company. Oh, wearing short skirts and pinafores like a child serves its purpose, and very well too! Yet I will be glad, for once, to have you dressed as you ought. Ah, Madeleine," she said in lilting tones, "you will look so lovely at the theatre in your new gown. I fear Mlles. Brigitte and Claudine will be pricked with envy at being seen with you."

Mattie ceased her spinning and clutched her hands to her breast. She was brought to a complete standstill. *How can I* possibly *manage my way through this?* she wondered frantically. The sisters had not bought themselves tickets to attend the play with her, nor even if they had, she certainly couldn't meet up with them in a dress. No, not even such a beautiful dress.

"Er, Brigitte and Claudine. Ah, um, er . . ." She couldn't think how to respond!

Misled by this halting speech, Tante Agathe nodded in contentment. "Mme. Leteuil assures me that they are good girls, so traveling as a group, you should be safe enough with them. Will you leave for the theatre directly from the shop? I notice from your ticket that the play begins at eight, leaving you insufficient time to return here that evening, change your clothing, and then get across the river before the performance starts. Perhaps you should dress at Madame's and consider staying the night with her and the girls."

Mattie could scarcely credit how easily some problems were solved. "What a good idea!" she exclaimed in relief. "I shall take my new clothes with me that morning, and when the play is over, I can go back to Madame's. I am sure you are right, and space can be found for me to remain there overnight."

Mattie ignored the slight, guilty feeling which threatened. She reminded herself that she hadn't stated outright that she would wear her new gown to the theatre, nor had she said Brigitte and Claudine would accompany her. A lie of omission was only a "white lie," after all, and not such a price for her conscience to bear. Her first chance to see an actual play was not something she wanted to give up!

And indeed, nothing should have been easier than implementing this plan. Although, when Mattie explained the way of it to Mme. Leteuil the next day, she was astonished to meet with an obstacle.

"Absolument, non," the modiste practically shouted, free to raise her voice since she had sent her two shop assistants off to bring their lunches back from one of the local pot houses. "I tell you, Mattie, I forbid this! Oh, what can you be thinking of? A young mademoiselle like you, going unattended after dark? Never. Never, I say!" Madame's thick eyebrows shot upward and then gathered, their regular curvature emphasized as she shook her finger before her.

Much taken aback, Mattie wondered that her employer should take issue. "But I intend dressing as Matt," she explained, thinking this solution obvious. "Certainly, I wish I could wear the wonderful gown that you and Tante made for me, but I know it's impossible under present conditions. Oh! And I do want to thank you with all my heart for your part in providing me such splendid presents. The gloves you found for me! The shoes! But mostly, as you might well imagine, it is the marvelous dress which I cherish. I never thought to own anything like it—it is quite the loveliest thing ever!"

She gave her still-irate employer an unselfconscious hug. Observing some softening in Madame's aspect, she proceeded in reasoned tones. "But please, don't feel you must fret about me going out alone. I expect to pass unnoticed, for boys are wont to roam the streets at any hour. One more will likely go unremarked."

To Mattie's surprise, the dressmaker's softening proved itself only temporary. *"Mon Dieu!"* she exclaimed, her black frown commencing anew. "Do you think that any assurance to me, Mattie? *C'est insupportable! C'est le ..."*

Marie Leteuil promptly launched into an inspired series of swear words in excited French, replete with Parisian vernaculars. She punctuated each addition with a veritable frenzy of gesticulating arms and hands.

However, since Mattie's knowledge of French expletives was somewhat inferior to the list in her English vocabulary, she could make out only the more common of her employer's utterances. Several words left her completely at a loss for comprehension, and Madame's ever-changing and fast-moving gestures gave her little clue. Inappropriately, she thought she must remember to encourage Madame to enlighten her sometime.

"But Madame," she finally broke in to say, "Brigitte and Claudine chose their birthday surprise for me with such care and without even knowing that, marking the end of my teens, it was a very special occasion. And they were so exceedingly proud to present me with the ticket! Oh, I really cannot now refuse! What would I say by way of excuse?"

Stifling her flow of maledictions, Mme. Leteuil fell silent. She scowled at Mattie with terrifying ferocity, while her black, half-moon-shaped eyebrows worked themselves up and then back down again in rapid succession. It was very like watching a pair of great fuzzy caterpillars climbing along a twig.

Unconcerned by the fearsome exhibition, Mattie pleaded, "Please, *do* but consider, Madame. There isn't any other way to accomplish my going, for I cannot go out dressed as *ma tante* expects, neither can I wear a pinafore and mobcap. That leaves us with 'Matt.' Unless, of course, we devise yet another identity for me?"

The modiste's heavy brows climbed to new heights, and she pressed her hands to her temples. *"Mais non. Non!"* she cried out. "You have too many rôles and costumes as it is!"

"Well, I will have to agree with you there, and so I simply must pose as a boy. And why should I not? I traverse these streets all day long and know most every corner and shopkeeper. 'Tis true I haven't ventured out quite so late before, but the pavements are the same ones, aren't they?"

"Hardly!" snapped Madame. "Although the streets may look the same, the people who inhabit the city after dark are not what you are used to. There are thieves, purse snatchers, even cutthroats who come out in force under the cover of darkness. Well do you know it!"

Mattie tried again. "But surely, there are just as many of those in London at any other time. Perhaps they do move about more boldly at night, but it is the law for every corner post to have a lamp, and every house as well, so there's not so much danger as you might suppose. None will bother about a shabby young boy, off to a night of revelry. Do I look like someone with tuppence to spare?" She struck an attitude in her baggy boy's dress.

She won her point at last.

And so it was that after every sort of warning, repeated numerous times, the sixth night of July saw a slightly built lad crossing north on Blackfriars Bridge, headed for Hay-market Street. The boy was clothed in baggy tan knee breeches and an overlong vest worn under a brown worsted jacket, together with a pair of brown-dyed cotton gloves, each one singly buttoned at the wrist. All were freshly laundered and brushed, leaving nothing especially memorable, nor even particularly notable, about him.

Mattie felt all the excitement of an adventure just ahead. Not since the mad escape from France ten years ago in '93—the year Louis XVI himself was summoned to the guillotine—had she felt this way. The urge to hurry, along with the tingling sensation of remembered fear, came back to her in a rush of memory.

She wasn't really afraid tonight, of course. Nonetheless, as Mme. Leteuil had suggested, London did appear strange at dusk. With the shops closed up and the streets stretching emptily ahead, the city became more mysterious, more thrilling somehow. Anything might lurk just around the next turn in the pavement, anything at all! And Mattie was stimulated to be out and moving amidst a myriad of new possibilities.

She observed nothing out of the ordinary as she approached the theatre from Cockspur Street. It seemed fitting that the waiting line of ticket holders stood silent with an air of hushed expectancy about them. It perfectly matched her mood. Bouncing up on her toes to see inside, she caught a glimpse of not a few society grandees whose colorful toilettes added richness and glamour to the occasion.

When Mattie's turn came to give over her ticket, she was handed back the torn stub which designated her seat number. "Have a nice evening," the attendant said brusquely, his eyes already skimming past her for the next person in line.

So I jolly well will, too, she thought without heat.

Easing her way through the crowded foyer, she was quickly caught up in the grand opportunity for obtaining a closer look at the gathered Elite. Luxurious crêpes, pastel gauzes, and étoile satins delighted her eye. She couldn't resist imagining herself amongst them, enfolded in whisper-soft, rose-tinted silk. Not daring to tarry too long, however, she soon moved on.

As she gained her way into the auditorium proper, Mattie began a search for her place. At last locating the aisle seat bearing the number matching that of her ticket stub, she saw that the seat was already occupied. A heavyset woman who might politely be referred to as *embonpoint,* but never dignified by the term *substantial,* sat lumpishly in the chair assigned as her own. Beside the woman was an even fatter man, most probably her husband, Mattie decided.

They were dressed in what must be their own peculiar ideas about what constituted appropriate attire for the occasion. Wrapped in yard upon yard of stiffened fabric made up in billowing petticoats and thickly wrapped neckcloth, according to their individual needs, the couple made an impressive sight. But to youthful opinion—when one considered the time of year and the gathering heat inside the quickly filling theatre—they looked overdressed to the point of discomfort.

Mattie came up alongside and rechecked the number on her stub. She again looked at the markings embossed on the little plate affixed to the aisle-side chair, then tugged at her vest and said, "Excuse me, ma'am, but I believe you are in my place."

Though seated hard by where Mattie stood, the ample-sized woman didn't so much as raise her head. The man in the next seat over, however, leaned forward to answer in a surprisingly belligerent manner. "An just whot is it that makes ya think it? Show me the slip whot says ya should sit here, 'stead of us. Show me, is whot I says!"

Obligingly, Mattie produced her little green stub and held it out for his inspection.

Without saying anything, and with startling dexterity, the man reached across his seatmate and nimbly pinched the pasteboard from betwixt Mattie's fingers. He examined it for only the briefest instant, then crammed it into his pocket. Without another word spoken, he sat back and faced the stage.

Mattie didn't know what to think. Such behavior was beyond her experience! "Excuse me," she began again, "but sir, you've not returned my ticket stub to me. Nor," she added, staring hard at the woman, "have you relinquished me my place."

This time, neither the man nor the woman looked up.

"Sir? Sir!" she said more sharply, giving up on the woman and trying to regain the man's attention. "I must insist that you give me back my ticket and allow me to take my seat!"

At the sound of her raised voice, the man ponderously heaved himself to his feet. He squeezed past the woman with some degree of effort and stepped out into the aisle. His bulk forced Mattie back a pace. His expression taunted her, even while he appeared to address himself to his still-silent companion. "Mabel, is this here boy pestering ya? 'Cause if'n he is, I'll be sending for the usher straightaway. We paid good money for these seats, and I have the receipts to prove it."

To Mattie's disbelief, he then reached into his pocket and lifted out two green stubs—one of them hers!

It dawned on Mattie that she had been duped. She

looked at the two stubs, audaciously held just beyond reach, and wasted no more time in argument. Usually, when faced with someone who seemed disinclined to do the right thing, like certain ones of Madame's customers who balked at meeting their bills, she could find a way to cajole the person into making the proper payment. Mattie suspected that her customary methods were insufficient to the purpose tonight, however. She realized she must have help in persuading this couple into more honest ways.

Reversing her direction in the aisle, Mattie fought her way back through the incoming crowds to reach the ticket taker at the entryway. She gave him a brief review of what had transpired, but without so much as a glance spared in her direction, he said in sullen tones, "Nothing I can do about it, now is there? I've plenty to do right here. See the manager if you've got a complaint."

"Very well," she answered him just as tersely. "Where might I find—"

The attendant cut her off with a curt motion in the direction of an interior door. It was marked with the title of the appropriate personage.

Mattie looked round to the place pointed out and swallowed back her ire. It was no one's fault but her own if she had been taken advantage of; there was no need to try and vent her anger on an innocent theatre employee, nor even a manager, she resolved. No, indeed. She wasn't going to let senseless resentment mar her evening. She went to the indicated door and rapped on it twice, then turned the knob to enter.

The doorknob didn't budge. It was locked. She knocked twice more but still couldn't obtain a response.

The crowd was thinning in the lobby area, for the play was about to commence. Mattie turned back to the ticket collector, who was by now not so thoroughly occupied. Somewhat desperate by this time, she again asked where she might find the man in charge—"For no one answers at the office door, and I really must take my seat before I miss anything," she beseeched him.

The attendant looked up from his work, finally. "Well, you can't remain without a ticket, boy. If someone's made off with yours, it's too bad, it is, but the manager's the only one who can bend the rules. And since he apparently ain't here, you'll just have to leave. Try us again on another night."

Dumbfounded by the injustice of this request, Mattie held her ground. "Then you will please find the manager for me. At once!" she demanded. And because more precise diction seemed to offer a greater likelihood of effectiveness in her present situation, she also consciously left off any vestige of the accents that went with her costume to add, "I assure you that I am going nowhere until I see the appropriate person."

As if in answer to her boldness, the voice of authority came from behind her. "What is the trouble? What is this boy doing here? No loitering, no loitering, I say! Don't you know there is a performance about to begin?"

This, issued in the harassed intonations of a very busy man.

Mattie turned to discover herself at eye level with a veritable midge of a fellow. She might be a little on the small side herself, even allowing for her sex, but the newcomer was astonishingly tiny, for all he was a grown male.

"Come, now," he warned. "Speak up. What is the difficulty and why are you just standing about out here?"

Taking her cue from the value he seemed to place on his time, she offered an abbreviated explanation of her predicament. But instead of acting to provide her with a solution—like removing the offending parties and reinstating her in her seat—the manager would only shake his head while he tut-tutted under his breath.

"Nothing to be done. Not a thing!" he said when she had finished. "How do I know you aren't trying to make whole cloth from this piece of work? I certainly can't judge without proof."

"Well, I'm here, aren't I?" Mattie argued logically. "If I'd no ticket for my entry in the first place, how do you suppose I got in?"

The manager sputtered in obvious exasperation. "But the couple you say cheated you out of your place came inside by some means or other too, didn't they? Someone has got himself admitted fraudulently tonight, but how can I know who?"

"Easily," she rapped out, anxious to have this done with. The sound of opening applause, so close, yet so far away, was deafening in her ear. She gestured toward the by-now interested underling. "This is the attendant who accepted my ticket in the first place. He'll remember me; he even spoke to me when he tore my admission ticket. He said, 'Have a nice evening.' "

The manager turned round to his employee. "Well, what about it, Judson? Do you remember this young man? Speak up! Speak up! Did you take in this boy's ticket?"

"Well, I own might have done so," the attendant answered prosaically. "On the other hand, mayhap I didn't. Can't say for certain, since I seldom look at the numbers which swarm through here on a big night, and it's my habit to wish everyone what comes by me a good evening. Him knowing my ways doesn't prove much, it don't."

Mattie could barely prevent a groan of frustration from gaining audible outlet. To aggravate matters, another round of applause broke out in the auditorium. She had to clench her teeth against the temptation to wail like some thwarted infant. "Oh, but you cannot mean to forbid me to see tonight's play. It's Shakespeare's *Richard III!* There must be something you can do."

The small man seemed in a fidge to get about his business. "Unfortunately not, young man. There's not so much as an inch of space left, for we sold out three days ago and have already issued all the standing-room passes we can allow. We're not so large as the Opera House, you know; so unless you have a friend inside who will give up his seat in your favor, I'm afraid you cannot remain. I wish I could help you, I truly do, but there is nothing more to be said."

Mattie's earlier feelings of high excitement and fine expectation shriveled, reduced to naught. While she tried to appreciate the manager's position, she felt sick with dismay that her planned evening was now so hopelessly ruined. A great lump formed low in the back of her throat, and it took every effort to disguise her grievous disappointment. Still, Tante Agathe had taught her better than to inflict an unwonted show of personal emotion upon others, so she dropped her eyes to the floor for a moment, struggling to conceal her unhappiness.

"You will permit me to add a word?" came a voice in quiet tones just beside her. "I believe Master Serinier counts me amongst his friends. Right, lad?"

Startled, Mattie looked up. She knew the voice, she recognized it instantly, but hadn't seen the gentleman's approach for she was too engrossed in her troubles. Optimism at once replaced gloomy resignation.

"It's his lordship!" she cried with new energy, taking in his sizable, yet preeminently elegant form.

In a coat of rich russet above black satin inexpressibles, nary a crease nor a pucker marred the magnificence of the earl's evening wear. Wide, wide shoulders tapered smoothly to a flat, trim waist, while black clocked stockings fitted an enviable calf with every sign of perfection. Black patent evening pumps gleamed over the curves of his well-formed feet, and a full two-and-seventy inches above that, waves of dark gold hair, brushed and burnished, lay with a healthy sheen. The earl also bore evidence of that special, freshly shaved look peculiar to the well-groomed male, a look confirmed by the clean scent of imported sandalwood soap.

Mattie had never been so glad to see anybody.

The rest of their little company seemed to agree. The theatre manager bowed low and bid his lordship a good evening, while his underling, no doubt considering it above his place to address such a celebrated Go-Amongst-the-Goers, merely bowed.

"Oh, I *am* so thrilled to see you," Mattie confided to the earl, removing her hat and tucking it beneath her arm. "You'll scarcely credit my foolishness, I know, but I've stupidly let someone cheat me out of my ticket. I ... um. Oh, dear!"

She whipped around, turning her back on their little party. Reaching to an inside pocket, she brought out a ridiculously small square of linen to blot furiously at suddenly streaming eyes. "You will please excuse me for a moment?" she whispered over her shoulder.

Niddle-noddied widgeon, she mentally chastised herself as she daintily blew her nose. *What makes you to behave so absurdly? And now, of all times, when help may well be to hand!*

Mattie just couldn't understand why the appearance of his lordship had sent her into tears. She had felt the most intense sense of relief when she had greeted him; she'd found herself quite overwhelmed! But did she seriously expect the earl to swoop right in and straighten out all of her difficulties? Such fustian! She knew herself capable of managing on her own—if, perhaps, not so well in this instance. Nonetheless, she certainly could bear the consequences of her folly without crying on anyone's shoulder. Not even such very broad shoulders as those his lordship presented.

Ignoring the overset youth, the manager inquired in tones laced with disbelief, "Your lordship knows this young man, then?"

The earl answered on a preoccupied note. "I do." He was at the moment busy bringing forth his own larger handkerchief, which, with a tap on Mattie's turned shoulder, he passed into her hand. "Better, lad?" he asked in solicitous tones.

The friendliness of his gesture nearly set Mattie off anew. Mortified by her display of nerves, she sniffed cautiously to ascertain that there would be no telltale drip, before, chin up, she turned back to face the men. Her natural contralto deepened to gruffness in her embarrassment.

"I must beg your pardon, my lord. And both of you as well," she said, her look encompassing the two theatre employees. Putting away her small handkerchief, she next carefully folded his lordship's linen into a neat square. "I do thank you," she said simply, extending her hand to return his handkerchief. She held her back straight as a cane.

70

He seemed oddly uncomprehending. He stared at her with a puzzled look, making no move to recover his property. Horrified that she may have committed some gaffe, she watched in dismay while a well-remembered, distancing quality began creeping its way into his eyes.

This caused her to remember something else. Her accent! She'd left it off practically from the moment of entering the theatre. Nothing for it but to pop back into her regular style, lest his lordship begin to speculate. If she took care not to overdo the thing, the earl might not realize the change before she'd overlaid her speech with more appropriate inflections and reestablished herself as Matt-the-errand-boy.

Despite these intentions, however, something about his by-now frozen look prompted her otherwise. Spontaneously, she blurted out, "Ye gods, man! Cat got yer tongue? Does yer wants yer wiper or not?" Slapping her hat back atop her head, she adopted a truculent stance, mounting one fist tight against her hip. "An' yer could also enlarge on what I took to be yer offer of a place inside. We ain't just gonna' stand here all night a-playin' flap-jaw, are we?"

"Here now! That's no way to speak to his lordship, boy," the manager put in anxiously.

Truth be told, Mattie hadn't meant to speak out so strongly, nor to take advantage of the large gentleman's offer. But with *that look* facing her, she had felt herself compelled to take any action which might dispel it.

For a moment, it appeared that her aggressiveness had turned the trick. The earl's expression cleared, even as she started speaking. He fixed her with his impossibly blue orbs. "No, no," he said to the manager, not taking his eyes off of hers. "It is quite all right, really. And as for the handkerchief, young man, you may continue to use it, display it under glass for a treasured memento, or throw it away as it suits you."

Mattie was entirely shocked. She had intentionally delivered her words to the earl on a challenging note, thinking to provoke him into a response as she had once before. The last time she had tweaked him, he had come down off his high ropes, lost that ghastly emptiness in his eyes, and had come to meet her halfway. Instead of which, this time, he'd verbally shoved her! He didn't even seem to want his linen returned, acting as if it was soiled past redemption.

Mattie began to understand how it might be that the man had no friends. His manner tonight was downright uncivil.

And to think, she had actually wanted to see him again, *wanted* to know more about him. She felt confused and enormously hurt. She had to bite hard on her lower lip, which she feared was beginning to tremble.

Again, he surprised her. He readdressed her in lambent, almost comforting tones. "There now, don't take on so, lad. I only meant to convey that the handkerchief was of no importance to me. I am afraid I'm more accustomed to giving than to receiving, and I'm sorry for refusing you the way I did. However, as you've so rightly reminded me, we needn't stand about out here any longer. Come along. There's plenty of room in my box for you."

It would be hard to decide who was the most astonished by this surpassing generosity: the manager, who lost his bustling-busy air and openly gawked, his assistant who simply stared, or possibly his lordship, upon whose countenance could be discerned the odd tinge of confusion.

Mattie didn't waste any time dwelling on Dame Fortune's reversal, though. Beaming with renewed trust, she again passed the handkerchief. She was pleased to see his lordship make her a brief, but polite bow as he accepted its return. Cocking her head up at him, she chirruped, "Off we go, then, milord. Why, the night'll be over if we don't get the gams into motion!"

With continued courtesy, the earl gestured for her to come up alongside him before he turned to lead the way toward the second-floor corridor. Unaware of it, he curtailed the length of his stride, enabling shorter steps to keep the pace with ease.

"Gams?" his lordship next whispered down at her, even as he slowed their passage. "I had thought I was up on all the latest canting terms, but that was 'gams,' you said?"

"Well, o' course. Stampers, pins, shanks—yer *gams!*" came the whispered reply.

"Ah. Legs, you mean."

"Ain't that what I just said? Don't knows nothin' much, now *does* yer."

Chapter Five

In the dimly lit corridor of the Theatre-Royal, Haymarket, the Earl of Staffield felt the almost forgotten sensation of a huge smile winding its way across his face. Recovering himself in time to enter a box not far from the stage, he motioned for his guest to come inside and choose a seat. Four red velvet upholstered chairs stood awaiting their pleasure, for his lordship expected no other guests tonight. He watched interestedly as the boy looked each one over before moving to the second seat back. Obviously, the youth intended to leave his host of the evening with the best-positioned chair.

What an odd creature it is, the earl mused, quietly assuming a place. *Brash kiddie one minute, court manners the next . . .?*

But Vincent was not behindhand in returning the consideration. He took the third seat down, leaving the first seat nearest the stage vacant, just as he would have done for a more important guest. In point of fact, the lad had earned his respect—and piqued his interest, too—especially when he very politely removed his floppy-brimmed hat upon their entering the booth. The boy settled himself almost primly in his seat, his hat resting quietly in his lap, just as it ought.

While the players went about their parts, Vincent was glad of his decision to let the youngster have the better place. It allowed him to watch each changing expression as the lad seemed instantly to immerse himself in the drama enacted before them. His young friend frowned and gasped and postured along with the actors, giving his onlooker more enjoyment in the production than any in recent memory.

With an indulgent eye, Vincent settled himself farther back in his seat. A smile played across the corners of his mouth as he reflected upon the various anomalies surrounding his young guest.

From their first meeting, he had found the cocky young errand boy uncommonly attractive, notwithstanding the fact of his being of the lower orders. With his downy-smooth cheeks, delicately winged brows, and eyelashes quite as lush as any girl's, Matt nevertheless proved himself to be a singularly staunch little fellow. His was a ready impudence coupled with manners of the highest polish, as witness the way he handled his hat, his handkerchief, and even his words. To be sure, the lad's rough accents seemed to come and go from one utterance to the next.

Vincent next mouthed an unrefined word of his own, remembering tonight's witless delay in accepting the restoration of his linen. Small excuse that the boy's sniffles, in combination with the assumption of improbably cultivated accents, had somehow misled him into suspecting the youth of acting the toad. But he should have known better than to think the lad *coming*, since Matt had refused a boon from him once before—and in no uncertain terms! Still, so strongly did Vincent detest all forms of flattery, he had been slow to recognize his mistake.

Unfortunately, he had then compounded his error by telling Matt, all well meaningly enough, to keep the borrowed handkerchief, speaking out in an unthinking way which had led to another misunderstanding. The boy had shown his mettle, though, speedily accepting the apology and even throwing back a lively quip. Young Matt had pride, yet was remarkably quick to forgive.

Vincent decided that therein lay the secret of the little urchin's charm: He was an enigma, albeit one of an unusually animated variety.

The earl sighed softly, no longer seeing young Matt as he considered his own life more deeply. It seemed like eons ago since he had felt much enthusiasm for anything himself. His estates were managed by an able steward, and his family concerns were limited to the occasional polite visit with his one remaining cousin, a young matron with two young sons still in the nursery. It left Vincent with little to do but see to his own amusements, no different from other young Bloods and Bucks on the town.

Mondays and Thursdays saw the earl at Tattersall's capacious tap and betting rooms. Tuesdays meant Bond Street, first to his tailor's and then on to one of his clubs, while Wednesdays usually led him to the theatre, followed by a look-in at the gin-spinners or perhaps some popular gambling hell. Fridays and Saturdays were most often spent on the road in various driving contests, as were Sunday afternoons, with the whole repeated again on the following week.

Assuredly, he interspersed trips to Brighton and Newmarket Races in season, took part in all types of field sports, and made time for an assortment of *ton* parties.

But lately, he'd found himself bored by it all. He'd begun roaming yet farther afield, placing higher and higher stakes on ofttimes ridiculous wagers in the company of men who drank longer and deeper with each passing day. All in the name of amusement.

Rumors of his exploits were beginning to close doors to him amongst the highest sticklers of late, but what cared he for that? Was having invitations to five Society entertainments of an evening any better than a man's partaking of five bottles a night? Not that he imbibed quite so much on a regular basis—yet. But he could appreciate those of his sporting friends who did. For a bumper with one of the Fellows of the Fancy was at least as amusing as sharing the latest *on-dit* with the bandboxed sort of creatures who exemplified London's Beau Monde.

But the lad proved an effective diversion. Quick to take umbrage and just as quick to laugh, the boy reminded Vincent that, for some, life still held immense interest.

"Capitol!" the little lad cried out sometime later when the lights were turned up for the intermission. "What a famous *go* this is, for true!" Quick brown eyes gleamed with excitement while small hands moved rapidly in applause.

Retaining his seat, Vincent made no effort to hide his smile. "So, you are enjoying yourself, I take it?"

The lad's fervid clapping continued unabated. "Well, o' course, I am, milord! Why, the stage sets and backdrops look real as real can be! An' did yer happen to see how Mr. Elliston spoke that last line with his eyes all squinnied up? I can't wait to see what comes next. What a complete hand he is!" With a last burst of applause, Matt resumed his seat, an enraptured look upon his face.

As host, Vincent felt compelled to add comment. "Well, Matt," he said mildly, bent on enriching the lad's experience, "Robert Elliston is new in the part and is very good with it, I agree. And as you've already noted, when Shakespeare wrote the play, be sure that he penned those last lines purposely. Then, just as now, men of the theatre use such tricks to make certain we return for the next act."

He couldn't but be entertained by the boy's corresponding look of bright interest. Matt wriggled around in his seat to face him.

"I know just whatcher means." The youngster sounded thoughtful. " 'Tis like at the end of the third act of *Othello,* when Bianca says, ' 'Tis very good; I must be circumstanced.' Ye-es, Shakespeare must have wanted to make sure that the actors could keep an audience drawn. Oh, capitol, indeed!"

Vincent hid his amazement at this bit of erudition, merely asking, "You attend the theatre often, I gather?" He considered that if the lad was a regular theatregoer, it would go a long way toward explaining his occasional divergence into refined speech, also tonight's unexpected dissolution into tears. Those who involved themselves with matters thespian had a penchant for histrionics, did they not?

"Naw," the youth denied on a throaty chuckle. "This is my very first time ever. I had the ticket as a birthday gift from two friends who, same as me, work for Mme. Leteuil at her dressmaking shop in Southwark. That's why I was so anxious when it seemed I couldn't stay and see the play. Brigitte and Claudine would be so awfully disappointed, yer sees.

78

"Oh, by Jingo!" the little fellow interrupted himself to add. "I almost forgot to make yer m' thanks, milord. An' I hopes yer can forgive me for jumpin' at an opportunity to join yer like I did. I s'pose yer thinkin' me a regular understrapper, bent on hitchin' a ride without payin' the fare! But I did have a ticket, or at least"— Matt pointed over the railing to an overdressed couple nearest the aisle—"I did till those two snatched my stub and refused to give it back. Can't blame the manager for not believin' me 'bout it, though. But you do, don't yer, milord?"

For the second time that evening, Vincent felt remarkably nonplussed as he looked into Matt's wide, trusting eyes. There was something extraordinarily appealing about those eyes, their color reminiscent of fine Spanish sherry and framed by long, silky lashes, the same shade and texture as the blue-black curls surrounding the clever little face.

Before he quite realized it, Vincent found himself constrained to mend matters. He apologized for the difficulty suffered and volunteered to bring the boy a spot of wine from the counter belowstairs.

"Oh, no, nothing for me, although certainly I do thanks yer," the lad declined. "I 'spect I've already put yer to much too much trouble, and anyways, I'm too excited to swallow a thing. I'll just sit close here while yer sees to yerself."

Apparently wanting to view the other theatregoers, Matt turned back to the auditorium to commence an inspection of the night's attendees. Vincent had the impression that the youngster longed to hop up and peer over the railing so as to better to see what went on, but the lad held to his seat, squirming only slightly from time to time.

A smile again tugging at his lips, the earl set off on his own business.

After he had left, Mattie rested one small hand on the box front's deckled railing and willed herself to relax. She supposed her restlessness came from sitting for too long in one place, surrounded as she was by so many new sights and sounds. Being in company with a handsome gentleman could have nothing at all to do with her disturbed state, of course, but wasn't it wonderful how his lordship had happened along and offered her a place as his guest; this, after she'd so often wished for another meeting?

Unable, or perhaps unwilling, to pursue the thought too closely, she fixed her attention on the crowd. Shifting clusters of people milled in the aisles, while scattered groups remained in their seats to chat and fidget with half-penny play programs.

Soon enough, however, it was the crème de la crème occupying the other raised booths who drew her rapt attention. A slope-shouldered beau impressed her as he moved between boxes; his pomaded wig of daffodil yellow made his progress easy to follow. A young débutante's high, nervous giggle next caught her interest, even while fluttering aigrettes and sparkling gemstones pulled her eyes this way and that.

Picking out the girl with the piercing laugh, Mattie felt an urge to go over and comfort her. She wanted to assure her that, with such lovely looks as she had, there was no need for her to feel uneasy in any gathering. But Mattie's own confidence took a plunge when she happened to notice that she was herself under close observation!

Directly across the theatre, in the box exactly opposite, a Fashionable Beauty, sitting alone, held a gold-framed eyeglass raised in her direction. She used it to cast what was, unmistakably, a disapproving glare. Mattie took note of the lady's pale blond locks, coiling silkily over and in front of one white shoulder, reaching down, almost to the bottom of the deep vee of a sumptuously plunging neckline.

That neckline revealed a truly amazing depth of figure. Rich shirring of dark green gauze further amplified a bosom which, to Mattie's mind, had little need of enhancement.

"What-ho?" she muttered under her breath as the lady continued to stare.

Mattie couldn't believe that anyone could tell that her own jacket was of naught but simple worsted, or at least, not from such a distance. And Mme. Leteuil had arranged her freshly starched neckcloth beautifully, she was sure, so she couldn't imagine what the lady across the way adjudged so at fault. But the fair-haired beauty, sitting tall and regal, projected an undeniable look of dislike.

Why ever should the lady be so irked? Mattie had to wonder. What reason for tossing her pretty head and looking down her nose at someone as insignificant as the ostensible Matt Serinier? Failing to come up with any sort of answer, Mattie consciously dismissed the strange occurrence and resumed her own perusals.

Not one minute later, though, movement from the opposite box again drew Mattie's eyes. A large gentleman had entered the box, and it was *her* large gentleman. Having very good eyesight, without a need to resort to any sort of magnification, she watched as the earl sat down beside the Beauty. He moved his chair closer, lazily settling one long arm along the top of the lady's seat back. He looked comfortable, as if he belonged there.

The fashionable beauty promptly dropped her glass to her lap and leaned back against the earl's arm. A lovely smile replaced previously pinched lips, and she seemed prodigiously gratified. A fan appeared in her gloved hand to replace the opera glass. Spokes covered in glittering, gold-threaded silk were spread as she set that item into flirtatious motion.

Mesmerized by the artful maneuver, Mattie leaned forward to better observe the lady's gracefully applied technique. When the fan languidly tap-tapped against the earl's chest in emphasis of some remark, Mattie mimed the motion. She was fascinated by the ease with which each coy movement was performed. She took in the lady's every affectation, from the way she simpered and arched her long neck with her shoulders tilted back, to the coquettish manner she had of opening and closing her fan. Mattie thought that not even Brigitte's practiced skills could have managed it better. The blond lady had a certain genius for using her smiles, her posture, and her fan to hold his lordship's attention.

On one level, Mattie was wholly admiring. But on another, deeper level, she discovered a stirring of regret. Not for her was the use of these wiles to lure a man to interest. She could pull her shoulders back all she liked but still would have no deep bosom to display to appreciative eyes. Her long quilted vest and the soft cotton binder she wore beneath her shirt were all that was needed to disguise her own less-than-generous female shape.

Possibly, she could benefit from knowing how to properly wield a fan. However, poking people in the ribs was, to Mattie's mind, a somewhat questionable practice. "Hrumph. Likely I'd only plague somebody into a temper," she grouched under her breath.

And indeed, she realized, that was just what was occurring. Even as she watched the blond lady nudge the earl a second time with her fan, it could be seen that his lordship was not best pleased. A certain stillness in his posture told Mattie that his eyes were assuming a withdrawn look, although she was too far away to make out his actual expression. Moments later, after the golden fan was thrust at his shirt front yet again, the Earl of Staffield stood up, sketched a bow, and took his leave.

Quick resentment arose in Mattie's breast. She was incensed that the lady had been so incautious with her stratagems, when any fool could tell that his lordship was becoming irked. The earl deserved more consideration from the Beauty than that!

"Pawh," Mattie muttered in disgust. She turned away from the gauze-clad blonde and let her eyes roam over the remaining booths.

When the lights were dimmed for the resumption of the performance, Mattie's host had still not returned. She rapidly scanned the crowd to see if he had stopped to visit elsewhere but couldn't locate him. One thing she did notice, however. The couple who had cheated her out of her place were no longer there. Before she had time to wonder at it, though, a soft, rustling sound from behind her, together with the pleasantly sharp-sweet smell of sandalwood, told her of his lordship's return.

"In case you've changed her mind," he said quietly, reclaiming his seat. He placed a glass of cooled white wine on the edge of the small table set between them.

"M' thanks!" she whispered back, flashing him a grin.

There was no time for more words. The stage curtains began their slow, majestic parting in preparation for the second half of the play.

Mattie sat motionless in expectation. But as the actors picked up their lines, her attention was again diverted by renewed activity in the theatre box just opposite. Another man entered the booth across the way to join the lady of the richly made gauze gown. When he, too, positioned his arm along the lady's chair back, it aroused Mattie's curiosity. It would appear that, like the earl, the man was on close terms with the Beauty.

Displaying dull brown hair, teased and curled into a fluffy do, the newcomer looked like nothing so much as a just-brushed water spaniel. The resemblance made Mattie decide that the lady had far more need of spectacles than of an opera glass! There could be no other explanation for anyone's accepting the current company after having had the benefit of his lordship's attentions.

Where the earl was a magnificent, well-looking man, the newcomer lacked his lordship's erect and graceful bearing, his lithesome athletic figure, and had nothing in comparison to the earl's handsome coloring and features. So when the lady in the green gown ignored her companion to continue directing her glass at their box, Mattie was sorely tempted to stick out her tongue and wiggle it, just to see if the foolish woman would be unobserving of that as well.

Before being tempted beyond her limits, though, Mattie realized that the lady's companion was taking up another set of opera glasses. He, too, brought them to bear upon the earl's box. "Oh, the very deuce," Mattie groaned, reaching up to touch the folds of her neckcloth.

"Beg pardon?" whispered her host.

She felt his lordship's eyes on her. And now that she considered it, she thought the earl had been watching her for most of the evening himself. That being the case, mayhaps he could explain why the blond lady, and now the newcomer, all held her under such close scrutiny.

Wanting to get the thing out into the open, she turned and fixed the earl with a look of inquiry. "Is there somethin' partic'lar frumagemmy in my looks tonight, milord? Yer've been eyein' me most of this long while, I notice, and so've those two across the way. Do I really look so out of place, does yer think?" Her long, winged brows came together in consternation.

His lordship shifted his gaze and looked out across the auditorium.

Almost immediately, the pair in the opposite box commenced acting yet more strangely. The lady, evidently taking note of the earl's interest, at once lowered her glass. She glanced briefly at her companion, then tossed a dazzling smile across their way before turning to face the stage.

The man, without removing his eyes from their box, seemed aware of the lady's movement. He loosed his hold from her chair back and placed his arm in a more intimate position, tucking it underneath hers. He appeared to stare across at them all the harder.

"Well, dish me!" Mattie ejaculated softly.

She looked askance when the earl only chuckled. "No, lad," he said in reassurance. "Isn't you they're so interested in; rather, I believe I am the object of their disparate apprehensions. You see, Lady Hedgewick was earlier miffed when I wouldn't offer her my escort tonight, for all the not-so-subtle hints dropped my way. She was sure her husband wasn't coming, you understand. Now, her ladyship is concerned that I am already losing interest in the game—before it's even begun—while I suspect that Lord Hedgewick fears exactly the reverse. It's rather amusing, really."

Mattie's throat went completely dry. She ignored the play she had so wanted to see, ignored the actors and the fabulous sets. Galled by his careless answer—his insolence!—she reached to take a sip from her wine. She scarcely noticed that it was of the very first quality.

Oh, she could see well enough. In fact, she saw with absolute clarity. And what she saw was not merely one but *two* gentlemen who had been overly complaisant.

"Then, yer knew all along that the lady had a husband?" she accused in sharp whisper. "So just why did yer go to her box during the intermission? And for all the world to see!"

The earl seemed more interested in watching her return her wineglass to the tabletop than in making her an answer. She was careful to make no sound while she set the vessel down. He gave an infinitesimal shrug, the meaning of which she couldn't at all interpret, before he apparently recollected himself.

He lazed back in his seat. His reply, when it finally came, bordered on the insouciant. "Oh, come now, Matt. You cannot possibly be so naive. Lady Hedgewick is a remarkably lovely woman, and even at your young age, you should understand that married ladies are permitted certain freedoms within our society. As for myself, I find that the spice of danger accompanying such liaisons adds a particular piquancy."

Mattie drew herself up straighter in her chair. She could hardly give credence to the words she had just heard uttered! Her pert little features molded along severe, condemning lines. "But yer can't mean t' say that

86

yer'd dally with a lady precisely *because* she's married. That's nonsensical. Caper-witted! It can only lead to a rare rumpus!"

His lordship's eyes glazed over with disinterest. "Unlikely," he coolly returned.

But if he considered this answer sufficient, he was soon to learn otherwise. Remembering what her friend Billy had told her, and especially the part about dueling, Mattie persevered. "Be good enough to tell me this then, milord: Did you, or did you not, give me yer name as Staf*field?* Yer sees, I have a time learnin' new names, I do, so I couldn't rightly recall it when some'un suggested as how yer might be known as the 'Invincible Vince.' Leastways, I hadn't thought to believe yer was *that* one afore now." Though she kept her voice down in deference to their neighbors, her tones lacked any hint of admiration.

With a slight twitch of his wide shoulders, his lordship answered merely, "My friends call me Vincent."

Her own voice continuing low, more from the thickness of her anger than from any concern for others seated in the adjoining boxes, Mattie yet managed to inject a certain derisiveness into her reply. "Friends, is it? *Ha.* And have yer gots so many of 'em that yer can fly into the face of bespoken nuptial vows without anyone bein' upset with yer? No kind of friend I know of would ignore it when they see this kind of trouble brewin'. Friendships command more honesty. Why, any *real* friend would be a-tellin' yer to leave be, did they know even the half of it!"

"Well," his lordship responded, more aggressively than before, "as to that, there are precious few secrets in the *ton*. Nonetheless, I can assure you that no one has spoken to me about my budding relationship with Lady

Hedgewick. Such criticism wouldn't be at all proper! Matt? You aren't seriously intending to do so now, are you?" He looked shocked by the possibility.

"Damme, if I don't!" she instantly hissed back at him. "The lady's problems with her husband aren't your concern, maybe, but it's the outside of enough that yer should aggr'vate the situation. Sure, that one's a beauty," she continued in a somewhat thinned voice, looking across at the daringly cut green gown. "But she's a married woman all 'a same. Yer've no business in it." Her voice took on strength. "No, no business at all, I says!"

Again, Mattie became aware that she had let her tongue get away from her. Better she should keep silent, enjoy the play, and let his lordship go to hell in a hand-basket, if that's what he wanted to do. He was a grown man—a very well grown man, at that—with no need of advice from a stupid young miss who had cried tonight, merely at the sight of him.

She felt a deep swell of anger follow. She was angered by the Fair One who should have held herself unattainable and angry with the earl who had turned out to be little better than a *roué,* pursuing a woman for the sheer danger in it. She was, moreover, angry with herself for caring so very much.

No more. In a huff, she spun about and reaffixed her eyes firmly upon the stage.

"Lad?" came a soft query through the shadows.

Steadfast in her intentions, Mattie refused to turn her head.

"Lad," came the whispered voice yet again. "I rather think that even had I a thousand friends, the loss of one would still be no light matter."

She shifted in her seat to steal a quick look at him.

88

The earl quirked a funny but charming little smile back at her, then raised a finger to cover his lips. He pointed meaningfully toward the front. Oddly satisfied, she gave him a brief, acknowledging nod, then restored her attention to the stage.

At the end of the performance, her host stood up with her to join in the applause for a few minutes before returning to his seat. She continued clapping, as did most of the audience, for several minutes more as, indeed, the players had acted out their parts with verve.

"Bravo. Oh, bravo!" she called out with many another.

To be sure, Mattie felt a measure of relief at having some physical activity to engage in. Too many incidents had occurred within too short a space for her emotions to entirely harmonize. She was fast coming to a decision, though. Just as soon as it was time, in only a few minutes more, she would bid the Earl of Staffield a final adieu—he, a man whom she had once thought she would be proud to recognize.

It scarcely occurred to her that the idea of any real acquaintance between a peer of the realm and a lowly errand boy was glaringly preposterous. No matter. For despite his lordship's implied concern over their friendship, she understood that any degree of mutuality was impossible with a self-confessed libertine. Immaterial that the earl had treated her with every consideration, or that awareness of him had lately been haunting her thoughts. She was determined that anyone with his rakehell ways could be no friend of hers. Her friends were chosen with care and for their individual merits.

The actors at last made their closing bows and exited the stage. With her resolve well in place, Mattie picked up the wide-brimmed hat she had left lying behind her on the seat. Positioning the hat under her arm, she said gruffly, "I s'pose it's time I was leavin', too. Again, I do thanks yer, milord."

On a sudden urge, she started to hold out her hand to offer him a farewell handshake. She remembered just in time that, while a lady could instigate such an action, a mere boy must never behave with such pushery. Engaged as she was in her rôle as Matt, she must wait to see if his lordship would offer his hand first.

The earl, however, seemed to have something besides leaving on his mind. "You'd oblige me greatly if you would resume your seat, lad," he said quietly. "There's no reason for us to rush, is there? For I think that you and I have something to discuss."

Uncertainly, Mattie subsided into the red velvet cushions of her chair. She had already steeled herself for the unpleasant task of dismissing the earl from interest; whereas now, she felt somehow glad for the delay. Being at such cross-purposes was new to her. It was highly discomfiting too!

When she was seated, Lord Staffield held her with his dark-eyed gaze. He spoke in compelling tones. "See here, Matt, I want us to come to a better understanding. Oh, I realize you are displeased with me, and no denying it either, but I meant what I said about not liking to lose a friend—not even the least of them."

He seemed to mentally gauge her diminutive size, while she stared back into depths of midnight blue. She clutched at the brim of the hat which rested in her lap, for the moment unable to remember her reasons for wanting to leave. She found herself wishing she could claim more years than her part tonight allowed. She longed for more adult height, more prepossessing dimensions, more feminine curves and wiles. Absorbed in these thoughts, she was startled when, most unexpectedly, he reached over and, with strong fingers, ruffled her uncovered hair.

Her skin leaped, her pulses flew. . . . She lurched back in her seat!

Mattie was aghast at her own wildly improper reaction. She blinked at her companion, then blinked again, marveling that she should respond so. She could only pray he wouldn't divine her thoughts. She hoped he would suppose her movements natural to a boy, since boys were notorious for avoiding fond gestures.

"Aw, that's just ridic'lous, milord," she managed to get out. "Best we just leave it alone. No reason yer should care a jot for my opinion, now is there?" Although determined to present every semblance of calm, she couldn't resist pushing herself farther back into her seat.

Dark eyes caught and stilled her. There was not the least hint of boredom about them now. Despite the dimness, the earl looked intensely interested.

His gaze then dropped and he glanced down to his white-gloved hand. He inspected it minutely, for all the world as if he'd never seen this particular arrangement of five fingers before! With a puzzled air, he looked at Mattie's hand, then slowly returned searching eyes to her face. It appeared that he wanted to say something, but he seemed not to know just what it was.

Mattie had enough problems of her own without worrying herself about any words his lordship might be trying to shape. *What is it about the man?* she fretted. *He has but to speak, to make the most casual of gestures, and I'm sent all topsy-turvy.* " 'Tis the devil's own mischief," she muttered aloud.

Evidently construing her remark as a return to their

original topic, the earl seemed quite happy to get back to the discussion. He immediately answered, "Yes, well, possibly you are right, Matt, and the devil is in it. But I do wish you'd try to understand what goes forth. Oh, I know it's difficult at your age to realize the whole, but I assure you, the lady is not unwilling."

Such patent condescension flicked Mattie on the raw. Sherry-brown eyes kindled in outrage. "So, yer thinkin' that makes it right? Why, it's not even her ladyship yer so interested in but only the chase, I'll vow!" She shook her head in disgust. "And whatever else I mayn't understand, it's yerself who doesn't appreciate what's important 'bout this. 'Tis the *people* who matter, don't yer sees? They are what's really important! And yer'd be a better man for staying away from Lady Hedgelight—"

"Um. That's 'Hedgewick,' Matt."

"What? Oh. Very well," she groused. "Lady What*ever*-her-name-is. But regardless of that, what must be considered here are the principal facts. You know very well that her ladyship has already bound herself in a contract meant to stand for a lifetime, so it's easy to see that both she and her lord will be made terribly unhappy if you don't leave things be. A lawful husband will feel miserably unable to please his wife, all the while she herself yearns for a state of freedom which will likely never be hers. And you? You will, at most, have a moment's worth of exhilarating memory but precious little else for your trouble. That's if, and I do say *if,* you aren't called out and killed!" Vexed past all reason, Mattie flounced round in her seat, turning her face resolutely away from him.

Her inflections had changed again. But if the earl remarked the improvement, he gave no indication. He only sighed, deeply, then addressed her straight little back. "Lad, you're full of pluck, and no mistake, for I don't know of another soul who would dare to lecture me as you do." She heard him exhale another long, slow breath before he resumed. "I suppose you could be in the right of it, though. It is possible that I have been wrong in thinking of my other acquaintances as true friends."

She winced to hear the dull constriction in his tones. She didn't even have to turn around to know that his eyes had again assumed that inwardly drawn, flat look which she most hated to see, that look of hopeless ennui. Worse was the knowledge that, this time, she was the cause for it.

"I'm sorry, sir," she mumbled, feeling not a little ashamed. "I was only tryin' to help—to makes yer recognize just what it is yer're about."

She waited for a moment to see if he would respond, but only silence resulted. Hunching her shoulders, she growled, "Well, yer might also know I've a way of stickin' my conk in where it shouldn't ought to be. Oh. An' in case yer're a-wonderin', milord, that means m' nose."

His words were infinitely slow in coming. " 'Conk,' is it?" he asked finally. "Also known as a sneezer, a gig, or a trunk?"

She heard the change in his voice. Definitely. Unable to stop herself, she turned back to meet his now-lightened eyes with a great smile of her own. "An' don't forget smeller!" she crowed.

Having thus reestablished their earlier camaraderie, the earl drew himself to his feet. With a vast air of solemnity, he held out his hand to her.

Aware of the honor intended, she jumped up and extended him her hand. Fine white kid enfolded brown-dyed cotton. A soft current of warmth seemed to flow back and forth. In a voice turned husky, Mattie held her grasp firm while she shook his hand and said, "It has been my pleasure, sir."

"No, Matt," he replied in still deeper tones, matching her grip with the gentlest additional squeeze. "The pleasure, I think, is mine."

Chapter Six

After her amicable parting with the earl, Mattie stepped onto the flags bordering Hay-market Street, lost in a mood of bemusement. She had found that leavetaking handshake satisfactory in every respect, the evening's earlier reverses notwithstanding. All things considered, she felt remarkably lighthearted.

Full darkness had fallen during the hours since she'd first entered the theatre. The out-of-doors felt wonderfully refreshing, cooler and cleaner than during the day. Streetlamps glowed softly on every corner post, and Mattie rejoiced in the feather-light touch of a summer night's breeze as it caressed the curve of her cheek. Just the chance to stroll along the pavement, without having to rush, felt very fine indeed. She had no appointments to keep, no packages to carry, and time was at her disposal.

Mme. Leteuil wasn't even waiting up for her. Tomorrow was a business day, so Madame had given her a key to the shop after receiving Mattie's promise that she would awaken her when she returned. But who was to know whether she came in at this particular time or later? She needn't light a taper when she roused Madame to report herself safely arrived, so the exact hour wouldn't be known.

Mattie was on her own. She reveled in the liberty. And with no necessity to hurry in making her return, she also decided that she could benefit from a moment's reflection.

Practically from the moment she'd started up Blackfriars Bridge, tonight's entire outing had been almost too exciting to bear. Her first venture into the city after business hours, she had nearly missed Mr. Elliston's fine performance, had been rescued by an earl, and had seen a great drama enacted from a booth of the first style of elegance. She had also argued with her host on a matter which, strictly speaking, could not be considered her concern. But the result of all this was that she had, just perhaps, made herself a new friend.

Briefly, Mattie puzzled over her strange reaction when his lordship had so-casually mussed her hair. The effect had been quite *electrick.* Her nerves had jumped and skittered about as though he had touched her soul. A poetical notion, that. And an absurd notion too, Mattie just as quickly concluded. In this manner she disregarded a singular and most extraordinary occurrence.

She did own that having the large gentleman's friendship seemed somehow important. She couldn't imagine why this should be, but there it was. And for all of his ofttimes glaring faults, she admitted to finding the earl an attractive man, a man with a rare generosity of spirit. She especially liked the sound of his voice—warm and frequently gentle—and admired the ready way he had of explaining himself whenever he discovered he'd displeased.

Above all else, though, she loved looking into his

eyes. She seemed able to read meanings from those eyes, more so than in most people.

And Mattie made a practice of looking closely at everyone around her. She found it useful in her own efforts at maintaining a disguise. Tonight, for example, she had studied the theatre employees, the actors, and the society grandees alike. She had judged the effectiveness of this gesture, that posture, even paying attention to the precise tilt of a smile.

One particular lady, a woman with silky blond hair and a daringly décolleté gown, came to mind. Unconsciously, Mattie thrust out her chest, arched her neck, and fluttered an imaginary fan. She slowed her walk to a decorous pace and offered a flirtatious look to a pretended admirer. Upon apprehending what she was about, though, she pressed her lips together and made a distinctly vulgar sound.

"Hulver-headed simkin," she grumbled into the night.

Irked by the focus of her thoughts, Mattie stopped and fussed with the set of her coat. She could not, however, prevent herself from wondering just what it might have been like had circumstances permitted her to arrive at the theatre in the dazzling new gown Mme. Leteuil and Tante Agathe had made for her. She then would have been just as stylish as any, would she not? In a dress like that, she would have appeared beautifully feminine. Lush green gauze might be all very well, but it couldn't compare to the exquisite make of her gift, now could it!

Mattie next recalled what the earl had said about his being unaccustomed to receiving gifts. An untrue statement if ever there was, for Lady Whatsits had certainly been offering something. But his being the "Invincible Vince"—how Mattie did hate that sobriquetical bit of nonsense—he was probably far too used to such favors to be at all appreciative. A man with his reputation would have scores of people falling all over themselves just for the boon of his company.

That idea struck home. Could she have hit upon the actual problem? A man apparently of some aptitude, a nobleman of wealth and distinction . . . was it not likely that he attracted the endless attention of all and sundry? And how difficult, surely, in the face of such adulation, not to lose sight of one's true self. What unhappiness must result!

Thoughtfully, Mattie gauged the importance of being recognized for deeds well done and for accomplishments of some real merit, rather than being known for whatever titles and honors devolved upon one at birth. Her own antecedents outshone most of the English nobility, come to that, but did it make her a better person? She thought not. Her breeding had value only if she used whatever talents she possessed to the best of her ability. And those talents needs must be directed toward some purposeful activity, not vainly frittered away.

Agathe de Serinier had taught her well.

Sounds coming from somewhere nearby gradually impinged on Mattie's engrossed consciousness. Jangling bits, stomping hooves, and wheels crunching on cobblestones. She looked up to realize that she had been standing for some time at the end of Hay-market Street, quite lost to the external world. In the meantime, any number of carriages, chairs, and a fast-growing crowd of people were collecting in front of a house across the way, almost under her nose.

Recognizing the address, Mattie's perceptions bounced back to their norm. Evidently, some late entertainment was planned at Carlton House, the noble home of George the Third's firstborn son and heir.

Like a marionette guided by the toymaker's strings, she allowed herself to be drawn in closer. Flambeaux marched along the stuccoed outer walls of the great residence, rippling in an ever-changing show of yellows and bright oranges. The captured flames emitted whuffling noises as they danced a set with the roving nighttime air.

Advancing nearer, Mattie was enchanted by the sounds of lighthearted laughter and charming music coming from within. *How very lovely,* she thought. In her mind's eye, she pictured well-dressed couples swirling gracefully in time to the violins' bidding, while other, equally fashionable guests engaged in no-doubt brilliant conversations. The erudite Mr. Sheridan would likely be just behind those doors, the inimitable George "Beau" Brummell, and of course, England's First Gentleman, the Prince of Wales himself. With her eyes half closed in unaccustomed yearning, Mattie envisioned the scene.

She didn't linger thuswise overlong, however. She bethought the time and of how it could be much better spent. Tonight presented her with an unlooked-for opportunity to make a visit to a friend of her own, and Charlie Coomber's watchhouse was less than twenty minutes away. While not so well known as the habitués of the Prince's home, Ol' Charlie was quite as important as anyone else could be—and the more so for being her friend.

Mattie had first met Charlie Coomber nearly four years before while he was working as a rent collector in Southwark. They'd got up an acquaintance when she had returned a receipt book which had inadvertently fallen from his pocket, and they had been chums ever since. She didn't see Charlie quite so often now, for he had changed employment at the first of the year and had become a watchman for the Mayfair district. His duty hours prohibited their meeting in the ordinary way, so the chance to see him tonight was entirely too good to miss.

Picking up her pace, Mattie pursed her lips in a low whistle. She was unaware that she repeated the tune she'd heard issuing from Carlton House. Cats on the prowl halted at the sound, and as she passed them by, she made a game of counting each one she saw. By these means she dismissed the weight of previous thoughts. For to her, no amount of cogitation was so important as participating in the present. She was happy in her new goal.

She moved rapidly westward and then made a turn to the north. And just as she had assured Mme. Leteuil, every corner held a lamp and each front doorway bloomed with light. What Mattie hadn't before realized, though, was how little real illumination these measures provided. The golden circlets formed by each lamp barely extended beyond their protective glass enclosures. So meager was the total output, in truth, that it served only to increase the depth of the shadows in the long stretches between. She owned to a sense of relief when the glimmer of light emitted from a niche on Chandler Street declared her destination.

Built to give shelter from untoward weather, the small wooden house, typical of its kind, was just large enough for a rough bench seat and a lantern hook. Similar watchboxes stood in every neighborhood, supported by an annual assessment on the residents of each district. The citizenry also paid for a man to stand guard, the watchmen thus employed collectively known as "charleys." Happenstance had provided Charlie Coomber with a name of particular aptness.

"Ho, there," she greeted, grinning widely as she thrust her little face inside the box.

Ol' Charlie leaped up with alacrity and immediately came out to shake her hand. His black tricorn hat remained forgotten on the bench, along with the grubby scrap of paper and a worn pencil stub he'd been using when she had come upon him. Towering a foot and more above her, his head was quite as bare as any fresh-laid egg. His uncovered pate shone with a familiar brightness in the lamplight.

Mattie was delighted to see that the spindle-shanked old man had not changed appreciably in the months since she'd last seen him. His grip was quick and firm, while his eyes curled at the corners in well-remembered good humor.

"Lookee, if it ain't young Matt come to see me!" he cried. "Been an age, son, been an age. An' you not grown an inch!" At her stricken expression, he looked abashed, then quickly consoled, "Well, now, just you give it time, boy. You'll sprout up as fast as Michaelmas daisies and afore ever you know it."

It wasn't that Mattie was so terribly sensitive about her height in the ordinary way; she rarely attended the fact that practically everyone she encountered was rather taller than she. It was only that Charlie's remark had put her in mind of the Fashionable Fair One. Unhappily, for the space of an instant and for the second time that evening, she had found herself lacking. She quickly pulled herself together, though.

"Aw," she said, standing as tall as she could, " 'tain't so important, is it? Yer've more inches than most yerself, Charlie, but haven't yer ever wanted to be a mite smaller, so's yer could be more comfortable, like?" Indicating the box behind him, she couldn't resist a wag. "Now just you take this here watchhouse, for instance. A mite cramped for a long-shanks like yerself, ain't it?"

Turning to judge the inadequacies of the indicated wooden structure, the old man answered her with a smile. "Well now, since you mention it, Matt, I do see that a fellow your size might have more'n a few advantages. I can hardly bend my bones enough to sit meself down inside, whereas you wouldn't have a speck of trouble. An' when it rains? Lord, love me! I can hardly find the means to keep dry."

"And do let's consider that bench," Mattie quipped, all innocence. "Why, long as it is, I could stretch right out an' take a snooze. You ever think o' doin' that, Charlie?"

Unexpectedly, the old man met her teasing with a surprising show of solemnity. "No. Never once, Matt. Give you my word, I haven't slept a wink on the job and do all my restin' of a day now. I know what my responsibilities are, and I always, always give 'em my best."

This too-somber alarmed her. It was so unlike her jocular friend. Anxiously, she asked, "Charlie, is there somethin' wrong? Has someone accused you of not performin' yer job properly? Is that it?" She squinted up at him, trying to see past the shadows created by the lantern's thin light.

Moving the rattler slung from the loop on his hip out of the way—the noisemaker's purpose being to give the alert when assistance was needed—the old man bent to one knee where he could better meet her eye. In a voice filled with dejection, he explained. "It's housebreakers plaguing me, Matt. As clever a bunch of ken-millers as ever dubbed a lock. Thrice in the last four weeks they've cracked houses under my protection, and there's already talk of replacing me with someone more wide awake. Lord Thornbaugh's house was first, then Mrs. Endicott on South Audley Street lost a diamond necklace worth thousands. Right after that, Lady Rothshaw's home was broken into and her entire jewel collection stolen. A curious thing, too. Each time, the dubbers have taken nothing but jewels—not that they haven't got a deal of value from that!—but nary a silver spoon nor an ormolu clock's gone missing withal."

"But no one blames you, surely," she protested. "Burglaries, er, that is, *ken-millings,* happen all the time! Anyways, I can't see what clocks and spoons have to do with it. Pinched is pinched, ain't it?"

The watchman twisted to reach inside the shelter box behind him, bringing forth the scrap of paper he'd been working on before her visit had interrupted him. He angled the sheet toward the light and pointed to it. "Just lookee here, Matt. This is a list of all what's been taken. I thought to make my own copy from the Bow Street occurrence reports, thinking it would provide me with a clue as to where the goods might be fenced. It being naught but jewelry helps in narrowing down the possibilities some, but what with there being more'n two hundred pawnshops in the city, I don't see how I'm to investigate every one. Still, some mighty influential people have been hurt by my failure, so you can understand that I have to try and locate the articles afore I lose my post. An old man like me, how else can I earn my bread? I need this job, I do," he said sadly.

His despondent look went straight to Mattie's heart. How else, indeed, could Charlie Coomber earn a living?

Young men came up from the countryside almost daily, she knew, and every one of them was eager for work. It would be a simple thing to replace her old friend with someone younger and more active, leaving poor Charlie with little prospect for much besides the workhouse. And if the old fellow planned a search of the pawnshops during the daylight hours, then worked his shift through the night, he would soon be exhausted and really *would* fall asleep on the job.

There had to be a way she could help. She was young, fleet of foot, and she was willing.

An idea began churning its way to the surface.

"Could yer makes me a copy of that list, Charlie?" she asked, her little face earnest. "Me an' some other fellows I know of could take over checkin' on the pawnshops for yer easily enough—an' who knows? We might uncover the goods right off. But for now," she said, tugging her friend to his feet, "let's us take a turn around this here neighborhood. Yer can also be tellin' me more 'bout what all's been happenin' of late."

The long-legged night watchman professed himself agreeable. He stood and lifted the lantern from its hook then clapped his black tricorn atop his bald head. After seeing his box secure, he took up a staff of gnarled wood, making a last check to be sure he had his rattler belted firmly at his side.

One figure rising cathedral-tall, the other mouse-hole short, Ol' Charlie and young Matt set off down Chandler Street.

The dark-haired tavern maid sidled over to the table, carrying the requested pints of porter. She preened a bit as she approached her customers, for The George on

Hay-market Street took on only the prettiest girls, a fact of renown which made her aware of her worth.

Unfortunately, this particular young woman was not so aware that her serving skills were somewhat less precise.

As she set the two tankards down, the first gentleman watched the carelessly handled liquid splash over and onto the table's surface. He saw a dark ring spread out from the base of his container. His table companion ignored a similar mishap when the second tankard was released, being too busy at maintaining an appreciative eye on the pretty tavern wench. When she tarried to allow one well-rounded breast to brush suggestively against the first gentleman's richly colored russet coat, the second man shook his head.

"Damme, Vincent. How do you *do* that?" Mr. Evant asked admiringly.

The earl offered no answer. He merely extended one long, thickly muscled arm to pull the willing girl down to his lap. With his free hand, Vincent next reached inside his coat, searching for something to use as a wipe. He knew that if he picked up his porter as it stood, the moisture gathered at the bottom of the tankard would drip on the serving maid's apron. And because this made his third pint since coming in from the Theatre-Royal across the street, and the wet ring had grown betimes, he decided it was time to rectify matters.

Locating his handkerchief, the earl pulled it out. He stared at the neatly folded square. Then, with an arrested expression, he put it back, unused, into his pocket.

Mr. Evant disregarded this rather strange behavior. He was far more interested in the dark-haired addition to their table than he was in remarking anything else.

Sounding plaintive, he said, "I'll swear by all that's holy, Vincent, I just don't understand it. Here I am, willing to give up my lead hand to have the women notice me like they do you; instead, they fall all over themselves trying to gain your attention. Good gad, you'd think I was tedium personified!" His expression lugubrious, he struck an attitude.

Vincent smiled and gave the girl on his lap a teasing wink. "Well, my pretty miss, what say you to that? Is our friend here so unpleasant to look upon? Give us the truth, if you please."

The serving girl giggled and glanced over at Mr. Evant, who promptly rearranged his features to present his most winsome smile. "Oh, Lor' love ye, dearie!" she achieved on a titter, before turning back to the earl. She then wrapped her arms around Vincent's neck and leaned close to whisper a confidence into his ear. "Ye arter be un'erstandin', though, milord, that I knows jest who ye are. An' a girl like me is bound to be dead smit by someone so *Invincible*. Why, an' never doubt it," her voice lowered with promise, "I'd do near anythin' for a famous man like you. Oh, anythin' a'tall." She shifted her hips in a bold, intimate move while pressing herself invitingly against his broad chest.

Receptive to this piece of flirtatiousness, Vincent reached for one of the dark, crimped curls which dangled loose at her temple. Deliberately, he drew his fingers down the captured strand, idly testing it against the overhead lamp for color and for texture. He was disappointed when no shimmering blue-black highlights met his eye. And with or without gloves, he recognized a certain coarseness in comparing the tavern maid's hair to the much darker curls he had touched earlier on this evening.

He instantly dropped his hold on the barmaid's hair. He was gripped by an awful fear! *Good God!* he protested in silent panic. Could his strange discontent of late have led him to—dared he even think it—*unnatural desires?* Could he, a man amongst men, have found little Matt so attractive as to mean . . .

Vincent's mind bolted and shied in an urgent search for answers. His dismay was unbounded when he next remembered the powerful jolt he had felt upon rumpling young Matt's hair.

But *surely,* he amended, forcing himself to calm, it was no more than an unexpected response to the lad's own shocked reaction. As for whether his current companion had hair so fine as another's, it was nothing more than simple curiosity which had compelled him to compare the two. So what if he had found Matt's movements, manners, and person more refined than another's. It didn't really mean so very much. None of it meant a thing. Nothing, that is, unless—

Vincent looked closely at his seatmate. In the strictest concentration, he examined the line of her jaw, the curve of her neck, followed by a minute inspection of her hands. He realized that something didn't quite ring true when he compared the girl in his lap to his memory of young Matt.

He raised a clear mental picture to his mind's eye. . . .

It was rather like looking at a man with a muff.

Before he could follow this intriguing thought further, however, a slight stir amongst the patrons announced the entrance of a new customer to The George. In some distraction, Vincent looked up, and at once found himself calling upon every ounce of the discipline he had developed through years of competition in strenuous sporting events.

Expunging every last trace of expression from his face, he sat quietly, waiting for the moment when their table would receive notice. That time was not long in coming. The gentleman established their presence and began moving their way.

Gently removing the tavern maid from his lap, Vincent prepared to greet Lord Hedgewick.

Chapter Seven

In a matter of days, Mattie had her friends Billy and Kevin organized and off on their new assignments. She had made each of them a copy of Charlie Coomber's list of stolen goods, then had added her own prepared notes which detailed the likely pawnshops and jewelers where they should begin their search. Billy had helped her by pointing out which shops might have sufficient affluence to purchase the missing items, because, stolen or not, the price offered by any knowledgeable fence would still likely be high.

Neither Billy nor Kevin had ever met the Chandler Street watchman before. But because he was one of Matt's good friends, they had pitched in to help with a will. They had begun by dividing up the city into manageable sections, commencing their search for the specified gems on a high note of excitement.

With Charlie's descriptions to aid her, Mattie had even drawn up a remarkably like sketch of a three-piece amethyst parure which she thought might be easiest to spot. The amethyst pieces were not so distinctive, nor so valuable, as to require particular concealment by a dishonest shopkeeper, but Charlie had learned from the jewels' owner, Lady Rothshaw, that they were easily identifiable nonetheless. The tiara had a large misfaceted stone at its center, as did the matching necklace, and the amethyst bracelet had a finely braided wire on its fourth link gone missing. Mattie had considered these facts well before deciding upon a method which might uncover the jewels.

By pretending to act the part of agents for a wealthy master desirous of purchasing just such a set of bright violet gems, and by describing to shop owners the supposedly wanted items without revealing the sketch, one of them should soon uncover the goods.

Three times a week, the youths met at the Bluebell to discuss their progress. The idea of capturing thieves gripped everyone's imagination and added a deal of spice to their days. Though as time passed by without anyone discovering a single, identifiable bauble, their initial enthusiasm had palled. They began to feel the abysmal frustration marking failure.

"Oi've less'n a score more places left ter search, Matt," groaned light-haired Kevin as he looked over what was left of his list. They had been six days on the hunt. "Sure, Oi've seen some roight pretty gew-gaws, stap me if I oin't, but none what fits the bill. An' there's only the lowest sorter ploices yet ter be checked. What'll we do when there's *no* more shops ter give the look-in?" He folded his list and laid it down on the table. "Why, they might a'been shipped off ter some Egyptian har*eem,* for all we knows." He looked exceedingly glum.

Mattie felt quite as depressed as young Kevin. When she'd awakened at Mme. Leteuil's that next morning after hearing of Charlie's troubles, she had disregarded her short night's rest and had hurriedly dressed in her boy's garb, feeling wholly optimistic. She had been sure her idea of searching the pawnshops between errands would save the day for old Charlie. She had expected that three sharp-eyed youths could accomplish the deed in no time. Yet now, she was not nearly so certain of success. Even Billy Tomkins seemed to have no idea about how they were to proceed when there were no more shops remaining to be inspected.

"If only we could 'appen onto that lot while they were at it one night," Billy said now, brushing back an errant thread of straight brown hair. His vision, not strong under the best of conditions, had no need of further impediment. Impatiently, he added, "And Matt, uncoverin' the sparklers is no more'n a part of the problem, neither, 'cause even if we do come up with the goods, we still 'ave ta prove who took 'em, don't we? That is, if yer friend Charlie is to come out of this a' right."

Caught up in her own anxieties over the question Kevin had raised, it took Mattie several seconds to absorb what Billy had said. In a burst of realization, she startled the two boys by leaping up from her seat. "O' course! That's it!" she cried, looking down into their upturned faces. "An' we know the district as well as any, don't we?" A bright grin stretched from ear to ear; she dropped back into her seat, fully satisfied.

Kevin's freckled face crinkled in confusion. "Naow, whatcher be meanin' by that, Matt? What's our knowin' the district have ter say ter anythin'?"

She quickly explained. "Oh, but it's such a simple thing, fellows. So simple that I don't know why I missed thinkin' of it before. We've only to join ranks and form our *own* watch patrol. If we take turns, none will lose too much sleep, and sooner or later, somethin's bound to happen. 'Sides which, 'tis been more'n a week since the last break-in, makin' the odds strong in our favor. The *dubbers* are sure to strike again. And soon!"

The idea of coming upon housebreakers in the very act appealed to youthful minds as only heroic deeds can. Agreement was instantaneous. Within minutes, schedules were arranged, signals agreed upon, and enthusiasm rekindled.

Mattie was especially excited. Having once accomplished a late-night adventure without anyone being the wiser, she felt every confidence in her ability to slip off undetected for a night in Mayfair. All the easier since, like Marie Leteuil, Tante Agathe was no light sleeper. Mattie was sure she could do her part without the least cause for concern.

After hearing of this newest plan offered for his support, Charlie Coomber continued in hope.

"Zounds! So this is where you've been hiding yourself." The boisterous greeting came accompanied by a hearty guffaw.

"As you see," Vincent replied, not for an instant looking aside. He held his position, keeping his full attention on the business before him.

A fine sheen of moisture spangled the Earl of Staffield's wide brow, and his thick, sun-streaked blond hair glistened and shone dark with sweat. A line of perspiration also patterned the back of his loose-fitting cambric shirt, worn above a comfortable pair of buff-colored nankeen breeches. Contrary to any appearance of overexertion, though, he breathed quietly and without undue labor.

Comprehending the importance of the given situation,

Sir Guy Chittenham stepped back out of the way and dropped into a crouch on the wooden plank flooring. Though the rails weren't up, affixed to the corner posts set permanently into the floor, it was obvious that a bout was in progress.

A short-statured and somewhat corpulent fellow, affecting a flaxen wig under his broad-brimmed white hat, squatted nearby. "Townshend," the baronet mouthed in silent greeting.

The man thus acknowledged, a highly placed official with the Bow Street Runners, answered by way of a friendly flutter of the fingers.

Sir Guy eased his bulk to rest further back on his heels to await a full resumption of that activity which his entry had threatened to disrupt.

While the baronet settled himself, Lord Staffield's opponent, who was also the owner of the spacious sparring room where these several gentlemen were gathered, stolidly ignored all but the task at hand. He feinted twice to the right with short jabs, his bright blue eyes never leaving Vincent's breastbone. Bobbing and weaving, he closed rapidly to deliver a swift left to the earl's apparently unguarded jaw.

The glove never connected. Lightening fast, Vincent shifted and threw out a strong left of his own. His reach was a full inch the greater, and he used this advantage as he followed with a powerful right. Then another right. And a third. It was a hit!

His opponent, also a large man, was unharmed in any serious degree. He had seen the blow coming, and while unable to wholly avoid it, he had nonetheless managed a move of the head which had minimized its worst effects. He now danced back lightly and smiled. Once at a safe distance, he absently massaged his abused cheek with one thick forearm, his eyes brimming with mischief. "Oh, that was well done, my Lord Staffield! Very well done. I see you've lost none of your science! Now, let us see if we can bring up the pace a mite."

A flurry of punches and jabs and audible gasps soon had Sir Guy and Mr. Townshend back on their feet. Gentleman John Jackson, England's retired boxing champion, was clearly in topping good form. He amazed his audience with his neat accuracy and his speed. The room soon resounded with the high-pitched susurrations of air displaced by the velocity of four broad fists, together with the occasional thumping noise when someone's glove made contact. Sweat flew in profusion with each man's movements, sprinkling the air with a quantity of fine crystal droplets.

For long minutes, Vincent held his own. His eyes glittered with the intensity of profound concentration. The dark stripe down the back of his shirt expanded, even while another, matching stripe grew and spread along the front. His nostrils flared out, begging for additional oxygen. Doggedly, every muscle strained to the utmost, he focused solely upon his next move.

Gradually, however, the earl's determination was outstripped by the opposition's superior abilities. John Jackson, the best of the best, managed to cut in under his guard with a marrow-bone stop which put him squarely on his backside.

The ingloriousness of his new position didn't perturb Vincent in the slightest. Grinning broadly up at the man who had floored him, he arose easily, controlled his breathing not so very easily, and graciously conceded the match. "You couldn't resist going me one better, could you, John? But perhaps it wasn't so quickly accomplished as you had expected?" He next added honestly, "Not that I could have lasted much longer, in any case. All in all, though, I don't think I made too poor a showing. What say you, sir?"

Mr. Jackson agreed without stint. "Oh, aye, my lord, that was quite a piece of work, especially for someone who's not donned the gloves these last months on end. With a bit of cooperation, I don't doubt we could have you back up to snuff in a trice. Your wind isn't what it should be, I'll grant, but it's nice to know you've not forgotten everything I've taught you. Aye, the moves are still there," he declared roundly.

" 'Deed, they are!" exclaimed Sir Guy, passing each man a clean huckaback towel to dry his face. His own countenance bore a look of undisguised admiration. "Knew you were good"—this said to Vincent—"but I'd forgotten you had *this* kind of talent, man! You could teach me a thing or two, what?"

Mr. Jackson looked thoughtful while he blotted the sweat from his neck. Significantly, he remarked, "Now that, gentlemen, is a truly grand suggestion."

Vincent, at a rare loss for meaning, glanced around their little group. Sir Guy's expression mirrored his own blank look, while it appeared that the round-bodied little policeman from Bow Street had perfectly understood. In fact, Mr. Townshend looked positively knowing.

The earl turned back to the boxing saloon owner for the needed clarification. "What, precisely, do you mean, John? Are you suggesting that I set myself up to teach? Give lessons in the fistic arts?" At the champion's brisk nod, he snorted. "Well, that's hardly what I consider proper sport. I'd far rather train to—"

"To what?" Mr. Jackson interjected forthrightly. "To strip off the gloves and compete for prizes like any bully boy at Southwark Fair? Is that what you would

115

have?" He slapped the spent towel over his shoulder in an unusual sign of impatience.

From the corner of his eye, Vincent caught a growing smile on Mr. Townshend's face. For some reason, the sight irritated him. "Well, no, of course not," he answered Mr. Jackson somewhat stiffly. "But certainly I can find suitable competition without going up against professionals."

The champion seemed to disagree. He shook his head as he answered, "And just where, my Lord Staffield, do you think to discover this 'suitable competition'? You won out over every amateur pugilist not above two years ago. Now then, what I propose is that you take another road, try a new avenue for your talents. Consider. There are any number of men with a mature man's weight who would necessarily feel silly sparring with someone who matches them in having little by way of skill, but who cannot approach them for size. Men like Sir Guy here," he reminded with a gesture, "for whom, regrettably, I haven't adequate time. You could assist such men—and help yourself, as well—for there's many a lesson to the teacher. Oh, I can attest to that. Aye, and first*hand.*" Eyes all a-twinkle, he dabbed tenderly at his still-reddened cheek.

The dapper little policeman from Bow Street chose the moment to enter his own brand of encouragement. "And may I be permitted to add that the activities here at Mr. Jackson's have the additional benefit of being legal?" Catching no one's eye in particular, he expanded on this seeming non sequitur with what, at first, seemed another. "Oh, yes, indeed, yes. The law takes a dim view of a good many things. There is, for example, the purpose which lately brought Lord Hedgewick before the practice targets over at my friend Joe Manton's shooting gallery. Perhaps it was in preparation for a certain dawn meeting which occurred yesterday? Or, at least, that's as I understand it."

Vincent was both affronted and unaccustomedly embarrassed. Evidently, the officer knew about his exchange of shots with Lord Hedgewick, the duel having taken place only the morning before and under terms of the greatest secrecy. The challenge had been issued at The George, though, and with all the world looking on, so Vincent supposed that he shouldn't feel surprised if the news had already reached interested ears at Bow Street.

Fortunately for everyone involved, Lord Hedgewick's shot had gone wide, practice or no, after Lord Staffield had deloped. The matter had therefore been successfully concluded with everyone's honor—and person—intact. But to Lord Staffield's mind, it was a private affair and not one to be so casually bruited about. He resented Mr. Townshend's inference.

Vincent tried to return his attention to Mr. Jackson's proposal. Yet without his quite realizing it, indignation crept to the fore. "So, you would have me become a teacher, John? Me? A *teacher!* Well, I'll have you know that I'm not about to start playing the nanny for some inexperienced, *in*competent, *inept* bunch of—"

His remaining protest died a quick death as he caught sight of Sir Guy's crestfallen look. Vincent recollected himself sufficiently to realize the actual cruelty in what he had just said; within seconds, right reason resumed its place. The Bow Street Runner's intrusive and public remarks might have put him into a confounded ill humor, but that was no excuse for having insulted his friend.

And well did Vincent know it. "In something of a pet, aren't I?" he muttered.

Shrewd to the very echo, Mr. Jackson correctly assessed his changed mood. He used the opportunity to bring out further arguments, saying in persuasive tones, "I can appreciate that this would mean a new touch for you, my lord, but I ask you to look at the thing fairly. If you supplied lessons, you would be obliged to keep up the frequency of your sessions, if only because you would have students who were counting on you. As I pointed out earlier, too, the benefits of regular exercise would accrue to get you in prime condition, and you would be helping a few fellows, besides."

Vincent stole another look at Sir Guy and was dismayed by his friend's now-hopeful expression. And indeed, he realized, John Jackson was the "Gentleman" in every way for having made his point without once playing the bear like he himself had.

The truth slowly, slowly sank home. Vincent began to consider that the champion could be right, and that there might well be any number of men, both young and not-so-young, who would enjoy learning more about the manly science of boxing. The idea had a certain appeal.

But for an earl to set about schooling them?

Once again Mr. Jackson broke into his thoughts. "Oh, I know. Believe me, I know." He sighed as though he had heard the earl's every unspoken doubt. "Your interest has always been primarily in the competition. But surely, my lord, you can appreciate that there's much more to the sport than that! It's the feeling of fitness which results from good hard labor, the strength you develop in lungs and limb, not to mention the knowledge that you can defend yourself with naught but your own two hands. I'm asking you to consider giving of your

118

free time—for, of course, I won't insult you by proffering any monetary form of recompense—yet your time could not be better spent! You'll find yourself paid in a better coin altogether. Aye! That's what's important here."

A previous admonishment about the "importance" of things jangled loud in Vincent's memory. He deliberately squelched the reminder, however, deciding that, by damn, the competition *was* important. The chances taken, the thrill of winning . . .

But no. Vincent had to concede that while winning had once been of the utmost consequence, it had lately seemed much less so. And today he'd enjoyed his round with the champion, even knowing that there was no chance for the ultimate victory. It had been enough, more than enough, just to last as long as he had and to get in a hit or two.

He admitted, as well, that earning Mr. Jackson's compliments on their impromptu mill had felt very fine. It had meant something, unlike the mindless cheering of mere lookers-on who hadn't participated in any measure. Receiving accolades from someone like John Jackson was real praise. He didn't have to wonder if his titles, or his wealth, or merely the enthusiasm of the moment had played a part.

Making up his mind, the earl swiftly divested himself of his practice gloves. He said laconically, "The day after tomorrow then, Guy. One o'clock. We'll meet here."

Vincent was immeasurably gladdened by the sight of his friend's face, now beaming at him with elation.

Regrettably, Lord Staffield's own pleasure was to prove itself short-lived. When Sir Guy and Mr. Jackson turned aside for a moment to discuss the particulars of Sir Guy's upcoming tuition, Mr. Townshend availed himself of the chance to beg a moment of the earl's time. It would seem that the officer had not yet done with him.

"Yes, what is it?" Vincent said brusquely, not bothering to disguise his annoyance.

The Runner had the grace to appear remorseful. He also had the intelligence to choose his wording with care. In conciliating tones, he said, "My lord, I must own myself guilty of the very thing which I am sworn to prevent. For I broke the peace between us. My position demands that I uphold the law at every point, it's true, but you'll perhaps understand that there are, in many instances, distinct difficulties in carrying out my duties. I cannot rightly make accusations from hearsay—neither do I outright charge you with any specific fault—yet I feel bound to speak out when I know a crime has been committed."

Mr. Townshend's reputation was of sufficient measure for Vincent to respect, albeit grudgingly, the man's good intentions. "I suppose you must, at that. Although," he added more sternly, "for my part, I prefer to see Bow Street expending more effort toward protecting the innocent citizenry from becoming unintentional victims. I have in mind the spate of burglaries so recently committed in my neighborhood."

It was the policeman's turn for embarrassment. "Er, yes. Just so. The three jewel thefts, you mean." Mr. Townshend shook his head in dismay.

"Exactly. And what are the Runners doing about these incidents, I ask?"

The little policeman again shook his head. "Well, Grosvenor Square does center a wealthy area, so it naturally attracts thieves from time to time. But as for this particular set of prigging coves ... um. Ahem! What I mean to say is, this set of, er ..."

Prigging coves, he had said. *Prigging coves,* no less!

The rotund little officer, struggling over his lapse into an indelicate use of the language, was clearly horrified. For a representative of the Home Office, one whose presence was de rigueur for every Queen's Drawing-room and chronicled court levée, any slip in speech, and while in polite company, must be mortifying in the extreme.

The earl choked back a laugh. He refused to succumb to the temptation to add to the officer's discomfort. It had never been Vincent's way to try and get even for every least offense, no matter how much he might have resented earlier being put in a similar condition.

Having some skill in canting himself, he sought to put the little man at his ease. Breezily, he said, "So it's no mere gang of draw-latches, then, but a bene crew of bowman prigs? Must be rare *flash* ones," he affirmed, "to put a leary cove like yourself on the fret. But why so? The rum-dubbers only cracked a few kens and brushed off with the goods. Nothing so smokey in that. Happens all the time! No reason to make a hurricane of it, now is there?"

Mr. Townshend seemed much gratified by the earl's method of response. Relaxing at his lordship's so-flattering condescension, he sought to explain further. "Oh, but, indeed, there are several details which are quite extraordinary, my lord. To begin with, nothing but pocket items have been taken. Furniture, rugs, plate, and all larger items, however valuable, are left untouched. And when you've seen the results of as many, er, ken-millings as I have, you'll know that this sort of thing is unusual. Most unusual."

"Well, if that's the case," the earl responded with a sharpened look, "then you've only to investigate the domestic staff of the residences involved. Or so I should think. For it sounds as if the stolen items are passed on, hand over hand, to an outside accomplice. It could explain why only small pieces are removed; quite possibly, there have been no break-ins at all."

"Oh, a right smart answer," Mr. Townshend said with strong satisfaction. "And just what I thought at first myself. However, I'm afraid my investigations don't support the theory. Both Mrs. Endicott's and Lady Rothshaw's houses had the latch plates completely torn off—indicative of intruders—besides which, neither house has taken on a new servant for ages. The same holds true for the first burglary, that of Lord Thornbaugh's residence. However, if you think you'd be able to spare the time, there is a way you might be of help, my lord."

"And how is that?" Lord Staffield began to look interested.

The little man from Bow Street proceeded to explain.

Chapter Eight

A short time later, and after washing away the signs of his labors, the earl began arranging a fresh neckcloth. He pressed the lightly starched cloth into precisely spaced folds as, with meticulous care, he lowered his jaw, very slowly, to his chest. He then raised his chin to a comfortable level. When satisfied that his care had achieved the proper result, he eased heavy shoulders into a well-tailored coat, adjusted his hat and his gloves, and exited Jackson's Rooms.

He set out, his steps brisk. With the day only slightly more than half over, he became aware that the remaining hours held something less then their usual burden. It was warm, the afternoon temperature perfect for a stroll out of doors, and somewhere along Bond Street, Vincent thought he might find a shop having a copy of *Broughton's Rules*. A review of the pugilistic code was in order. Inasmuch as his own copy of the book was so much thumbed over as to be virtually useless, a new copy was needed.

The earl enjoyed his explorations into the booksellers' wares. He extended his search to St. James's Street before he located the appropriate text; in the same shop, he made the happy discovery of two other books of similar interest. He decided to add these to his purchase. He had the lot wrapped in sturdy brown paper before leaving the shop, feeling eager to get home and begin his studies.

It would be no great matter to extricate himself from that night's casually accepted engagements, he considered, since sometime in the last hours, whatever previous plans he had in mind had radically changed. He wanted time to make a review of the current boxing rules. He had also to determine what methods to employ in developing students who needn't yield the palm to anyone. Although Mr. Jackson might think it sufficient to "teach a fellow a thing or two," Vincent was resolved on a deal more than that. Such students as placed themselves under *his* instruction would have not only the opportunity to learn the noble science of boxing but would, more importantly, be encouraged in an appreciation of its art.

Anticipating a pleasant evening, the earl started back up St. James's Street. But as he prepared to pass by Lauriere's, that eminent jeweler to no less than the Duchess of York, he was deflected from his expected course. He spotted young Matt ahead under a floppy-brimmed hat, just leaving that famed establishment.

Vincent fell into step a few yards behind. As the boy darted nimbly over the flags through the oncoming traffic, Lord Staffield, unnoticed, availed himself of a fortuitous opportunity to evaluate the lad's appearance. He attended the youngster's lithe figure, his eyes narrowing in close scrutiny over each line of Matt's slender form. In due turn, he also paid heed to every detail of costume.

Costume, indeed. The garments which before seemed

nothing more than ill fitting, with each quick movement, now appeared to be the result of an unusually clever bit of tailoring. Having spent many an hour being fitted up at Meyer's, Vincent thought he recognized the signs. The drape of fabric over horsehair padding was evident to his newly critical eye; he surmised that Matt's dress had been effected by a very accomplished professional.

Oh, yes. He saw that Matt's jacket had been intentionally designed to disguise a definite narrowness of shoulder and—no doubt of it!—a certain overfullness of hip. The long vest, quilted and with its buttons placed just so, was well suited for the purpose of hiding what could be an entire series of curves. Adding up this ocular evidence, Vincent's conjectures took on substance.

He acted at once. He hailed the "boy" and was rewarded by the sight of a piquant little face turned his way. The youth whirled round and came scurrying back down the pavement to meet him, respectfully doffing his hat, a lively smile of recognition lighting his fine features.

Vincent perused those features with care. "Matt, well met," he said crisply.

"And a very good afternoon to yer too, milord!" the "lad" chirruped in a familiar rough-edged contralto. "Goin' my way, is yer?" Without waiting for an answer, Matt fell into step alongside him.

Vincent found himself charmed—thoroughly *charmed*—by the low timbre of that husky little voice. He wondered that he'd not paid it much attention before! Bemused, he reduced his pace, wondering how it was that he ever could have thought the young scamp to be of the masculine gender. He must suppose he'd been fooled by his own expectations of anyone who dressed in similar clothing.

There was no mistaking it, though. The fragile bend of jaw, the light bones in brow and cheek, and equally telling, the dainty taper in Matt's uncovered hands—those delicate fingers never belonged to any boy!

It was just as he'd suspected since that night at The George, when he'd made a mental comparison between young Matt and the pretty tavern wench.

Curiously enough, Vincent discovered he wasn't in the slightest put out over being the victim of such a take-in. Most probably, Matt had his own—or rather, *her* own—reasons for the rôle she played. At any rate, that aspect wasn't Lord Staffield's concern. He was too relieved at having his suspicions confirmed to fret over-much about whatever game the little elf was involved in.

Keeping the pace, with no notion that there was aught amiss, Matt tilted her chin and fastened on the sight of the paper-wrapped parcel beneath the earl's arm. "Looks like yer've been out sportin' a bit o' the blunt, milord. What is it yer has there, anyways?" she asked him brightly.

Vincent made some noncommittal answer, being absorbed as he was in yet another observation. Matt, to his so-recently opened eyes, proved not only to be a female, but one he suspected of having more years to her credit than he had ever supposed. Along with the mature depth of her voice, there was a certain firmness in the way she held her head, a promise of adult purpose in her eyes. He thought it unlikely that she had left her teens behind, but no sooner had he formed this conclusion than he became shockingly aware of another. If dressed in the proper clothes, Matt would make a regular little beauty!

What a diverting idea *that* made.

Matt's attention meanwhile remained affixed on his package. "Well, burn my breeches!" She gave a low whistle. "If'n that ain't a load o' books? Never say they're yers, milord!"

Her reaction was most unflattering. It was, however, distracting. It served to remind Vincent of just what it was that he liked best about his young friend. Matt had pluck. She teased him, delighted him, and by some special magic, seemed to brighten time itself.

On the instant, Vincent decided to keep his knowledge of her sex concealed. By holding silent, he could continue his enjoyment of her company without risking any change in their relationship. And it was a relationship he was coming to enjoy more and more.

Any matters of good fellowship notwithstanding, though, he determined to give her back a bit of her own. "Now just how do you suppose," he asked, looking at her askance, "I should make my answer to that? Do you think the act of reading beyond my skills? While I'll have to admit that I've not done so much of it lately, I would have you to understand, Matt, that the shelves of Radcliffe Library were not unknown to me in my youth."

Her fine winged brows flew aloft. "Oxford? Yer was a scholar then?"

"Well, no. Not exactly," he owned. Vincent was surprised that she'd caught the reference. "However, neither would I say that my years at school there were a complete waste. Difficult as it may be for you to believe, I did manage to keep up with my class at Magdelene."

She slowed and gave him an astonished look, her mouth rounding in awe. Smooth and cherry-pink, her lips made a perfect O. "Lor! So's there's more to yer than meets the eye. Oh, I knew it. I just knew it!"

"Why, yes," came his answer, the tones faintly sardonic. "One often finds the most accurate information by taking care to seek beneath the surface." A jewel-like clarity in his Kashmir-blue gaze warned of a deeper meaning.

Matt picked up her pace and tugged at the set of her vest—uneasily, his lordship thought. After a few moments, she seemed to collect herself to inquire, "So, tell me, milord, just what kind o' books be they? I hadn't s'posed a tip-top Corinthian like yerself 'ud be much on collectin' the latest novels."

She then stepped out ahead of him, extending her arm and letting her wrist droop as if holding a fashionable walking stick. She reduced her stride to mincing steps, stopped, and turned back to face him. She set both hands to rest atop the imaginary cane. She next threw up her head, arched her eyebrows, and dropped her lids in a ridiculous and amazingly supercilious manner. Her imitation of a beau on the strut was perfection. Assuming an odd falsetto, she trilled, "La, that dear Mr. Coleridge has such a *marvelous* way with his pen. Too, too sublime, is he not?"

Vincent exploded into a hearty shout of laughter. His large frame shook with amusement. "No, Matt, you're correct. For I've neither novels nor poetry here, I'm afraid. These volumes relate to the ring. *Boxiana,* if you would know. I had thought a bit of reading on the subject might prove helpful to me in my latest endeavor, you see."

An arrested expression on her pert little face rather pleased him. But as for just why she should show an interest in his reading material—or why he should feel so gratified that she did—Vincent couldn't fathom.

As they recommenced walking, he found himself explaining his intentions further. "It's like this, Matt. John Jackson convinced me to take on a few pupils of my own, informally, of course. He hasn't the time to see to everyone who comes to him for instruction, so I will merely be giving him a little assistance. And as you were once at some pains in pointing out, I could do with a few more constructive activities, while this"—he thumped the brown paper wrapping—"promises benefits to all parties."

Matt gave another low, amazed whistle. "New copper, is it?" she asked. She bobbed her head appreciatively. "Egad, sir, that's tearin' fine. Glad to hear it!"

"Are you, indeed? I wasn't sure you'd approve. There are those, I believe, who might consider it as, ah, none of my business." She missed the teasing glint in his eye.

"Oh, but it is. 'Deed it is!" She stopped and planted her feet squarely on the pavement, bringing their progress to a halt. Her eyes flashed up at him from beneath her wide hat brim, her long, silky black lashes reaching all the way up to the base of her eyebrows. With a great scowl, she admonished, " 'Tis somethin' yer has a talent for, now ain't it? 'Course, I've heard plenty 'bout yer prowess in the ring—why, 'twould seem that even Mr. Jackson believes in yer. But by yer doin' this, by providin' them as what needs 'em with lessons, yer've found a splendid way to broaden an interest. An' it's hardly the same as before, is it? Yer situation with Lady Whatsits, I mean. This can't *hurt* anyone."

His amused look informed her that she must needs rethink her words.

"Aw," she said gruffly. "Yer knows what I mean."

Her smooth cheeks took on a hint of pink at either side of her straight little nose. She didn't dodge his glance, however, when she added, "Leastways, Lord Staffield, I think it's a capital thing yer're a-doin'. Bang up to the marker. First rate!"

Vincent regarded Matt's sincerity. He also noted the correct use of his name. Both provided him with a sense of accomplishment.

By way of returning Matt's courtesy, he turned the conversation away from matters pugilistic. He changed subjects to what he thought would be more suitable for one of her sex. "Well then, enough about my doings, Matt. I'm interested in knowing what handsome bauble has caught your attention. I saw you leaving Lauriere's. Are your employer's customers grown so plump in the pockets as to require diamonds sewn onto their gowns? Or possibly, you were looking for a pretty trifle for yourself." He gave her a quizzical look.

"Oh, hardly that!" Matt chortled. "Jewels may be all very well, but they looks best when, unlike meself, there's no need for the ready money. Sad to say, Mme. Leteuil hasn't yet attracted such a wealthy clientele either. Too purse-shy by half, the lot of 'em. Anyways," she said next, her little face beginning to sparkle with cunning mischief, "I have it from a reliable source that diamonds ain't at all *bon ton* this season. Hadn't you heard? 'Tis rubies as are in style." At his expression of distrust, she merrily proclaimed, "Oh, gives yer m' word. 'Tis to be ruby buttons on mantelets, rubies scattered 'cross sleeves and hems, and ruby-dotted streamers made to dangle from every cuff!"

Again, the earl made no effort to contain his laughter. Her impertinence surpassed belief. "And next, I suppose, you'll be telling me that I must instantly arrange for a ruby-mounted cane."

Skipping a step forward, she answered mendaciously, "But o' course, milord!"

They parted on good terms at Piccadilly, Matt excusing herself to finish the day's errands. Still chuckling, the earl continued along his way.

And all through the following day, while poring over regulations concerning the duties of bottle-men at ringside, Vincent found himself subject to the occasional grin. Over the surface of his desk top, now littered with books, sporting magazines, and sheets of notations from his own hand, he stopped from time to time to look up and draw in a breath of fresh air from his opened library windows. He smiled at the memories of yesterday.

He'd popped in a hit over Jackson's guard, something which didn't happen to the champion more than once or twice in a year. He'd also agreed to join ranks as a professor of the noble science of boxing, an idea which had already begun to prove very much to his taste. Before yesterday was done too, he had acceded in another, equally fascinating request put to him by the rotund little man from Bow Street.

But above and beyond these happenings, it was the memory of his encounter with young Matt which sent the corners of Vincent's mouth into upward motion. The youngster's irrepressible spirits were a constant source of wonderment. Matt's other and better hidden assets were not so easily dismissed either, for no matter how artfully dressed—from her slim, hosiery-encased ankles to the top of her inky-dark hair—Matt's contrivances no longer obscured the truth. And the truth of it was that a young boy's clothing covered a tiny, but perfect, female body.

Recollection of a rich, husky contralto made Vincent's smile grow wider. The thought of long black lashes, setting off alert, sherry-bright eyes, warmed him from the inside out. Why, those eyes looked ready for anything! There was mischief peeping out from those eyes, mischief, and what mostly seemed to be an enormous and quite genuine care for those lucky enough to inhabit Matt's world.

How strange that he, a gentleman born to every advantage, should find so much pleasure from sharing a laugh with a little dab of a miss. Why, she was scarcely *half* his amplitude. Vincent laughed quietly to himself, then returned his attentions to the project before him.

There were other and rather more sizable fellows he must contend with on the morrow.

Chapter Nine

The streets surrounding Grosvenor Square lay quiet, enveloped in the hushed, velvety silence of the small hours past midnight. Hackney carriages, normally jostling one another for position in this area of wide lanes and magnificent residences, had long since gone to rest, leaving their stands soundlessly vacant. Unnourished lanterns, hung at doorway and at corner post, flickered uncertainly here and there.

Occasionally, one would blink out.

Mattie whistled under her breath as she ambled down the pavement. Her fourth night out in half as many weeks, it hadn't taken long for her to realize she must pace herself so as not to tire too quickly. There were dozens of back alleyways and countless entryways that wanted checking before her circuit was complete. Conscientiously, she investigated each one before moving on to the next.

She didn't travel alone. A near-grown kitten rode with its front paws braced atop her shoulder. She had acceded to its demands for attention when it had come upon her path at the last corner crossing. The cat now rested with its furry chin nestled close to her ear, purring its pleasure in shared company.

"A fine lot you are," Mattie grumbled, adjusting its hind feet more comfortably inside the crook of her arm. "At home to a peg, now aren't you? And when, really, you should be off and scouting out your territory. Like me! I'm doing my part in helping Ol' Charlie—that's the night watchman hereabouts, if you don't already know it—to keep this neighborhood safe. Oh, couldn't you at least get down and go look for a mouse or something?"

The animal quieted for a moment and nosed Mattie's ear. It soon settled back and resumed its feline buzzings.

"Useless cat," Mattie muttered in disgust. She ran a hand down the animal's silken fur, her gentle touch at variance to the tenor of her speech. "Hrumph. Foolish beastie. What I better stand in need of tonight is a dog. A dog could help me keep watch, instead of merely taking up space on my arm."

As if in some understanding of the situation, the cat lifted its head and wriggled its willingness to be let down. Mattie carefully lowered the creature to the pavement. Once freed, it darted off into the shadows.

"Ingrate." Mattie chuckled.

A lack of gratitude had little to do with the cat's swift retirement, however. A large white blur of the canine order whizzed past just seconds later, in hot pursuit of Mattie's feline friend.

"Oh no you don't," Mattie cried softly, immediately joining the chase.

With shapely legs grown strong from years of trotting the streets, she caught up to the dog in no time. She grabbed hold of its trailing leash and voiced a command for halt. Reluctantly, and after making a final lunge—a lunge which Mattie answered with yet another and still sharper word—the dog complied.

134

"Ahhh? Ah-*ha*," Mattie exclaimed, examining her prize. "*C'est un beau toutou—un caniche. Bon accueil et heureuse recontre, Monsieur Compatriot!*"

Indeed, Mattie's newest companion was, at least by breeding, originally from France. The long, tightly curled hair, the stylishly trimmed face, feet and tail, made up the typical grooming details of the French poodle wherever it might be found. Poodle dogs were also highly valued here in England, Mattie knew. And from this particular animal's meticulous grooming, together with the fine craftsmanship of the leather cord in her hand, she judged her find as belonging to someone who appreciated his possessions.

She looked back in the direction whence the dog had come. Not a soul was in sight. She was determined, nonetheless, to try and find the poodle's rightful owner. Taking the leash firmly in hand, she directed, "*Venez, monsieur, s'il vous plaît.*"

Obedient to her request, the white-haired poodle started off in a long-legged lope.

Mattie had practically to run to keep up. At every corner she managed a pause to look both ways for signs of any movement, before proceeding on to the next block. Her vigilance was soon rewarded. Just as she reached the limits of Avery Row, she spotted a man ahead who seemed to be casting about and calling something. And while she couldn't be sure with his back turned away as it was, she thought it sounded like "skittles."

She hailed him as she neared. "Ho there, sir. Is this what yer're a-lookin' for?"

The dog, at least, seemed certain. He strained at the leash and commenced whining in recognition before even Mattie's first word was uttered. And when the man

135

faced round, Mattie had his answer as well. His expression, revealed by the glow of the corner lamp marking the opening to Grosvenor Street, was one of profound relief.

"Oh, blessed be!" he cried. "Is this my Skittles found? Yes, yes, there's a good boy. My very own good Skittles." He crouched down to fondle the miscreant's white silky ears, crooning praises all the while.

The poodle promptly instituted an enthusiastic reply, applying a profusion of wet doggie kisses which soon had his owner's curly-brimmed hat knocked from his head to the pavement.

Mattie couldn't see that the otherwise smartly dressed gentleman minded in the least. But she was amazed by the foolish endearments which followed; "Bweautiful Skittles" and "My pwettiest good boy" filled her ears. After a good many more such effusions, her amazement increased when she felt the weight of the purse which the gentleman would press upon her.

"Oh, but you must!" he insisted when she gave signs of protest, "for I'll not have it said that Frederick Byng—that's me, don't you know—has neglected to pay what's owing. That sort of shag-bag behavior wouldn't do. Not *do*, I say. Please, I beg you will take what is, after all, but small recompense for the singular service you've done me. Oblige me in this, won't you?"

His earnest look convinced her. Without further compunction, she accepted the reward. It was nearly half an hour later, though, after she had stopped beneath a guttering streetlamp to count out the amount received, that she appreciated the extent of Mr. Byng's largesse.

Emptying the contents of the little sack into her hand, her eyes grew large as she beheld the amount. It was five golden guineas. Five.

"If that don't just beat the Dutch?" She gave a little hop of excitement. "Well, split my windpipe and call me 'Ben'!"

Gleefully, she twirled up on her toes. For the five gold coins, when added to her other savings, would make enough to buy a certain apple green Brussels carpet. And wonder of wonders, with a full six shillings to spare! Tante would never have to suffer cold floors again. Wouldn't the old dear be surprised! Mattie wanted to shout, to run, to be waiting at Mr. Biggersley's carpet warehouse when it opened later that morning.

With effort, she contained her impatience. Tonight, she shared Charlie Coomber's responsibility for securing the surrounds of Grosvenor Square, and only two evenings prior, there had been a fourth house broken into. This time, it was a prominent Member of Parliament who had his jewel case taken. The thieves had discovered it behind a hidden panel within his shaving table.

Fortunately, the burglary had occurred one street beyond Charlie's territory. However, poor Charlie feared he might not be so lucky again. Mattie had to agree.

So, for the two hours remaining to her service tonight, she must continue alert. She would finish her current round and make her report at Chandler Street; after which, she must hasten back across the river so as to slip into bed before her *grand-tante* awakened. She tucked the little coin sack deep inside the pocket of her vest. There, it seemed to tingle with promise. She determinedly ignored it, though, resolved to keep her mind on present business.

Just now, at this very moment, another burglary could be in progress.

Indeed, the night's adventures were not yet over. Faint, rhythmic sounds reached Mattie's ear, coming from the other side of the lilac bushes planted along the perimeter of the small oval park centering Grosvenor Square.

Instantly, she hunched her shoulders and ducked her head, using the densely planted hedge for concealment. The thudding noises repeated themselves, and as she worked her way in closer, she realized that they came in time with someone's heavy breathing. The soundmaker didn't seem to be on the move, though, since the noises continued from the same location.

Mattie stole down the flags, searching for a break in the hedge. When she reached a point near the source of the sounds, she discovered an opening in the bushes, blocked by a small, wrought-iron gate. Evidently, it was where entry and egress from the little park took place, and where, of a day, the area's residents went for enjoyment of the square's pleasant atmosphere.

But this was not daytime, and there shouldn't be anyone here.

A pair of lamps guarded the entrance, making it impossible for Mattie to peek around the last bush without disclosing her presence. The entry gate wouldn't shield her from view either, for the ironwork was pieced together like so much lace. But there must be some way for her to see inside without being seen. And she couldn't help wondering what she was to do if there was more than one person there. Perhaps there were two, or even three.

It might be the very gang of thieves she searched for.

Running her gaze down the length of the hedge, Mattie discerned an aperture at the base of a lilac bush a few feet away. Ignoring the warning bells in her brain urging prudence, she inched her way over and lowered her cheek to the pavement. Peering through the foliage, by the glow of the lamps lighting the gate area, she caught sight of a man, not ten steps beyond, wearing naught but a shirt, breeches, and shoes.

He was a very *large* man. The satiny gleam of golden-blond hair, the well-formed size of him ... she identified the earl positively. But as for what he was doing, Mattie couldn't imagine. She was even more puzzled when, without any reason she could see, he dropped to the ground and began pressing his fingers into the muscles of his left leg.

"Damn," she heard him say softly.

At that, she jumped up and hurried in through the gate. "Oh, what is it? What's wrong, Lord Staffield! Can I help?"

The earl jerked his head up and ceased rubbing his leg. For several long seconds he sat and stared up at her, then began the struggle to his feet. "Where the deuce did you come from?"

She thought he sounded cross. She didn't answer, though, being too intent on watching his movements. He seemed to have some difficulty with his balance, for he staggered slightly, giving her to fear that he might actually fall! Mattie knew her size was inadequate to be of much use in such a case.

She was relieved when, unaided, he successfully managed his way over to the park bench where he had left his hat and coat. He sat down heavily and rummaged through his belongings to pull out a chased silver flask. Removing the outer cap—actually, a small drinking cup—he unscrewed the inner top and poured out a quantity of liquid.

It sparkled clear and colorless in the light from the nearby gate lamps.

"Care for a drink?" he asked politely, holding out the little cup.

She shook her head "no," and he downed the contents himself. Apparently, not satisfied, he then raised the flask to his lips and drank off the whole.

Of all the nasty *things!* Mattie grieved. Known by such names as Blue Ruin, Jemmy, Stark Naked, and Daffy, gin had brought ill health and penury to countless pour souls. In nearly every part of the city, Mattie had seen the victims of the beverage, wandering aimlessly through the streets as they clutched at telltale bottles. She harbored no doubt that the clear liquid contained in the earl's pocket flask was, indeed, gin.

She planted her fists on her hip and scowled. She had at first been fearful of encountering thieves, and then, when she had seen the earl go down without any apparent reason, her initial fears had been replaced by anxiety. But the reality before her left Mattie feeling disappointed and angry.

"*Pawh,*" she exclaimed in her husky-voiced way when he set the flask aside. "Looks to me like yer should know when yer've had enough o' Sot's Comfort. Why does yer have to drink that stuff, anyways?"

The earl returned her a quizzical look, then glanced down at his flask. An instant's thought told him what Matt had meant, and while he could have reassured her, he was too caught up in a feeling of hurt that she would misjudge him so.

In point of fact, Vincent had found sleep troublesome tonight because of muscles made sore and tight after a week spent in unaccustomed exertion. Jackson's Rooms were open three times a week, and Vincent had met

140

with enthusiastic students on each one of those days. Tonight, when overtired limbs had convinced him to stretch out some of their stiffness, in consideration for his sleeping servants, he had slipped outside and come to the square. Not knowing how long it might take him to accomplish his task, he had filled the flask before leaving home—with water.

Rather than reveal the truth, however, some wayward imp, likely encouraged by the sight of the impertinent, dark-haired beauty standing so militantly before him, inspired his reply. He lifted the empty container and shook it meaningfully. "Matt? Are you going to advise me to give up the company of Madame Geneva? Would you have me avoid *all* the ladies of my acquaintance, not just the married ones? But how ungenerous of you! A man needs a softer influence, now and again. What, would you leave me nothing to enjoy?"

She seemed to attend his words seriously. "Aw," she grumbled, relaxing her pose and moving to take a place on the park bench just down from him. When she was seated, her heels dangled above the ground. She extended one foot and scraped a toe along the dirt at her feet. "I s'pose yer're thinkin' how I'm the sort to forever carp over what's good fer yer and what ain't. But *yer* was the one as said we might be friends. An' who can be comfortable-like when yer're a-tipplin' away? Sure, a spot of wine or a bumper of ale is one thing. But gin? Gin is a *mean* bit." She screwed up her face into a hideous expression of distaste.

The earl felt a shade guilty. He knew he shouldn't lead Matt on so, for it was scarcely a month, no, nor even a week ago, since her concerns might have had merit. But he shrugged off the feeling, remembering that he wasn't the only one engaged in deception this night.

To be sure, when the cramp in his leg had sent him to the ground and he had heard Matt's warm contralto—well! And then, when she had stood so anxiously before him, he could scarcely fail to note the softly rounded curve of her thigh before it disappeared beneath her overlying coat and thickly quilted vest. The sight was so intriguing, so altogether enticing, that had it not been for the gathering pain in his leg, he might have reached out and pulled her closer to him . . . run his hand along those sweet curves to touch . . .

Vincent allowed the imp on his shoulder to tempt him further. Deliberately, he slurred his words. "So you don't shink—think—a man should imbibe as he wills, eh, Matt? Well, I'll give it thum sought; ah, some thought."

With devilish intention, he leaned back and stretched out his arms to the sides. The length of his reach permitted him to clap a hand on Matt's shoulder. As if unaware of it, he allowed his hand to remain at rest a bare inch from her neck. He felt wickedly pleased with the result. Beneath his fingers Matt stiffened, even while she turned toward him with an expression of shocked inquiry.

Giving her a smile as benign as any his friend Mr. Evant might have made whilst under the influence of Bacchus, Vincent adjusted his hand to follow her movements. He gave her shoulder a light squeeze, and delighted in the feel of the gathering tremors under his hand. Lazily, he asked, "So, what about you, brat? What are you doing out this way? I'm in my own neighborhood, after all, but unless you've recently changed addresses, you're a long way from home, aren't you?"

Mattie struggled over her answer. His lordship, wearing little more than skin-tight breeches and a thin shirt of white lawn, displayed proportions of such manliness as must appeal to any feminine eye. In all certainty, the renewed wonder of his midnight dark orbs, focused upon her own, sent frissons of delight coursing through her. Add that to the feel of Lord Staffield's large, yet beautifully shaped hand, even now lingering lightly upon her shoulder, and the combined sensations were unbearable. Her only recourse was escape.

Using his question for her excuse, she bounced off the bench and withdrew the little sack the poodle man had given her. She shook the coins into her palm and concentrated on what they meant. "I've been gettin' myself a bit of good fortune is what. Just look you here, milord! A handful of golden boys came my way this night."

His lordship studied the amount. "But Matt, how . . ."

"I put myself in the way of doing a fellow a service, is all. And this here's what I gained for my effort." She jiggled the coins in her hand before counting them back into their sack.

Observing the care with which she tucked her treasure into her pocket, Vincent couldn't resist teasing, "Well now. Such riches are surely beyond what any *one* person can enjoy. Have you decided how much is to be my share, Matt?"

She seemed to take no offense, for her eyes began to twinkle. "Aw, yer really are bosky, ain't yer? 'Cause if'n yer was sober, yer wouldn't be 'spectin' me to go snacks and share my loot. But I'm no cock-robin cully, so yer're fairly out with that idea. I'll have yer to know that I earned this money. Though the amount, I'll admit, is more'n I ever expected."

Her easy slide into thieves' cant—*go snacks . . . loot . . . cully*—caused the earl to forget about his hurt at being thought a drunkard. Instead, he remembered Mr. Townshend of Bow Street and the charge laid upon him by that gentleman. The Runner had asked him to keep watch for any odd malingerers in the neighborhood—for the burglaries had each one occurred at suspiciously convenient times, times when the owners were from home. Matt's being here, and at such a late hour, was very much out of the ordinary.

Cautiously, he asked, "But what kind of service brings such a large reward, Matt? Explain, please."

She remained unaware of his apprehensions. "Oh, it wasn't anythin' much, really. I just happened across somethin' that someone was lookin' for. I'm always on the lookout for ways to make myself useful, yer might knows, an' if a bit o' the blunt comes into m' hand as a result, 'tis all well and good, I says."

"So, this is something which you do often?" Vincent persisted. "You have come here, and at such late hours, before?"

"Well, o' course I have!" She looked surprised by the question. "I've been here, let me see now . . ." She paused in thought. "Four. Yes, four times besides tonight. Yer sees, I've a friend who stands to be in some trouble if'n I don't lend him a hand."

The earl's feelings of disquiet grew, expanding at speed. Could the chit actually have some connection with thieves? Vincent didn't want to believe it. But he couldn't imagine what other purpose Matt might have for working under the cover of darkness. Anxiously, he sought to clarify matters.

"So you venture out at night, come to Mayfair on a regular basis, as a favor for a friend? But Matt, what exactly is it that you do here, and what friend are you speaking of?"

But she, in turn, became cautious. No one must know if the old night watchman required support in doing his job, particularly not one of the area residents who were responsible for Charlie's salary. She tried to sound nonchalant. "Well, I can't say as I *have* to be here, and certainly not every night. I takes a turn only one evening, now and then. As for my friend, he's just someone with business here, someone who wants a little assistance from time to time."

She was intentionally avoiding any mention of specifics. Vincent was sure of it. He turned her words over in his mind, weighing the possibilities. She had said she had been here on four occasions before tonight, and so far, there had been four burglaries in the area. Then, with a sinking sensation, the earl recollected having seen Matt exiting Lauriere's last week. Lauriere's!

As anyone might know, it was common practice for jewelers to deal in pawn and to purchase outright when they could. And many items presented for sale were of dubious provenance, either because of the seller's discretion, or for less valid reasons. Ascertaining whether an item was stolen or not depended mainly on the perspicacity of the jeweler involved. Thus, and any reputation for honesty notwithstanding, Mr. Lauriere could still be fooled into accepting stolen goods.

Vincent's muscles began to tighten again, this time in fear. He said, somewhat hoarsely, "You—you indicated earlier that you needed money, Matt. But I understood you already had an employment. Is the remuneration from that work so insufficient to your needs?"

She returned to her seat on the bench before answering. Without using the slatted back for its intended purpose, she ignored it to sit facing him. Her own back straight, although unsupported, she positioned one foot atop the bench seat between them and confided, "More than sufficient, in the ordinary way, but I have a special need for every penny just now. You should know how it is with me, though. I won't take money I haven't earned. *Not* that I don't stand ready to put myself in the way of earnin' it, howsomever!"

She grinned, and Vincent felt strangely reassured. Still, he couldn't help wondering just how far Matt might go in an effort to "earn" her money.

He repositioned himself so he could face her. Likewise, he drew his inside leg onto the seat, and absently massaged his sore calf. Hating and yet fearing the necessity, he spoke as if following a stray thought. " 'Pon my word, Matt, it just occurred to me. I can't remember if I fastened the door when I started out tonight. Do you suppose any will discover it?"

"Ye gods!" she exclaimed, sounding greatly concerned. "Bad enough a rum dubber can pick a lock in a pig's whisper, but to just hie yerself off an' leave yer door on the latch? That's naught but askin' for trouble! We had best go and check!"

She made as if to rise, but he hastily stayed her. "No, no need." He patted the little pocket at his waistband. "The key is right here, I just realize, and I now recall using it when I left the house."

He watched her closely. He didn't *think* her response was incriminating, for surely, Matt's familiarity with thieves' jargon needn't be of any significance when one considered her equal ease with upper-class accents. But he had to learn more. He had to know whether she had any connection to what the little man from Bow Street had referred to as *prigging coves*.

146

Vincent realized something else. Even if Matt was involved, even if she had been assisting thieves, he was as sure as he ever had been of anything that she had acted in innocence. Her straight little back and sparkling bright spirit—that spirit which was Matt—could never participate in anything underhanded. Not knowingly.

He regarded her look of wide-eyed innocence and vowed to do everything in his power to preserve it.

First, though, he had to learn the extent of her involvement. To this purpose, he said, "I take it, then, that you are aware of the malefactors that lately have been plaguing us in Mayfair. I don't suppose you would have any ideas about it, would you? Anything you'd care to mention?"

He couldn't bring himself to probe further than that. He observed Matt's guileless eyes and was too embarrassed to press her. No, he felt sure Matt wasn't involved and waited only for her words to prove it.

Instead, her answer sent Vincent's confidence spiraling downward, where it fragmented into sharp shards of chaos.

"Well, 'o course I do!" Her voice lifted in eagerness. "I knows all about it! And did you know that Lady Rothshaw had her whole collection of jewels stolen, even her set of amethysts—tiara, neckpiece, and the matching bracelet? All of her jewelry was taken, down to the most paltry item! I also knows that the houses robbed, every last one of them, kept *their* doors locked," she added pointedly. She then mused, "It is shameful how some folks will prey upon their fellows, though, don't yer thinks?"

Vincent responded almost sternly. "Honesty is indeed a thing of great worth, Matt. It is my opinion that in any

147

kind of commerce—whether in business matters or in more personal relationships—trust is needful if people are to deal well together."

She bobbed her head at this. "Yer're in the right of it there, Lord Staffield. Unfortunately, 'tis *dis*honest efforts which too often take the reward."

The earl couldn't know it, but she spoke while considering how old Charlie must feel for having lost the trust of his employers. And how awful it would be if someone made off with her savings, so carefully tucked away beneath her mattress! She sighed and her voice deepened slightly. "Do you know, I'm minded of that couple at the theatre—the ones who tricked me out of my ticket—remember? But they couldn't have enjoyed themselves much, I'm thinkin', for I noticed as how they left before the second half of the play. An' even if I shouldn't admit to it, I'm *glad*. While I, on the other hand, had a perfectly splendid time."

Despite his seesawing emotions, Vincent felt the tension drain out of him. "Ah, but then," he said gently, "just supposing that pair of cheats had wanted to stay and instead were, um, convinced that a certain influential patron took exception to their remaining?" Then, in more imposing tones, "The cause of justice must ever be served."

Quick to understand, Matt cried out, "Well, of all things wonderful! You actually did that?" She searched his face for the answer.

The earl said consciously, "I did."

She gave him an admiring grin which went a long way toward renewing his belief in her innocence. However, when she begged to excuse herself from his company, then dashed off to the north instead of the south toward her home, Vincent experienced the strangest sensation.

He sensed danger afoot.

Chapter Ten

Early the next day, Lord Staffield commenced a series of visits. He went first to Bow Street to discover whether there were any reports of new thefts in his neighborhood. To his indescribable relief, he learned that there had been none. He then made a request. Much fussing and grumbling resulted, but a mention of Mr. Townshend's name soon put a stop to that.

It took some time before the clerk could complete the desired transcription, but the earl remained patient. He left with a list of the items stolen during the recent burglaries in his neighborhood. With that in hand, he went directly to see Mr. Lauriere.

He didn't know whether to be relieved or sorry when nothing came of this next call. The jeweler had items for sale of most every description, but nothing which fit Vincent's list. Mr. Lauriere did comment, however, that a young boy had been in, and not so very many days before, also looking for a parure of amethysts such as his lordship had specified. Close questioning, however, revealed that the boy had merely wanted to *find* such jewels, not sell them.

From there, the earl continued on to make a visit to

a certain French dressmaker's establishment in Southwark. Once arrived, he learned little, confirmed much, then encountered another puzzler.

On the pretext of wanting a gown as a gift for his cousin, Vincent studied samples of Mme. Leteuil's work. He satisfied himself that the dressmaker's skills were adequate to have devised Matt's costume. He found this unsurprising. Also, Madame's reluctance to respond to his carefully put questions regarding the shop's errand "boy" made it plain she supported Matt's deception. This, too, was as he expected. But when one of the pretty grisettes volunteered that Matt resided with an old aunt, then mentioned the Serinier surname, Mme. Leteuil's reaction did surprise him.

The modiste dismissed the young seamstress and launched into such a series of circumlocutions as nearly made Vincent's head swim. The only thing of importance he could abstract from her words was the fact that the Serinier name was conspicuous for its absence. It made his lordship suspicious. Matt had given out the name readily enough at their first meeting; what made Madame react so?

Vincent pretended to notice nothing unusual, however. Selecting a length of Selisie linen, he made out a cheque on his bank and arranged for an appointment to bring his cousin to the shop for trim selection and fittings. He then quickly took his leave. He wanted to be gone before Matt should return.

He went only as far as around the corner to the King's Head. He made himself comfortable at a table near a window, one that afforded him a view of any who might enter Mme. Leteuil's shop. It being close to the end of the day, he ordered coffee, thinking it unlikely that he would have to wait long.

151

His surmise proved correct. Within the half-hour, he saw Matt come breezing into the dressmaker's. A little while later, a young girl, wearing a billowy, blue-and-white-striped pinafore, came trotting back outside.

Vincent had no difficulty identifying the ink-black curls and those energetic movements. He dropped a few coins on the tabletop and sped off after her.

Matt moved so swiftly that, despite his longer stride, the earl lost sight of her when she turned east and cut across Gravel Lane. Luckily, he again caught a glimpse of telltale stripes just as she entered Williams Court. He saw Matt skip up the front steps at one building and go inside. Stepping within the same edifice moments later, Vincent heard the sound of a door closing overhead.

He hesitated at the bottom of the stairwell, then slowly made his way on up to the next floor. Supposing he did figure out which apartment was Matt's, what came next? he wondered. If she discovered she had been followed, she must realize that her disguise had been pierced and would hardly thank him for that! Instead, it was everything likely that she would become leary, and just when he might need her trust in order to help her. He consoled himself with a reminder that, at least last night, there hadn't been another burglary.

Still, the little rascal had done *something* remarkable to have obtained those coins she had showed him. And whatever it was, he wanted her out of it. So, beginning with the newest mystery, the mystery surrounding her surname, he must discover what it was that young Matt was about.

While he stood in the corridor and considered how best to proceed, a woman in a plain cotton apron stepped out into the hallway. She acknowledged his greeting and, with a question in her eyes, advised him that she was the landlady of the building. She asked if he would be so good as to state his business.

His earlier experience with Mme. Leteuil now acted as a warning. He improvised, "Yes, certainly, ma'am. I am searching for an émigré family named Cherinier. Someone told me that they lived near here, but I don't have the exact address. Can you direct me?" He gave the landlady a purposely disarming smile.

Her features relaxed and she smiled back, disclosing a missing eyetooth. "Cherinier? No, I'm sorry. You must not have the right building. I have no tenants by that name. Oh! But I do have a Madame *Serinier* and her niece living on the top floor. Could they be who you mean?" She gave him a hopeful look.

Vincent perceived that, unlike the dressmaker, the landlady had nothing to hide. "No," he responded, allowing a note of regret to color his voice. "I'm afraid it cannot be the family I seek, unless I have the name wrong. But stay, what can you tell me about these Seriniers?"

Apparently delighted to retain the attentions of such a handsome gentleman, the landlady opened her budget. "Oh, a lovely old lady and her great-niece—they've been with me for several years now. Of course, I don't usually hold with having foreigners in my house, but those two have never given me a moment's trouble. Even if they are of the nobility."

Vincent could almost feel his ears rise. "But what say you, ma'am? They are aristocrats?"

The landlady looked pleased at having impressed him. "Well, I've drawn my own conclusions, of course, for they neither one will discuss the matter. But what else should I suppose after seeing Madame's credentials? I might never have suspected a thing either, ex-

153

cept that when they first came here, I insisted on having their references. A widow like myself can't be too careful when letting out her rooms, you understand." She patted the faded curls peeping from beneath her matron's cap and tossed him another gap-toothed smile. This one was distinctly coquettish.

"Er, of course, ma'am." Vincent smiled back. He felt uneasy about using his charm in such a calculated manner; nonetheless, he continued as he had begun. "But are you so sure about them? It seems to me that nearly everyone who comes from France these days claims exalted connections."

At this, the earl was made to realize that he need not further distress himself about the effects of his charm. The landlady no longer looked in the least friendly. "That's as may be," she reproved him, her smile gone on the instant. "But as I've already told you, my tenants aren't the sort who puff themselves and put on airs. Madame supplied me with her letter of introduction only at my request. That letter referred to Madame Agathe and Mademoiselle Madeleine *de* Serinier. And it was signed by Henry Dundas, the Viscount Melville himself!" When he still looked skeptical, she huffed, "As for that, you may be sure I checked with the Ministry. They confirmed that the document was genuine, also that the de Serinier were of the highest standing in France, before the turn of affairs there put them to flight."

Vincent so forgot himself as to exclaim, "By God, *what* a bender!"

The landlady gaped openly at him, then began to look even more incensed.

Comprehending his blunder, Vincent exerted himself to soothe the woman's wounded sensibilities. He apologized, saying he hadn't meant to cast aspersions on either her or her tenants, explaining that it was the mention of Melville which had sent him flying into the boughs. He submitted that he was himself a staunch Whig, rather than of Henry Dundas's party.

And that really is *a bouncer,* he thought in disgust. For he had no more interest in Lord Melville, or anyone else in Pitt's old ministry, than he did in Australia! He had merely given out the first excuse he could think of in his shock at learning that Matt was not just any female but, mayhaps, a young lady of standing.

A lady? Matt? *His* Matt?

The earl left Williams Court in short order, having first stumbled his way through yet another apology. He made his way home in a daze, concentrating upon what he had learned. In his judgment it was bad enough for Matt to scamper through the streets wearing knee breeches and hose, but if she should prove to be of good family . . . It made things worse, much worse.

Questions swarmed around in Vincent's mind like so many agitated bees. Why would Matt act and dress the part of a lad, then change into that ridiculous girlchild's garb before returning to Williams Court? How much, if anything, did her great-aunt—a woman "of the highest standing," whatever *that* meant—know about Matt's midnight forays into Mayfair? And Matt's employer, Mme. Leteuil, why had she treated him to such an absurd spate of tergiversations at the mere mention of the Serinier name? And what, for God's sake, had any of this to do with housebreakers?

He had to learn more. Soon. For unless he was badly mistaken, his sprightly young friend was in a fair way to being run off her legs.

By the next day, Lord Staffield had decided upon another route for obtaining the needed facts.

Waiting only till the hour struck ten, he dispatched a footman with a message to his cousin's home in Tenterden Street, just off Hanover Square. The following hour saw the earl enter her ladyship's morning room, where the baroness, Lady Ellengood, sat at a cylinder-style writing desk. Bills and receipts and a many-columned book for household accounting lay scattered, higgledy-piggledy, across the tabletop.

"Vincent, dear coz!" she cried, rising to greet him. Her movement caused a small avalanche of paper to tumble to the floor. "My goodness, you're very punctual. And"—she squeezed out as she endured his powerful embrace—"you are very vigorous, too!"

Lady Ellengood ignored the mess and pushed him away to have a better look at him. He stood quiet while she made a survey of his coat, darkest blue and lovingly formed by Mr. Meyer's clever hands; his cravat, yellow silk and softly knotted, à la Belcher; and a pair of glossy black boots, worn above fine doeskin pantaloons of some neutral color.

She rendered up her verdict. "Oh, vigorous, indeed. You look better than I've seen you this age!"

His lordship merely cocked his head to one side and commenced his own inspection. "Thank you, Sal, I think. And I suppose I should say the same for you, even though you do begin to look as if you'd swallowed a whale. But I thought it was months yet before you added a third to your nursery."

Her ladyship grinned proudly and patted her growing middle. "Well, Jeremy *does* have twins running in his family. And the doctor says, since I'm only now entering my fifth month, there is a possibility of presenting my lord with a pair in due time."

The earl grinned back at her. "The deuce, you say! My best wishes to you and Jeremy both, then. And if you don't mind, I will also remember Nurse with a special gift come Christmas. Managing your growing brood is apt to keep her busier than ever. Hmmm. Might be easier for everyone if you merely presented your husband with a whale."

The cousins had been close throughout the years of their childhood, and while they saw rather less of each other in these latter years, they still stood on terms of such intimacy that neither felt any reservation about making personal remarks. They were of an age and shared the same dark-blond good looks, if Sally Ellengood's eyes were not so dark a blue as her cousin's. Neither was she so tall nor so heavily boned, and despite Lord Staffield's teasing remarks on the subject, the rounded softness of pregnancy well became her.

After the two young sons of the house had been called for, admired, and duly sent back to the nursery, Vincent brought up the purpose of his visit. "Sal," he said, choosing his words with care, "do you recall ever having heard of a family named Serinier or, possibly, de Serinier? Since George's grandmother was French, I thought perhaps you would know the name."

Her ladyship did, to be sure! In next to no time, Vincent learned that the name of Serinier was particular to only one family in France, and that before the profound political upheavals marking the last few years, the de Seriniers had stood within the first ranks of the thirty-eight peerages comprising the French aristocracy. The earl was further informed that the Ellengood family might claim a connection of sorts, since Jeremy's great-grandmother's sister's third daughter—Vincent thought he had that right—had, in '62, married someone on the distaff side of the de Serinier house. He also learned how Sally had once actually met Madame *la Marquise,* Agathe de Serinier.

Highest standing, indeed.

"Oh, it was years ago," she expanded, noting the intensity of his interest. "It was just after Jeremy and I were married and were making the rounds of his grandmother's people in France on our honeymoon. I remember her especially because she came to my defense—and before even we'd been formally introduced—when someone derided my choice of dinner dress. I had worn a calicoed muslin, you see, thinking it unexceptionable for a little family gathering. But when I came down to dinner, I discovered that, instead of the small group I had expected, half the nobility of France was in attendance! Had I known beforehand of their coming, I would have chosen a different gown, but I—"

"Sal," Vincent interrupted her at last. "I have no interest in knowing who wore what nor in how many people came to some long-ago dinner party. Get back to the subject. Please!"

Her ladyship stopped and fussed with a small, silk-covered pillow, rearranging it at her back. She drawled in artificial tones, "My, my, my, Vincent. A bit touchy today, aren't we? Perhaps the change I remarked in you is not *all* to the good; ordinarily, you are the soul of patience. But no," she interjected at a new thought. "That's not quite right, is it? It hasn't been patience at all! Not really." She frowned, then withdrew the pillow she had just positioned and brought it forward. She began folding it into halves. "Rather, I believe it's been indifference which has characterized your aspect of late.

158

World-weary indifference—brought on, no doubt, by the sort of diddle-daddle, stick-at-nothing life you've been leading." Her expression grim, she took the doubled pillow and attempted to stuff it behind her.

Vincent winced and passed her a matching pillow from his own chair. When she couldn't seem to get it situated with the other, he stood and came over to help. "Better, Sal?" He struggled to adjust the two pillows. "Give you my word," he said in some concern, "I don't see how anyone can manage with such a burden as you carry. We men have it easy, I think." After he had helped her to get herself more comfortably established, he returned to his seat. "In any event, Sal, I regret having been such a rudesby and interrupting you the way I did. But never mind about exposing my character. I have a reason for wanting to know what you can tell me about the de Seriniers. It is important."

Sally Ellengood settled herself deeper into the cushions. "This is all somehow of a piece, isn't it," she observed shrewdly. "I mean, here you are, and for the first time in months, looking awake and aware and—oh, I don't know—there's a new spring in your step. And you must realize that I have been terribly anxious about for you, racketing around like you've been doing. You were for all the world looking set to become another one of those beastly Care-for-Nobodies, with no more feeling than an old shoe! And then that dreadful business with Lord Hedgewick. Oh, Vincent, I was so afraid when I heard!"

"We needn't go into that. Surely."

"Oh, but we shall go into it! Because if my condition hadn't prevented me from getting out more and learning of it sooner, I would have been on your doorstep long since, demanding that you should keep away from

Maryanne Hedgewick! She always was a vain, silly chit. While as for you, coz, you might have known better than to involve yourself there. What on earth were you thinking of? On second thought"—she gave a naughty chuckle—"don't answer that."

He shifted in his seat, accepting that his discomfort had little to do with his missing pillow. Matt's pronouncement about his friends had been right on the mark, it seemed. His real friends, friends like Sally Ellengood, had no compunction about reading him the riot act when they thought he needed a scold.

"Oh, very well," he said, resigned to the criticism. "But someone has already set me straight regarding my recent activities, rest assured. And there is no danger of my repeating mistakes. I can still recognize good advice when I hear it."

"Then, some friend of yours spoke out?" The baroness sounded relieved.

"Yes, a friend," he answered quietly, realizing a simple but important truth. And it wasn't Mr. Townshend of Bow Street whom he had in mind!

Vincent was also, albeit slowly, adjusting himself to the idea that Matt, no, *Madeleine,* was born of a noble house. It explained so much. Her delicate mannerisms, her sometimes use of correct speech, her familiarity with the works of Shakespeare—she had even recognized Radcliffe as being the library at Oxford! And *his* new knowledge made it crucial for him to act toward her protection. It was his duty as a gentleman, most certainly as a friend, to expend every effort to ameliorate the little elf's situation as soon as possible. More than that, Vincent realized, if she were ever to take her rightful place in Society, he

TAKE ADVANTAGE OF THIS SPECIAL OFFER, AVAILABLE *ONLY* TO ZEBRA REGENCY ROMANCE READERS.

You are a reader who enjoys the very special kind of love story that can only be found in Zebra Regency Romances. You adore the fashionable English settings, the sparkling wit, the captivating intrigue, and the heart-stirring romance that are the hallmarks of each Zebra Regency Romance novel.

Now, you can have these delightful novels delivered right to your door each month and never have to worry about missing a new book. Zebra has made arrangements through its Home Subscription Service for you to preview the three latest Zebra Regency Romances as soon as they are published.

3 **FREE** REGENCIES TO GET STARTED!

To get your subscription started, we will send your first 3 books ABSOLUTELY FREE, as our introductory gift to you. NO OBLIGATION. We're sure that you will enjoy these books so much that you will want to read more of the very best romantic fiction published today.

SUBSCRIBERS SAVE EACH MONTH

Zebra Regency Home Subscribers will save money each month as they enjoy their latest Regencies. As a subscriber you will receive the 3 newest titles to preview FREE for ten days. Each shipment will be at least a $11.97 value (publisher's price). But home subscribers will be billed only $9.90 for all three books. You'll save over $2.00 each month. Of course, if you're not satisfied with any book, just return it for full credit.

FREE HOME DELIVERY

Zebra Home Subscribers get free home delivery. There are never any postage, shipping or handling charges. No hidden charges. What's more, there is no minimum number to buy and you can cancel your subscription at any time. No obligation and no questions asked.

must manage the thing without stirring up too many questions.

From his cousin or anyone else.

Finding his way to a solution even as he spoke, he said, "So, and with your permission, Sal, I'll get back to the original topic, my reason for coming today." He sat forward in his chair. "You see, I've learned that there is a Madame Serinier who resides here in London with her great-niece. For my own reasons, I'd like to help them. And if they really are *de* Serinier, and it seems likely that they are, then I could use some assistance. That is, if you would be so good?"

Sally Ellengood looked astounded. She sputtered, "But—but Vincent! Do you mean to sit there and tell me that Agathe de Serinier is alive? She and a great-niece actually survived the Terror and made it safely away from France? Oh, I cannot believe it!"

"Yes. Or at least, I think so. And I understand that they've had the same lodgings in Southwark for some years now."

"Southwark?" Her ladyship goggled anew. "But that's *no* place for them. Why, the Agathe de Serinier I recall was one of the most elegant, most naturally dignified women I think I've ever had the privilege to meet! Oh, she was never one to stand upon ceremony, just the opposite. But Southwark?" She set down her coffee cup with a snap. "Give over, Coz. Do. Just what goes forward here?"

He recollected how Matt—*would he ever get used to thinking of her as Madeleine?*—had said she needed money. Uneasily, he answered, "I cannot say for certain why they have chosen their present address, but I suspect it is the result of some shortage in funds. However," he inserted more strongly, "I believe I may have

161

figured a way of resolving their difficulties. With luck, all of their difficulties."

In a few brief sentences, he outlined a plan.

Lord Staffield returned to Williams Court later that same afternoon. With his cousin's description to aid him, he ascertained that the elderly woman in the upper-floor apartment was, indeed, the Marquise de Serinier. And from the top of her old-style lace cap to the tip of each beautifully tapered finger, Vincent agreed with his cousin's assessment.

Madame *la Marquise* was a woman of great distinction.

Vincent introduced himself and extended his apologies for coming to her unannounced. He then furnished Madame with a fine bit of bobbery about how this omission was due to his excitement at having at last located her. He said that he was most anxious to discharge an old debt to the de Serinier, one he hoped she would acknowledge on her family's behalf.

"It stems from an arrangement made between certain persons, regrettably no longer with us," he glibly explained. He added a suggestion that, since the affair was of a private nature, he would appreciate Madame's forbearance in not asking such questions as, in honor, he must refuse to answer.

The old lady allowed him to come inside. She requested him to select a chair from those at a scarred old deal table and bring it nearer to hers by the window. When he had done so, he handed Madame a note on his bank, "Entrusted to me on the de Serinier account," as he put it.

Madame Serinier, for so she insisted upon being

called, regarded the amount inscribed. All tranquility, she folded the paper and laid it on the little worktable at her elbow. She returned him her full attention.

"It shall be as you wish," she said, her voice pleasantly euphonic. "And with due respect for the departed, I will ask of you no questions, nor will I attempt to discuss the matter any further." Having lived through uncertain times, Madame seemed to recognize the dangers attending too much curiosity.

Relieved to have this portion of his mission thus successfully accomplished, Vincent moved on to the next step of his plan. He presented Madame Serinier with yet another note, this one a letter of welcome from his cousin.

In her note, Lady Ellengood expressed herself eager to renew old acquaintance. She warmly reminded Madame that they shared a family connection, one which she and her lord husband were most anxious to recognize. She gave it as her fondest wish that Madame *la Marquise* and her great-niece should consent to take up immediate residence with them at Tenterden Street and included her hopes that she would be further allowed the privilege of introducing them into the London *ton*. In the most tactful terms possible, Sally also slyly hinted that, for an unmarried girl in Mlle. Madeleine's position, the move offered an opportunity of unmistakable merit.

Without being aware of this last notation in his cousin's letter, Lord Staffield, too, assumed that Madame Serinier must be glad to avail herself of the means for returning to Polite Society. He had wondered about whether to wait for the old lady's consent to Sally's invitation before presenting Madame with his cheque, but his first concern was to satisfy whatever compelling need for money was, even now, keeping "Matt" out on the streets.

As for her great-aunt, whether in funds or no, why should anyone hesitate over such a golden chance for further improving her circumstances? The earl believed the old lady's acceptance was a foregone conclusion. So when Madame Serinier began shaking her head "no," Vincent felt something akin to fear.

Had he misjudged, after all? By giving the old lady the money at the start, however nice his reasons for doing so, he *had* eliminated a powerful argument for her removal to his cousin's home.

Glancing around the tiny apartment, searching for any means by which to bolster his case, Vincent was suddenly struck by an irregularity. Along with the few pieces of furniture—all of a quality much in keeping with what was to be expected of rented rooms—lay a rich Brussels carpet. He was so astonished with this oddity that he blurted out, "But that is a very fine carpet, Madame! Surely you could not have managed to carry so large an item with you all the way from France?"

Madame Serinier showed no signs of discomposure at his indelicately phrased mention. She seemed content to answer. "Yes, isn't it lovely? It was a gift from my little Madeleine. She says she purchased it because she knows the color is my favorite, but as you note, it must have commanded a very large price, indeed." Smiling softly, she considered, "But then, my Madeleine is a very resourceful young lady, is she not?"

Vincent wasn't about to comment on *that* statement. With a dread feeling, he ventured, "Then, the carpet is a new addition?"

"Just this week," the old lady confirmed.

The earl submitted to the obvious conclusion. He understood why Mattie had claimed to need "every penny" and where those pennies had gone; certainly, he could not help having noticed Madame Serinier's infirmity. But Vincent also had to wonder what more the little madcap might think needful. He had to convince the old lady to remove to his cousin's at once!

In tones of some urgency, he insisted, "Madame, you may think the sum now at your disposal is ample for any need, but I assure you, it cannot compare. The amount is inadequate to provide the kind of luxury which will be available to you at the Ellengoods'." Seeing no sign of capitulation, he entered yet another inducement. "And as my cousin must have assured you in her letter, she and the baron are in all ways regretful for not having realized your situation sooner. You and Mlle. Serinier are family!"

But it seemed that nothing he could say made any impression. For all she'd abandoned her title, Madame Serinier, apparently, had a full complement of pride. She would only reply, "But I do not wish to go to the Ellengoods'."

The earl was, by this time, fighting desperation. Such single-minded resistance to his pleas had him very near to the end of his tether.

He stood to his height and demanded, "Madame, please, you must listen to me! This is not a mere matter of your wishes, nor my wishes, nor even Lord and Lady Ellengood's wishes. It is the younger generation which concerns me. It is wrong for you to persist with this— this *withholding* of yourself from your family. It's wrong and abominably shortsighted!"

Agathe Serinier elevated her well-defined chin to an imperious level. Although seated, she conveyed the impression of staring down her nose at his six feet of masculine height. And yet, at the very same time, she somehow retained her pleasant mien. "What is that you say? Young sir," she corrected in lilting French accents, "believe me when I tell you that you know nothing of it. My past refusal to involve myself with my relatives—my *distant* relatives, I remind you—was a decision made because I regard my claims as insufficient to beg anyone's support. My position today is the same as before. I choose to be no one's encumbrance."

Truly distrait by this time, Vincent charged, "So, you think that's the way of it, then? Oh, I beg to differ with you, Madame! For in case *you* don't know it, my cousin Sally already has two young sons, two boys who know nothing of their French heritage. And if it interests you to learn of it, a few months hence, there will be an addition to her nursery. And have you forgotten that you have a great-niece who is excluded from any real knowledge of her English relatives—unjustly prevented from accepting her rightful place in the world? Shortsighted? Oh, yes. I'll stand by my words if you won't reconsider. It is you who deprives these young people of *your* support!"

He wanted to speak further. Very much. He wanted to tax her with her responsibility to a young lady who gadded about town in boy's dress—one whom he was determined to see safe under Sally's roof. But he said nothing more. He wasn't sure how Madame might react, wasn't even sure how much she knew about "Matt's" activities. And he didn't want to jeopardize his position by bringing up a subject which might embarrass the old lady past forgiveness.

His circumspection was rewarded. Agathe Serinier sat silent for a goodly space of time, with only a touch of

166

abstraction about her dark eyes to show that she was in any degree overset. With an admirable show of calm, she finally rendered her decision.

"Very well," she said as mellifluously as ever. "I shall write at once to make arrangements with the baron and his wife. If they truly have a place for me as a member of their family, Madeleine and I will go to them as soon as they are ready to receive us."

Vincent made no attempt to disguise his exultation. "Oh, but that is very *fine*, Madame! Be sure, you will not regret it."

While Madame Serinier set about penning her reply to Lady Ellengood, she looked up at him without any sign of hauteur. In fact, it was with some hesitation that she said, "My very dear Lord Staffield, I do hope you realize that I am grateful to you, though I should know by now that it is never too late to learn better how to go on. Ah, but even you, good sir, cannot really understand how important this change in our fortunes will be to us. I shall be able to invest in Mme. Leteuil's business, just as I've long wanted. And no more hours of stitchery, no more pinafores for my dear little Madeleine. Oh, won't she be surprised!"

"Indeed," his lordship answered. "I should rather think she will be at that."

Kashmir blue eyes gleamed in expectation.

Chapter Eleven

"Fiend seize it," Mattie mumbled, throwing her weight into her work.

"Madeleine?"

"Oh, sorry, Tante. But this thing *will* escape me at every turn."

For the second time that week, Mattie contended with the unwieldy yardage of an apple green Brussels carpet. Without Mr. Biggersley available to help her roll and tie, the work was proving amazingly arduous. Nonetheless, Mattie had an inkling that it was something more than her current labors which was making her to feel so hagged.

When Tante Agathe had three days ago imparted the news of Lady Ellengood's generous offer, then had mentioned £5,000 which had—and altogether inexplicably!—come their way as well, Mattie had felt soaring elation. No more damp rooms to bring her great-aunt discomfort and plenty of strong footmen to help the old dear up or down any staircase. Mattie flew into high alt.

That joyous feeling was quickly supplanted, however, when she had learned that the glad tidings had come by way of their soon-to-be hostess's cousin, the Earl of Staffield. "Dismay" was the polite term for what Mattie had next felt, but *"lurched"* was the word she had used.

For this heretofore unfamiliar locution, Tante Agathe had promptly requested an explanation. But Mattie had been too caught up in emotion to oblige.

Mattie could easily appreciate how the change in their prospects would affect Tante Agathe and Mme. Leteuil. Her *grand-tante* could, at long last, return to the society of cultured people, people who knew books and music and art. Mme. Leteuil would be able to relocate her shop in a fashionable area, one where her business was sure to thrive. But as for how she herself was affected? Well, that was more difficult to predict.

A good deal depended on Lord Staffield's reaction when he discovered her identity. When he saw her dressed as a female . . . ecod! Whatever must he think? Would he judge her a sad romp? A heedless baggage? A *rantipole?* Was that how it would be? Just the thought of it sent Mattie into agonies of apprehension.

There was also every likelihood that the earl would reveal what he knew about "Matt" to Tante Agathe. His lordship might well feel himself obliged to disclose how Mattie had been spending her days—and nights. Tante would be so mortified. All gods forfend such a thing! Neither must Mme. Leteuil's involvement be exposed; the modiste had only been trying to help. But was there any hope of averting disaster?

Then, another possibility occurred, a thoroughly dismal one. Lord Staffield might say nothing at all and merely look bored by the whole. He might, Mattie realized, simply shrug off her ruse as unimportant—might consider the hours which they had spent together as entirely insignificant. The notion caused Mattie to lose her grip on the Brussels.

Soon enough, however, she got back to the job at hand. But even as she tugged and pulled, fighting weighty lengths of Brussels carpet, her mind continued turning and twisting about. Finally, shoving her knee into thicknesses of densely woven yarn, she wrapped twine binding around the carpet's middle and made the final knot. "There now, just you stay put," she ordered.

Tante Agathe looked up from her place by the window where she was herself busy finishing up a last bit of work, an embroidered Salisbury pelerine for one of Mme. Leteuil's customers. "Ah, Madeleine," she said somewhat mistily as she tied off the last silk strand, "have you any idea of how proud I am of that carpet? From the instant I saw it, I loved its every thread. Such richness. And what better time for its arrival? We had so few nice things left to us. But now? Your gift makes an impressive addition to carry with us to Lady Ellengood's. So much time it must have cost you to save the money needed. So much effort! But soon, life for us will be very different, you'll see. We can put these last years behind us."

"I suppose so," Mattie rumbled, doubtful. For it seemed to her that, rather than having the past behind her, it was even more probable that previous deceptions were about to catch her up. And still further deceptions were needful in her future. Tomorrow was her turn at helping out Charlie Coomber.

With a tiny shrug, Mattie returned her attention to more immediate matters. She made a last look around the apartment. She felt a sense of accomplishment at seeing the newly bound carpet bisecting the tiny room and, along one wall, the collection of small boxes and crates, every item neatly sorted and packed. Slipping out of her old cotton pinafore, the same short length as the sturdy twilled-fabric dress she wore, she went to add it to the box containing her other clothes. It wouldn't do to arrive at the Ellengood's wearing a striped pinafore. 'Twas bad enough that there hadn't been time for Mme. Leteuil to provide her with a full-length gown.

Opening the packing box, rose-tinted silk attracted Mattie's eye. The sight inspired an idea. All of a sudden, she knew how to forestall his lordship from upending Tante—or from overlooking herself. Floss silk was the answer! In her beautiful gown she would dazzle him, enthrall him, make him so enchanted with her that he would forget about everything which had gone before. No man, not even the most jaded roué, could ignore such a gown! Mattie tossed her pinafore high into the air, letting it fall where it may.

But there was no time now. No time to change clothes. The Ellengood carriage was expected at any moment.

Mattie scooped up her pinafore and wadded it nohow. She realized that her idea had not been such a very good one after all, considering that it was not yet two of the clock. She would appear foolish if she donned silver-threaded silk so early in the day.

Much put about by this realization, she began stuffing striped cotton into the packing box. She spread the garment width-wise so as to fit it inside. Frustrated when it couldn't be accommodated so easily, she removed the pinafore and began folding it otherwise.

"Madeleine," her *grand-tante* admonished gently. "You're as restless as an eel. Calm yourself, little one. It won't be long before the Ellengood coach comes to collect us, I am sure, so put your things away and—"

She looked out the window to view the street below. "Ah. Here it is now. Are we ready?"

Mattie and her great-aunt were soon seated inside a very new and fashionable barouche. Two smartly gloved-and-powdered footmen rode in the dickey behind, and in what Mattie considered an especially good omen, no Lord Staffield appeared with their escort. There was still time to divert him before he spoke to Tante Agathe.

Lost in a rêverie wherein his lordship was struck dumb by her petite female attractions, Mattie was surprised when the carriage jolted to a halt. She had been so involved with her own thoughts, she had failed to take advantage of the novel view of London's streets as seen from a moving carriage. But here they were in Tenterden Street, stopping in front of a large three-storied house, trimmed in Purbeck stone.

One footman jumped out and began lowering the steps. The other stood by, waiting to assist the ladies from the carriage. Hoping she wouldn't look too out of place in her worn old shoes and childishly short skirts, Mattie climbed down and followed Tante through the Ellengoods' front doors.

The reception provided them upon their entrance was all that anyone could wish. Tall and fair of feature, the baroness glided up, clearly thrilled by the addition of two females to her household—"To even the balance, my dears, for I was quite outnumbered before!"—while Lord Ellengood shook hands and professed himself delighted to welcome them as "family I had feared long since lost." The two young sons of the house appeared equally pleased: Rhodney, the elder boy, and Jacob, the younger, greeted them with bouquets of flowers, picked that morning from the back gardens and by their own hands, as they proudly announced.

The daisies, poppies, and pinks may have looked slightly the worse for this handling, but no one seemed to notice.

"Ooo-oh. Smells splendid!" Mattie opined, accepting the bunch meant for her.

Indeed, the carnations included in her posy were the more fragrant for having been partially crushed by youthful fingers.

"And you must everyone call me 'Tante,' " her great-aunt decreed, happily accepting her flowers. "If we are to settle here for a time—"

"Oh, but we'll have none of that!" Lord Ellengood broke in at once to say. He was a big man, almost as big as his wife's cousin, and congeniality poured from his every feature. Not even Tante, who could be quite sensitive upon occasion, took offense when he continued, "Be very sure that, now that we've found you both, we will not allow you to disappear from us again!"

"Perhaps, then, yes," Tante Agathe replied graciously. "But what I meant to convey was what I had tried explaining to her ladyship in my letter—"

"It's 'Sally.' " This time, it was Lady Ellengood who interrupted. Neither did anything in her manner give cause for offense.

"Yes, thank you," Tante acknowledged. "But what I mean for everyone to understand is that I wish for no guest's status. I would prefer it if Madeleine and I—"

"That's 'Mattie,' " came a laughing contralto from their midst. "For 'tis only *ma tante* who refuses to see that such a large name for one so small as me is rather too much to bear."

The elderly lady for a moment looked set to dispute

this. However, seeing the twinkling eyes surrounding her and the depths of everyone's goodwill, she essayed a smile and conceded the point. Before she could finish her request, though, her hostess took over again.

"Yes, yes. I understand you perfectly, Tante Agathe." Sally Ellengood didn't falter at according Madame *la Marquise* the preferred title. "And I shall be most happy to have you participate in our household however you will, but we can work out those details later. First, I want to show you the rooms I have chosen for your stay and make certain that you have everything you need to make yourselves feel truly at home."

The two little boys grabbed for Mattie's hands straightaway, chattering excitedly to her as they led the way up the stairs. Or rather, Rhodney chattered, while little Jacob mostly giggled. The pair, aged five and three, seemed to take her in instant affection; although Mattie wasn't sure if it was because she looked so much of a young age, or whether it was simply because hers was a new face to them. Either way, she felt absurdly happy to be amongst the Ellengoods.

Her happiness was not unbounded, however. No one had mentioned Lord Staffield yet, leaving her to wonder what had become of him. Of course, it might be just as well not to know the hour of her doom. For when he did appear, if she couldn't present herself so as to prevent it, there was sure to be a regular blowup!

Others did not share her trepidations, however. Halfway up the stairs, Tante Agathe paused, causing her host, who was supporting her steps, to stop alongside her.

"But where is Lord Staffield, if you do not mind my asking? I had so hoped to see him here. For you must know that had it not been for him—had he not sought us out and, subsequently, been so persistent in his appeals—we might never have come to you today. No, nor any other day, for that matter." At the baron's stricken look, the old lady soothed, "The connection between our families *is* a remote one, you must admit, and I had feared to impose myself or my little Madeleine upon anyone. It was Lord Staffield who made me see your offer in a different light. He brought me to understand how my presence here might rightly be considered in the way of an asset. Such an estimable young man. So kind!"

Intrigued by this novel view of her cousin, Lady Ellengood, one step below Mattie and two ahead of her husband, turned round to answer sweetly, "Oh, yes. Vincent will join us for dinner tonight. And I've no doubt we all look forward to seeing him. I, for one, most assuredly."

Only Mattie heard it when Sally, upon resuming her climb, muttered, "Vincent? Estimable . . . *kind?* Pshaw."

"But why not? It isn't as if I have anything else to wear."

"I said no, Madeleine." Tante Agathe looked unusually stubborn.

"What then? Do you expect me to go down to dinner in the same clothes I wore when we arrived this afternoon—in a dress which is not a tenth part long enough to give me a decent appearance? Oh, but 'twould be an insult to our hostess if I came to her table as I am. I must wear the silk, Tante. I must!"

The old lady, seated on the edge of Mattie's mahogany-framed bed, motioned the maidservant provided by their hostess from the room. Before the girl left, Mattie took back the rose-colored gown which the maid had been holding in readiness.

"Madeleine," Tante said with some firmness, as soon as the servant was gone, "you should know without my telling you that it is inappropriate to wear such fine stuffs for a small family gathering. Have you forgotten our lessons on the subject so soon? Yes, I, too, am sorry we have nothing else for you to wear, but it is only for this once. Mme. Leteuil has promised to come early to-morrow to begin replacing our wardrobes."

Unconsciously, Mattie stroked the shimmering silk while she gave her great-aunt a searching look. Tante's dinner dress was scarcely better than her own much-worn twill, she had to acknowledge. The old dear still looked elegant, though, even clothed as she was in a slightly rusty-looking black taffeta, with its old-fashioned laces pulled tight to close the back, instead of the more modish buttons.

Mattie sighed and glanced over at the cheval glass. At least Tante didn't have an excess of black stocking exposed below her hem.

But what did it matter if Mme. Leteuil came tomorrow with every item needed? Who cared a fig for that? Mattie was far more interested in tonight's all-important first appearance before Lord Staffield. Nothing could compare to the fabulous floss silk, no other gown imaginable. And she had to convince Tante to let her wear it now, tonight, while her clothes press still stood empty!

She couldn't recount this aloud, of course. Instead, she said coaxingly, "Don't say I mayn't wear it tonight, Tante. Please. This is my first real sit-down dinner party and I want to look my best. Please?" Oh, she *so* wanted the earl to see her in exquisite pink-on-rose.

"But Madeleine, I tell you again, it is too grand for a

family occasion. It was quite unexceptionable for you to wear it to the theatre with your friends, and were more guests expected, it would be proper for you tonight. However," she said, speaking more slowly, "I fear I will have to agree with you on one point. Though your birthday gown is inappropriate for this evening's wear, so also is your present dress." This time, it was Tante Agathe who sighed. "No, little one, I am afraid you cannot go down, looking as you are. We shall just have to take our dinners up here."

Shaken to her shoestrings by this unexpected setback, Mattie cried, "Oh, but surely there is no need for you to miss the company at dinner, Tante! I don't mind eating alone. I never meant this to happen. Truly!"

Tante Agathe made a dismissive motion with her fingers. "Now, now, of course, you didn't, dear. But I won't leave you to a solitary tray, never think so. I will make our excuses to Lady Ellengood—ah, *Sally.*" Unlike this last-named person, Tante Agathe didn't find it so easy to address others in the same informal terms which she accepted quite readily for herself.

Mattie found none of this easy. Before the change in their fortunes, she had known and understood her responsibilities and had fulfilled each one as she deemed fit. But only look at the results of her efforts tonight! She had achieved nothing whatsoever of worth.

For one thing, she had come as close as ever in memory to arguing with her *grand-tante.* Shameful. She had also managed to condemn herself to dinner while confined to her room; at the same time, she had compelled Tante Agathe to give up her own evening in the society of those below. Reprehensible.

Mattie was more used to making good things happen. What, she had to wonder, had so suddenly caused her world to turn itself topsy-turvy? Could there be a basic wrongness in wanting to conceal events which would only hurt her great-aunt?

Mattie thought not.

Then, was there aught amiss in the means she had chosen, about her scheme to beguile his lordship? Certainly, something had brought on all these unlooked-for and undesirable repercussions. In the corner of her mind, Mattie saw the glimmer of an answer. *Alors! She saw the answer as plain as day!*

Feeling very much ashamed of herself, Mattie owned to the truth. She immediately went to return the silk gown to her clothes press. For the answer was, she realized as she bent to straighten out the flounces at the bottom of the gown, that even supposing four-feet-and-something really could entrance his lordship, it would be wrong to attempt to divert a man from his honest purpose by such means.

There was a word for that kind of substitution. It was not a very pretty word, either.

"Wrong coin," she mumbled beneath her breath.

"What's that you say, dear?" Tante asked from her place on the bed.

"Er, nothing, Tante. I was merely agreeing with what you said earlier about the appropriateness of, um—things."

Tante Agathe looked serene.

And Mattie was put to the trouble of rethinking how she could convince the earl not to give away her secret. By fair and virtuous means.

Fair and virtuous means.
Throughout the next day, the words hammered them-

178

selves continuously inside Mattie's head. She went about in a stupor, barely aware of the finished gowns Mme. Leteuil had brought with her. Spotted gauze failed to interest, book muslin left her unmoved. When she was asked her preference between this color or that for other gowns which the modiste proposed, Mattie's gaze drifted off into nothingness. Over and over, the modiste had to repeat her instructions for Mattie to lift an arm or turn a quarter before obtaining her compliance.

After half a day of this, Tante took to exchanging troubled looks with Marie Leteuil. Neither woman had ever seen the little miss so immobile—so lethargic!— and for such a space of time. Finally, Tante made some excuse for leaving the room, crooking her finger at the dressmaker to indicate that she should follow.

Lady Ellengood came upon them as they were closing the door to Mattie's bedchamber. "My dears?" she said questioningly.

Tante Agathe for a moment looked nonplussed. It was Mme. Leteuil who answered. "It is Mattie," she whispered, checking to see that the door was shut tight.

"My great-niece," Tante added unhelpfully.

"Then, she is ill?" Her ladyship made as if to reach for the knob so as see for herself.

The dressmaker stayed her with a quick wave of the hand. "*Non, non.* It is nothing like that; we were merely concerned because little Mattie is ordinarily bursting with energy. *Alerte.* But today she is quiet. *Oui.* Too quiet." With a flick of her thick black eyebrows, the modiste expressed her bafflement.

"Yes, she is very quiet—exceptionally so," Tante confirmed. "I cannot think what might be wrong with her."

"Well," said the baroness, looking thoughtful, "perhaps she is merely suffering from a touch of homesickness. I don't know her very well yet, of course, but it would be in all ways understandable if she was missing her old home and friends, don't you think?"

Beginning to smile, Tante Agathe struck her cane softly on the carpet beneath her feet. "But yes. If only I had thought sooner. Madame"—she turned to the dressmaker—"we should have realized how it would be. Had we done so, we might have had Brigitte and Claudine come with you today." Not noticing the alarmed look this prospect engendered, Tante turned back to Sally Ellengood and explained, "There are two other girls employed at the dressmaking shop. They are good friends to my Madeleine, having all worked together for, oh, nearly a year now. My little one must feel lost without them."

With very good reason for not wanting the two pretty sisters anywhere near a high-born young lady who, to them, was once a delivery boy named "Matt," Mme. Leteuil spoke out quickly. "But perhaps it is not so much that Mattie is missing anyone—one day is hardly overlong to be apart from one's friends! *Non, non!* Instead, I think she is *inaccoutumée,* unaccustomed, to any sort of idleness. At my shop, she is always the one to be up and doing. You would never believe how she frets when there is not enough work for her to do! But what can she busy herself with here?"

Marie Leteuil had asked no idle question. Upon Mattie's insistence, she had brought in more than just *new* clothes today. Although, what *la petite* wanted with her old costume, the dressmaker couldn't imagine. But to her certain knowledge, Mlle. Madeleine Serinier could be up to nearly any sort of mischief.

Unaware of the modiste's concerns, Lady Ellengood

180

looked wise and rolled her eyes meaningfully toward the nursery floor above. "Well," she said rather dryly, "if that is the only problem, I am sure my boys would be more than happy to help out. They quite dote on Mattie already, you know, and if you think she would care to spend, say, an hour or so with them in the afternoons, Nurse and I would be prodigiously grateful for it. But I must warn you, those boys of mine could exhaust any number of Matties."

But from the moment the idea was suggested to her, Mattie grinned and agreed that it was just what she would like. Thereafter, she twitched and wriggled during the morning's fittings until freed to be with the boys. Her elders were pleased as the day advanced to hear shrieks, squeaks, thuds, and high laughter come floating down from the nursery floor.

Mattie was her old self again. Almost her old self, that is.

For as the days passed by without anyone hearing further from Lord Staffield, Mattie became ever more agitated. She suffered being pinned and hemmed, tucked and trimmed, till she thought she would surely go mad.

It took no more than that first day at the Ellengoods', though, and that one morning's fit of abstraction, before Mattie gave up her *brooding* and decided to pay more attention to the development of her wardrobe. It may have been wrong to think of playing *la coquette* for his lordship, but that didn't mean she shouldn't enjoy new clothes! Still, fittings were a tedious process.

Mattie's afternoons served her better; actually, they served a dual purpose. After a good romp with the two Ellengood boys, she discovered herself free to disappear into her room for a "nap." That allowance permitted an agile youth in a fawn-colored slouch hat to scramble out a window at the end of the hall, down a leaden drainpipe, and over the back garden wall.

Mattie never missed a meeting at the Bluebell. Of a surety, her efforts on the old charley's behalf were facilitated by the move to Tenterden Street. Her kinsmen's address was right on the verge of Charlie Coomber's territory, making it a simple task to slip away as needed to make her nighttime rounds.

Unfortunately, while Mattie's clothes press filled and her friendship with the Ellengoods prospered, her other purposes were not so well served. No house had been broken into of late, nor had she any opportunity for encountering the earl.

And she did so want to have her confrontation with Lord Staffield over and done! Either he would accept her new identity, or he would condemn her as a harum-scarum chit, not worth the knowing. Either he would reveal her exploits to Tante or be convinced, somehow, to hold his tongue. Or in that most dreaded possibility, he might say nothing to her, nothing to Tante, nothing to anyone else. He might take one look at Matt-now-a-Madeleine and recede behind an impenetrable wall of dull-eyed disinterest.

Whichever it was to be, though, one thing was already certain. By the end of a week, Mattie hadn't a particle of patience left to her.

Chapter Twelve

"Take more time with it, Guy. Use some science. Flailing away at your opponent like that makes for a good show, I'll grant, but it won't serve to bring down your man. Here, I'll go through it again for you."

With slow, well-controlled movements, Vincent demonstrated the proper way to strike a right-handed blow in the close. He followed it with a reverse, immediately twisting his upper body away so as to set up for another right.

"Zounds! It looks demned easy—when *you* do it."

"It is easy. Just let each motion flow, one from the other." The earl showed Sir Guy the way of it again, this time more slowly yet. He was pleased when his friend imitated his moves exactly, and then, receiving Vincent's nod, went through the motions a second time at speed. He clipped the air smartly, right where Vincent's left ear had been only a split second before. "Oh, that *was* well done. You almost had me, too!" his lordship approved.

For an hour and a half each week, Lord Staffield met with Sir Guy Chittenham at Gentleman Jackson's elegant sparring rooms. Eight other students claimed a like share of Vincent's offered expertise, their instruction taking three days out of every seven. The earl hadn't intended giving lessons to so many, but he hadn't the heart to disappoint anyone who asked.

There were those who had come to him because of his reputation as a serious sportsman, men whom John Jackson had recommended for their interest. There were other men who, self-conscious about their apparently apt size, coupled with their actual fistic inabilities, had thought it less intimidating to be taught by an amateur. But without regard for what had brought them to him, Vincent had made time for each man.

Never had the list of subscribers to Jackson's Rooms been longer. With the news of Lord Staffield's participation, the gymnasium at No. 13 Bond Street—however popular it had been before—now was constantly filled to its capacity. And Mr. Jackson was heard to comment, quite beside himself with glee, "Oh, the earl is a wonderful glutton. Aye! A downright glutton!"

Jeremy, Lord Ellengood, concurred. He, too, had taken the opportunity to sign on as one of Vincent's students. Of a size with Sir Guy, Jeremy was too large a man and too inexperienced a boxer to benefit from the lessons offered by smaller pugilists. His session today had preceded Sir Guy's, but he had waited around for Vincent to finish, since his wife was insistent that he should bring Lord Staffield home with him this evening.

Vincent's eyes lightened in amusement when Jeremy made to follow him into the changing rooms. He had a pretty good idea about what was wanted and had every intention of complying, but he couldn't resist the opportunity for tweaking Jeremy on another matter beforehand.

Entering the room set aside for the gentlemen to exchange their clothing, Vincent kept his back to the door. He looked around for a moment as if not recalling where he had left his apparel. In fact, his real purpose was to ascertain that there were no witnesses while he harried his cousin-in-law. Satisfied, he turned back round and, with a casual air of surprise, said, "Oh, hullo there, Jeremy; glad to see you stayed behind to watch my next lesson like you did. Really, I had meant to suggest it before myself, knowing you could learn from Sir Guy's style. I'm pleased you came to appreciate it on your own."

Lord Ellengood's response was just what Vincent had hoped to provoke. For once, the affable gentleman looked a trifle put about. He, too, glanced around to be sure he wasn't overheard, then protested, "Style? All that heedless swinging and thrashing, sent off in any which direction? You call that 'style'? Why, I managed better my very first lesson!"

"Hmmm. Perhaps." Vincent appeared to consider the matter. "But that was your first lesson. Things are different now. Sir Guy has made real progress since then."

Jeremy looked indignant. "And you think I haven't?"

"Well," the earl replied, using the same, pensive tones as before, "if you mean have you surpassed my other students in your knowledge of form, I'd have to answer you with a 'yes.' But there is rather more to boxing than an accumulation of physical skills. It requires an eagerness, a willingness to fend off every attack and return it forthwith. Sir Guy has that eagerness."

"And I suppose you think I don't?"

Vincent answered him frankly. "Jeremy, I can teach a man the best way to deliver a hit. I can teach him the best way to counter one. But what I cannot do"—he paused for emphasis—"is teach a man the *when* of it. Oh, I don't mean just speed. You've speed enough and have a good sense of timing besides. What you lack, however, is the will to give and take a good hard knock-down blow. What conceivable use can there be for knowing what to do or how to do it if you won't put your skills into practice?"

The baron all but sneered, "But I thought that's what I came here for. Practice."

"No, no, I mean putting what you learn to the test. Take today's lesson, for example. When I told you to *set to,* you obediently raised your fists and jabbed neatly at the air in front of my face. I said, 'Hit me,' and you obliged with a punch that wouldn't have done damage to Sally's daintiest glassware."

"But Vincent, what was I supposed to do? Actually hit you?"

"Damn right, hit me. Mill me down. Launch me across the room, if possible!"

"But—but what if I broke your nose or something? Really hurt you? I'd never forgive myself! I can't simply haul off and smash a fellow's face. Just step in and take my swing."

"No? Then what happens if, say, some cove insults Sally or the boys—threatens them, tries to hurt them? Is it your intention to scare the blackguard off with some prettily executed jabs, thrown into the air? Maybe you intend to confuse him with your fancy moves, the correctness of your positioning, before you offer him a few swipes that never really connect. Is that how it's to be?"

"Well, no. But that's different! A man's got to defend his wife and children, don't he? Under those conditions, I guess I might *go at* a fellow."

"Under those conditions, Jeremy," the earl said wryly, "you don't 'guess' about what your actions will be. You don't posture or pose, and you don't give the scurrilous

186

dog a warming-up round. No. You wade in and deliver him a full set of fives. Hammer him. Knock him into tomorrow! And Jeremy," the earl said next, his dark eyes intent, "to do that effectively, you must be ready to strike, and strike hard, the very moment it is needed. That's why I want to see you taking every practice session seriously. A habit of holding back can be as dangerous as any criminal."

Looking much affected by these words, the baron returned, "Well, yes. I do believe you may be right."

"So then. At our next lessons, when I say *hit me*—"

"I draw your cork! Spill your claret!"

Vincent nodded, his purpose accomplished. He would see his students, every single one of them, prepared to meet any situation head-on.

This matter settled, the earl prepared to confront a little situation of his own. He had deliberately delayed making a return visit to Tenterden Street, but now it was time. He would accept Sally's importunings.

After that first night, when neither Matt, or *Mattie*, as Sally now called her, nor her great-aunt had appeared at dinner, he had sympathized with their predicament. He would not have come himself if he had thought about it more; he should have realized that they could have not suitable clothing to appear in company so soon. He had made himself scarce thereafter. Sally's notes suggesting that "Tante Agathe" particularly wished to see him had been answered with polite excuses.

Until now. Now it was time to see *la petite émigrée*— and dressed as she ought.

Mattie stood in front of the cheval glass and stared at the exotic creature she had, somehow, magically become. Intricate shell-pink embroidery, intermingled with the occasional strand of silver, swirled across high, firm breasts before passing along her tapering waist to slide delicately, deliciously downward, giving emphasis to the shape of softly flared hips. Any least movement set floss silk into currents of subtly changing hue ... pink-to-rose, rose-to-pink ... drawing attention to a mysterious succession of deeply feminine curves and contours. The tips of rose-colored slippers peeped out from beneath the garment's narrow, double-flounced hem, as if anxious to do their part in supporting such magnificence.

"So, what say you *now,*" Tante Agathe affectionately scolded. "You see, it is just as I told you, Madeleine. Nothing could be more suitable. Though I still do not understand. A week ago you were anxious to wear your birthday gown, and yet, for tonight's assembly, you tried to refuse it. What objection could you have?"

"Well, I just thought that, since I've other dresses to choose from now, I could wear—"

Tante Agathe's hurt look silenced her. "Then, it is no longer your favorite, Madeleine?"

"No! I mean, of course, 'tis still my favorite gown, Tante. I think it always will be! I only meant that another gown might have done me just as well. That's all."

"But what nonsense is this? Tonight marks your introduction into *le bon ton,* into good society. Everything should be of the best for you."

With a fatalistic shrug, Mattie began pulling on white, sixteen-button-length gloves.

She had tried so hard *to keep to her resolve.* "Fair and Virtuous" had been her watchwords for days!

But nothing seemed "fair" about greeting Lord

Staffield in a dress cunningly designed to turn his man's brain into lustful mush. And as for being "virtuous"—ha! Lady Hedgebird had appeared more virtuous! For without the cotton binder, the one which Mattie usually wore, two shockingly evident swells of flesh at Mattie's corsage gave all the proof needed for her claim-of-place within the ranks of adult womanhood.

Ruefully, Mattie turned away from the looking glass and shook her head. It sent her freshly washed blue-black curls into pretty disarray. Unconscious of this enhancement to her appearance—short, disordered curls were all the rage amongst the Fashionable Ones this year—Mattie went over to allow Tante Agathe to help her fasten up her gloves.

Doomed, Mattie thought dejectedly.

A tap at the door brought distraction. Sally Ellengood came in, wearing a sky-blue Selisie linen which none but Mme. Leteuil could have cut and sewn with such distinction. The lines of her pregnancy were scarcely evident, so cleverly had the folds of material been gathered and draped.

Before Mattie could wonder at it, Sally's two young sons tumbled into the bedchamber behind their mother, chiming in excited chorus, "Mattie, Mattie! Look at you! Look at Mama! And oh, at Tante, too!"

Indeed, all three ladies were looking well. Mademoiselle Madeleine in her birthday gown, Lady Ellengood in crisp blue linen, and dear Tante Agathe, always dignified, wearing another of Mme. Leteuil's creations, this one in Naples yellow.

"Oh, my dears," Sally applauded, much impressed by her guests' improved appearances. "How superb you look. Superb! And is that really you, Mattie?" Her ladyship gave an exaggerated gasp. "Goodness, I knew you were a taking little thing—but now? In that dress? Oh, top of the trees, my dear. Bang up to the nines!"

Mattie grinned, her doldrums vanished. *So what if she was on her way to destruction?*

She was going down in style.

Lady Ellengood had something to add. "My own lovely gown tonight was a gift, so I thought perhaps you might each enjoy a present as well." Giving her boys the office, she sent them from the room for a moment to return with two goodly sized boxes. They were enshrouded by quantities of somewhat mangled-looking white paper, one bearing a dark-rose-colored ribbon, the other, a yellow.

Three-year-old Jacob presented his burden, the box with the yellow ribbon, to Tante Agathe. "Self!" he said importantly.

Agathe Serinier might never have been favored with children of her own, but she had the knack for understanding them. "Indeed, Jacob," she said gravely, "and you wrapped it very nicely, too." She opened the box to bring forth an elegant length of warm Norwich silk. "Oh, what a glorious shawl!" she sang out softly. In a burst of affection, she enfolded the little boy in a generous hug.

Jacob giggled his pleasure.

His older brother, meanwhile, handed Mattie her box. It held a similar item, a long scarf made of silver-spangled gauze. She immediately danced over to the glass to try it against her gown, every expression of gratitude rushing from her lips.

Little Rhodney watched for a moment, then bounced his way over to where she stood. He consciously composed himself. All solicitude, and with an eye to his

190

mama for her permission, he begged the favor of escorting "Mam'selle" downstairs.

Mattie was terribly impressed when this request was accompanied by a neat little bow; after which, Rhodney held his arm out to her, stiffly, and bent just so. His actions were in perfect mimicry of how his father might have done when offering a lady his support. Here was a boy after Mattie's own heart!

His fond mama looked tempted to consent. But she refused, saying gently, "No, Rhodney, I am afraid you are too young yet, although you do Mattie honor with your request." At his downcast look, she offered him a palliative. "However, I do consider tonight a special occasion. So if you and Jacob will promise to be very quiet about it, I shall allow you—and just for this once, mind—to watch from the upstairs landing until we leave."

Her proposal turned the trick. The boys ran from the room, squabbling over who should position himself where, so as to obtain the best view.

The evening's plan was for Lords Ellengood and Staffield to accompany the three ladies to the Jerseys' home. Frances, the fourth Countess of Jersey, bore a connection to Jeremy's family, closer even than Tante Agathe's. Lady Jersey had therefore declared it her prerogative to introduce Madame *la Marquise* and Mademoiselle de Serinier to the *ton*. They would begin the evening with a dinner for forty at table, to be followed by a reception with upward of two hundred couples invited.

Sally Ellengood was nothing loath to fall in with these arrangements. Not only was she relieved of the responsibility for effecting a similar party herself, but with the socially preeminent Lady Jersey's sponsorship, Mattie's acceptance into the best Society was assured.

Of course, the prospect of such social success meant little to someone like Mattie. She had no fears about making new acquaintances and gave that aspect of tonight's events no more than a passing thought. Tonight, she hoped for only one person's good opinion—an opinion she feared would be unduly influenced by a seductive, rose-colored gown.

Abruptly, Mattie's mood swung into one of wretched self-castigation.

When the ladies started for the stairway, the boys forgot their mother's instructions and gave out a rousing cheer. This, in turn, alerted the gentlemen; Lord Ellengood and a footman came bounding up the steps to render assistance to Tante Agathe and the baroness. While Sally rendered her sons a cautionary look, prompting them to better behavior, the baron offered Tante Agathe his arm. The strong-looking footman secured Sally's progress, following his master's lead.

Mattie hung back for a moment to fuss with the set of her scarf. Again she wished she were not quite so richly dressed . . . so, so feminine. But it was not in her nature to dawdle or dilly-dally. She straightened her back, took a deep breath, and set her foot on the first of the steps.

She felt as if she walked atop a basketful of thin-shelled eggs.

And there he was. He waited at the bottom of the staircase, watching as she made her descent. He was all gold-gleaming hair above dark-eyed pools of blue; she had to appreciate that his were such looks as went beyond handsome, beyond those of ordinary men. And he was such a tall man. Tall and very large. *Hadn't she known all of this before?*

No. Not like this. Not with this heart-stopping awareness which made her almost forget to breathe. How like a stranger he appeared in his dark maroon coat and spotless white vest over flawless, form-following black breeches. Like someone she scarcely knew.

In a flash, Mattie recollected how much more strange *her* appearance must seem to *him*. She remembered the importance of this meeting and refocused her attention, trying hard to decipher his expression. But what she saw within his blue-eyed gaze made her forget to feel glad that no weary-eyed disinterest greeted her. It was as she had predicted.

Lustful mush.

A tinge of color crept into Mattie's cheeks. She became suddenly and altogether uncomfortably conscious of fine silk swishing across her ankles; of a slight pressure at her elbows, where her gloves were stretched the tightest; and of a faint current of air, moving across uncovered skin when someone opened the front door. She got down to the bottom of the staircase somehow, her own eyes beginning to plead with his for understanding. She had rather he forget how she looked and accuse her for her sins outright!

But when he spoke, it was only to offer the usual words expected with introductions. "So delighted to be meeting you, mademoiselle," he said quietly. An odd, almost teasing glint flickered around the edges of his eyes. "And may I address you as 'Mattie'? Sally has suggested that I might. I would also be pleased if you would call me 'Vincent.' All of my friends do, you know."

She thought he sounded kind.

Kind?

While Mattie uttered what she trusted were appropriate replies, she was set to wondering about the change in his expression and about his tone of voice. Could she have been wrong, thinking he had been overwhelmed—lost to good judgment by the sight of her in her beautiful gown? Surely, he recognized her! And yet, he gave no sign of surprise at seeing her. But when no further hints were given while wraps and hats, sticks and canes were adjusted—no, not even during the whole of the ride to the Jerseys'—Mattie had to doubt for meaning.

Whatever else, though, she couldn't doubt that *warm* look in his eyes when she had first appeared. His response to her gown was the one she had feared.

She believed she might just cry.

Chapter Thirteen

Lady Jersey's dinner was the grand affair which years of Thursday lessons had presaged. Tante Agathe's many lectures now reminded Mlle. Madeleine Serinier of which fork to choose, of where to set down her goblet when the wine course was changed, and of when and how to properly address her fellow guests. And a good thing it was, too, since she and her *grand-tante* were ensconced in those seats nearest their host's at the table. The cynosure of all eyes, Mattie's responses were blessedly practiced unto habit.

Yes, I'm very well, thank you, my lord. . . . Oh, of a certainty, your grace.

Her converse proceeded without effort.

Lord Staffield's rank obtained him a place opposite Mattie's and only a few chairs down. And while Mattie never caught him staring precisely, she was aware of his watching her in the same way she knew the touch of sunlight. One didn't have to see some things to know they were there. The only peculiarity was that, as the meal advanced, her awareness of the earl's attention seemed gradually to relax her. By rights, she knew she should have instead been sent into the highest fidgets!

The only way Mattie could interpret this rare state of affairs was that she must be merely basking in the aftermath of a disaster which had not occurred. Tante so far had not had to face any unpleasant truths about her great-niece, nor had Lord Staffield shown either disgust or indifference at the sight of a young lady in a flowing floss silk gown.

Au contraire, Mattie thought with a tiny grimace.

But a way to prevent any repeat of his lordship's all-too-explicitly appreciative look occurred with the first serving of soup. It struck Mattie that she had successfully diverted his lordship from an unwanted disposition beforetimes, had she not? Adjusting the table napkin in her lap, she bided her time, satisfied that she knew how to resolve her situation with the earl.

She gave her attention to her host, an elderly gentleman approaching his seventieth year. She soon had Lord Jersey so at his ease that he confessed of his own most pressing concern—a troublesome bilious complaint.

Mattie entered into the subject with spirit. She treated him to a knowledgeable comparison of the merits of tincture of arnica, Dr. James's Analeptic Pills, and Godbold's Vegetable Balsam. "And I had the information," she assured her enraptured listener, "from the apothecary on Clifford Street. Oh, and never doubt it, he will be able to provide you with just what is needed!"

The great man quickly extracted her promise that, after the next remove, she would tell what she knew about gout.

Mattie then turned her attention to the dinner partner seated on her left. Of an age with her host and an esteemed Member of Parliament, he kept her entertained with an involved account of his latest triumph at billiards. She had never seen the game played and so was fascinated. She didn't realize how she charmed the honorable gentleman—a twattling old proser, some would have said—by giving him her complete attention. The dinner was thus passed pleasantly.

At the end of the meal, Mattie observed the countess giving a discreet signal to her butler. The servant promptly moved to a set of doors, opposite to the ones by which they had entered the dining room. Mattie laid aside her napkin and gathered up her gloves in preparation.

She knew from Tante's instructions that the ladies would remove to a selected withdrawing room, with time to freshen themselves in expectation of the arrival of the gentlemen. After which, the company would repair to the ballroom. There, the Jerseys, the Ellengoods, and the two guests of honor would form a receiving line for the newer arrivals.

Matters did not proceed in quite that way, however. When her ladyship rose, so did everyone else. It seemed that the second set of doors did not open the way to a withdrawing room but to the ballroom. The entire company was to enter it directly.

For a moment Mattie was confused. She quickly collected herself, though, reasoning that it was only to be expected if her great-aunt's knowledge of English conventions had proved fallible. After all, this was Tante's first real experience with the London *ton,* too! Mattie's eyes twinkled as she started for the door with the others.

She had quite a struggle to get her gloves back on, *sans* assistance. She fell behind somewhat, but picked up her pace when she realized that her great-aunt was already passing through the doors on Lord Jersey's arm. And she could swear she felt Lord Staffield's looming presence, close at her own back! It was as though his gold-streaked hair had absorbed not only the light, but also the heat from the sun. Heat she could feel spreading across the nape of her neck—like an itch.

The advantages accruing to those of small stature offered opportunities which Mattie knew very well how to exploit. When she came to the doorway leading into the ballroom, she paused right at its center. This resulted in no perceptible impediment to the flow of traffic.

A faint odor of sandalwood told her when it was time. Sure that the earl was exactly behind her, she simply stepped to one side and slid her hand beneath the gentleman's arm. Casually, she recommenced walking right along with him.

"Scamp," she heard him grumble.

Her own voice brimming with laughter, she peeped up and whispered, "Right yer are, milord! A reg'lar smoke-merchant. That's me!"

Apparently, the earl was as anxious as she for private conversation. Retaining her hand, he avoided the receiving area and adroitly maneuvered Mattie across the ballroom. He bypassed those dinner guests who were starting to convene in little clumps here and there, stopping only when he reached the long windows at the far side of the room. He turned a stern face upon hers.

" 'Smoke-merchant,' indeed." His voice came out in a growl. "I might have expected you to say something of the sort. Howsoever I am inclined to agree with your assessment, though, I will remind you of where you are. Your choice of language has no place here. Do you understand me, young lady?"

This was *not* the reaction Mattie had anticipated. She had meant only to remind him of their old friendship; then, to try and convince him that he mustn't betray her to Tante Agathe. Now, she didn't know where she stood with him. He seemed primarily interested in ripping up at her for her manner of speech!

Well, she thought prosaically, better that than to fix her with another of those too-*warm* looks which had so discommoded her at the start of the evening.

Quick as the thought came to mind, she tugged at an imaginary cap and gave a respectful bob of the head. " 'Tis ter be nothin' but just as yer says. Why, I'm at yer every command, yer worship!" She was tempted to try rolling a few vowels or dropping a few aitches for him, too, but from the forbidding look on his face, she concluded that this might be going too far. But at least he was seeing *her* and not her gown. She ceased her twitting and deliberately smoothed her accents.

"My lord," she said forthwith, "by your leave, I would like to suggest that any discussion of my selection of words is nothing to the point." From the corner of her eye, she could see the receiving line beginning to form. Hurriedly, she added, "I had expected you would be surprised to see me tonight—to learn who I am. Yet you said nothing of it."

His look remained stern. "Oh? You supposed it required some gift of genius to put one 'Matt' and one 'Mattie' together, then come to a conclusion? Well, some of us *remember* names, and as I understand it, de Serinier have never been particularly thick upon the ground."

So he *had* known to expect her. It relieved Mattie of at least a portion of her concerns. "Well," she said more slowly, "but not so very many people would know such a thing, would they?"

"Oh, good God, Mattie." He frowned, making his aspect yet more severe. "Don't you realize that only one would be too many? Not even Frances Jersey's influence could protect you if anyone learned how you were used to spending your time."

She finally understood what was bothering him. It was really quite sweet. He was obviously concerned that her previous rôle as a common delivery boy should not be exposed to the *ton*.

She said, trying to appease, "Yes, but Tante and I have resided here for close on eight years, and none have remarked it before. Besides, when I do give out the name, 'tis soon enough forgotten. And if I had considered it—which I don't think I did—I would have expected you to forget it as well."

He growled again. This time, whatever it was he said, it was something unintelligible. As near as she could guess, though, he was wanting to know more about how her situation had originally come about.

Reaching to adjust the seam at the elbow of her glove, she explained. "It is all because I cannot sew. No, I can't—not a stitch," she reiterated, catching his disbelieving look. "Oh, Mme. Leteuil tried and tried to teach me, but in my hands, thread tangles into beastly wads of fluff, while pins jump from the cloth and run away to hide."

He stared at her left elbow. "Somehow, *that* I can believe."

She immediately quit fussing with her glove. She relaxed her hands at her sides, just as Tante had taught her. "In any event," she resumed when he had left off staring, "we agreed that I should pull my weight by making deliveries and running errands. It was the only way for me to be useful, the only thing we could think of."

" 'We'?"

It took her a moment to understand the question.

200

"Oh, you mean, who else knows about my taking on the part of a boy? No one but Mme. Leteuil. You must understand' that she and I were afraid that if anyone else knew, Tante might somehow find out. And I would honestly rather have *anything* than that happen! Tante has always felt very badly about having to let me out to work; I don't know whether she could ever recover if she learned how I dress, er, dressed, on the streets."

"But sometimes you appear as a young girl." It wasn't a question.

Mattie thought back rapidly. She supposed Lady Ellengood had mentioned how she had been attired that first day. She then remembered Sally's gown, the blue Selisie linen. "Then—then you have been to Madame's shop, haven't you! But when I saw Sally's gown tonight, and she said it was a gift, I hadn't really considered that there might be some connection. I should have realized that I'd not seen her being fitted up at the house. You took her to the shop!"

"And just how had you supposed I obtained your great-aunt's direction in the first place?" he said stiffly. "Yes, I arranged for the gown with Madame, after which, I waited at the King's Head, before following you home. Now. You were saying?"

Instead of the idea of Vincent's stratagem dismaying her, Mattie discovered that she felt rather pleased. He had gone to some trouble, and possibly, he had done so as much on her account as her *grand-tante*'s. She didn't think this was the time to ask further about it, though, and so said merely, "Thank you."

She dropped into a pretty curtsy, not noticing how her words had startled him. By the time she looked up, his face was expressionless.

She hurried to finish her explanation. "You are correct. I dressed as a girl to go back and forth to the shop, but that much 'twas done by Tante Agathe's permit. As I became older, Tante didn't like my having to travel on foot all the way from Williams Court, and she agreed I might attract less notice if I used the same clothes, year after year." With a sudden, merry little smile, Mattie added, "And it wasn't so difficult as you might think! Especially for one who attained her adult height by the age of thirteen. "But sir"—her voice turned suddenly serious as she willed him to understand—"you must, please, say nothing of my other costume. It would quite destroy *ma chère tante*. Really, it would."

There wasn't time for more. Jeremy Ellengood approached them, sent to fetch Mattie and bring her to her place in the receiving line. Necessarily, she had to suffer the baron to lead her off.

Over her shoulder, she sent the earl a most affecting look.

As Mattie left to fulfill her duties, Lord Staffield's eyes followed her. He hadn't missed that last, silent entreaty and had understood to a nicety what it was meant to convey.

He was now certain that the elder Serinier was unaware of her great-niece's more indecorous activities, something which Vincent thought good to know. He also understood that Mattie wanted nothing so much as to keep the old lady in ignorance, which was also to the good. Additionally, Mattie appeared anxious to remain on the same easy footing with him as they had enjoyed before . . . and that was best of all.

The earl grinned to himself, accepting this last as a challenge.

From the moment she had started down his cousin's front staircase, floating softly toward him like a dream that comes just before dawn, any intentions he might have had for Mattie's future had begun to shift and change. This was not the energetic lad of his first acquaintance, nor even the impudent youth who had rebuked him for his choice of flirts, chided him for his drinking, and charged him to change his ways.

This was Mattie. A staggeringly beautiful young woman who happened to have an amusing gift for mimicry. One who, more importantly, cared about everyone around her and helped where she could. To be sure, she was also a most imprudent young lady who had scampered about the streets—sometimes after dark!—and to who-knew-what purpose.

"My God, but what a little beauty she is," he cried softly.

He was startled when his comment received a reply!

"Oh, there never was a neater turn-out. Dash it all."

Their host's son, George, and Vincent's friend, Nicholas Porterby, sauntered up to him. Viscounts both, the one styled 'Villiers' and the other, Lord Maines, they had noted the earl's tête-à-tête with the evening's guest of honor and now were wanting to discover the extent of that interest. But with Vincent's overheard words, they had their answer.

"Twenty quid to you, Nick," George Villiers said next, laughing, while he reached into the pocket of his handsomely made snuff-colored coat. "Seems Mama was wrong, after all."

At Vincent's quizzing look, he confided, "Nick here insisted that I didn't stand a chance at gaining the young lady's attentions ahead of you. Said you'd single her out and dazzle her silly—and do it in an instant, too! But when Mama told me that the lovely mademoiselle was on the lookout to make a good match, I thought sure she'd give me her first notice. Everybody knows I'm in the market for a wife. Bet Nick twenty guineas, thinking I couldn't lose!"

"Well, I did try to warn you," Lord Maines drawled, phlegmatically pocketing his winnings. His long-jawed, weather-browned face appeared as lugubrious as usual; in fact, the only difference in his aspect this evening, despite his good fortune, was the whip points missing from his lapels. He sighed then said gloomily, "I knew how it would be, though, more's the pity. I might have liked to make the run myself. But no. I suppose, mere mortals can't compete."

Vincent didn't at all care for the way the conversation was going. "Nick—George, what are you two talking about? And what exactly did Lady Jersey say to you?"

Lord Villiers was the first to answer. "Oh, she didn't say anything to Nick. Said it to me. But since the three of us fellows are of an age—twenty-nine, aren't we?— it's only natural if we entered the lists for the young lady's favors all at the same time. Shame you beat me out this round, though, Vincent. I'll just have to hope for better luck, maybe later this evening." He turned to Viscount Maines. "But am I right, Nick? Mama didn't say anything to you about it, did she? Or did I miss something?"

"Nothing I recall," his fellow viscount agreed, locking his arms over his lean chest before languidly positioning one shoulder against the window frame. "I have a good memory for what's said to me, don't y' know," he added mildly.

Vincent smothered his annoyance and redirected his question. "George, I want to hear what your mother said

204

to *you*. About what Mattie said to *her*," he appended, hoping to forestall further digressions.

George shook his head. "Well, I don't think Mlle. de Serinier spoke to Mama about anything since—"

" 'Serinier,' " his fellow interposed.

"What? But that's what I said, Nick."

"No, you didn't, you said *'de* Serinier.' And it's not. The young lady and her great-aunt want to be known as 'Serinier' now, not 'de Serinier.' Told you, I've got a good memory."

Lord Villiers turned to Vincent. "Is that right, what Nick said? Do we say 'Serinier' or 'de Serinier'? Which is it?"

The earl somehow contained himself. " 'Serinier' only, without the honorific," he managed calmly.

"Oh, well, if that's what they prefer, then I suppose there can be no objection. Anyway, what I started to say was, unless she's spoken to Mama about it tonight— which would be a trifle unseemly, come to think of it, so I'm sure she hasn't done anything of the sort!—Mlle. *Serinier* wasn't the one who gave Mama the information. Never said otherwise, did I?"

Again Lord Maines interrupted, this time remarking to Vincent, "That's right. He didn't, y' know."

Vincent purposefully relaxed himself, thinking that a light hand on the reins would move this pair of peers along faster. "Then who was it that informed Lady Jersey that Mlle. Serinier was bent on making a marriage?" he asked with what he considered a remarkable degree of control.

He was rewarded when George answered promptly, "Your cousin Sally, of course. The ladies are always after a bit of matchmaking, aren't they? So when Mama heard, she decided our *petite belle* might just do for me.

Quite right. She would, indeed!" Stealing a look at his aging father through the growing crush of guests, he then said in more subdued tones, "It's time and more that I got about the business of setting up my nursery, I believe."

Vincent followed George's glance and understood. Enough so that he didn't even take George to task for referring to Mattie as "our" little beauty. Not that Vincent felt the least inclination to permit anyone other than himself to pursue Mlle. Serinier. He had decided that Mattie was to be his alone.

And he would have her realize the fact very, very soon.

Chapter Fourteen

Mattie wondered whether anybody noticed that her cheeks were growing numb. They didn't seem to, however, since everyone just smiled right back, made her their compliments, and continued on into the ballroom. Hundreds of people passed through Lady Jersey's doors. Apparently, it was the custom for each invited guest to bring along two more, until Mattie felt sure half the city sought entry.

Lady Jersey had sent for chairs for her husband, Tante Agathe, and the *enceinte* Sally Ellengood nearly an hour ago, and still new guests arrived. Being on her feet had never been a problem for Mattie before, but she was beginning to shoot envious glances toward the innocently seated trio. Nevertheless, she kept her smile in place, reminding herself that she might be more thankful that tonight's wasn't a dancing party.

When she was at last released from duty, Mattie headed unerringly in Lord Staffield's direction. The dark gold gleam of his smoothly brushed hair had been easy for her to keep track of throughout her term of service, so she made her way to him at speed. She had to be sure he understood that he must not reveal her secret to Tante!

He seemed to sense her presence. Before she reached him, he excused himself from the group of gentlemen with whom he'd been chatting and, without a word, accepted her lead through the now-opened long windows and onto the terrace beyond.

Mattie dodged a potted ivy in a stand and headed for an unoccupied corner of the terrace. Nervously, but without roundaboutation, she faced the earl and asked straightly, "Have you decided, sir?"

It took forever before he answered. "Yes. Yes, I have," he said. "If we can effect a pact between us, I believe there will be no need for me to make a report to your great-aunt."

She had all she could to keep from squirming. "A pact, sir? What kind of pact?"

"Oh, well, nothing too involved. I give you a promise and you exchange me a promise. The usual sort of thing."

She anxiously studied his expression. She could read nothing in it except a degree of watchfulness, just at the back of his eyes.

After a few moments, he continued, "You see, I want your solemn word that 'Matt' will run no more errands for anyone. Not ever again. Not on *any* account. Under the circumstances, I think that's reasonable, don't you?"

She hesitated for the space of an instant, then decided she could comply. Her assistance to the old charley on Chandler Street could not be considered an "errand," and so did not fall under his lordship's terms. "I agree. Is there anything else, my lord?"

She wondered if he would think to prohibit excursions such as the one she had been on the night when she had gone to the Theatre-Royal, Hay-market. She had no objection to giving in on that point either, but instead, the earl seemed to have something else on his mind.

"Actually, there is another thing," he said quietly. His eyes seemed to darken as he allowed them to travel from her face down to her feet. Slowly. "I also want your promise to at least try and keep to that style of speech which corresponds with your clothing." When his eyes had returned to hers, he extended in unexpectedly crisp accents, "That is a lovely dress, Mattie. Don't spoil it. Speak French or proper English, as you prefer, but no more canting, please. In return, you may trust me to do everything in my power to assure that your great-aunt never learns of your previous rôle. No more than you would I like to see her hurt."

Considering that she had just been subjected to another one of his lordship's outrageously intimate *oglings,* Mattie had more than a few reservations about entering into any agreements whatsoever! Nonetheless, thinking it prudent, she kept the thought to herself. *"D'accord,"* she answered just as brusquely.

Still, it seems he had one more proviso to add. "Oh, and I say there, Mattie?" This time, a flicker of some lighter shade of blue sparkled down at her. "If you would be so good, I also wish you to understand that I would appreciate it greatly if you would, henceforth, avoid all those 'sir's and 'my lord's.' Address me simply as 'Vincent.' I don't think—no, I could not possibly bear it if I was again to hear myself referred to as"—his massive shoulders commenced a slight shaking while his voice came out sounding strangled—" 'your *worship.' "

It was that same light she had seen gleaming from his eyes when she had accepted his "introduction" at the

Ellengoods'. This time, she knew what it was. He was funning her!

She had no fault to find with that. "Agreed!" she gurgled, succumbing to a burst of laughter while the earl looked on indulgently.

Catching her breath, Mattie fell silent. Again, she discovered his eye dark upon hers. The warm night air carried the scent of late summer flowers to her nostrils and also another familiar fragrance, that of his lordship's tangy, masculine scent. These elements combined with something in the earl's stance, causing Mattie to feel strangely uneasy. She immediately acted to counter the feeling by saying brightly, "So, um—Vincent, shall we adjourn to the ballroom? For we've failed our hostess miserably by being absent all this while, and everyone must be wondering what has become of us."

He held her with his eyes for a moment longer. But in the end, he merely nodded and took her inside.

This time it was the earl who provided guidance. With the benefit of his greater height, he readily located her great-aunt. She was comfortably settled on a small sofa, surrounded by a company of notables who were, apparently, delighted at having Madame *la Marquise* out of "retirement" and back within their society. With a bow, his lordship saw Mattie placed beside the old lady, then excused himself and left them.

Mattie was more than pleased just to have a place to sit down! No matter how soft the fine leather of her embroidered, rose-colored slippers, she had been on her feet rather long. So long, in fact, that she blamed their condition for the odd quiver in her knees. Fixing an interested look on her face, she was also glad of her youth, since it made it unnecessary, if not downright offensive, for her to join in the ongoing discussion. She was free to pursue her own thoughts—free to draw her own conclusions.

Retrospection wasn't an easy thing for Mattie, but she realized that her ever-changing relations with Lord Staffield seemed frequently to demand it. With a brief mental shrug for the absurdity, she began reviewing the terms she had just agreed to with his lordship.

Oh, she realized that she had come dangerously close to the line but decided that her consent to the earl's dictates had compromised no principles. His failure to mention anything about her going out and about for other reasons—when he knew perfectly well that "Matt" had ventured out on a pleasure jaunt—well, it clearly left her uncommitted on that point. Anyway, her first obligation was to secure her *grand-tante*'s peace of mind. She also had every right to help whatever friends she chose to support, and nothing in her agreement forbade her to meet with Billy and Kevin; there was nothing to prevent her from helping Ol' Charlie.

"Errands" were not involved.

Certainly, she realized she would have to take particular care from now on. Most of the guests tonight likely resided in or near Mayfair, and many of them probably had houses in Charlie's own district. The numbers of people who might recognize her were therefore vastly increased. But since she had so far encountered only one poodle dog owner and the Earl of Staffield himself while out making her rounds, Mattie was not overly concerned.

She had only to be sure and stay out of Vincent's path when she was in the area at night.

"Yer're sure 'bout this, Kevin? Completely, an' no mistake?" Mattie leaned forward, her voice low, aware

211

that the Bluebell had other customers who might overhear this discussion.

Kevin Howe thrust out his chin and stabbed a freckled finger at the scrap of paper lying on the table between them. "Sure Oi'm sure!" he whispered hoarsely. "It's them roight enough, the same as in this here pi'ture yer drew us, Matt. Bracelet, necklace, headpiece. All of 'em just loikes yer said. Oi gave out that story we made up—said as how Oi had an employer who was lookin' ter buy some o' them purple amethyst-stones—and the man brought 'em out, quick as quick may be. They was sittin' in a tray under his counter, just waitin' ter be sold ter the first comer."

Making up the third party at this meeting, Billy Tomkins also held his voice down. "But what about the broke wire on th' bracelet, Kevin? Did ya' remember an' look for that?" The dark-haired boy could be counted on to ascertain every element.

"Naow, how *stoopid* does yer toikes me ter be, anyways? An 'Oi thought at first Oi had it wrong, since Oi made out it were the seventh link which showed the damage. But then Oi realized Oi'd counted from the wrong end of the clasp. It turned out ter be the fourth link, after all."

Mattie sighed, lifted her old felt hat, and ran an impatient hand through her hair. She settled her hat back into place, then remembered to tug it lower across her forehead. She was taking special care at concealment these days.

"Well," she said, "the next question is, fellows, just what do we do 'bout it? This Mr. Chigwell didn't buy the stuff directly but tells Kevin he got it from Hamlet's. What we're needin' now is to learn who sold 'em to Mr.

Hamlet. This makes the first clue we've had since we started. We can't let it go by!"

"But it ain't gonna' be so easy ta check a thing like that," Billy pointed out. "Proper gudgeons, we'd be, goin' up ta Mr. 'amlet an' askin' 'im ta tell us what 'e knows 'bout a set of stolen sparklers. Exceptin' maybe Rundell & Bridge, 'e's the most important jeweler in the city. No, this ain't gonna' be easy," he repeated.

"Maybe, but then again, maybe not," she said thoughtfully. "I think I have an idea. I'll let you know if it worked when we meet again on Wednesday. Or, no, not Wednesday." She stopped and considered for a moment. "Let's us make that Saturday. I'll be needin' the time to make the thing work, I 'spect."

Mattie did indeed have an idea about how to obtain the needed information. Mr. Hamlet might refuse to answer questions from a common delivery boy who presumed to enter his premises, for as Billy had noted, the jeweler was the richest tradesman on the West End. But perhaps Mr. Hamlet would be less suspicious if a Mlle. Serinier visited his jewel room. A clever *Society* miss might be able to find out who it was that had brought Lady Rothshaw's amethysts to his worthy establishment . . . and how Mr. Chigwell's dingy shop in the Limehouse district had ended up with them.

Matters were not to proceed so smoothly, however. Mattie not only missed Wednesday's meeting at the Bluebell with Billy and Kevin, but to her dismay, by lunchtime Saturday, she was no closer than ever to Mr. Hamlet's shop in Cranbourn Alley. She marveled at how simple it was for "Matt" to slip away from the Ellengoods', and how impossible for a well-dressed young lady to do the same.

It began to look as though her only alternative was to

come up with some plausible reason for visiting the jeweler's outright. But wouldn't Sally just stare to learn where she wanted to go? Tante Agathe might have come into a spot of money, but it was hardly enough to justify a claim of interest in the merchandise at Hamlet's!

After leaving the Ellengoods' table, Mattie went upstairs for her usual romp with Rhodney and little Jacob. The whole of the time they played at Bear-leader, Hot Cockles, and other such rollicking games, she kept cudgeling her brain for a means to get to Cranbourn Alley. But even after she shut the door to her bedchamber for her afternoon's supposed respite, no plan recommended itself. Not one notion.

She was preparing to change clothes for her meeting at the Bluebell, when someone knocked at her door.

"A moment please," she called out, hastily cramming shirt, vest, and knee breeches back underneath her mattress. She made a quick survey of the drape of the bedcovers to be sure everything looked normal, before going to answer the door.

"Oh, good. You're still up," Lady Ellengood said cheerfully, glancing toward Mattie's apparently undisturbed bed. "I had hoped to catch you before you were at your rest. You have a caller downstairs."

"Someone is here to see me?"

"Well, and just what is so unusual about that?" her ladyship asked with a laugh as she stepped inside the room. "We've had company every day this week, haven't we? And I must say, I have never before enjoyed the prospect of being a stay-at-home"—she patted her expanding midsection—"but this time, it's going to be so much different. Oh, Mattie, I cannot tell you how

214

happy I am that you and your *grand-tante* have come to us. This is such fun, isn't it?"

"Famous fun," Mattie responded dryly.

Sally didn't seem to notice anything lacking in this reply. She went over to Mattie's bed and perched herself on a corner of the mattress.

Mattie could only pray that no suspicious lumps would bring themselves to her ladyship's attention. Why did Sally have to chose to sit down on the very corner under which she had just stuffed her boy's costume! Mattie took a seat at the bench by her dressing table and tried to look indifferent.

"Now, let me see." Sally counted off on her fingers. "We went to Lady Jersey's on Friday last. The next day, and indeed, on every succeeding day, we've enjoyed visits from at least a half-dozen people. That makes it"—she added up her fingers—"upwards of forty people who have come to call! And of that number, I am sure we've seen *all* of the young men you met at the Countess's." She clapped her hands together. "Is it not too, *too* exciting?"

"Very exciting, yes."

This time, the young matron perceived Mattie's tone. "Oh, dear, you really are tired, aren't you? And it's my fault. I should never have encouraged you to spend so much time with the boys. We shall just have to start limiting your hours in the nursery so that you needn't go into seclusion to recover yourself every day. I won't have you fagged to death on our account! Do forgive me, I hadn't realized!"

Mattie at once objected, "But no, Sally. It isn't that I'm tired. Not in the least." She jumped to her feet, her thoughts racing. "I'm only, uh . . ." She rapidly scanned the room. Espying a likely excuse, she dashed over to the fireplace and grabbed up a book from the mantel. She hugged it tightly to her chest. "Reading! That's what it is. I just love to *read*. I hope you won't think too poorly of me if I confess to having used the boys as my excuse for indulging in a favorite pastime. I never meant anyone to think badly of *them* for my daily disappearance."

"But Mattie, when I came in you seemed so—"

"Guilt! I felt guilty about stealing away from everyone the way I have been these last couple of weeks."

The look Mattie gave the young matron was sincere, if misleading as to its cause. She certainly felt *guilty*, but not for the reason offered. Before the feeling quite overpowered her, however, Sally apparently remembered what had brought her to Mattie's room.

"Oh, silly me, I've left Vincent waiting all this while!" she cried. "He wanted me to see if you might like to go for a drive with him." Sally paused then, a look of puzzlement crossing her face. "But how peculiar," she said, looking rather bemused. "What a remarkable thing for him to do."

Seeing Mattie's startled expression, she hastened to explain. "Oh, goodness, I don't mean to imply that there's anything peculiar about someone's wanting your company, Mattie; that's not it at all! I just think it strange that Vincent does." When Mattie looked even more dumbfounded, a giggle slipped out and Sally tried again. "How troublesome this is to explain. What I mean is that my cousin has come to dinner almost daily of late, but he isn't known for seeking the attentions of young ladies. Or no, I don't suppose that's right either." She sighed and looked a little perplexed herself.

With dawning comprehension and a certain décolleté green gauze gown in mind, Mattie hugged the volume she'd removed from the mantelpiece tighter against her chest. She said in droll tones, "Mayhaps, what you mean to say is *eligible* young ladies."

Sally's face danced. "So you *do* understand. Yes, that is it exactly! In any case, I am thrilled to see Vincent taking an interest in you. Oh, but wait." Her face fell. "I'm doing it again, aren't I? I am imposing on you, Mattie, and I don't intend any such thing. If you would prefer to be left alone, that is how it should be."

Mattie hated to miss her meeting with Billy and Kevin, hated all the shifts she was being put to lately. But she knew that a drive with his lordship just might serve. "Why, I shall be delighted to drive out with your cousin," she said with some firmness. "You may tell him I'll be down as soon as I gather my things."

When she entered Sally's drawing room a few minutes later, Mattie was a trifle flustered. She had refolded her boy's attire and stashed it more neatly beneath the center of her mattress where the maids were unlikely to discover it, then put away her book, grabbed up a hat and tied it on any which way, remembering to go back for gloves only after she had reached the foot of the stairs.

All week long she had hoped for just such an invitation from one of those gentlemen callers Sally had seemed so pleased about. Mattie had considered that a casual drive with one of them might provide her with the opportunity she needed for making a brief stop at Cranbourn Alley. Instead, she had received scores of invitations for evening entertainments—entertainments which she had so far refused, pleading Tante's rheumatism and Lady Ellengood's promising condition. Her real objection to nighttime excursions was, of course, their potential for interference with her commitment to Charlie Coomber.

But Mattie was under no illusions. Any attempt to diddle Vincent into taking her in the direction she wished to go was going to be extremely risky. A prime *deep one* like the earl would be down to her tricks in no time! Even so, she had to try to help the old night watchman by whatever means became available.

Upon noticing her entrance, the earl took in her appearance and rose from his seat near Sally's. He walked right up to her. "Lift your chin," he said softly.

Mystified, Mattie complied, which allowed him the room he needed to begin retying the ribbons to her bonnet. She restlessly shifted from one foot to the other while he efficiently completed the business.

He stepped back to assess his handiwork. "Much better," he said. "But Sal was just explaining how she delayed you, so I must be flattered that you responded to my request as speedily as you did." He looked on Mattie with approval.

She had to wonder at it, for hurry had caused her to seize the first bonnet and jacket which had come into her hands. Providence, however, and Mme. Leteuil's artistry had assured that each item of dress made a perfect foil for the other. Over a tansy-colored gown with a high, double-buttoned collar, her tiny spencer jacket was of finely striped merino. The spencer included a line in the exact same shade as her dress; it bore another small stripe of a rich sherry brown, chosen to match Mattie's eyes. The hat which had given so much trouble was a shapely Dunstable straw, with stylishly gallooned ribbons in colors to compliment the whole.

Mattie could more readily admire Lord Staffield's mode of dress. Finely woven Bath coating in the darkest of blues, a light Valentia waistcoat, and tan-colored chamois breeches, worn above lucent boots—he was an enviable figure of a man. If her appearance pleased him, his was no less appealing to her discerning eye.

"Ready, then?" he asked, evidently satisfied that her attire was set to rights.

After seeing her seated beside him in his carriage—a sporty two-wheeled curricle pulled by a matched pair of bays—he directed his groom to remain behind at his cousin's to await their return.

"We won't be gone above an hour and so won't be needing Phipps to hold the horses for us," he assured Mattie while he started up his team. "We go only as far as Hyde Park. I thought you might enjoy seeing the *élèves* who come out to take the air. And by starting off so early as we are, we should be able to complete the circuit before the Row becomes too crowded."

But Mattie had no desire to view whatever Elegants thronged to Rotten Row this afternoon. Her needs lay precisely in the opposite direction! "Oh, but must we go to the Park?" she protested.

The earl was too busy making the corner onto New Bond Street to look at her while he replied, "I do beg your pardon. Mine was but a suggestion. If you'd prefer to do something else, we can go wherever you like." He sounded a touch mifty.

"Oh, your idea is a good one," she soothed. "But, well, I was rather hoping we might drop into Mr. Pollard's Printing Shop." Having successfully utilized a similar ploy earlier on, and recalling the imprint of the book she had snatched up from the mantelpiece, Mattie thought the device might find merit one more time. "The companion volume to the book I'm reading may be had at his shop off Leicester Square—just down

Cranbourn Alley. Although, of course, I wouldn't want to put you to too much trouble," she finished demurely.

He straightened out his horses after completing the next turn into Oxford Street. "Very well," he said when he was free to look up. She marked a slight frown upon his wide brow. He continued, "We can still make our drive in the Park first, if you like; after which, I shall let you down at this Mr. Pollard's place. But only for a moment. Will that do?"

"Oh, yes, thank you!" she answered eagerly. "I shan't be more than a minute!"

Released from her cares for a space, Mattie set herself to enjoying the ride. They passed through the Cumberland entrance to Hyde Park at a spanking pace, Vincent's practiced maneuvers never once giving cause for alarm. No, not even to someone unused to traveling at such a height and behind a team of powerful horses.

They slowed and began down the long, irregular circle known as Rotten Row. The August sun glittered off the backs of his lordship's team, while a light breeze off the river kept afternoon temperatures comfortably within bounds. Soon, Mattie was caught up in amazement at the variety of rigs and riders which joined them on parade. She was interested to observe an odd, shell-shaped equipage being pulled by a pair of dock-tailed creams, and then was distracted to discover that a handsome barouche-and-six on the approach held the person of George, the Prince of Wales. Sitting beside him was one or another of His Royal Highness's cronies.

"Remember, have a care for your language," the earl cautioned when the Prince hailed them and called for a halt.

Mattie flushed at the warning. There was no time for

any display of umbrage, however, before they reached the Prince's carriage.

Lord Staffield drew his team to a smart stop alongside the barouche. He doffed his high-crowned beaver and bowed from the waist, returning the hat to his head with an elegant motion. "What say you, good sirs?" he greeted. "Out to take the dust on this fine afternoon?" He grinned at the Prince's passenger. "Lord Hutchinson, I express myself astonished to see you here in town. I realize that the press of state business sometimes compels our Royal Highness to leave the pleasures of Brighton, but I had thought nothing could bring you here at this time of year."

However reluctantly, Mattie had to be impressed at Vincent's unaffected manner in the presence of such august company. She was soon equally impressed by the Prince, whose much-celebrated charm ever rendered the exchange of informal pleasantries possible.

"Why, we have come to be introduced to *La Petite Belle*, of course," the Prince advanced. "We heard how it was all the crack to be seen visiting with this young lady"—he turned a winsome smile on Mattie—"so we thought we'd best to come and make ourselves *au fait*. Wouldn't do to be behindhand in these matters. Oh, no, not at all!" he insisted, emitting a good-natured laugh.

After Vincent had completed the introductions demanded, the Prince gave his full attention over to the earl's passenger.

"So you are the one causing all the flutter amongst the peacocks, mademoiselle. I knew you at a glance! Give you my compliments, too, for the tales of your beauty were in no wise exaggerated, I vow. Although"—he wagged a reproachful finger at her—"you might appreciate that you have deprived us of more than one of our favorite guests at the Pavilion this last week. But wait, I have it!" he exclaimed on a thought. "Perhaps you would care to come down to Brighton. We would be pleased to see you at the Pavilion, what?"

Mattie opened her mouth to offer a diplomatic refusal, when Vincent answered for her.

"I'm afraid that might be rather difficult at this time, Your Highness," he entered smoothly. "Madame Serinier's current state of health does not permit her to travel any great distance, and as Your Highness is no doubt aware, my cousin Sally is in expectation of a happy event but a few weeks hence. Mlle. Serinier must regret the missed opportunity."

Mattie could scarcely disguise her wrath! She should have answered for herself. What possible reason was there for Vincent to interfere in such a way? Had it to do with that comment about *watching her language?*

Something of her upset must have made itself evident to the Prince. He smiled sympathetically at her and said, "Now, now, no need for disappointment, mademoiselle. We shall consider the invitation open until it is accepted. Be sure of it."

Summoning a smile from somewhere, she replied as brightly as she could, "Your Royal Highness is too gracious."

"Yes, so very good of you," Lord Staffield murmured politely.

When the Prince had driven on, Mattie rounded on the earl. "Just what on this green earth made you to speak for me like that? I believe I could have managed for myself!" Long, silky black brows snapped together in a fine scowl.

"Then, did you want to accept Prinny's invitation?"

"Of course not! Is that what you thought?"

"It was one consideration."

"One?" she asked, her voice growing deep with warning.

He didn't seem to regard it. "One. The other being that I was afraid, even if you didn't desire to go down to Brighton and participate in the Prince's entertainments at his Pavilion there, you might not be able to refuse His Highness in proper form."

She thought about that for a moment. When she spoke, her tones came low and furious. "So, what you are saying is that you wondered whether I had sufficient tact to decline His Highness's offer without appearing discourteous. And perchance, you feared that I would suddenly forget myself and sink into low accents which might embarrass you. Vincent Charles Houghton, you will at once beg my pardon!"

He was so disconcerted by this demand that he dropped his reins for a moment, causing his horses to bridle and break stride. Immediately recollecting himself, he frowned and tightened the pull on the leathers. When his team had settled back into a steady trot, he clipped out, "And what should *I* apologize for? I'm not—"

She interrupted in a clear contralto. "You must apologize to me for your ridiculous suspicions—your lack of confidence in my sense of fitness. If I had wanted your assistance, I could have *asked* for it! Perhaps it might help you to recall that, for over a dozen years, I have been accustomed to adapting my language. Can you switch from French-to-English-to-cant and back in the breath it takes to sneeze? Can you claim—dare you claim that concern for your listeners has led to you choose the words most likely to appeal? Hrumph!" she muttered, deep in her throat. "At least I *care* when I abuse somebody's feelings."

Mattie didn't know when she had been so angry. No, she did know. She had *never* been so angry! The thought drifted past that she might just be whistling her chance at Hamlet's down the wind, but so be it. "Monster," she grumbled, staring blindly ahead.

After some few minutes, the earl spoke, almost as if to himself. " 'Monster,' is it?" He paused. "Also known as a wretch, a churl, or a dastard?"

She sniffed in disdain. "The kind of man who would go out on a hunting field—and then *shoot* the poor fox!"

All was silence. She had issued the ultimate insult to any sportsman.

Then, she heard a chuckle. Once started, he couldn't seem to stop. He laughed so hard he had to pull his horses to the curb and clutch his reins between his knees. And soon Mattie's own laughter nearly tumbled her over the edge of her armless seat.

Chapter Fifteen

Less than twenty minutes later, Mattie had conceived the most prodigious gratitude for the convention which ordained a heavy brown wrapping around each new book sold. Her absorbed interest in Volume Two of *The Peerage of Great Britain and Ireland* might otherwise have been more than a little suspect.

"Are you coming in?" she asked the earl when he drew his horses up before the Ellengoods' house on Tenterden Street.

"Not this time, elf," he answered. "I'll pop in tomorrow, though; Sally's invited me to supper. However, I intend coming by somewhat earlier to pick up the boys. I promised them a boating expedition."

Mattie gasped, "You're jesting. You must be! Sally told me that your relations with Rhodney and Jacob were strictly *en passant*. Do you really plan on taking them out in a boat!"

"No," he pronounced, leaving her to shake her head in confusion. "When I said 'boating expedition,' I meant we are going to Green Park with the toy ships I gave them last Christmas."

"Oh?" she said cautiously.

"Yes, you see, when I heard about how you found those rascally boys so entertaining, I decided to look them over more closely myself. I discovered that they were somewhat likable, after all."

"And such sober, well-behaved young gentlemen," she said, keeping her tones bland. She had found that there was something about the earl's *uprightness* lately which made it impossible for her to resist trying out a *hum*.

It was his turn to sound cautious. "But what's that you say? I understood that they had the reputation for being lively little fellows."

"Lively? Rhodney and Jacob?" She fixed him with disbelieving eyes. "Well, they never complain of suffering any boredom," she owned truthfully, "but then, they aren't the ones who must be at pains to entertain anyone, are they? Oh, it sometimes exhausts me entirely for trying to hold their interest. Why, little Jacob can go hours without saying a single word!"

None of which was a lie, Mattie thought with fiendish enjoyment. Both boys could jump from one game to the next, within the space of a heartbeat. It gave her no end of trouble to finish anything started. And as for three-year-old Jacob, he really could babble the most long-running stream of nonsensical gibberish anyone *ever* heard.

The earl looked surprisingly disappointed. But by the time his groom got to his horses' heads, and his lordship came around to hand Mattie down from the carriage, he apparently had reconsidered. "Mattie?" His eyes glittered with shafts of blue light. "I won't say I have never been caught on a blind suit before, but before you try to come the double-shuffle with me again, perhaps you should understand something."

"And that is?" Her eyes developed a matching sparkle.

"Well," he said, quite as blandly as any, "you might just remember that I am capable of being led only so far. Beware. A day may come when you discover my ideas about giving 'Tint for Tant.' "

Mattie was still grinning when she got upstairs to her room. She tossed her parcel onto the mantlepiece, put away her outerwear, then plumped herself down on her bed.

"What a wonderful day!" she cried aloud in glee. The earl, who had been acting awfully *uppish* ever since seeing her go into long dresses, was at last recovering his humor. That was important. Censoriousness was no more becoming to him than that dreadful, rackety image he had presented to the world aforetimes. The man she knew, the man he really was, was the charming gentleman who had showed concern for a scruffy lad who had taken a fall to the pavement. He was the man who had given that same "boy" a seat in his theatre box and then had apologized—and in his own delightful style—for behavior which had offended.

And he wasn't pursuing women of dubious character these days. He was pursuing students. From a discussion she'd heard between Vincent and Jeremy Ellengood after dinner the evening before, Vincent was serious about teaching his fellows the science of boxing, virtually to the exclusion of all else! Mattie wrinkled her nose. It didn't sound like any kind of activity which she might enjoy. But she shrugged her small shoulders, thinking that at least boxing was done to a purpose.

And another thing. Mattie realized that, even on the

night of the Countess of Jersey's party, she hadn't once seen the earl at drink. Oh, he might take a glass of white wine at the start of a meal and a glass or two of red later on, but he seemed to imbibe nothing more. She knew. She watched him closely.

The day seemed one destined for making discoveries. By the greatest good fortune, Mattie had also learned who was behind the burglaries. Well, to be more accurate, she had marked two likely suspects and had eliminated a third. For when his lordship had let her down at the bookseller's and had chosen to remain on the street with his horses, she had made use of the opportunity. She had dashed inside the printing shop, pointed out the needed item, then slipped out a back door while her package was being wrapped. Accustomed to the ins and outs of tradesmen's buildings, Mattie found it naught but the simplest matter.

Her idea was to come from behind to Hamlet's corner entrance, knowing the earl's position farther along the street must prevent him from seeing her. But as she was hurrying past the rear of the jewelry shop, someone began opening its heavily barred back door. After making the corner, curiosity caused her to turn and look back down the alley.

All she saw was the outside of the door, below which, she made out a worn pair of shoes. Tarnished buckles over scuffed brown leather, the man tarried while he spoke to someone inside the shop.

"An' yer wants 'um Saturday next?" came the guttural accents.

Mattie was sure that the speaker was the man whose shoes she could see, because the response emerged with a more muffled, distant sound.

"Yes," said another man from inside the building.

"And be sure you come at this same time. Will that be a problem?"

"Naw. Me an' Willy can do it well enough. So that's Bird Street, No. 21, and after darkmans next Froiday, roight?"

"Right. The Darcys are attending the concert at the Rotunda that night, and her ladyship will be picking up the repaired items that afternoon."

"But what if she wears 'um ta the Gardens?" asked the man with the tarnished buckles. "It's them big emeralds we wants, oin't it? A foine thing it 'ud be, us goin' ta all this trouble jest ta have nothin' ta show fer it. This here's the first new dose we've had in nearly three weeks!"

A deprecating snort came from the speaker inside. "Not the least chance of that, my man. No lady would wear something so expensive to a public garden. Not even to the Rotunda at Ranelagh's. You can take my word for it, Mrs. Darcy will leave her jewels at home. And as she was so obliging as to tell me when she brought the necklace in to have the catch repaired, she keeps her jewelry in a leather case, beneath a large tin of pomatum in the third drawer of her dressing table. Foolish of her, really."

"Oi'm after 'um, then. Jest be ready ta tip me the dues . . ."

Mattie waited to hear no more. She hurried on inside Mr. Hamlet's jewel room and had boldly asked for Mr. Hamlet.

When the assistant who came forth to greet her owned that he was only person available—it being the owner's practice to attend a guild meeting every Saturday, he said—she presumed she had her thief. She was sure of it after she inquired about some amethysts her "footman" had located at Mr. Chigwell's shop, and the assistant went all over pale.

But he seemed to recover quickly. "Oh, there's no need to discuss the matter with my employer, miss. Those pieces were my own dear departed mother's," he emphasized with a soulful look. "Sadly, necessity forced me to sell them away, for they weren't of sufficient value for this establishment's clientele, you understand. But I fear that, knowing I am Mr. Hamlet's assistant, Mr. Chigwell must have assumed the items had a connection to the business here. Foolish of him, really."

Mattie was out of the jewel room and back to the print shop in jig time, excited over what she had learned.

A decision about what to do with her knowledge was not quite so easy, however. Mattie rolled over on her stomach and cradled her chin on her elbows.

She could go to Bow Street and make a report. Yet even when her evidence was added to what Mr. Chigwell could tell, most probably only the shop assistant would be caught and charged. Whether the shop assistant subsequently gave information on his accomplice or not, Buckle-feet and his henchman might get away.

Mattie wanted more. She wanted all three miscreants arrested, and she wanted Charlie Coomber to keep his job.

Thus, her dilemma. If Charlie was to be the hero of the hour, he must have an active part in apprehending the thieves, proving to all that he was capable of protecting the neighborhood assigned to him. To do that, though, he would need something more than a gnarled old staff and his rattler. He would need . . .

But of course!

Mattie had her solution!

* * *

By any account, the Right Honourable the Earl of Staffield was a Corinthian of the first order. A dab hand at the reins and a neat one in the ring, he knew himself *fly* to every rig and row in Town. He did, in truth, have ample reason for feeling a measure of confidence in himself.

Vincent believed that he had likewise convinced Mattie that he couldn't easily be gammoned. There must be no rubbing shoulders with the coalheavers and costardmongars in St. Giles, nor any other of that ilk, for he wanted the curly-haired little minx for his own. He was playing for keeps with her.

"Well, are you in, or are you out?"

"Hmm? What's that?" Vincent looked up.

"Do you want to stay in or not? Guy just raised the bid, Nick is in, and so am I. Now, are you playing this hand or aren't you?" Mr. Evant shoved his green visor farther back on his head, a look of expectation on his face.

"Oh." Vincent glanced down at his cards.

He had come to White's after letting Mattie off at his cousin's, thinking to pass a pleasant evening. It had been a while since he had found time to stop in at his club, and he had always a partiality for the late suppers they served. Sir Guy, Lord Maines, and his friend Mr. Evant had wandered in not long after him, and inasmuch as no one had any particular plans, they had all sat down to a round of cards. It was an activity Vincent had expected to enjoy.

"Out," he said.

He went back to his musings.

What a one she is, he considered proudly. Mattie

came up to scratch at each and every call. She took what she could "earn," as she put it, but was just as quick to deal out a leveler if someone handed her too much. Neither was she shy in the close. She went toe to toe with him over his any least mistake, any small error of judgment. If she thought he dallied with women or drink—or merely mislaid his house keys!—she took him up on it right smartly. His Mattie was pluck to the backbone.

The little lady could plant quite a facer, too. Less contentedly, Vincent toyed with a painted wooden counter, recalling her disparagement of his much-valued sense of sportsmanship.

He concluded, though, that her response had been no more than a fair exchange for his own earlier slur. She absorbed life's blows, then returned one just as stout. Year after laborious year, she had done the needful, helping to support herself and her great-aunt. But he'd be willing to bet that she had never lost her smile, never gone into a funk over having lost her rightful position in the world. So, while she seemed to expect a lot of him, Vincent decided that it was no more than she expected of herself. She was a match a man could take pride in.

"I tell you, he isn't listening."

Vincent rolled an ironical eye to the speaker. "Am I missing so much, then, Guy? It's not just more of the same prittle-prattling foolery? Don't tell me you were discussing Trevithick's latest steam device, or perhaps, the late Tax on Income."

Sir Guy guffawed. "Bless me, Vincent, it's no such thing! The topic is of much more consequence. Assure you, it is!" He laughed again.

"Well, my bet's as good as entered in the Book," said Mr. Evant. "We were just speculating, however, about whether you'd care to add to it, Vincent." He pushed his visor up higher on his head, then reached to take a swallow from the wineglass beside him.

"Damn right, you should be in on this, Vincent," Sir Guy put in. "After all, this concerns you closer than the rest of us."

"Oh, speak for yourself, Guy," Lord Maines repined. "I haven't completed the course yet, y' know. The young lady may actually prefer my suit when all's said and done." He twiddled with a silver whip point dangling from his lapel.

"Against Vincent?" Sir Guy's mirth commenced anew. "No offense, Nick," he chortled, "but that's about as likely as that bob-tailed nag of your friend George's winning the next race at Newmarket."

The viscount's narrow features twisted into a wry smile. "Well, it's an outside chance, I admit, but it could happen. On the other hand"—he looked round the table and sighed—"I told George to pull his horse while he can still get his track fees refunded. I suppose I should heed my own advice and step aside, too."

"Oh, I give up," Vincent said, beginning to smile. Nick's long-faced look was about to send *him* into laughter, and he didn't have a clue as to what everyone was talking about. "Will someone please take pity on me and explain what it is I'm supposed to put my money down on?" he begged.

"What'd I tell you? He *wasn't* listening!" Sir Guy was practically beside himself by this time. He slapped his thigh and stamped his feet in merriment. He got out between gusts of laughter, "You're supposed to bet on yourself, Vincent. Yourself!"

Vincent looked from one man to the other. "For? Or against?" he asked, his mouth starting to twitch.

Sir Guy was too convulsed by laughter to answer, while Nick merely looked mournful. It was left to Mr. Evant to explain.

"The mam'selle," he said concisely.

Whatever inclination for amusement Vincent had felt before vanished without a trace. Maintaining an impartial look, with slow deliberation, he placed his wooden counter down on the table. He felt every succeeding word like a blow.

Unaware of the possible effects on his listener, Mr. Evant said, "Well, I'm betting the little lady chooses a partner-for-life before the first Winter Assembly in October—too many bees buzzing around La Petite Belle for things to be otherwise, I'd say. And Guy has it that because you had dinner with her at your cousin's on one particular night, and he got a punch past you the very next day, you are already smitten with the pretty young lass." He gave Vincent a quizzical look. "By gad, Vincent. If that's the way of it, then, as your friend, you should tell me. I want the chance to add to my bet!"

Vincent had learned how to guard his expressions from the first time he had taken a fall from a horse. He had been six years old and hadn't wanted to let his mother know he'd been hurt. She was a woman who, never having enjoyed the best of health herself, suffered the severest anxieties over the well-being of her only son. And later, after his parents were gone, he had found the talent useful. A man holding a winning hand shouldn't announce the fact too soon, nor should an opponent in the ring know when a vulnerable spot was hit. But he had never found it more difficult to hide his feelings than now.

None but the most perspicacious of observers might note that the lightness of his tones was at variance to the dark, attentive look in his eyes. "How do you plan to enter these concerns in the Betting Book?" he inquired without inflection.

Mr. Evant was not so observant. He said eagerly, "I'm thinking to write mine as: 'A Certain Young Lady of French Descent shall fix her Interest on or before October 1 of this Year.' Guy's entry will have to say something like: 'A Fixed Star in the Pugilistic Hemisphere shall announce his Intentions toward A Certain Young Lady, no less than 45 Days hence.' Our proof, of course, must be an announcement, chronicled in the London news sheets."

"I see." Vincent forced himself to continue pleasant. He turned next to Lord Maines and asked evenly, "So who besides you, Nick, is interested in Mlle. Serinier? Is there anyone in particular?"

"Oh, well, George *was,*" the viscount answered him. "But after she followed you around all night at that reception we went to at his mother's, and then she turned him down for a perfectly unexceptionable invitation this past week, well, what was he to think? She's new on the town, ain't she? Yet she showed no interest in making up a party with him for the theatre. She stayed home and took supper with your cousin—and with you, if I don't mistake."

Vincent ignored the implication. "You do realize that her great-aunt cannot find it easy to accompany her," he managed smoothly, "while Sally may not wish to go out much at this time."

"No, that can't be it," the viscount disagreed. "Lady Jersey sent word that she would be happy to play chaperone. But La Petite Belle turned thumbs down with a farrago of prettily made excuses which, George said, he knew for the polite lies they were."

Vincent thought of the night Mattie had so enjoyed her first play. He knew she wouldn't easily give up another such chance. But he kept his features in repose, despite this telling indication of Mattie's true feelings. He wanted to shout in triumph but said only, "Then where does that leave you, Nick? Are you seriously interested in Mlle. Serinier?"

It didn't so much matter, except Vincent considered it wise to know his competition.

"Yes, and no, really."

Vincent held his breath.

"Yes, I like her very well . . ."

The blood from his body seemed to pool at Vincent's feet.

". . . but I can't say my interest is serious."

The earl breathed out slowly.

"Can't blame her if she has set her sights on you, though." The viscount swung a fist to Vincent's shoulder. His eyes crinkled at their down-tilted corners. "You're the best friend I have, don't y' know? So if the little lady will have you, then I'm for it!"

"Oh, I'll drink to that," said Mr. Evant.

Simultaneously, his three friends rolled their eyes to the ceiling and groaned.

"Er, tomorrow. I meant, I'll drink to that tomorrow." Mr. Evant set down his glass, without so much as a sip, then straightened the pack of playing cards before returning to his duties as dealer.

Chapter Sixteen

"Come in," Madame Serinier sang out when Vincent knocked at the door to her sitting room. "Oh, how very good it is to see you, Lord Staffield!" She pushed her needle beneath the last, silvery stitch she had set into some bit of white fabric, then dropped the whole into the workbox beside her. "But I'm afraid Madeleine isn't with me, my lord. She is usually to be found in her room during this time of day. Shall I send for her then?"

Vincent came in and closed the door behind him. "Actually, I wasn't looking for your great-niece, Madame. It is to you I would speak."

The old lady offered him a seat, then folded her hands placidly in her lap. "Will you care to take tea or, perhaps, some other refreshment?"

"No, nothing for me, thank you." For some reason, he felt a trifle awkward. Usually, he was comfortable in Madame Serinier's company. He decided to make certain *she* was at her ease, before bringing up the point of his visit. "So, please tell me, Madame, how do you fare here? Do you find everything to your satisfaction? I know you had some initial misgivings."

"Why, thank you for asking, my lord. And I am happy to say that you were right on all counts. The Ellengoods are just as you described them, and the boys are absolute darlings. It may please you to know that young Rhodney has already learned his letters *and* his numbers in French. As for Jacob"—she gave an affectionate laugh—"there never was a sweeter little soul."

Having spent an incredibly strenuous afternoon with the boys in Green Park a few days before, Vincent was at pains not to cry exception to this encomium. He had found Jacob dangerously interested in first the milch cows which roamed the area, then the reservoir, and then back to the milch cows; while Rhodney chased after his brother, the cows, the park deer, or anything else that moved! Apparently, toy boats were not fast enough to hold their attentions for long.

Vincent had since determined that, come next Christmas, he would gift them with a merry-trotter.

But to their doting kinswoman he said simply, "Yes. Quite so. And, ah, Mme. Leteuil, how does she go on? Everything all right there?"

"But yes, we are making excellent progress. The new dress shop will be open before the first of next month; the workmen have almost finished the inside painting. And since the reception at Lady Jersey's, I cannot tell you how many ladies have begged for the name of our modiste. Oh, we shall soon see as many new customers as anyone could wish!"

"It sounds as though everything goes well there, then."

"Oh, we have dealt with a few complications, of course," the old lady confided. "We were in something of a coil when the two girls who assist Marie Leteuil received permission from their parents to marry—they have been walking out with the young men of their choice for some months now, I believe. Neither Marie nor I could think what we were to do about replacing them! But it seems there will be no problem about them continuing to work, after all. Thanks to Madeleine." She smiled in contentment.

Vincent wondered what Mattie could have to do with it. It was his understanding that, insofar as the two grisettes were concerned, "Matt" had moved to Yorkshire. Mattie's only contact with the girls these days was through letters "posted" by Mme. Leteuil.

"It was your great-niece who found the means to settle the matter?" he asked, curious. "Is that so?"

"My, yes, and she managed it beautifully, too!" Madame replied. "When my little one learned that the girls had at last had word from France, she suggested that, as our wedding gift to them, they should each have a small interest in the new shop. Their young men were thence willing that they should carry on with their work for Marie. Was that not a clever resolution?"

This was a question he could respond to with enthusiasm. "Entirely clever, Madame! Mattie is that and so very much else besides." He drew in a fortifying breath and came to the purpose of his visit. "That is why I wished to see you today. Perhaps you will think me precipitous, but your great-niece and I have been spending a deal of time together recently—out for drives and our evenings spent here—more than sufficient for me to know, and to know beyond any doubting it, that she is the woman I would marry. She is so, so incredibly alive! There can be no one like her. Not anywhere!" A radiant smile lit his face. "And I have some reason to think," he

239

said, his voice filling with warmth, "that she has a like care for me."

Madame Serinier nodded. "She does, yes." At his quick, searching look, she revealed, "Oh, Madeleine has said nothing specific about it, but I know what I see in her eyes when anyone so much as mentions your name. Hers is a look which cannot be mistaken. As for 'precipitous'?" She laughed in pleasingly musical notes. "Well, we French are not like you Englishmen, who seem to believe that young lovers need time to know their minds. Whatever thoughts the mind contains are ever summed up in the *heart.*"

Vincent supposed he hadn't considered it from quite that perspective before, yet he rather thought *la Marquise* was right. He said, "Just as well for me that you are her guardian, then. My cousin-in-law might have delayed my application beyond bearing, all the while thinking himself prudent for it."

"It is well, indeed." Her eye fell dark upon his. "My dear young sir," she said then, more intently, "Madeleine is twenty years old. You are familiar with the ordeals she has suffered? The losses of home and family? If so, you must appreciate that she has experience aplenty of life. She also has her own special way of surmounting each difficulty as it comes."

He responded with another wide smile. "How true. But lest you think me too top over heels to realize it, Madame, I am also aware that Mattie inclines, perhaps, to move so swiftly forward at times that she forgets to look at what's behind."

"Just so!" the old lady trilled, looking enormously pleased. "In turn, you can understand why I believe you needn't delay in putting forth your proposal. My little one could have no patience for a more deliberate suitor.

And I have your cousin Sally's assurances that, although your past might have involved some foolishness, you, my lord, are no fool."

Vincent had no similar accolades to bestow upon his cousin. He recalled that it was Sally's hints to Lady Jersey which had inspired George Villiers to pursue Mattie's affections. Vincent dismissed his resentment, however, recognizing that the Swells would have been stirred to interest without anyone's interference. At least the members of his particular set of friends had agreed to refrain from penning entries in White's Betting Book regarding Mlle. Serinier's marital future.

With that very future in mind, he said, "Then I have your consent, Madame? I may address your great-niece?"

"I will send word for her to come. We shall have her answer at once!"

But the earl was not to receive any immediate answer. Mlle. Serinier was not in her room, nor could a search of the house discover her.

In the inevitable, ensuing uproar, Lady Ellengood came to report that no carriages had been called up, neither were any of the maids gone to accompany the mademoiselle on any errand. "I just don't know where she could be," Sally said in some alarm. "Surely, Mattie would not have gone out by herself, would she?"

Vincent didn't even have to think about that one. "She would," he declared positively. With some understanding of how such a statement might add to everyone's upset, he added with more compassion, "Sally—Madame, you both know that Mattie is long accustomed to going about on her own. I'm certain she must have decided to check the proceedings at Mme. Leteuil's new location, never thinking that anyone might be concerned over her absence. It is but a few streets away; to Mattie, that might not seem very much of a distance." When the two ladies appeared to accept this, he bowed. "So. By your leave, I will just go and bring her back home. You will not regard it if I don't bring her here directly, I trust?"

They both shook their heads, at the same time, looking not a little bewildered.

"Good. Because there are one or two things I want the chance to say to her first!" Starting for the door he muttered, "Oh, and what I *won't* have to say to that young lady."

Mattie knew something was wrong the minute she climbed in through the window at the end of the upstairs hall. She could hear raised voices, echoing hollowly up the front stairwell, accompanied by the sound of hurried footsteps. From above and below, doors were opened and then closed again in a steady succession.

"Blown!" she whispered, dashing down the hall to her room.

She scrambled out of her shirt and breeches and exchanged them for a day dress as quick as a fish turns in water. In mere moments, she left the bedchamber on tiptoe to steal a peek from the landing.

The hall underneath churned with servants. From their excited comments, wafting up from below, Mattie deduced that it was just as she had feared. She was indeed the object of a search!

"Dished," she whispered next.

There was only one thing for it. She ran back down the corridor, tucked up her skirts, and started down the leaden drainpipe. She managed surprisingly well, too, until she perceived that coming down was not going to be the problem. A complication arose when she crossed the back garden and came face to face with a twelve-foot-high, two-foot-thick, stone wall.

Her regular practice was to climb to the top of the stonework, beginning with the aid of a corner planting of wisteria. The sturdy vinelike plant enabled her to reach a stout oak branch which dipped over into the Ellengoods' property from a tree planted in the alley. It was Mattie's practice to get a grip on the oak, then swing her heels high enough so as to clamber onto the top of the mortared wall. From there, she had only to climb down the tree itself, so to reach ground level.

From this side, though, and in a fragile gown of elminetta cotton, it seemed impossible to perform these same moves.

The Ellengoods' back garden had a gate, of course, but it was kept locked. This, in case Rhodney or little Jacob should take it into their heads to wander. Mattie had no idea where to find the key; she had never needed it before!

Well then, the wall it would have to be.

She had let down her skirts after reaching the bottom of the drainpipe which passed alongside the upstairs window. Now, concealed by a screen of yellow-flowering laburnum, she hitched the delicate fabric up again, using the ribbon at her waistband to secure it. Once sure that the gown would hold above her knees, she began carefully working her way up the thick tangle of wisteria. It seemed to take forever, but in time, she grasped a hold on the heavy oak branch.

Her first attempt to swing her feet to the wall's summit failed. She bit her lip and concentrated harder, summoning up every ounce of her strength. The second try succeeded. She was soon standing to her height on the stonework, brushing the errant bits of leaf and bark from her hair and hands. While hidden from view by the spreading tree leaves, she readjusted her skirts, preparing for the next climb down.

"You intend going out—*again?*"

"Ye gods!" she yelped, her voice coming out hoarse and frightened. Only quick reflexes and a nearby oak limb saved her from toppling right to the ground!

She stared down into dark, knowing eyes, then relaxed a mite. "Oh, it *would* have to be you," she grouched. "Did you know I was missing?" She then had to blush for the vapidity of mind which would frame such a ridiculous question.

"Yes," Vincent answered. He sounded calm. "I have been out looking for you, as a matter of fact."

"Oh."

Mattie felt smaller than she ever had in her life. The superiority of her position didn't seem to matter a whit; neither did his tranquil expression relieve her. *Done up out of hand,* she realized, thinking of what must come next.

"Well, I didn't mean for anyone to discover me," she said, her voice roughening in distress. "But there were a couple of friends I had to go see. And you might as well know," she rushed on, wanting the worst behind her, "that I went out as 'Matt.' And I was just now leaving again, hoping to slip back into the house where I could begin making my apologies to everyone."

His lordship no longer looked calm. "What?" he practically shouted. "We had an agreement, you and I!"

"We did. Yes, we did." She could scarcely look at him. "But I didn't go against any of the terms we made, not really, because I—"

His disgusted look cut her off. At her silence, he reproved in razor-sharp tones, "Well now, let me see if I understand all of this. You have been out visiting with no-saying-what sort of old *chums*—people who know you as a little dandyprat of a boy, I presume?" At her reluctant nod, he continued, "And these are people whom you call 'friends,' yet who aren't privileged to know your actual identity. Am I being accurate so far?" When she nodded again, he resumed, "But was it not you who once explained to me about how 'friendships command honesty'? Do I state that correctly? Isn't that what you said?"

Mattie wished she were *under* the wall, not on top of it.

"Yes. Yes, I said that," she grumbled, giving a tug to the just-tied ribbon at the front of her gown. "But I've already told you where I had been and what I had done."

"Dammit, Mattie!" he expostulated, making her drop her hold on the ribbon. His eyes shown nearly black in outrage. "So our pact—everything we said to each other!—it means exactly nothing. Am I to conclude that *I* have no importance to you, either?"

She gauged his expression for but the briefest instant. "Catch," she suddenly commanded.

And with no more warning than that, she jumped off the wall and straight into strong, hastily upraised arms.

Now that she was where she could obtain a better look at him, she confirmed that it wasn't so much anger in his eyes as it was hurt. Her own eyes filled with sympathy. "Oh, but I didn't mean to grieve you so. Truly, I didn't!" She made a quick little movement to regain her feet. When he loosed her, she straightened her skirts, spread her feet slightly apart and locked her hands behind her. "You will listen to me, won't you?"

He didn't seem too happy about it. Nonetheless, he gave his consent. "Very well. I'm listening."

Gripping her hands tightly together at her back, Mattie returned his stern look and said, "You had my oath that I would not run errands for anyone. I haven't. You had my promise that I would not speak in accents at variance to my mode of dress. I have complied with that as well."

He winced. Visibly.

"Oh, I know things haven't gone quite as you intended, but if you think on it, you must be glad!" At his staggered look, she said hurriedly, "Because otherwise, there could have been no agreement at all, don't you see? I'd not have come to terms with you if it meant denying friendships I've kept for ages—why, I've known Billy and Kevin ever since they took their first employment!"

He seemed to unbend a little. "I take it that Billy and Kevin are very young men? Boys, perhaps?"

She smiled. "Well, at the age of thirteen, they should prefer to hear themselves called *young men,* I don't doubt. Billy makes deliveries for Yatewoody Stationers' Shop, and Kevin distributes handbills for Astley's Royal Ampitheatre." She frowned, then said more slowly, "I'm not sure what's to become of them, though. Billy very much wants to become an engraver, but Mr. Yatewoody would have it that Billy's sight is not strong enough to justify granting him an apprenticeship. Billy didn't have a vision problem when he began working there, but now, and after three years' time invested at Yatewoody's, what is Billy to do? There's not much chance of another printer's taking him on, even if he could make up the fee and begin again."

The earl pursed his lips and shook his head. "And I suppose the other lad—Kevin—suffers some similar affliction."

"Oh, no. And Philip Astley treats his employees wonderfully well! 'Tis just that Kevin's father, who also works at Astley's, thinks Kevin should advance to become a trainer with the 'Dancing Dogs.' Kevin likes dogs, but what he most wants is to perform with the equestrian acts. His father won't hear of it, though, since dogs cost less than a horse. And while Mr. Astley doesn't care either way, Kevin cannot go against his parent. Sometimes Kevin feels badly about it." She looked a bit sad herself.

"So you meet these two boys and exchange tales of woe?"

"Well, of course not!" she cried, stamping her foot. "No one complains—Billy and Kevin are jolly good sorts! But after so many years of taking coffee at the Bluebell together, well, you get to *know* a fellow. Don't you sometimes feel concern about the outlook for some one of your friends?"

Vincent thought of Mr. Evant. "To be sure," he supplied rather dryly. He then recalled himself to the present. "However, young lady, we completely stray from the point. Not to gloss the thing over, you have been running an underhanded *rig,* and it must cease. If you feel you need to remain in contact with Billy and Kevin—or anyone else—you will just have to write them a letter. I can arrange it to come to them from Yorkshire or Jamaica or wherever you like! It matters not. But this time, no under games, Mattie. You will not go visiting as 'Matt' again, or I shall consider our pact null and void. Agreed?"

Visiting, he had said.

"Agreed," she said.

Chapter Seventeen

"Oh, but this is better than a play!" Mattie gurgled happily.

Her partner whirled her into the next figure of the dance, his lips thinning in what she supposed must be a smile. Since it came from beneath that *slicing* nose of his, she wasn't altogether sure. Upon closer inspection, though, she noticed telltale crinkles in the deeply tanned skin at the corners of his eyes, proving that he was, indeed, smiling at her.

"So glad you are enjoying yourself, mademoiselle. Dare I suggest that your presence renders the evening even more delightful?" The long-faced gentleman then made her his bow, it being the end of the set. He again spread his lips and crinkled his eyes at her.

Mattie laughed and dipped into the curtsy appropriate for a viscount. She might have trouble keeping names in her head, but she had drilled for too many hours with Tante ever to forget a title or what courtesies were due to each rank. "Flattery, my lord Viscount? Oh, well, that I can always approve. Say on, sir, say on!"

He seemed pleased by her notice. But before he could add anything more, a second gentleman joined them.

"Mademoiselle Serinier," he greeted, "Sir Guy Chittenham—your most obedient." He bowed.

She was glad that somebody tonight had thought to identify himself properly. "Yes, of course—Sir Guy!" she acknowledged gaily. "And I believe I've promised you this next set, have I not?" She twirled her fan with a delicate twist of her wrist, just as she had so often longed to do.

The baronet immediately offered her his arm and heaved a great chuckle. There was no misapprehending *his* cheerful smile. He then took leave of the viscount, saying, "Ta, Nick, we're off!"

Assuredly, this was better than any play, Mattie thought, accompanying Sir Guy back onto the floor. Music surrounded her. Laughter and the sounds of a hundred conversations rose from every spot in the room. A series of performances, comedies, mostly, were being enacted here and there, as people vied for one another's attention.

She was a player, too. She tossed her head, fluttered her fan, and pranced about like everyone else. And the best of it was that she needn't remain still for a second. She could step out and *dance*. How she loved it!

Lady Ellengood had warned Mattie not to be too disappointed by the sparse numbers expected for the Wingarths' ball tonight, since it was weeks yet before the Winter Season began. Much of the *plus grande monde* was out of town, being either at a country estate, with the Prince at Brighton, or off on a jaunt to the Lake District. A few were away on foreign tours. But Mattie looked around the ballroom and saw a veritable ocean of Fashionables. She decided they more than sufficed.

She hadn't wanted to come, initially. There was a burglary to be thwarted only two nights hence, and she had intended to restrict her social obligations until after that situation was resolved. It had proved impossible for her to refuse, though. Lady Wingarth's invitation had been sent directly to the Ellengoods' house, instead of being carried by one of Mattie's admirers. The baroness and Madame Serinier had been pleased to send off their acceptance, leaving Mattie with nothing to say in the matter.

Somehow, Tante and Sally had got it into their minds that they were doing Mattie a service, too. Following a certain episode of truancy yesterday, they had decided that Mattie needed to go out. Mattie hadn't been able to think of any way to explain that she really didn't want to go, so there was just no way to avoid tonight's attendance.

However, starting with the first note of music played, she had ceased to repine. Her dance card had filled within five minutes of their arrival, almost as fast as she could greet the gentlemen whom she had met previously—and sometimes, too, before Sally could provide introductions for the others. Mattie had been caught up in a sea of heads, bending over her dance card as the gentlemen had rushed to pencil in their names.

She had relished every moment since. Whether her dance partner was discovered to be young or old, large or small, she had found each and every one congenial. And she had still more to look forward to.

The last line on her card had been signed by the Earl of Staffield.

He stood next to Tante Agathe's chair now, seemingly content to remain on the sidelines where Tante and his cousin Sally had established themselves for the evening. Tall and handsome in a dark coat of some faintly plum-colored material, his white cambric neckcloth showed brilliant against his tanned features. He hadn't danced with anyone so far, but Mattie cared only that they had their dance together.

With a swirl of her bright-hued primrose skirts, Mattie disguised her interest in the little card tied to her left wrist. The final dance was but two sets away.

After she completed the gavotte with Sir Guy, the baronet returned her to her great-aunt. He stayed on to visit with Vincent, while Mattie looked about to see who was her next partner. Evidently, it was to be the gentleman who was just threading his way through the guests toward them. He seemed vaguely familiar.

Mattie at first thought it must be someone she had met amongst their callers to Tenterden Street. Then, when he came nearer and spoke to her, she recognized him. She had encountered this man before, certainly, but not last week nor in Tenterden Street. It was weeks and weeks ago. They had met on Avery Row.

". . . a knock-down blow!" Mattie heard the baronet saying to Vincent from somewhere over her shoulder.

How right you are, she silently replied. For if her new dancing partner should happen to remember her as well, it would raise a breeze of the very first order!

"Mr. Bang," she addressed him nervously.

He grinned. "Well, I don't suppose I have ever been called *that* before."

Before Mattie could apologize for getting his name wrong, he handed her onto the dance floor.

While the other couples spread apart for a tarantella, he said, "Mr. Brummell would have it that I should be known as 'Poodle' rather than Frederick Byng, because I never go anywhere without with my dog—a poodle, you must know." When Mattie involuntarily glanced

252

about, he laughed. "No, no. I'm not so lost to propriety that I would bring Skittles along to a ball! But the Beau is correct about my partiality, so I think the nickname suits. But tell me, mademoiselle, do you like poodles?" Before she could answer him, he answered himself. "Well, I'm sure you do. You are French, after all!"

Although he was a pleasant young man, just as she had remembered, Mattie was still unable to relax. Mr. Byng seemed to examine her with some especial care, his stare becoming progressively more intense as their dance proceeded. She was hugely relieved when she learned that it was only her hair which had excited his interest.

"*Just* what I desire in my next pup," he announced when the music ended. "A little curly-haired black one would do me about right! But I do wonder," he said, studying the color of her gown, "if we shouldn't have a yellow collar. 'Twould be most elegant, don't you think?"

She accepted this as the compliment intended. "Why, yes. Yellow should be perfect, sir!"

One more baronet and she could dance with the earl. It seemed fitting that, when the time arrived, her dance with Lord Staffield would be performed to the music of the graceful polonaise.

As the violins began in three-quarter time, Mattie smiled up at Vincent. The smile he returned bathed her in its warmth, till she felt the heat of it spreading over and through her. His look was lustful but it suddenly occurred to her that it was very much more than that! Beneath that look, she felt herself expanding, growing, far beyond considerations of mere physical size. She felt herself grow to meet a man's appreciation of her as a woman.

Together, they began the slow movements of the dance. The stately Coup de Talon, practiced for so many hours, was completed without effort. Through the Chassé Coupé and the Pas de Valse, Mattie drank in her partner's eyes, eyes of a color to equal the finest Kashmir sapphires. She realized, at last, what it was to be in love.

When had this wondrous thing happened?

Mattie neither knew nor cared. Her attention was all for the gleam of candlelight on dark gold hair, all for the man at her side. He so readily gentled his strength, softening his voice and his jewel-like blue eyes, until she felt she might melt away. At each turn of the dance, when gloved hands touched, her fingers burned and trembled at the contact.

And he knows what I'm feeling, the thought rang through her mind. *He knows,* her heart repeated.

As, indeed, he did.

Vincent's gaze never left her. He absorbed the sight of shimmering, sherry-brown orbs, so intriguingly outlined by lashes which extended up and up, nearly to the base of wide-swept black eyebrows, and confirmed his heart's desire. He hadn't yet had the opportunity to declare himself to her, but he looked down and, wordlessly, revealed how he felt.

He saw the response he yearned for. Banished forever was the dreary resignation, the deadening ennui which had so long plagued him, replaced by the energies of one preposterously small little lady. Life had real meaning now.

He transferred to Mattie's other side, as the movements of the dance required. With a tiny flicker of regret, he also recalled yesterday's backhanded turn, when Mattie's latest bit of deviltry had so effectively blocked him from presenting his proposal as he'd planned. But her husky-deep voice, startled and uncertain, when he had first discovered her atop the garden wall had almost instantly turned low and dark with concern. She had literally leaped into his arms, anxious to soothe whatever hurt she had wrought . . . never thinking that she might have caused *herself* an injury. What an amazing young lady she was. And what wouldn't she be at next!

Vincent's eyes glowed with anticipation.

Tomorrow would bring a new day. He would see Mattie home to his cousin's tonight, but tomorrow he would plight her his troth.

Sally's drawing room was filled with callers. The baroness was busy at entertaining the usual circle of acquaintances who had stopped by for her regular "at home" day, and Mattie was likewise occupied with those young gentlemen who considered it all the *go* to be seen among Mattie's suite. Tante Agathe sat and sewed, chatting away with this one and that, bringing everybody of any age under her charming spell.

Mattie had all she could do to get in a "how-do-you-do" to Vincent when he entered the room. She suspected something was afoot, though, for there was a curious tenseness in his manner which she had never seen from him before. Add to that the memory of the look she had exchanged with him last night at the Wingarths' ball, then that oddly *expectant* expression on Tante Agathe's face just now—the old lady had actually set aside her needlework when he had come in—and Mattie began to understand what it meant.

Most young ladies would have been vastly pleased with such a forecast. Mattie, however, was not most young ladies. She didn't want Vincent making any avowals until after tomorrow night! For when she had slipped out to tell the old charley on Chandler Street about the burglary planned for Friday, advising him to spread the news to Billy and Kevin, she had learned that the situation was even more urgent than she had supposed. The old man had just received notice of his dismissal, effective as soon as a replacement could be found. The residents of his district had insisted.

Vincent was one of those residents. Mattie didn't know his precise views on the subject, but this was no time to put it to the test. No, if Vincent proposed now, she must refuse him an answer. She couldn't allow herself to become affianced with less than the whole truth between them, but neither dared she disclose her plans for aiding the Chandler Street watchman. No matter how great her need to make Vincent hers—no matter how much she wanted and needed a full and forever commitment—it would have to wait.

Ol' Charlie's troubles were more immediate.

Not that Mattie intended to avoid the earl altogether. She could no more stay apart from him than she could give up air! Where else might she discover a man who would reprimand her soundly for having played ducks and drakes with their agreement, and then go with her to Tante and Sally, giving silent support while she made her apologies for her unauthorized absence? There could be no other man like him.

But despite her wishes, the press of guests continued to prohibit Mattie's actually exchanging more than a few words with Vincent.

Sally had caused a cold collation to be set out in the dining room. As the morning grew late, she announced that those so inclined should feel themselves free to partake. Most of the guests began moving in the direction indicated, but Tante Agathe said she would remain at her seat, if Mattie would be good enough to bring her back a plate.

Mattie hoped the earl might excuse himself and take the opportunity to come with her. Instead, when he saw her start from the room, he strolled over to stand beside her *grand-tante*. When she returned from her errand, she discovered that he was still there.

"And your first appointment is at what time today?" Tante was just saying.

"Half past one," Vincent answered.

"So then, with three students on Thursdays, that makes nine altogether. My, my!" The old lady bobbed her head. "What a very busy man you are these days." She looked up and accepted the plate of food Mattie held. "Thank you, *ma petite*. And you included some of the Strasbourg. How nice!" She turned back to the earl. "It is my favorite dish, though Madeleine shuns it as being too pungent for her taste. But you are not having anything, my lord? I don't mean to detain you."

"No," he said, passing Mattie a cogent look, "and since your great-nice didn't bring back a plate for herself either, perhaps she might like to accompany me into the garden for a walk. With your permission, Madame?"

Oh, no! Mattie thought. *Please, not yet.*

But before she could enter any objection, Tante Agathe replied, "Certainly, my lord. I am sure no one shall mind, so long as you do not detain her for too long."

Mattie could see little choice. Besides, her heart had leaped with such joy at the thought of having even a moment's privacy with Vincent that she could not bring herself to refuse. Something extraordinary had flared up

257

between them during the sweet strains of the polonaise last night, something she could not deny.

"Mademoiselle?" He offered her his arm.

At one side of the room was a painted wooden door leading out to Sally's garden. They passed through it to enter the narrow path which meandered first this way, then that, before leading to the back gate. The path was outlined in Purbeck stone but was crowded by a profusion of late summer blossoms, pushing away from overburdened stems. Mattie had to walk right next to the earl to keep her pale orange skirts from becoming dusted with bright yellow pollen.

Near the back wall, Vincent stopped and turned to face her. They were out of sight of the house. Dark, fleshy leaves of laburnum shielded them to one side, and the wisteria-covered wall hid them from view on the other. There could be no interruption to their privacy.

Fearful, not of the large man before her, but of what he might intend to say, Mattie reacted by doing the only thing she could think of. She raised up on her toes, extended her arms till she could reach the back of his neck, and pulled his head down to a level with her own.

Sun-warmed lips met hers without any least sign of resistance. His touch came as light and natural as a butterfly's when resting on the petals of some dainty garden flower. With apparent ease and infinite gentleness, Vincent gathered her fully into his arms. He lifted her higher and yet higher, allowing her better access with each move.

The change in positions delighted her. Her only object had been to prevent his lips from speaking, but the impulse was lost as an entire series of new sensations replaced her every thought. *Oh, he loves me!* her heart sang.

She discovered that lips could dance to the tune of unheard music, each measure soft, slow, and stirring. She learned the feel of broad shoulders, heavy with muscle, beneath her searching fingers. The rhythm of his heartbeat—or mayhaps, was it her own?—played gently against her breasts, pressed closely against his wide chest. Unaccustomed languor set her to swaying in time to their kiss. She felt warm, impossibly warm, and loved.

She clung to him. She was lighter than the air he breathed, more solid and more a part of him than the most vital organ. Vincent felt Mattie's exploring lips and hands, and his heart rejoiced at each show of her enthusiasm. She abandoned herself to him without heeding the cost, wanting nothing from him but what she could give. A tiny wisp of a woman, she was generous with her love.

His heart swelled inside his chest to accommodate that love. Their kiss went on and on, past any knowledge of time. Vincent didn't think he ever wanted it to end.

The sound of someone's calling softly after them jolted Vincent back to the present. How long had they been out here?

He swiftly set Mattie on her feet, grinned at her dreamy-eyed state, and put his finger over his lips. "Stay, my sweet. I'll just see who it is." With that, his fingers flew to readjust his neckcloth as he stepped forward to see who had come.

He was surprised to see Madame Serinier coming round the path. She walked at no great speed, but in the warm weather and with her cane to aid her, she moved with little difficulty. He was relieved to note that her expression was one of inquiry, not censure.

"Lord Staffield? Oh—indeed," she said tranquilly as Mattie came up behind him. "Come here, little one," she instructed.

When Mattie did as she was bid, the old lady crooked her cane over her arm and began straightening the ribbons gone awry at the front of her great-niece's gown. Making a tisking sound under her tongue, she finished her task and again gave the earl a quizzing look.

"My lord," she said in her gentle way, "unless I mistake matters, you progressed in one area, but were diverted from your purpose in another. But there is not time for anything further now, for your presence out here has been remarked. You also have less than ten minutes before you are expected elsewhere." Coffee-brown eyes gleamed softly with amusement.

Disbelieving, Vincent withdrew his watch to confirm the hour. A crown of black curls impeded his view. A piquant little face gleamed up at him.

"Tante's right, you know. It reads well past one o'clock!" Mattie made little shooing motions with her hands. "Go. Quickly, Vincent, before you are late!"

Her adorable, gurgling laughter followed his hurried departure.

Chapter Eighteen

Mattie had been given the choice. Would they attend tonight's private musicale at the Finburys' house—or stay home, entertain themselves, then go to the Rotunda at Ranelagh Gardens for the 5-shilling concert tomorrow? Tonight, Mrs. Finbury was offering a display of her daughter Eliza's vocal talents for the *ton*'s edification. On Friday, Ranelagh's would present a concert in instrumental music, with fireworks to follow. In consideration for Sally and Tante Agathe, neither of whom really enjoyed being from home for two nights in a row, they would not try to do both.

Mattie said she would prefer the Finburys'.

In part, her decision was made because, if they stayed home tonight, Lord Staffield would likely come to the point with her. While the thought of more such kisses as she had enjoyed this afternoon was a most agreeable one, Mattie knew that, this time, she would also be put to the question. Vincent was not the type to be distracted from his purpose overlong.

As for accepting an engagement for Friday night, that was, of course, impossible. It was all very well for the emerald lady to toddle off to the Rotunda, leaving her valuable necklace at home, but Mattie would, meanwhile, be off for No. 21 Bird Street, making sure those same emeralds *remained* at home.

At least Mattie needn't concern herself about avoiding the earl over the daytime hours tomorrow. Vincent would be acting as umpire for a sparring benefit at Wimbledon Common. The current Champion of England, Jem Belcher, had suffered a severe injury to his eye, and the Fellows of the Fancy were rallying to the lad's support. The earl expected to be occupied the entire day.

"Oh, yes, we must hear Eliza sing," she declared over dinner that night. "She has a rather nervous disposition, you might know, and when we became acquainted at the Wingarths' ball over supper, she confided to me that she had quite got the horrors about having to perform in front of so many of her mother's friends tonight."

"Fine with me," Lord Ellengood said, looking up from his chine of mutton. "I'm off with Vincent tomorrow and doubt I'll be up to disporting at Ranelagh till all hours, after putting in such a day. Poor Jem," he muttered, shaking his head.

"Yes, dear, we are all very sorry for what happened," Sally said comfortingly. "Mr. Belcher was playing racquets when he was hurt, wasn't he? How awful for him! I do hope he gets through this all right."

Vincent laid down his fork and answered, "Well, I've been to see him and there's no doubt he will live, Sal, but I'm afraid he will have only the one eye to rely on now. He says he won't let it keep him out of the ring, but the benefit tomorrow is to assure that if he does return to boxing, it will not be due to any financial necessity. He's only twenty-and-two years of age—just a boy, really."

Apparently, he noticed Mattie's fumblings. Without a word, he reached into his pocket and handed her his handkerchief.

She bowed her head to dry her eyes and cheeks, blowing her nose as quietly as she could. "Sorry," she said gruffly to the table at large, when she had herself under control. "But I do think it is wonderful what you men are doing."

"Certainly, it is," Tante Agathe said gently. Then, as Mattie sniffed again, Tante changed the subject. "Now. About Miss Eliza Finbury. Is she not the one with the rather odd laugh, Madeleine? Will we enjoy her performance, do you think?"

Sally interjected in the drollest of tones, "Well, I daresay that, whatever else it may be, her singing will be very *high.*"

The Ellengoods, Lord Staffield, Mattie, and her great-aunt all fell into chuckles. Miss Finbury was known for her giggle, an annoying affectation which was, according to most who heard it, rightly described as "piercing."

It was also the very quality which had drawn Mattie to her in the first place. Miss Finbury was, in truth, the same young lady who had attracted her attention some weeks before at the Theatre-Royal, Hay-market, on the night she had shared Vincent's box. When Mattie had heard the sound again in the Wingarths' ballroom, she had sought out the girl immediately.

"Eliza will come about soon, though," Mattie next advised everyone. "She just wants a little confidence of her own. However, tonight should help allay her fears and, hopefully, put that awful laugh of hers to rest."

"Then you may count on us to give her all the applause anyone could wish," said Sally kindly.

"Oh, but, no!" Mattie objected at once. "You mustn't do any such thing!"

The baroness looked confused. "But if we are to help her gain confidence—"

"No! Don't you see? That is what's wrong already!"

Only Tante Agathe appeared to understand. She inquired softly, "Her mother?"

"None other," Mattie replied with some strength. She looked around the table. Abruptly, she arched the small of her back and elevated her chin a notch. She opened her eyes very wide to blink them once, at the same time, turning her head, ostrich-like, to slowly blink her eyes a second time. She sucked in her cheeks, pursed her lips, and said in ludicrously superior tones, "Ah! My Eliza. *So* exceptional. There can be no one to compare! *Such* a perfect pattern, a brilliant of the first water, and always so terribly *distinguée.*" She deliberately mispronounced this last, in the English fashion. "Ah, but, my dears, it is too bad other girls cannot be born with the graces—ah! and the *talents!*—of my own lovely Eliza."

In seconds, everyone at the table was scrambling for handkerchiefs and napkins. This time, it was tears of laughter streaming from their eyes. Mattie's depiction of Mrs. Finbury was to the very life.

"So, just what is it," Vincent finally squeezed out, digging his elbows into aching sides as sobs of laughter continued to rack him, "that you intend to do for the girl, Mattie?"

"Oh, do tell us!" Sally got out between bursts of laughter.

"Why, I intend to tell her that she was horrid." A hush fell over the room. Mattie took in the stricken faces and said seriously, "Oh, yes, I will say it was all ghastly screeching and turned me perfectly sick."

Again, only Tante Agathe seemed to understand. "She knows this plan of yours?"

"Well, of course." Mattie grinned. "And she also has my promise that, after she's heard the worst I can think of to say, she shan't feel nervous in company anymore. I am no musician, and so I told her! So what Eliza will understand is that she need not to care for my opinion whether real or feigned, good or bad. People hissing doesn't always mean you are bad. Applause, nor even all of her mother's assurances, proves that she has done well! She must decide for herself when an opinion ought be of some consequence."

"Hear, hear!" Jeremy roared happily, pounding his fist on the table. "Finally, a French philosophy I like!"

"And I expect every happy result," Vincent pronounced proudly.

Some hours later, while standing near the doorway to await the carriages which would take them back home from Mrs. Finbury's, Vincent leaned over and asked Mattie in lowered tones, "You do know, in spite of what you said to her, that Miss Finbury's singing was excellent tonight, don't you?"

Mattie's eyes lit. "Wasn't it, though? She has the voice of an angel."

"Will you ever tell her so?"

Mattie grinned up at him. "Oh, yes. Just as soon as I'm certain she's learned to giggle properly."

Her own laughter bubbled forth then, sounding quite like a young woman's should.

But by eight o'clock on the following evening, Mattie was as anxious as Miss Finbury had ever thought of being.

Jeremy had come in from Wimbledon Common while the three ladies were still at their dinners, so they had kept to the table until he could dress and return downstairs to have his meal in their company. They had learned that the benefit was a success—Mr. Jackson himself had made most of the arrangements—and Jeremy had been pleased to assure them that the enthusiasm of the attendees had exceeded even the most optimistic predictions.

"Gentleman John and Vincent went on over to Jem's house to deliver the day's results," he told them. "I don't doubt the young man will rest easier for it, too. I would have gone with them myself, but we agreed that it might cause the lad too much excitement if very many of us were to show up on his doorstep."

Mattie, too, wanted every detail of how the day had proceeded, but by the time Jeremy could satisfy all of his questioners, it was almost full dark and high time for her to be gone. She summoned up a yawn. Within five minutes, Sally was holding her hand over her mouth for the third time, and Tante Agathe was putting away her needles and thread.

Jeremy rose and helped his wife to her feet. He then went to assist Tante Agathe. He echoed Mattie's thoughts when he said, " 'Pon my soul! I'm glad we didn't plan on going to Ranelagh tonight." He smothered a yawn. "I'm more tired than even I had expected to be."

" 'Night everyone," Mattie called out a few minutes later, closing the door to her room. "And *do,*" she said, hurrying over to lift her mattress, "get to your beds and sleep *well.*"

Down the drainpipe and over the wall, Mattie was glad of the quarter-full moon which lent her efforts speed. She made it to Chandler Street, just as her friends were about to leave.

" 'Bout time yer got here, Matt!" Kevin cried excitedly as she rushed up to the watch box where they waited. "Billy was just now soiyin' as how we needed ter get along an' set up in our positions!" The sandy-haired youngster seemed eager to be off.

"Sorry, fellows. Couldn't get away any sooner." She glanced around their little group. "Everybody got a whistle ready?"

Young Billy looked disgusted. "Wouldn't ya just knows it? Kevin fergot 'is. But Ol' Charlie 'ere had sense enough ta bring along an extra."

The lanky night watchman said quickly, "Now, now, it weren't the least problem, boys. I figured mebbe Matt might decide to have one at the last minute."

She ran a low, exploratory scale of notes through her teeth. "Naw," she said, giving her admiring young friends the wink, "my whistler's workin' fine. Learned to call up a bargeman from 'cross the river years ago!"

"That's it, then," the old charley said, looking not a little excited himself. "I'll take this end of the street, me being the biggest to hide. It's also the most unlikely direction for the priggers to make their approach. If any of us is seen, better it should be one of you kiddies—less suspicious-like. Now Kevin, remember that you're to stay on the far end of Bird Street. Billy to the common in the back, just in case they change their habit and decide to enter that way. And Matt, you being the smallest, you'll wait directly across from No. 21, so's to let everyone know when that pair of rum dubbers has made it inside the house. Once they're in, you boys hie off for the north, east, and west, just as we planned. Use those whistles all you like! What with there being only two o' *them*"—he smacked the end of his staff soundly into his palm—"I can manage right well till you boys reappear with some assistance."

Mattie and the night watchman had calculated everything to a fine degree. Since the previous burglaries had all been by entry through the front door, they were reasonably assured that this one must follow the same pattern. They had only to leave Charlie's lantern alight at his watchbox, making it appear as if he were still within and letting the housebreakers feel safe about cracking open the lock at No. 21. Once the burglars were inside Mrs. Darcy's house, there should be at least several minutes for the boys to fetch whatever watchmen were available from the three closest neighboring districts. The nasty lot would be lumbered for certain.

It hadn't been Mattie's first plan. She had thought they could pounce upon the thieves themselves. But Charlie had turned her down flat.

"A good punch up is just what I like best," he had stolidly maintained. "Though you may not think it to look at me, I've had plenty of experience at such, so you can trust me to give a good accounting of meself! But Matt, I'll go to the constable right now if you and the other boys won't keep yourselves out o' the way o' trouble. You'll have your jobs to do, and I'm relying on you to do them in bang-up style."

Reluctantly, she realized that the old man was right. He was the only one of them with any actual experience in a set-to. Also, she considered, taking up her place in the shadows of a porch column just across the street from the emerald owner's already darkened house, her old friend was probably in the right of it. With such a long reach as Ol' Charlie had, if anything was to go wrong, he probably *could* deliver the dubbers a well-deserved *quietus!*

At no great distance, two of the best-known pugilists of the day were taking leave of one another. One, a professional and a retired champion of the ring, and the other, an amateur of nearly as wide an acclaim, they were finished with their labors for the day.

"Bid you good night, my lord. All might not have gone off nearly so well without you. No one argued about a one of your calls!" Gentleman John Jackson stepped down from Lord Staffield's curricle. He chuckled as he started for his front door. "Not that anyone would be foolish enough to try and nay-say you. You'd have grassed 'em—done it instanter! Aye, and the fighters all know it, too. Well, shall we see you on Monday, then?"

"Yes, and thank you, John. Good night." Vincent saluted with his whip and touched up his team. He headed for home.

As was his wont when eating dinner alone, the earl had his servants to light the lamps in the library, where he would take his meal. While the room was being prepared, he went to wash away the day's dirt and grime. He came back down in a fresh shirt and comfortable breeches, topped by a long silk dressing gown. A steaming platter of sliced meats awaited, with several vegetables, breads, cheeses, and a pitcher of table beer set out nearby. He ate slowly, deliberately, trying to relax after the excitements at Wimbledon today.

They had seen a good turnout, just as Mr. Jackson had noted. But in spite of the huge numbers in attendance, there had been little actual disorder. Vincent had spent most of his time in the ring, assuring that the exhibition matches proceeded according to the rules while allowing none of the more serious consequences so common to regular bouts.

After he had done with his meal, Vincent rang for his servants to remove the remains. He gave his butler leave to dismiss the staff, thereafter to take their rest. It was getting late, and Vincent foresaw no further need of anyone's services this night.

When he returned to his room, however, Vincent became aware that he wasn't himself at all sleepy. He was instead feeling frustrated with all the delays attendant in asking Mlle. Madeleine Serinier to be his wife. And he must have a wife! He wanted and needed one lady in particular, a beautifully bound little package of energy. He wanted Mattie beside him for the rest of his days. He really couldn't wait much longer!

He thought perhaps a stroll about the neighborhood would better dispose him toward slumber.

Chapter Nineteen

Sitting alone and in the dark was horrendously taxing, Mattie discovered. It was also one of the more difficult things she had ever had to do. And notwithstanding the name of the street lying before her, not a single cat, nor even a dog seemed attracted to the area. There was nothing interesting to see or to hear—nothing to do but sit and wait, wait and sit.

The first hour hadn't been so bad. She had occupied a spot on a double-columned porch, fronting a house which contained, among other things, a scandalously irreverent bunch of servants. The lower window nearest her opened out from what was, apparently, the kitchen, so while the servants had gone about their final tasks of the day, their casual speech had drifted to Mattie's ear. She had learned that the house belonged to someone they referred to as "Her Stinginess," or alternately, "Old Lady Lick-a-penny."

Obviously, the mistress of this house was inclined to be close with her money.

Mattie had nearly laughed out loud when she had overheard a very young girl—probably the kitchen drudge, or maybe a tweeny—saying, "Sure an' when

Herself discovers tha' wee mousie under the lid o' her chamber pot tamarraw marnin', mayhaps she won't be sa' quick about forbiddin' us a nice kitchen puss. As if the price o' a few scraps of meat would empty tha' great lang purse o' hers!"

So did Mattie understand at least one reason why she'd not seen any of the furred, four-footed prowlers about.

When the servants finally doused the lights, closed up the window, and left to find their beds, Mattie darted up from her place. She had a light to snuff out herself. Using a funnel-shaped device, hung from a little brass chain attached to the lantern proper, she put out the lamp beside the front door. The street was empty, so she didn't think any would notice.

There was not much to do after that. She set about amusing herself at various mental games, knowing she must be still while biding her time. One game consisted of counting the windows, upper and lower, in the line of houses opposite her. She then divided their number by the panes which had lamps showing within. But as the evening wore on, Mattie found her games progressively less and less entertaining.

When the last window went dark, she began to fidget. Under her breath, she started humming every song she could think of. To be sure, she took care to be very quiet about it—if Ol' Lick-penny or one of the servants should hear, Mattie knew she'd be gapped for sure!

Several times, thoughts of the Earl of Staffield sought their way into a mind perforce kept idle. Scowling fiercely, Mattie pushed these thoughts away. She couldn't *do* anything about the earl just now, so she didn't want to sit around thinking of him. In her opinion, there had been quite enough of *that*.

Nonetheless, the memory of deep blue eyes or of the sound of Vincent's voice persisted in intruding. She didn't mind so much about the eyes, but the voice was something again.

Strictures about honesty came in that voice, and it was her own words he had repeated. While she knew she hadn't really been *dis*honest with him, the reminder of her words recalled her to certain omissions. Those omissions were adding up.

Her original "white lie" to Vincent had come about when she had introduced herself to him as "Matt." There had been nothing particularly wrong in that. He had no right to know anything more about her than what she had been willing to tell. Not one of her words had been an outright lie; her conscience remained undisturbed by his assumptions.

Next, she had let the earl believe that he had her agreement to keep herself in skirts. Mattie had to own that, for this last, she was left feeling slightly less comfortable.

When they had initially come to terms at Lady Jersey's reception, she had taken advantage of the situation, much as she had done when she had allowed Tante to think she was going to the theatre in company with Brigitte and Claudine. Mattie hadn't been wholly complaisant about her actions in either instance, but neither had her conscience pained her exactly. She had balanced her own desires against the likely harm and had made her decision. On both occasions, it had proved to be a decision she could live with.

But by the time Vincent asked for confirmation of their pact, things had changed—and rather drastically, too. She had known she loved him and that he loved her! Such love might not commit her to making disclosures about everything she knew, but it did forbid her to intentionally mislead her beloved.

For that, her conscience did pain her.

Gad, but I've sunk myself this *time*, she mourned.

But she didn't have long to grieve over her shortcomings. A pair of well-dressed gentlemen were treading their way unevenly along the pavement on Mattie's side of the street. They appeared to be the worse for drink. She ducked into the shadows.

Only after the men had gone by did she peep around the column and follow them with her eyes. They looked very much alike with their tall beaver hats and long, full evening capes. And yet, by the thin light of the moon, she observed something amiss. There was something notable about one of them, other than his tipsy, irregular gait.

Since when did a gentleman—however deep in his potations—wear shoes of broken-down leather topped by dull metal buckles?

On the alert, Mattie watched the two "gentlemen" shuffle nearly to where the old charley was hidden. To her relief, the men halted before reaching the corner and crossed over. They started slowly back up the footpath, this time coming up from the other side. She wasn't surprised when they stopped and lingered in front of No. 21.

Mattie was doubly cautious about keeping herself concealed. Her circumspection was repaid. The two men looked about them, then began ambling up to the doorway. The one she suspected was "Buckle-feet" dropped to his knees in front of the door, while the other man stood budge. In virtually no time, Mattie saw the door swing inward.

Both men entered the house across the way.

Not a moment after they had shut the door behind them, Mattie leaped from her place on the porch. She raced far enough down the street so that she wouldn't be seen from the windows of No. 21. She emitted a shrill series of chirrups, much like the sound a sparrow will make when a cat disturbs its nest. It was the signal to her friends that the burglars had *cracked the ken*.

Pulling her hat low against possible dislodgment, she took off running again. Only after she was well away would she begin a different tune, one which would summon another night watchman for help.

Old Charlie came bolting up from his hiding place. As they passed one another, he stretched an arm to give her hat a friendly tug. "Good work there, Matt. Off with you, now!" he whispered puissantly.

She ran as fast as she could. Past the first corner and on down toward Brook Street, where she could make the turn east. From there, she would go on to Hanover Square, where the next watchbox was located. Watching for any irregularities in the barely lit path which might cause a misstep, she set her feet to flying, faster than ever they had done.

Traveling in the opposite direction, although at a considerably slower pace, the Earl of Staffield stopped dead in his tracks. No matter that he had spent the entire day as a respected umpire at Wimbledon, he feared his vision had failed! For he could swear he saw "Matt"—floppy-brimmed hat, baggy knee breeches, and all—just evading the grasp of his district's night watchman!

It can't be, he reassured himself. But as the lad came at him at a spanking rate, and in a hat pulled too low to see much ahead, Vincent knew his *own* eyes told him true.

Quick as a housekeeper's broom, he whisked himself into her path.

As her small body hurtled headlong into his, he rotated a half-turn to reduce the shock. Still using her momentum, he whirled her around the corner and out of sight of the watchman.

Mattie found herself dragged down the steep, darkened steps of a below-street servants' entrance. The sharp scent of sandalwood, in such close confines, nearly overpowered her.

"Vincent? No, let me go!" she all but yelled.

His only response was to enfold her more tightly within his arms. When she squeaked in surprise, he flung her hat to the ground and covered her mouth with his.

She thought she might drown in sensation. Her first gasp for breath brought warm air rushing up from his lungs to fill hers, almost to overflowing. And just as if she had no other matters of weight to concern her, she gave a little shiver and surrendered herself to the intimacy, his embrace thrilling her from head to least tiny toe. She leaned into him—he at door level, she a step up. She wanted him closer, this very large man, much closer.

But for once, apparently, he recalled time's constraints. He pulled his lips away and said gently, "Be easy, my dearest, and trust me. Everything will be all right. I won't let anything harm you."

That brought her head up. "Oh, but you cannot understand, for I have to—"

He smothered her into his chest, one hand cradling her head. "Hush, hush, sweetheart," he murmured, stroking a thumb across dusky curls. "I'll take care of it, you'll see. Whatever it is, I'll take care of it."

No more than the earl was Mattie tempted into forgetting herself for a second time, though. "But 'tis Charlie!" she managed to rasp through layers of cloth. "He's going to—"

"I know, I know, Mattie, and it's all right. Really. He won't find you."

"Find me?" Her arms shot out then, heaving him back with some force. "Well, of course he won't find me! Vincent, I'm supposed to be helping *him.*"

Posthaste, the earl lifted her one step higher, where he could better meet her eye. "Explain yourself," he ordered softly.

Nearly frantic at the loss of time, she whispered back in a rush, " 'Tis the housebreakers—you know, the ones who have been making off with everyone's jewels! But we've finally caught them, just now, inside of No. 21 up the street! And Charlie has to hold them there till Billy and Kevin and I can bring more assistance. Oh, Vincent, I've got to go now, don't you see? They *need* me!"

She tried to turn away, urgently needing to get herself gone. She soon came to realize, however, that his arms were prodigiously longer—and stronger—than hers.

"Now, let me get this sorted out," he said quietly and seemingly in no hurry. He moved his hands to her shoulders, without quite releasing his hold. "I must assume that the one you refer to as 'Charlie' is, er, the *charley,* right? I know the fellow by sight, of course, but I don't suppose I ever thought to ask his name."

"Yes, *yes.*" She struggled, impatient beneath his big hands.

He didn't seem to notice. "So what that really means is," he continued, his voice rising by slow degrees, "for all of this time, *including* when you found me trying to relieve a muscle spasm that night in Grosvenor Square, you have been out looking for a pack of thieves. Thieves? Good God, Mattie!"

"Yes, Vincent, yes. As you say! But I have to go now and—"

"No!" he hissed suddenly, dropping his voice and giving her a little shake. "You are to stay right here. *I* will see to these thieves of yours, *and* these friends of yours, and anything else that *moves* tonight. And Mattie"—she tensed as his tones became charged with warning—"the only thing I had better not see in motion is you. Do you understand?"

"I understand!" She bounced from one foot to the other.

He released her then and started up the stairs himself. "Remain here until I come back," he growled as he passed her by.

She was still for only a moment. "But I won't stay here," she called up, "so there's no use in your thinking I will." She leaned down and grabbed up her hat where it had fallen to the doorstep.

He halted. He turned around. He seemed to swell to twice, no, three times her size. Perhaps the shadows merely created an illusion, yet standing above her as he was, she was dwarfed by any comparison.

"Young lady, I said you were to—"

"And I cannot do what you want!" she cut him off. "I have a responsibility! And I tell you, no matter what, this is something which I must see to. Myself! Oh, Vincent," she cried, "there is more than a handful of emeralds to be lost tonight, for Charlie will lose his *em-*

ployment!" She jammed her hat onto her head. Glaring up at him, she started up the steps.

As she approached, she couldn't quite make out Vincent's eyes. But his posture, looming powerfully above her, clearly revealed his anger. She kept moving forward until she was on the step just below his. She was determined that she would not be deterred, nor would she mislead him again.

She *could* see when the outline of his shoulders dropped a fraction. She hoped it meant she was winning her point. She brightened with an idea. Her voice gaining enthusiasm with every word, she made one more effort to make him understand. "If you won't let *me* do this, then *we* can! For if you really want to come too, I won't have to fetch another watchman, will I? Why, that would make everything *fine,* don't you think!" When he said nothing and didn't move, she stamped her foot for his attention. "But we have got to *hurry!"*

After that, she wasn't made to wait very long. The earl muttered low in his throat, "Abominable brat." But the hand he offered to aid her steps was sure.

Mattie grabbed for a hold and surged up the steps. As soon as they reached street level, she dropped his hand, starting off at a run. The earl caught up after a step or two, then kept stride right alongside her. At the sound of a shout from ahead, followed by the odd, clangorous racket of a watchman's rattle, as one, they burst into a final sprint.

Any number of people had already converged on No. 21. Someone in the middle of the street had even lit a torch, so that when she and Vincent arrived, they were treated to the sight of Charlie Coomber as he shoved two dazed-looking housebreakers into the light. Mattie

279

was tremendously gratified to see that one of them was Buckle-feet.

She tugged on the earl's sleeve in her excitement. "Just as I thought," she whispered up at him. "Everything *is* all right!" She caught a glimpse of a faint twitching motion, just at the corners of his lips.

Billy and Kevin spotted her amongst the milling crowd. Kevin reached her first, a wide grin splitting his face. "Did yer sees it, Matt? Did yer sees? Ol' Charlie here *basted* 'em! Me'n Billy got here jest in toime to see him *do* fer those two!"

Billy Tomkins, scarcely less excited, joined his fists and made a chopping motion through the air. "Coshed 'em both is what 'e done. The priggers never 'ad a chance ter fig'ure on what was what."

"An' Matt!" Kevin shrilled, pointing. "Would yer only looks at who all Billy called up? They was havin' a watchhouse meetin' up his way, so when Billy gave 'em the whistle, ever so many came out on the run!"

Sacrebleu! Mattie swore silently. Amongst the half-dozen or so other officers of the law, she recognized one portly figure in a flaxen wig and monstrous white hat . . . it was Mr. Townshend of the Bow Street Runners! *Some* names she *always* remembered.

She had good reason to fear that the presence of such a known *flash* one was a danger to her disguise. Vincent seemed to share her concern, for he immediately moved slightly to the front, preventing the play of torchlight from touching her. He then addressed Kevin, effectively distracting the boy from wondering at her near-disappearance.

"May I introduce myself to you, young man? I'm Staffield. Matt's friend."

From behind the earl's elbow, Mattie had to smother

a chuckle at the comical face Kevin made. His eyes grew so large, they seemed to swallow his freckles. His mouth opened too, but nary a sound came out.

It was left to Billy to reply. "Oh, s-sir," he gushed with a deal of enthusiasm, wrenching off his cap. He bowed, setting his dark hair asway along his thin cheeks. "I'm Billy Tomkins, an' as ya might knows a'ready, this 'ere's our other friend Kevin. We are honored at meetin' ya, milord!" Then, as if uncertain whether he had offered sufficient homage to a man he considered a tip-top Trump, he bobbed his head again. "*Greatly* honored."

"Honored!" Kevin cried, at last finding his voice. He, too, bowed deeply.

"Gentlemen," the earl acknowledged. He touched the brim of his hat. "It seems you have done well this night. Yes, very well, indeed."

The boys stood tall and looked wonderfully proud.

"Oh, and, of course," the earl added, his tones ineffably mild, "lest anyone neglects to mention it to you, we must not forget about the reward. As a resident of the district, I shall be pleased to see that you have it without delay."

"A reward?" squeaked Kevin.

"Reward?" Billy echoed. "But we didn't hear nothin' 'bout any reward. Is there one? Truly, sir?"

The earl answered with becoming gravity, "Why, yes. A hundred pounds goes to each of you."

Mattie was not to be stayed by such news. She leaned forward. "Charlie, too?" she asked in hushed tones.

"Certainly," Vincent replied, deftly pulling her back inside his shadow.

She grinned quite as widely as young Kevin.

Looking far less complaisant, Billy Tomkins spoke

up. "But it's Matt and Kevin 'ere who should have any rewards then, milord. Fer it was Matt as learned the assistant at 'amlet's shop were the *upright man,* after Kevin located them amethyst stones in a pawnshop over Limehouse way. We've all been a-searchin' forever—an' Chigwell's was nearly th' last 'un on our list—but afore ya be givin' me too much credit, I want their part un'nerstood."

In the middle of this speech, Mattie felt Vincent stiffen and thought she heard him groan. She decided she must be mistaken, however, when he bent his head to answer the boy. "Well, it sounds to me as though everyone's actions are to be commended. Although, as I understand it, the reward specifies that *all* persons who give material assistance are to have one hundred pounds. It wasn't a sum made to be divided amongst the participants. Oh, I say, you weren't thinking to go against the donor's wishes, were you?"

Billy looked uncommonly relieved. "Well, if'n that's 'ow it is, then I s'pose not! But, well, I wanted ta be sure, less'n mebbe I should give up my share an' let the others go snacks."

Again, Mattie felt Vincent stiffen. She couldn't imagine what was bothering him, more especially when he next suggested that she and her two friends should remove to a certain shadowy spot on the flags. He then excused himself, boldly strolling over to where Charlie was speaking with the esteemed gentleman from Bow Street!

She felt rather abandoned.

Even after the two housebreakers were hauled away for their meeting with the magistrate, Lord Staffield,

Mr. Townshend of Bow Street, and the old charley from Chandler Street continued in earnest conversation. Only one other official remained on the scene, a constable which Mr. Townshend had ordered to await Mrs. Darcy's return.

Charlie Coomber did most of the talking, supplying the portly Mr. Townshend with the details leading up to tonight's capture. "And what with those two priggin' coves caught with the goods and already bibble-babbling away like a regular pair of bagpipes," the old night watchman said finally, "looks to me like the matter is well settled!"

Mr. Townshend nodded and glanced at his occurrence book, where he had been jotting down notes all the while. He ran a chubby finger along the last page. "Then I won't need to speak to this—ah, here it is—this Mr. Chigwell until tomorrow," he said briskly. "All that's left is for me to take down what the young lads can tell me, particularly about the conversation the one named 'Matt' overheard as coming from behind Hamlet's shop. With *that* bit of evidence, I can have the last of the gang brought into custody."

"I think not," the earl interrupted.

Since he had scarcely said a word up until then, Vincent was unsurprised by the looks of astonishment which his statement engendered. The old charley seemed completely taken aback, while the rotund little policeman peered up from beneath the brim of his hat, then frowned.

Mr. Townshend promptly protested, "But surely, my lord, you aren't suggesting that I let the shop assistant go free!"

"Nor am I," Vincent responded, just as quickly. "However, I had thought you might prefer to have more solid evidence before you made your arrest. The testimony of a pair of felons, not to mention the word of some green young *chub*"—he allowed his very real scorn for Mattie's costume to color his voice—"will unlikely prove convincing in a courtroom." He then made a show of looking over to where the three boys stood. In the same, contemptuous tones, he said, "Your witness, I believe, is the one in that ridiculous, floppy-brimmed hat."

Glancing to the spot indicated, Mr. Townshend took his lordship's point. Even in the company of two other youths, the lad appeared shockingly immature. Mr. Townshend turned back to the earl. "Very well, I agree the boy is awfully young to impress a jury, Lord Staffield. And yet, without his evidence, I have no way, apart from the other thieves' testimony, to connect the shop assistant to a single burglary! Mr. Chigwell can only tell us that he purchased the amethysts from our suspect, nothing more. But you must have something in mind. Give over, my lord, do!"

Vincent appreciated the officer's willingness to listen. He only hoped his plan proved deserving of that interest. "Well," he said evenly, "with Bow Street's permission, there is a sure way to establish a connection between the shop assistant and the jewel thefts. If you'll accept my pledge of responsibility, I will take the emeralds and one of the thieves to Hamlet's tomorrow." He sketched a bow to the old charley. "Mr. Coomber's fine efforts have provided us with the means to complete the 'sale,' don't you know?"

The Runner subjected his lordship to another penetrating look. "But are you so positive, Lord Staffield, that you can convince one of those men we arrested tonight to participate in this scheme of yours? True, they

284

seemed eager to open their budgets when they left here, but that doesn't mean they'll be so cooperative tomorrow." When the earl merely grinned in a slow *knowing* sort of way, the little officer's eyes began to twinkle. He stepped back a space, in open appraisal of his lordship's inimitable and manly *cut*. "Er, yes. It may be that you can at that," he agreed.

The night watchman, quiet up till now, seemed to feel called upon to comment. He chortled and said merrily, "Oh, I can see that it's a right downy one ye are, milord. Down as a hammer, I'd say. And I've no doubt you're the man for the job if any *ever* was!"

The little man from Bow Street still required a bit more convincing, however. He considered the earl with some shrewdness. "Yes, perhaps so. But I cannot prevent myself from wondering, Lord Staffield, what makes you so interested in helping us out on this? Oh, I realize we discussed these burglaries some weeks ago, and you've done as I asked, keeping alert as it was convenient. Which, by the by," he interjected in more guarded tones, "I just recalled something. You obtained a list of the stolen goods from our offices, not so long ago. Did you know then what these boys were up to?"

"No," Vincent said truthfully. "I knew nothing more than you until tonight, although I did think to check a few places, Lauriere's for example, thinking I might encounter some of the stolen pieces."

"But why?" asked the man from Bow Street. "Why did you go to such trouble? And this plan of yours—it will require even more of your time."

Vincent answered him rather more stiffly. "It is *my* time," he reminded.

"This wouldn't happen to be just another hey-go-mad adventure to a young rip, would it?" Mr. Townshend asked sharply. "For I'll tell you right now, if that's the way of it, I can send another man out in your stead, needs be. What, I must know, is your interest here?"

Vincent knew the answer to this question. From the moment he had realized how deeply Mattie was involved—good God, she was a potential witness!—his participation was inevitable. He could not possibly allow Mattie to take the stand in a courtroom. Then, when her young friend Billy had used the word *snacks,* Vincent was reminded of how important it was to see Mattie freed of all involvement, and quite as soon as may be!

But he couldn't explain these considerations to Bow Street, of course. Instead, he said coolly, "A hey-go-mad adventure? Hardly, sir. Do you forget that this particular 'young rip' lives in this very neighborhood?" He flexed his shoulders in an overt display of temper. "I want those fellows rather worse than you do, I think!"

His performance seemed to turn the trick. Mr. Townshend relaxed and even smiled. "Right, then. I'll just be off for the station to make the arrangements necessary for tomorrow's activities. And I'll warn everyone to keep mum, too. We wouldn't want our quarry to get wind of what's in store for him before the fact!"

As the little man hustled off to get the business under way, Vincent thought it well past time for him to see Mattie home. Saying all that was proper to the charley, he also remembered to inform the old man of the "reward" he had earned. Before the earl reached Mattie and her two friends, however, another thought struck. He stopped, then heaved a tremendous sigh.

He had just realized. He would have to let Mattie enter the Ellengoods' house by the same means she had left.

Chapter Twenty

Mattie awoke late the next morning. The excitements of the previous evening had tired her, much more than the particular hour of her return to Tenterden Street. No lay-bed sluggard, however, she arose quickly and threw open the doors to her wardrobe.

A soft rainbow of colors greeted her. Most of her gowns were in white or delicate pastel shades of pink, yellow, or blue because of her age, but Mme. Leteuil had noted Mattie's glossy black hair and fine white skin and so had included some of the more vivid tones of green, orange, and even violet.

In consideration for Mattie's diminutive stature, Mme. Leteuil had taken care with the designs used for each gown. Collars and hems were trimmed with tiny ruffles and ribbons in bands of bright color, while skirts were invariably smooth, narrow lengths of fabric. Sleeves were given emphasis, and the bands used to separate bodice from skirt often had long sashes, flowing nearly to the bottom of each gown. Each detail was carefully contrived to give an appearance of height to the wearer.

Mattie looked over the collection. She was brought to

realize, of a sudden, that she would have only long dresses in her future. No more dashing through the streets in knee breeches and hose, she would be attired as a young lady for the rest of her days. She grinned. Skirts hadn't hampered her in the least during her romps with Rhodney and Jacob.

Besides that, it occurred to her that there was something utterly delightful about the feel of fine fabrics, flowing with elegance and grace at one's smallest movement. Occasionally, she had found that being dressed as a child made her *feel* like a child—insignificant and inadequate. She thought she rather preferred dressing as a young lady. And, if needed, she had already learned that skirts could be tucked up and got out of the way.

It didn't take Mattie but a minute to decide which dress she wanted to wear. She reached into her wardrobe and lifted out a yellow muslin, gaily sprigged with little violets surrounded by tiny green leaves. With slippers of bright yellow, their ribbons in colors to match, she would be dressed fine as fivepence. The shoemaker on Upper Thames's Street had been kept quite as busy as Mme. Leteuil.

And today, Mattie thought, she must look her best. Vincent would come to her. He told her that he would before they had parted last night, though warning her that he had things to see to first. He said it might be nearer the supper hour than early.

Mattie then gave a little gurgle of laughter. She had remembered how the earl had snatched her off the street and hidden her, actually thinking she had been trying to escape from Ol' Charlie. How absurd! Yet how like him. Vincent had wanted to assist her without even knowing what she was about. They had

289

talked it over for a bit on the way home last night; her smile grew softer, thinking of how deeply concerned he had been.

Her own concern had been reduced considerably by last night's events. For with the thieves caught, Charlie was secure in his employment. And with the reward money, her friends could each enjoy the future. Billy could get fitted up for spectacles at the oculist's with money to spare, Kevin would be able to buy a fine horse to train for the circus, and Charlie would have a substantial addition to set aside for his retirement.

The question was—what should she do with *her* money? After purchasing the Brussels for Tante, and then with her visits to the Bluebell to meet with Billy and Kevin these last weeks, she had to appreciate the unexpected gain.

Finished dressing, Mattie put her thoughts aside and skipped down the front stairs. She headed for the breakfast room, in hopes that Cook would have saved her at least a few of the sugared bread twists she so enjoyed. She was delighted to find a full dozen of them, waiting on the sideboard. She sat down with her plate and accepted the coffee a servant came in to offer, before she recommenced ponderation of how she might use her new wealth.

She determined that the first thing she must do was to select small, personal gifts for Brigitte and Claudine. Now that she was in funds, she wanted very much to choose something special for each of them as wedding gifts. Tante Agathe would gladly give her the money if she knew of Mattie's desires, but it was not quite the same as being able to give something solely from her own means. She remembered also that Rhodney and little Jacob had birthdays next month, and there was Sally's new babe to consider, later on.

Still, even after gifts for every occasion—including Christmas!—Mattie had more than sufficient for her needs. She supposed she would simply set the remainder aside or, possibly, invest it in Mme. Leteuil's business.

That decided, Mattie turned her mind to other matters. In particular, there was Vincent's retribution to consider. She had no idea of what might lie in store for her there; they hadn't spoken of it again on the walk home. But she wasn't overly anxious about it, just so long as it didn't mean postponing their engagement.

And he would never do that, she was sure. His last, funny little smile, when he had given her a lift up to the top of the back garden wall last night, had told her all she needed to know.

Oh, Vincent wasn't *pleased* by the events of the previous evening. But neither had she sunk herself beyond redemption. She had only to explain about her resolve to do better in the future and that would be that.

Having satisfactorily dealt with every issue, Mattie finished her coffee. She refolded her napkin and laid it beside her empty plate, then trotted back up the stairs. She wanted to see if Sally or her *grand-tante* had any plans for the day.

By four o'clock that afternoon, Mattie began to wish she had never asked if anyone had wanted any errands run. It seemed that Tante required a new assortment of silks for the embroidery she so enjoyed, while Sally hoped Mattie would have time to go by the Messrs.

Harding, Howell & Co., the drapers in Pall Mall, to see if the chintz she had ordered for new bed hangings had yet arrived. Sally also asked whether Mattie would mind stopping in at the Arcade, since one of the haberdashery shops there was the only place to find her favorite style of gloves.

To someone accustomed to such duties, it hadn't sounded like too much to do. Mattie had been glad to be of use. But when one has to travel by carriage, rather than on foot, shopping, she discovered, became somewhat complicated. A quarter of an hour was needed just to enter Pall Mall at one end and exit from the other!

As for the Arcade, well, Mattie owned that she had mostly herself to blame for the amount of time consumed there. True, the maid assigned to accompany her constantly lagged behind, ooh-ing and ah-ing over the assortment of wares displayed, but Mattie was every bit as slow herself, looking over each shop's merchandise, collecting ideas for the presents she would soon need for Brigitte and Claudine. The afternoon was all but over before she knew it.

She began to fear that Vincent would get to the Ellengoods' before she did if they didn't hurry along. But the city's streets simply would not cooperate. They continued crowded during the return journey, and their coachmen really could not proceed much faster than a snail's pace. For an instant, Mattie longed to leave the vehicle, hitch up her skirts, and run along home on her own.

Made restive at the slowness of transport, Mattie sat forward in her seat and concentrated on watching the strollers passing before the buildings on Bond Street. She saw one or two gentlemen of her acquaintance, out enjoying the day, and then, near the crossing where they would turn in to get to home, she saw Jeremy. He was standing on the corner, in earnest speech with the oddest-looking man. If she didn't know better, she might suppose Sally's husband had taken up with ruffians!

The fellow standing with the baron had a decidedly villainous aspect. He was dressed in a tattered and filthy shirt, belted loosely outside his waistband, and wore a pair of ill-fitted breeches above saggy stockings. He also sported a hat which, by any comparison, made her old brown felt look like the height of fashion! Discolored and hideously misshapen, it was the hat which disturbed her the most.

She didn't dwell long on Jeremy's taste in friends, though. She tapped the handle of her umbrella smartly against the panel, indicating to their coachman that he should stop. Even as close to home as they were, she thought it would be polite to offer the baron a ride for the rest of the way.

When the coach came to a halt, Jeremy looked round and waved. But when the baron started toward them, strangely, the odd-looking man followed right behind.

But the instant the fellow moved, Mattie knew exactly who he was. She had attended the mannerisms and bearing of individuals from every class of society, and for far too many years, to mistake the idiosyncrasies of someone previously studied. It was Vincent Charles Houghton, the Right Honourable the Earl of Staffield.

She knew her mouth gaped open, but she couldn't seem to prevent it!

He approached the vehicle, a slow grin lighting his face. "Oh, hullo there," he said.

Mattie noticed that the maidservant beside her on the seat relaxed, but her own reaction was entirely otherwise. *She* couldn't feel one iota of tranquility herself. "But Vincent," she gasped, "what can you be doing? And dressed like that? You look like the most tatterdemalion creature!"

"Ho! Doesn't he though?" Jeremy laughed. "That's precisely what I said myself. Here I was, sauntering along and tending to my own business, when he comes by me, just as you see!"

"But why?" Mattie continued staring at the earl. "What have you been doing?"

Again, Jeremy answered. "Oh, it really is the most amazing thing. Seems he's become a thief-taker! You will not have heard about it yet, since they've been keeping the thing quiet till now, but last night, there was another burglary attempt. Right up the street from us, too! Bow Street nabbed that lot, but there was a man left out—the arch rogue behind it all. So Vincent here"—he slapped a hand across his cousin-in-law's shoulders—"has been working a trap for the last of them!"

"You went to Ham—"

"*Indeed,*" Vincent swiftly checked her. He gave her a meaningful look.

She swallowed back what she had started to say, realizing that she had been about to give herself away in front of Jeremy. Vincent's reminder had come just in time. She asked instead, "But wasn't that dangerous, Vincent? I mean, the fellow you went to see could have been armed—had a pistol or something. Oh, Vincent!" she cried out, her eyes darting over his person as fear

294

egan to surface. "He must have been desperate when
ie discovered he was caught. You might have got your-
elf killed!"

"No such thing," the earl swiftly reassured her. Then,
vithout any reason she could see, his look grew entirely
oland. He continued nonchalantly, "And what is danger
inyway, when one is enjoying oneself? It all turned out
vell. So well, in fact, that I think even Mr. Townshend
vas impressed. Why, I have every hope that he may
iave occasion to make a similar use of me again." He
hen turned to Jeremy and, in the same smooth tones,
nquired, "I am still invited for dinner, I trust?"

The baron seemed unaware of anything awry. "Oh,
nost assuredly, you are. But you will go home and
hange first, won't you? I know Sally isn't easily
hocked, but as for this"—he gestured at Vincent's
iat—"it would be entirely *too*, don't you think?"

"Oh, no doubt," the earl said, removing the offending
irticle to examine it rather offhandedly. He then re-
olaced his hat in the most casual manner imaginable and
iade them adieu. He started away toward his home in
Grosvenor Square.

Just as soon as the Ellengoods' carriage had them
oack at the house, Mattie hurried inside. She ran up to
ier room and grabbed a pair of scissors. She dashed
oack out again, heading straight for Tante Agathe.

She barely waited for the answer to her knock before
he flung herself into her great-aunt's sitting room.
'Can you trim my hair before dinner, Tante?"

The old lady at once set down her needlework and
estured for Mattie to pull up a stool. It was not an un-
sual request; Madame Serinier had been tending her
reat-niece's hair for years. Madame had never suffered
er own braids to be shortened, preferring the tradition

of her coronet, but she understood the need for Mattie to wear her hair differently. It was fortunate that the clipped cap of curls was a style both fashionable and flattering to the clever young miss.

What had been begun of necessity, though, had continued as more than that. It had become a quiet time they shared whenever one of them felt the desire for a little closeness or, sometimes, just a little peace. And however strange it might seem, Mattie had never had any trouble sitting still at Tante's feet while her hair was combed this way and that, the scissors snip-snipping her short locks into order.

Haircuts meant the time when Tante had decided Mattie should know more about the process of becoming a woman, just after Mattie's thirteenth birthday. The physical facts had been discussed months before, but under the scissors, Mattie had learned to laugh at the sometimes discomfiting details. During another haircut, not long after Tante had heard about the death of yet one more of her dear friends who had been left behind in France, Mattie had begged for stories about the friendship, until the old lady was giggling like a girl at the memories. Haircuts also meant deciding which was a favorite flower, or a food least liked, preferences which might be overlooked in the ordinary way.

These were times deemed appropriate for matters both serious and small. Often as not, no discussion at all took place. Tante would comb and cut, while Mattie would sit quietly, simply enjoying a few moments in her *grand-tante*'s restful presence. Today, however, Mattie used the excuse of a haircut to bring up a source of botheration.

After the first stroke of the comb, she asked, "Tante, what if someone you love wants to do some-

296

hing foolish? Can you just forbid it, or must you al-
ow them to do what they want? But no," she an-
wered her own question, thinking of how Vincent had
ried to stop her from leaving to go and help the old
charley. "You can't make someone follow the path
you prefer, not really. While you might get in their
way for a time, in the end, if-'tis important to them,
hey will do as they please."

"Yes, dear," Tante Agathe said serenely. She read-
usted the cloth she had spread across Mattie's shoulders, so that hair shouldn't fall on her gown.

"So what you have to do," Mattie resumed almost at
once, "is convince them that what they plan is either un-
needful or better done by others. Or that they have prior
responsibilities which must be considered more fully."

"Certainly, dear," Tante agreed, making another
stroke with the comb.

"But why would someone who has other responsibilities"—Mattie thought first of the students
Vincent had in his keeping, and next of the wife she
hoped he would soon have in keeping—"go out in filthy
clothes to risk his neck, making the whole thing sound
like the most famous fun?"

Tante Agathe raised a curl at Mattie's crown to trim
a little from its ends. "I wonder which you would have
me the more concerned about, Madeleine," she mused
softly. "Is it the loss of dignity you fear, the degree of
risk, or do you not approve of someone's ideas of
amusement?"

Mattie considered this as she bent to allow her *grand-
tante* to reach the hair at her nape. It had been a shock
to see Vincent in that nasty hat, but if Tante should happen to see "Matt," the old dear wouldn't be upset for
any reasons of dignity! Mattie also had to appreciate the

297

importance of enjoying oneself, whether it was a part of one's work or not. Tante loved to sew, didn't she, even when it was no longer required for their income? "The risk," she replied, adamant. "But this would be a stupid, unwarranted risk!"

"Yes, dear," the old lady said, indicating that Mattie should turn her head a little to one side. "However, *ma petite,* it sounds very much as if you are faced with a decision. For if you are truly convinced that someone is become unconscionably foolish, then you must decide whether that person shall maintain a place in your estimation. Isn't that so?"

"Oh, I suppose," Mattie grumbled. But the way she felt about the earl, there was no question of simply dropping the acquaintance. She might have done, some weeks past—but now? Now she loved him!

"Perhaps," Tante said next, cutting a little more at the temples, "it is merely someone's *intentions* which confuse you. If you are listening only for what is said, it can prove misleading, I have learned. So, if you would have real understanding, I think you must discover *why* a thing is said."

At that, Mattie swung round to face the old lady, her eyes suddenly lit with awareness. She jumped to her feet, practically quivering in readiness to be off. "We are finished?"

"Why, yes, dear, I believe we are," the old lady answered, calmly closing the pair of scissors.

Mattie twirled away and out the door, the protective cloth forgotten. She left in her trail gossamer fine snippets of black hair, scattered in every which direction—most of them falling across the Brussels which covered the floor.

Smiling softly at this evidence of her great-niece's

haste, the wise old lady whispered, "Ah, but there is nothing quite like a *débauché* on the reform, now is there?"

Chapter Twenty-one

Upon taking his leave of Mattie and Lord Ellengood, Vincent proceeded homeward in a state of high elation. For every passerby who stared at the *outré* figure he cut, he tipped his hat and returned a jaunty grin.

Really, he hadn't meant for Mattie to know of his mission today. But Fate had decreed differently and had, as a result, done him a tremendous favor. That gawking look on Mattie's face when she had recognized him had made every penny paid for his groom's old hat well worth its price!

The hat was disgustingly dingy. It was lamentably farouche. It was also, and more than anything else, *inspiring*. Vincent congratulated himself all the way home.

Fate had, of a surety, provided him a boon. For within the moment of Mattie's fixing her disbelieving eyes upon his choice of headgear, Vincent had realized that he had an unlooked-for opportunity. He had discovered that he held the means to show one imprudent young miss just what it felt like to have the tables turned. It was time and more that those tables should be turned, too. The hours and days and weeks of anxiety over Matt-now-a-Mattie had been, in minutes, repaid.

Entering his bedchamber shortly thereafter, the earl instructed his valet to wrap and box up the article of justice. He had decided that this was one hat he would keep forevermore.

Vincent grinned so often, and so suddenly, that he very nearly cut himself shaving. He avoided any such misfortune, however, and completed his ablutions without mishap. Finally, when he had himself properly breeched, hosed, and shod, and with fresh linen beneath a coat of dark, woodbine green, Vincent was ready for the *coup de main*.

He made it inside Sally's front door.

Before he got halfway across the hall, however, Mattie appeared at the head of the stairs and immediately came flying down. Her feet seemed barely in contact with the steps, while she motioned for the footman who had answered the door to get along about his business. Vincent had but an instant to appreciate the gay yellow confection she wore—vastly becoming, he thought it—before she brought herself to a solid stop right in front of him.

Mattie locked her small fists against her hips. Her finely wrought brows pulled together in a great, ferocious scowl. Without preamble, she demanded, "Are you going to take up police business or not!"

He would swear that nothing in his expression gave him away, but she suddenly let out a loud whoop.

"So you really *can* be unkind," she crowed in triumph. "This was all *Tint for Tant!* Oh, you are a wicked, wicked man."

With the widest grin he had ever seen, she grabbed for the back of his neck, throwing herself into him. He had to catch at her or see them both lose their balance!

Vincent couldn't begin to guess how she had caught

on to his game so soon. For the nonce, however, he didn't find it appropriate to ask for explanations. He had a warm and very alive bundle in his arms, and his arms ached for nothing so much as this particular bundle. He promptly raised her up and nuzzled at her lips, suggesting they yield to him.

Quite as quickly as he could wish, Mattie fulfilled his desires. Some minutes later, she murmured, "Even?"

"Steven." He deepened their kiss.

From the top of the staircase, faintly French, lilting tones floated down. "All is settled at last, I see."

Vincent looked up to see Madame Serinier on the landing, his cousin Sally at her side.

"But how splendid!" the younger woman cried, at once starting for the steps. "Oh, coz, I've been hoping for something like this. How grand that you and Mattie are—"

"Sal," he cried out, halting her midstride. "I thought you told me that you weren't to try the stairs without assistance! You will wait right there until I come for you." A broad smile broke out across his handsome and newly shaved face. In a lighter voice, he amended, "But for the moment, I fear I cannot oblige. I expect very soon to find myself otherwise *engaged,* you understand."

The rolling boom of his laughter trailed behind him as he lifted Mattie further and carried her off to the withdrawing room. Once he was alone with his love, however, Mattie insisted that he return her to her feet.

When he had complied, she tilted her black eyebrows in query and said, "There are things of which we must speak, are there not?"

"Well, I certainly have something to say," he agreed.

"But I think that first I must tell you how you are to go on," she said, surprising him.

302

She went to perch on the edge of a low sofa, one which allowed her to sit with her feet firmly upon the floor. She indicated he should seat himself in a chair opposite.

When he had complied, she said huskily, "Now. I wish you to tell me exactly what happened today. Every detail. After that, I shall want to know what you meant last night, when you said you had been ministering to a muscle spasm that time I discovered you in the park at Grosvenor Square." Then, with a wholly mischievous look, she quipped, "It seems that I've been caught like fun on at least two counts. So if there's anything else I should know of, please, Vincent, you most tell me!"

He returned her a quizzical look. "On the square?"

"Definitely!" She gave an affirmative bob of the head.

He made himself more comfortable in his seat. With a keen sense of satisfaction, he appreciated that, with Mattie, he could speak as easily as if in the company of one of his sporting friends.

"Well," he began, "I went this morning to see the two men Mr. Townshend took up last night. I planned to call on the shop assistant, emeralds in hand, and with one of the burglars along to give credence to my story of being a *bene ken-miller* myself."

"Was it Buckle-feet who went with you or Willy?"

He had to smile at Mattie's methods of nomenclature. "Lew Cutty and William Fricks, actually. Come to think of it, though, Mr. Cutty does affect buckles on his shoes." At her look of impatience, he continued, "So, yes, if it matters, I decided to take the one you call 'Buckle-feet.' The pair assured me that I could pretend Willy Fricks's part, since the shop assistant had never seen him. The pair seemed entirely anxious to see to it that their cohort suffered at least some of the same punishment which they knew they must themselves endure."

"Ah," she said, sounding pleased.

"From there," he picked up his tale, "everything went much as expected. Mr. Townshend and another officer secreted themselves just inside the back door of the printer's shop so as to witness whatever was said. And where, I presume, you were stationed when you chanced to overhear the plans to break into Mrs. Darcy's house." He gave a wry smile. "Talk about being 'caught like fun'—you had me completely bamboozled with that story about needing to stop into Mr. Pollard's to purchase a book. That *was* when you came upon them, wasn't it?"

Her cheeks pinkened slightly. "Um, yes. Yes, it was. Kevin had learned that someone at Hamlet's might be involved, and I calculated that mine was the best chance of discovering more. I wasn't inside the bookseller's, though." She shook her head again, in the negative this time. "I had already passed the jewelry shop and was headed around the corner when I heard the two men talking. But do get on with it, Vincent! You had them caught in a crossbite, and then what happened?"

"Well, Lew Cutty rapped at the back door of the jewelry shop, and as soon as our quarry opened up, I flashed the stones where he could see them. It seemed to affect the shop assistant strongly. So strongly, in fact, that I had only to place one or two questions about the previous thefts, before he was reeling off an account of his prowess in disposing of each item. I believe most of the proper owners will, as a result, soon see their belongings returned to them."

Mattie made little hurrying motions with her fingers.

"But what came next! When the fellow realized that he was crimped—wasn't there some sort of kick-up? Oh, he must have been knocked out of his gears! Cock-a-hoop! Tell me what happened? What did he do!"

Vincent thought to criticize her freedom with the language, then reconsidered. He couldn't fault her for being concerned, when, obviously, it was his own well-being which concerned her.

Neither would he be completely candid, however. For in fact, there had been quite a street broil. The shop assistant had taken exception—violent exception—to being trapped, and Willy had thought to make use of the opportunity to try and make an escape. Vincent had found it expedient to push round the skulls a bit, putting a finisher on them both. But to Mattie, he said merely, "Why, Mr. Townshend made his arrest, of course. The last I saw of the shop assistant and Willy Fricks, they were quietly on their way to Bow Street." That much, at least, was the truth.

Mattie showed no disappointment for this accounting. "I am so glad 'tis done, then! Now, about that night when I came upon you in Grosvenor Square. I thought you were, er, *abroad*. But you weren't, were you." She didn't make it a question.

He grinned at her renewed display of ladylike reticence and answered with alacrity. "Not in the sense I think you mean. Oh, I won't say my flask has never been in the province of Bacchus, but on that particular night, I carried only water."

She shot him a sharp look. "Then why did you pretend to be overtaken? Vincent, I remember distinctly how you slurred your words. Why would you do such a thing? Surely you must have known what I thought!"

He returned her a sardonic look. "Indeed? And have

you never behaved a certain way, even badly, just because someone seemed to expect it of you? But as you've already noted yourself, I, like most people, can be unkind at times. I suppose kindness itself is an act of faith. Faith in another's basic goodness."

She held his eye without wavering. "I understand then. It is like your thinking I was involved with the thieves, yet you decided to help me anyway. Sorry," she said gruffly.

Vincent was amazed at how that last little word released him. In one brief utterance, Mattie had managed to include such wholehearted sincerity as could erase the pain brought by far greater crimes. None could know how much he loved this woman.

But it was time for Mattie, at least, to know his sentiments. Without further ado, he rose from his chair, determined that there had been enough retailing of matters which were become, after all, irrelevant. He didn't know how much longer it might be before they were interrupted, and there had been delays enough.

He bent to one knee, bringing his eye exactly upon a level with hers. "Mattie," he said softly, giving his eyes permit to show his deepest feelings, "I love you, sweetheart, and I want you to know that I—"

"But *yes!*" she shouted suddenly. In a blur of bright yellow, she hurled herself off the sofa to sail straight into his arms, nearly tossing them both to the floor!

As it was, Vincent was put to the trouble of countering her move by seeing them both seated flat on the carpet, side by side.

She was content with this placement for less than no time. She at once rolled herself onto his lap, clapping her little hands along either side of his face. Evidently, she had it in mind to take control of their further converse on the subject by the simplest available means. She covered his lips with her own.

Vincent didn't think he had ever enjoyed such a kiss.

They were returned to the present only when sounds of persistent tapping obtruded. Lifting Mattie back to her place on the low sofa, Vincent went to see who desired entrance, at the same time feeling not a little grateful that whoever it was had knocked first. Before turning the handle, though, he looked to be sure Mattie had reordered her skirts.

As usual, she was well ahead of his wishes. She was already sitting as prim and upright as anyone could want. Only a small smile—much like a naughty pup who was making off with someone's favorite slipper—gave her away. He smiled a little himself, then swung open the door.

"*Now* have you settled it between you?" Madame Serinier said by way of greeting. Sally and her husband stood just behind, gleefully awaiting his response.

"Why, yes, we have," he answered coolly as the trio filed into the room. In rather more rueful tones, he added, "And we shall want a special license, I think. I hope Mattie will agree, but I *know* I shan't care to wait above a single week longer."

Chapter Twenty-two

True to this statement, Mattie hurried everyone into the preparations necessary for an immediate wedding. She was astonished to learn that her gown was long since made up, a glowing white satin with long, heavily embroidered panels—each one depicting in silver the yew leaves which heralded a member of the Staffield house. Tante Agathe presented her with the finished garment, as serene and complaisant as ever.

"But, of course, I knew you must choose him," she said when Mattie challenged her for an explanation. "For this is true love, is it not? Oh, no great discernment was needed to predict this outcome, my little one, of that, I can assure you."

Mattie could only embrace the old dear and remind herself not to forget to extend her thank-yous to Mme. Leteuil as well.

The Ellengoods were not much behindhand in their own offers of assistance. Jeremy ordered in so much champagne that even Vincent stared, and Sally happily saw to the musicians and caterers and Mattie-knew-not-what-alls as the young matron went about making ready for the swiftly approaching day. Even young Rhodney and little Jacob did their part, deciding which flowers from the florist's samplings should be used for decoration.

Vincent had declared that by Friday next, they should see the thing done. Mattie hadn't thought him impetuous in the least! But she was startled when he had also insisted she accompany him to Mr. Hamlet's for the purpose of selecting her rings.

As they left in the earl's curricle, bound for Cranbourn Alley, she quizzed him about it. "Vincent, why did you not just pick what you wanted for me to have? Surely it isn't customary that I come with you, is it?"

Because of the traffic, both before and behind them, her betrothed made answer with his eyes on his team. "No, I don't suppose it is the usual way of things. But I decided we should go on this errand together, since I really wasn't certain about what you might prefer. And to be honest, Mattie, I feared the consequences of a wrong decision. Just imagine what it might be like, having to wear something—and for the entire rest of your life!—which actually didn't suit." He shuddered in genuine horror.

She gave a throaty chuckle. "You mean, like, say, a hat which one didn't really care for?"

He shivered again and spoke with real feeling. "Exactly."

"But why to Hamlet's?" she asked next, lowering her voice so that the groom, brought along to tend the carriage in their absence, shouldn't hear. "We could have gone to another shop. For you must know that the contents of Mr. Hamlet's jewel room are prodigiously expensive! A plain gold band would please me very well, did you not know it?"

"Oh, yes, I knew." This time he did pass her a smile. "Although, if you shouldn't mind too much, Mattie, I would see to it that your first piece of jewelry is something very special. We shall have one ring for you to enjoy for its beauty and shall select another to serve as your wedding band. But in matters like this, I think, we should choose together.

She slipped her hand inside his arm and gave it a small squeeze. "Thank you," she said softly. But then, with more firmness, she reminded, "Still, Hamlet's, Vincent? I don't understand."

"Well, as to that"—he looked a trifle embarrassed—"you must know that Mr. Hamlet was excessively grateful for my little part in quietly having rid him of a potential source of mortification. He sent a note round to me, begging the favor of my custom."

This was something which appealed to any Frenchwoman's heart. "So he will make us a special price? Oh, but that's wonderful!" she exulted.

"Nonetheless, Mattie," Vincent cautioned, almost sternly, "whatever the expense, you are not to regard it. Understand?"

"*D'accord!*" she cried gaily. Another thing occurred to her. "Vincent?" she asked next, a small frown marking her brow.

"Yes, love?"

"Do you know yet when I'm to receive my reward money? You see, I shall need it if I am to pay for you to have a wedding ring; although, certainly, I realize it is not currently the English fashion for husbands to wear bands. But you will have one, won't you? Perhaps, even a gold band made to match my own?"

The earl appeared thoughtful for a moment, then said gently, "Why, yes, I do believe I shall like to have a wedding ring. Very much. And as for your reward money, rest assured that I have it right here." He patted his breast pocket.

Satisfied that she would be doing her part in what, after all, was a joint undertaking, Mattie sat back against the curricle's seat and smiled in undiluted pleasure.

Mr. Hamlet met them at the door to his shop with every sign of similar satisfaction. When Vincent told him of their requirements, the tradesman's face became wreathed in smile upon smile. "Diamonds? Rubies? Whatever you wish!" he declared.

"Perhaps we should start with the rubies," Vincent replied, a lightened glint in his eye. "I've heard they are all the crack."

Mattie had to laugh, remembering the day she had tried to flummery Vincent with that tremendous great *plumper* about the need of rubies for fashion. "Of course, we must consider those!" She gurgled. When her intended's eyes twinkled again, she said, more seriously, "But I would also see sapphires, Mr. Hamlet. Blue ones. I'll know the right shade when I see it."

Obedient to these requests, the jeweler brought out tray after tray of precious stones, both loose and already mounted. Mattie considered each carefully. She tried on any number of rings, finding several styles which she thought might do for her a lovely ring, and those Mr. Hamlet gladly set to one side. As for a center stone, though, she didn't find what she wanted.

Vincent sat in apparent patience, occasionally offering a suggestion. "I admit I like the sapphire best, Mattie, so what about this one?" he would ask, holding up a delicately clustered arrangement.

"Yes, I like the ring very well," she would reply, slipping it onto her finger. "But no, the stones are just too light."

Mr. Hamlet would lay the ring aside.

"And this?" Vincent held up a loose sapphire.

"No, too blackish," she would say.

Each time, Mr. Hamlet would either return the item to the tray as unwanted, or put it to the side for reconsideration. Finally, after Mattie had perused every jewel in his stock, the jeweler said soberly, "Mademoiselle, I believe I know what it is you are seeking. Forgive me for not having accommodated you sooner, but I rarely have a customer of such discriminating taste. If you will excuse me for but a moment, I will bring one other tray. It contains my finest merchandise." With a little bow, he left them.

Anxiously, Mattie leaned closer to her intended and whispered, "Oh, but Vincent, that means it will cost very dear! I hadn't meant—"

He hushed her. "I will determine that, my love. Let us first see what Mr. Hamlet has to offer, shall we?"

Only a little reassured, she agreed.

The jeweler returned to them with covered rosewood box. He slid open the latch to reveal a something over a dozen rings with a variety of precious gemstones—most of very large size. Mattie's eyes went directly to the smallest of the lot. In one corner of the box rested a ring with a teardrop-shaped sapphire, tiny diamonds set all around.

"That one," she announced in triumph.

She nearly bounced in her seat as Vincent lifted the appropriate ring from the tray and examined it. "I agree that it is exquisite. Just what I shall like to see in your possession, even years and years from now. But are you sure, Mattie? You may have something larger, if you prefer." He waved his hand over the rich array of rings remaining in the box.

"No, no," she said, adamant, watching the play of light across the sapphire's dark surface as Vincent turned it in his hand. "None can possibly compare!"

It was Mr. Hamlet who spoke. "Ah. Mademoiselle does, indeed, know her stones. What you hold there in your hand, my lord, is a fine example of the rare Kashmir sapphire, known from ancient times as 'the gem of the soul.' The blue is of a shade so rich, and so distinctive, that it is instantly recognizable to dealers the world over. But tell me, mademoiselle, how is it that you know of such things?"

Mattie smiled and reverently removed the ring from Vincent's hand. She held it up to his eyes.

It was the only answer she knew to give.

After they had selected a matched pair of thick gold bands for their weddings rings, the jeweler marked the sizes needed, and Vincent and Mattie were ready to leave the shop. Mr. Hamlet promised to have everything delivered to Tenterden Street as soon as may be and saw them to the door.

Just as they stepped outside to where Vincent's curricle awaited, another carriage pulled up. Two passengers were let down right in front of them. Dismayed, Mattie realized that it was Lord and Lady Whatsits who had once stared so at "Matt" at the Theatre-Royal.

No green gauze this time, but a smart day dress of vivid, conquelicot red enhanced the Fair One's lush figure. Her lord husband looked much the same, although Mattie thought perhaps his hair was not teased quite so high as before. Evidently, the couple were so intent on entering Mr. Hamlet's premises that they didn't even notice the earl and Mattie before the foursome came face-to-face.

Mattie felt Vincent tense slightly. "Lord Hedgewick—my lady," he greeted them quietly, his voice light and even.

Mattie was astonished to realize that the other couple looked exceedingly nervous themselves. The Beauty's husband anxiously darted pale eyes here and there, while his mouth was held to grim lines, as if in prospect of some grave misfortune.

As for his wife, despite her being taller and even more beautiful than remembered, she looked somehow, well, *small*. Mattie couldn't imagine what made it seem so, but there it was. The Fair One practically shrank in size before Mattie's very eyes.

Vincent began the obligatory introductions. Mattie was pleased that Lord Whatsits ungloved to shake her hand—as was proper for a gentleman to do when meeting a lady—and Mattie grasped his hand firmly. She then turned to her ladyship and took her hand with equal firmness.

"So pleased," the Beauty murmured, not quite meeting Mattie's eyes.

But Mattie was not content with that. She knew that the couple was uncomfortable, but such awkwardness was not to be borne. "My lady," she said warmly, "I am delighted to have your acquaintance. Have you come to Mr. Hamlet's for a purchase? How exciting! You must know he has the most marvelous selection; I've no doubt you will find just what is wanted."

Her topic seemed a felicitous choice. With more enthusiasm, her ladyship answered, "Oh, I do hope you are right. My Neddy"—she tucked her arm inside her lord's—"has promised I shall have a new ring, but we have been everywhere and I cannot find one I like."

Mattie grinned and made a pretense of looking over her shoulder at the shop, as if not wishful of being overheard. She leaned forward and, on tiptoe, whispered in her ladyship's ear. "Oh, well, if that is the case, then you must ask Mr. Hamlet to show you his *private* collection. He has a special tray of beautiful things which, I am told, he won't exhibit to just anyone. However, if you were to mention to him that Mlle. Serinier insisted, I am sure he will oblige you."

Her ladyship's lovely face lit at this intelligence. The two gentlemen looked uncertain for not having heard Mattie's words, but they relaxed perceptibly when the Fashionable Beauty said, "Neddy, I now have it on good authority that we shall find what I want here!" She practically dragged her husband into the jeweler's, waving and smiling her goodbyes.

Vincent assisted Mattie into his curricle. When he had himself seated alongside her, he turned to catch her eye. "And just what was that all about?" he asked, his mouth atwitch.

"But it was so much nothing!" Mattie answered airily. "I only told her ladyship about Mr. Hamlet's private jewelry collection. You do know, I trust, how the people of *ton* value *exclusivity,* don't you? And so, I suppose, the lady was just grateful for being put into the *know.*"

To Mattie's amazement, Vincent chuckled at odd moments all the way home.

The bells at St. George's, Hanover, rang with the happy tidings. A newlywed couple—one a handsome specimen of young manhood, tanned, and with dark

315

gold hair and wonderfully wide shoulders; the other a petite beauty with ink-black hair and flashing eyes—marched sedately out to the street and to a waiting carriage.

Two small lads of nursery age followed after the bridal couple, tossing pennies at the gathered spectators' feet. They were thrown with vigor, but in precisely that manner which their new "Cousin Mattie" had taught them as being the most efficacious—also the least dangerous—for the potential recipients. Other boys, somewhat older and more raggedly attired, scrambled for a share of the nuptial party's largess.

A very young voice piped up from amidst the gathered crowd on the footpath. "Lor! Whot a reg'lar pair o' Swells! An' would yer jest looks at 'ow they tips us the dues? Long life and best wishes fer 'em is whot *I* says!"

From her place inside the carriage, Mattie grinned and nudged her escort. Apparently, having heard the same message, Vincent promptly reached into his pocket and, with remarkable accuracy, sent a shimmering golden guinea flying right into one little fellow's hands.

And as the newly married pair started away down the street, an excited *"Coo-oey!"* floated through the air behind them.

A Memorable Collection of Regency Romances

BY ANTHEA MALCOLM AND VALERIE KING

THE COUNTERFEIT HEART
(3425, $3.95/$4.95)
by Anthea Malcolm

Nicola Crawford was hardly surprised when her cousin's betrothed disappeared on some mysterious quest. Anyone engaged to such an unromantic, but handsome man was bound to run off sooner or later. Nicola could never entrust her heart to such a conventional, but so deucedly handsome man. . . .

THE COURTING OF PHILIPPA
(2714, $3.95/$4.95)
by Anthea Malcolm

Miss Philippa was a very successful author of romantic novels. Thus she was chagrined to be snubbed by the handsome writer Henry Ashton whose own books she admired. And when she learned he considered love stories completely beneath his notice, she vowed to teach him a thing or two about the subject of love. . . .

THE WIDOW'S GAMBIT
(2357, $3.50/$4.50)
by Anthea Malcolm

The eldest of the orphaned Neville sisters needed a chaperone for a London season. So the ever-resourceful Livia added several years to her age, invented a deceased husband, and became the respectable Widow Royce. She was certain she'd never regret abandoning her girlhood until she met dashing Nicholas Warwick. . . .

A DARING WAGER
(2558, $3.95/$4.95)
by Valerie King

Ellie Dearborne's penchant for gaming had finally led her to ruin. It seemed like such a lark, wagering her devious cousin George that she would obtain the snuffboxes of three of society's most dashing peers in one month's time. She could easily succeed, too, were it not for that exasperating Lord Ravenworth. . . .

THE WILLFUL WIDOW
(3323, $3.95/$4.95)
by Valerie King

The lovely young widow, Mrs. Henrietta Harte, was not all inclined to pursue the sort of romantic folly the persistent King Brandish had in mind. She had to concentrate on marrying off her penniless sisters and managing her spendthrift mama. Surely Mr. Brandish could fit in with her plans somehow . . .

Available wherever paperbacks are sold, or order direct from the Publisher. Send cover price plus 50¢ per copy for mailing and handling to Zebra Books, Dept. 4411, 475 Park Avenue South, New York, N.Y. 10016. Residents of New York and Tennessee must include sales tax. DO NOT SEND CASH. For a free Zebra/Pinnacle catalog please write to the above address.

KATHERINE STONE —
Zebra's Leading Lady for Love

BEL AIR   (2979, $4.95)
Bel Air—where even the rich and famous are awed by the wealth that surrounds them. Allison, Winter, Emily: three beautiful women who couldn't be more different. Three women searching for the courage to trust, to love. Three women fighting for their dreams in the glamorous and treacherous *Bel Air*.

ROOMMATES   (3355, $4.95)
No one could have prepared Carrie for the monumental changes she would face when she met her new circle of friends at Stanford University. Once their lives intertwined and became woven into the tapestry of the times, they would never be the same.

TWINS   (3492, $4.95)
Brook and Melanie Chandler were so different, it was hard to believe they were sisters. One was a dark, serious, ambitious New York attorney; the other, a golden, glamorous, sophisticated supermodel. But they were more than sisters—they were twins and more alike than even they knew . . .

THE CARLTON CLUB   (3614, $4.95)
It was the place to see and be seen, the only place to be. And for those who frequented the playground of the very rich, it was a way of life. Mark, Kathleen, Leslie and Janet—they worked together, played together, and loved together, all behind exclusive gates of the *Carlton Club*.

Available wherever paperbacks are sold, or order direct from the Publisher. Send cover price plus 50¢ per copy for mailing and handling to Zebra Books, Dept. 4411 , 475 Park Avenue South, New York, N.Y. 10016. Residents of New York and Tennessee must include sales tax. DO NOT SEND CASH. For a free Zebra/ Pinnacle catalog please write to the above address.